THE SEASON OF
SECOND CHANCES

THE SEASON OF
SECOND CHANCES

A NOVEL

DIANE MEIER

ST. MARTIN'S GRIFFIN

NEW YORK

THE SEASON OF SECOND CHANCES. Copyright © 2010 by Diane Meier. All rights reserved. Printed in the United States of America. For information, address St. Martin's Press, 175 Fifth Avenue, New York, N.Y. 10010.

Designed by Meryl Sussman Levavi

www.stmartins.com

The Library of Congress has cataloged the Henry Holt edition as follows:

Meier, Diane.
    The season of second chances : a novel / Diane Meier. — 1st ed.
        p.   cm.
    ISBN 978-0-8050-9081-9
    1. Women college teachers—Fiction.   2. Divorced women—Fiction.   3. New York
(N.Y.)—Fiction.   I. Title.
    PS3613.E426S43 2010
    813'.6—dc22   2009013959

Originally published in hardcover in 2010 by Henry Holt and Company

ISBN 978-0-312-67411-3 (trade paperback)

10 9 8 7 6 5 4 3

FOR SARA-GWEN AND FRANK

I t takes a keen eye to tell a false start from a dead end. I was finished with New York. I wanted out. I wanted somewhere else, anywhere else. I'd taught at Columbia for fifteen years and was, against all odds, a full professor. I'd published three books of poetry that few had read, not even my mother, and a biography of Margaret Chase Smith that no one read, not even me. How I'd managed to shred that fascinating woman— a clear-thinking, hard-talking, Yankee senator from Maine who had the guts and fortitude to run for president against Goldwater, Rockefeller and Stassen—into tiny bits of endless detail that added up to nothing, certainly nothing human, was almost an act of genius in itself. I'd created a belabored pile of facts and figures, with no life whatsoever between the hardbound covers, wrapped in the dung-colored book jacket.

I am a teacher—a good teacher. I like the year in, year out repetition of the curriculum. I like the fact that my job is to impart knowledge and enthusiasm, managed within an environment where the risk is minimal; what these kids do in the future with the information and the potential they may or may not display is not my problem. I'm thoroughly entertained by them through the school year, and, for the most part, in the spring they move on. In September I get a whole new batch. It's redemption every fall. I have no arguments with this life.

But New York is another story. Within the vaulted halls of Columbia I've been rubbed raw by the administration, frustrated by the exclusionary snobbery of academe and driven wild by the politics and the postures we're forced to assume to maintain any standing in the community. One is obliged to align oneself with positions that refuse to distinguish common sense from pageant, and God help you if your thoughts stray from that which is predigested and approved by committee to block any offense that might be taken by bullies masquerading as thin-skinned victims.

Should one suggest that banding homosexuals together and creating a "team" that demands recognition might, *indeed*, buy the team a bus, but that this bus will certainly *not* be in the fast lane—you will be ousted from the bosom of this academic community faster than you can say "Boys in the Band."

But go ahead, I dare you, because I am finished with this. I am packing my bags and moving away from this tempo of insistence that everyone step to an insipid dance or be labeled a rabid, right-wing reactionary.

I am moving away from an apartment that, while it has a heart-stopping view of the Hudson, if one hangs out the window, is roughly the size of the kitchen in the old Victorian I saw in Massachusetts. Four flights up when you are thirty-four may seem like an adventure. Four flights up when you are forty-eight seems an increasingly steep Matter-horn. Try carrying three bags of groceries up those stairs for decades, and you will find yourself eating only food that can be delivered.

I moved to New York when I was thirty-one, rather late to come to the press and whistle of the men and the subways, and perhaps too late to learn the wit and timing of real New Yorkers. I watched and listened in awe and delight, but I was never of their league. I was too quick for Saint Louis, that was obvious, but not ever-ready for old New York.

Since childhood, I'd dreamed of Manhattan and wished for a way out of Saint Louis, but I had no plan. When the opportunity to teach at Columbia appeared, I found the courage to leap from the Midwest, and I didn't look back. I left a pretty little starter house in Clayton, a teaching assignment at Washington University and a husband of four years, for the canyons and the peaks of New York's promise.

In my first apartment, shared with a secretary from Revlon and a stewardess from Delta, I read Kerouac, Salinger and Allen Ginsberg again and again, as I had in high school and college when the image of New York—and the woman I would become—fueled my fantasies. I kept reading and waiting for it all to take, but it never did.

There was a television commercial for Chemical Bank on the air when I first arrived, in which an attractive young woman purposefully made her way up Park Avenue. The camera caught her long stride to somewhere important. She ran a publishing company, I imagined. She designed jet engines. Her game farm in Africa bred white tigers. She commanded respect and used other people's money. The tagline to the commercial: "The New York Woman. When her needs are financial, her reaction is Chemical."

I opened an account at Chemical Bank within days of landing in Manhattan. I wanted to be that woman. Four months after my move, Chemical merged with Manufacturers Hanover and my bank became known as Manny Hanny. In New York, I was always just a tad late for the party.

Change rarely happens in doses large enough to choke you. Every day you swallow a little more and expect a little less. So I don't remember the day I stopped hoping I would become that self-assured woman who knew where the important people lunched. I don't know when I last believed that I would grow into someone Susan Sontag would choose to meet for an early supper and a movie we might then hack to pieces. I didn't know I'd given up. And yet, when opportunity beckoned to fly yet another coop, I jumped headlong into the gale that might carry me away from the niggling shame that I never would become That Woman whose reactions were Chemical.

Amherst College has recruited me, rescuing my sorry ass from what had seemed a sealed and dismal fate. For reasons I won't question, lest they wise up, they're paying me far more than I'm worth to move to the wilds of Massachusetts and work with one of the living legends of literature and criticism on developing new ways of sharing, if not teaching, the written word. This is far more than good fortune. This is like finding an unmarked envelope full of hundreds on the backseat of a crosstown bus. Before they figure out their mistake, I plan to be ensconced in some ivy-covered office, so wrapped in bureaucratic tape they won't be able to unravel my contract.

The three-hour drive to Amherst in my old BMW had been easy and pleasant. The air-conditioning was working again, and encased in my cool bubble of air I felt protected from the heat of early August. The New York route into New England allowed me to drive along the Hudson until Riverdale and then catch the wide, tree-lined superhighway that unfolded vistas of the Catskill Mountains and the foothills of the Berkshires.

The feeling of freedom, driving into scenery as green and lush as a post-card of Ireland, was close to bliss.

I pulled into the Red Rooster, a hamburger joint on Route 22 that seems lifted from my Missouri childhood. Years ago, I'd stopped there with a musician with whom I'd had a brief fling. I picked the same picnic table where Roger and I sat in the middle of a very cold winter, downing hot dogs and Brown Cows, as the snow seeped into my city shoes. After a chilly night in a motel somewhere on a river in Connecticut, my hips and shoulders hurt and I wanted to be warm. It occurred to me, even back then, that I might be getting too old for romance. But I remembered the place with fondness, as I remember Roger with fondness; not perfect, but, all in all, not a bad memory. In his honor I had a Brown Cow, that sweet mixture of vanilla ice cream and root beer a friend of mine from England thinks tastes like ointment. I love this drink, but I haven't had one in—what can it be?—more than five years. Lord! More like eight or nine years. Time, as they say, flies.

Six months ago my secretary buzzed my intercom and announced a call from Bernadette Lowell. It was possible that Celeste might be play-ing a little joke, but Celeste has never displayed anything close to a sense of humor, and she is pathologically disconnected from academic life. She might as well be a secretary in a lumberyard (where, no doubt, as it is her nature, she would be disconnected from all things wood). Most of all, a joke in itself, Celeste would never have heard of Bernadette Lowell, who is about as famous an academic as one can be.

In my world, we don't herald the beautiful, the best dressed or the rich, but we do have the very occasional individual who breaks through the line between academy and popular culture. They publish, they lec-ture, they become regular guests on NPR and PBS, lending their studied air to whatever crises or phenomena the media believe must be explained to the dim public. They become our superstars; although, true to the nature of academics, we do nothing but denigrate them in our conversations and public attitude. In private, we maintain little shrines, Harold Bloom pinup pictures and prayers to the gods of academic poli-tics, that someday we might have our own tiny place in a *New Yorker* profile or within the gloomy embrace of Charlie Rose's roundtable.

Lowell had done her groundbreaking work thirty years ago, defining and developing the field of gender studies, making magazine covers and television appearances and creating unlikely best sellers out of academic research. She was now making waves with equally radical ideas about how humans learn, the pejorative nature of identifying and cataloging learning disabilities and an idea about graduate studies she was tagging Immersion Technique. Amherst College had given her a chair, made her a dean of graduate studies and stood behind her experiments. Most of academe was snickering, as usual, but everyone was watching.

Harry Fox, the resident glamour boy hotshot from Columbia's School of Journalism, recommended me to Dr. Lowell. I didn't know Harry well and was surprised to learn that I figured on his rarified radar at all. Harry's a type. Every school of journalism worth its salt has one. They come out of media and swagger across our campuses with insufferable style. They can be useful in bringing some real-life contacts, a bit of attention and often a trickle of money to our limited and insular stage, but they never do seem to fit in.

At any rate, at his suggestion and crediting him with the call, Bernadette Lowell asked me to lunch at the Algonquin Hotel in February, to see, she said rather coquettishly, if we "liked each other." I was, admittedly, a little intimidated, but I "liked" her fine. She is about seventy years old, give or take a few years; her hair is white as snow, cut like Buster Brown or a page in a Maxfield Parrish mural; but the first impression was that of power. She stood as I approached. "Dr. Harkness?" Her head was tilted and eyes bright, like a bird dog on the scent of a quail.

"Joy," I answered and extended my hand, met by her powerful and warm grasp. She is big, by any standards, in a strong, masculine way, and taller than my own average height by at least four or five inches. Her hands are large, and she wore a distinctive sapphire and diamond ring. She displayed a disconcerting combination of apparently shy reserve, fluttery infectious charm and a well of immense calm. I have yet to make sense of the expression of gravitas and willful strength all wrapped in a package of girlish delight; but there you have it. My father once referred to my brother's "life force," his immense energy, his distinct and unique personality, so defined and powerful, even in childhood. And that was the term, *life force,* that came to mind when confronted with Bernadette.

We discussed her plans for Amherst and the team of academics she hoped to build, and we talked about my situation in the barest terms. I played no games, I was completely candid. I would run from New York and Columbia, like a hound at the drop of a hare.

A month later, on the twenty-seventh of March at three o'clock in the afternoon, Dr. Lowell rang and offered me a job for far more money than anyone who teaches might ever anticipate. For this, I would have to commit to a minimum of four years, carry what would amount to my existing workload of teaching and join her Core Team, who would, in addition to our teaching schedules, develop Bernadette's new curriculum concept. There would be weekends and evenings required, although not so many in the first year, Bernadette explained, as the plan was just beginning. She wondered if she'd remembered to mention that the team would need to work together for a month in the summers. So what? I thought. I had no other life. Summer travel didn't much interest me; tooting around the world with hordes of tourists in months too hot for comfort. I had no country house, no partner and no children, underfoot or otherwise. My summers could easily be sold to Bernadette Lowell.

The real catch was that she wanted me, or someone, on board and in place by the beginning of the following term. Here, deep into spring, I had a semester to end, a position to relinquish, an apartment to sell and pack and move and an Amherst home to find by the first of September, at the latest. Bernadette was asking me to create a whole new life in a matter of weeks.

I was her first choice, she told me squarely, but if I could not see my way clear to agree to this move right now, she needed to get on to another candidate immediately. Not see myself clear to make the move? Had I not been plain? I was out of here. Whether I sold the New York apartment or not, my psychic bags were packed and I was, emotionally, already *in* Amherst.

My apartment was literally on the market for four days when it sold for more than the asking price. I hadn't even gotten around to clearing out the foyer. A parade of seven couples and a single man marched through my rooms in the first two days of the listing, attended by their real estate agents and mine. Everyone seemed to think that the apartment was such a gem, with its high coffered ceilings, parquet floors and the bowed window that looked out onto broad Eighty-sixth Street. Wait until you hear the bus, I thought, but I didn't say a word. I smiled when they talked about the light. I nodded when they mentioned the perfect proportions of the rooms. I knew it was a crowded, dark, mean little apartment with a fireplace that didn't work and too few closets. Two real estate agents mentioned that the building was promising to install an elevator at the back service stairs. I didn't tell them that our co-op board had been arguing about that imaginary elevator for all of the sixteen years I'd lived in the building.

I watched the potential buyers navigate the piles of books that made my living room floor a cityscape in miniature, and chat on about the potential of the place. Potential? We were standing in a dim and noisy crowded box, drafty, sometimes buggy and not quite near enough to a subway, a restaurant or a decent garage. This apartment was no prize. But I also wanted one of them to buy it; I held my tongue, and I held my breath. And lo and behold, after bidding against one another and pushing up the price by more than fifty thousand dollars, one of them did. I could only laugh. With real estate booms, as with comedy, timing is everything.

Now it was my turn. The college recommended a real estate agent, with the promising name of Donna Fortunata, to help me find accommodations, and we'd agreed to meet in front of the administration building. I pulled into a parking space directly opposite the entrance and recognized her immediately. She looked just the way her voice on the phone sounded. Donna was small and bright in the way women's magazines sometimes describe as perky. Her honey-colored hair was pulled high in a ponytail that made her look about twelve. She was wearing a pale yellow stretch-terry warm-up suit that seemed two sizes too small even for her petite, I imagined Pilates-enhanced, figure. A small gold chain gleamed around her waist between the low-riding bottoms and the shrunken little top.

Disregarding the warm weather, I was wearing a dark gray long-sleeved shirt, a black linen cardigan and black gabardine trousers. I didn't look like anyone on the streets of Amherst. Welcome to the world outside of New York, I thought. But Donna was bright and witty and frankly stunned at the price I'd gotten for a two-bedroom apartment in

New York, which allowed her to show me a series of interesting houses, all of which were buried deep in the mountainous and dark woods she described as the "desirable hills." In the Massachusetts countryside, it seems, they still think of these remote places as "town," and perhaps it does literally appear so on a map; but I know better.

Now, I've walked the streets of Harlem at all hours, and I've never hesitated to take the subway. I've never been afraid, as sirens wailed and voices—sometimes angry, sometimes drunk, sometimes plaintive—rose to the open windows of my apartment, through the nights and the years of my New York stay. And yet, the idea of being alone on a winter's night in the rattling woods of Massachusetts was decidedly unsettling.

After four houses where one could barely see (or remember seeing) a neighboring home, I asked Donna if she'd show me houses *in* town. The *real* town—with sidewalks. Sadly, she explained, there were few for sale at the moment, and none that matched my criteria.

And then she remembered a house. Her expression was pained as she recounted its details. It had been empty for years. And it needed work, she emphasized. A *lot* of work. Trying to follow her line of thought was confounding. The house was priced far below what I'd planned to spend, and it was a much larger house than I required. Still, it was near to school, in a lovely neighborhood, a rambling Victorian with a big front porch; but she hesitated. "It's kind of a white elephant. It needs *so* much work," she said gravely. "I think you'll find it daunting."

I could hardly believe my ears. If I understood correctly, it was *in* town, and there were actual sidewalks with neighboring houses. Daunting? Let's go there—now! My heart ran ahead. Let's leave the arena of wild bear and rabid raccoon and crazy men with axes, for the safety and comfort of a neighborhood, for the aroma of blueberry pies cooling on kitchen windowsills, for little front yards and the idea of biking to work. The concept of biking to work should have given me the hint that I was getting carried away. And why *was* it priced so far below all that we'd seen, and what did she mean by "white elephant"? "It's probably a teardown" was all she'd share, shaking her golden ponytail like Trigger refusing a fence.

We drove into a driveway of cracked and broken concrete, choked with overgrown forsythia and weeds. Through masses and tangles of what looked like a garden never tended, one could make out the wide, shingled porch, all strangled in vines with feminine quatrefoil corbels and a screen door of Victorian detail so fine it looked like the lace of old French underwear. Lest this sound too romantic, sections of the handiwork were missing, and the door was no longer on its hinges.

Inside was no better, though no worse. The stairway creaked and shifted to the point where I feared we might both end up in the basement, and regardless of the point of entry, I didn't want to see the basement at all. The toilets were rusty and the kitchen sink had a long brown edge and a deep green stain from faucet to drain. There was a white mineral kind of stalactite—or is it stalagmite?—buildup on the metal faucet handles, and mouse droppings littered the counter.

But there were broad-planked wooden floors, a fireplace with inset art nouveau tiles and a deep, bowed window and window seat, or at least half of one. The other half had been lifted away some years before, and the scar on the wall had never been repaired. Light streamed in the leaded windows and ran across the floor, long and yellow and warm and delicious. The first floor held a dining room and a living room and a room that could be my study. The idea of an office at home filled me with satisfaction. In New York, my extra bedroom overflowed with the furniture and household goods that had arrived more than a decade ago, when, as the last surviving Harkness, I took reluctant possession of the material remains of my family's lives. My "office" was my living room; stacked with papers and books, it had never been a place where anyone could be invited to relax or even visit. And, consequently, no one ever was.

Closets appeared everywhere in the old Victorian—under the stairs and on each side of the front door in a gracious entry foyer. A butler's pantry, large as my bedroom in the city, sat between the dining room and the kitchen.

The newel posts on the stairway and the paneling in the living room still held a kind of dignity and beauty missing from the architecture of our time. Light fixtures, pulled out of walls and ceilings, left gaping holes that didn't diminish the proportions of the rooms or the intent of those who built them.

As we walked through, surveying the dreadful conditions, Donna suggested that someone might want to buy it for the lot alone and the chance to build from scratch to their own requirements. Imagine, I thought, tearing this history out of a town, bulldozing the beauty of its bourgeois comfort and the graciousness of its past for a modern house with Sheetrock walls.

"Shouldn't someone be assigned to protect these old homes?" I asked. We heard a scratching, scrambling noise in the wall suggesting a squirrel, or something larger or wilder, had made its way to town from the "desirable hills." Donna's eyes were wide; I knew she wanted to leave, and I wasn't far behind.

Much as I appreciated this house, I knew Donna was right. It was daunting. I was in no position to take on such a task. I needed shelter and a place to work and grade papers. I don't cook, entertain or invite people into my home. I have simple requisites, but I need a house that can take care of me, not a house I would have to feed, burp, dress and send to Yale. Clearly, this was not the house for me.

I spent the night at an inn called the Lord Jeffrey, on the town green. Full of hunting prints, pewter mugs and Windsor chairs, the atmosphere was disconcertingly like *Holiday Inn,* the Bing Crosby musical, not the chain of bland motels. I suspected if one returned at Thanksgiving, the receptionist might be dressed as a pilgrim or a turkey.

The next morning, Donna and I saw four more houses in the scary, rugged wilderness, and one cheap and featureless condominium, far smaller than my New York apartment, in a treeless and grim development just out of town.

I asked Donna to spend more time hunting and made an appointment to meet her on the next weekend. This left only three weeks before my contract began at Amherst. Donna suggested that if worse came to worst, I could put my things in storage and take a room at the inn on the green until we found a place to buy that was simple and clean and ready to take my furniture. I hoped against hope that a move-in, postwar, suburban cape, close enough to civilization, or a town house in the fully booked ersatz-Shaker development down the highway toward Northampton, would, miraculously, become available. And, though it wasn't an ideal plan, Donna suggested that if we'd not found anything by the middle of September, I could rent a house, or part of a house, that might take me through a year, as we continued to look for a place to buy.

Still, the Victorian, with the crazy-quilt shingles, all decorative and different at each level and angle, stayed with me. I couldn't imagine myself living there, but the rhythm of its geometry and its distinct and civilized sense of place became an unspoken, unsettled, half-remembered poem that would not leave my mind, though it should have been so easily dismissed.

As I drove back into the city, the hot August evening turned sticky in that particular way only New York seems to develop; a kind of damp and greasy, sooty, airless atmosphere that holds smells of vinegar, decay, urine and car exhaust, like a stew brewing for decades. The walk from the garage, off West End, to my apartment on Riverside seemed endless, my hair was escaping, like live wires, from its long braid, and my head was wringing wet when I turned the corner and caught a blast of air that felt almost arctic. How can it be, in a city steaming as though Hell itself lived beneath the sidewalk, that the air off the Hudson might be cold enough to take your breath away, but not strong enough to permeate a city block? Except, of course, in winter, when the chill off the Hudson reaches its mean icy fingers to Central Park, and some days beyond, to Astoria, Montauk and all the way to Greenland.

The climb to my front door was exhausting, and the apartment seemed even smaller than I remembered. It was hotter than blazes, and the air conditioner took forever to cool down rooms barely large enough for me to turn in. My patience was thin. The week had been hard and hot and the issues in my leaving Columbia were not without their problems, although, for a change, they were largely procedural and bureaucratic rather than political.

There were few colleagues on campus in August, and perhaps fewer still I'd even considered calling to say good-bye. But on my last Wednesday in town I had dinner with two women of whom I was rather fond. Adele and Laura Grant were cousins, originally from New Hampshire. Laura and I had started teaching at Columbia the same year and had stayed in touch through our tenure. The cousins were related to President Grant in some distant way and had parlayed that relationship or their passion for family and historic lore—or both—into parallel careers in history, with the American Civil War their specialty. One taught at Columbia, the other at Brooklyn College, and they lived together in a Brooklyn Heights brownstone, and wrote together, like conjoined twins, surprisingly poetic academic papers that were well published and highly regarded. Their success was unusual for women in the business of academic military history, not in the least because they shared the credit to the point where no one knew where one of them left off and the other began. There was speculation that one did the research and the other wrote, but no one knew for sure. They never offered, and I never asked.

The Grant cousins looked rather alike, or perhaps they just dressed alike and had the same mannerisms. They tended to ample cardigans and pull-on pants in muted earth tones. Their shoes were always devastatingly wrong; solid pumps worn with slacks, or sandals and socks under an Indian cotton skirt. Occasionally, they would express themselves with a hand-loomed scarf of vivid color and hugely misplaced creativity, or a piece of craft-fair jewelry that tended to the visual pun. One had a pin with Grant's and Lee's silhouettes wrought of silver. Another counted an Abe Lincoln–in-repeat necklace as a fashion statement. Adele's hair was thinner than Laura's, and you could see her scalp through the pale orange waves that seemed air-puffed, like Cheetos, on her head. Laura wore glasses, though now that I think of it, Adele might have worn glasses, too.

I guess one might say they were my closest friends in New York, although we'd never been to one another's homes and we'd never talked about anything truly private. Still, I would miss dinners with the Grant Girls, as I thought of them.

They were a tie to my earliest days in the city, and it seemed we'd drifted into middle age when I wasn't looking. I remembered my Chicago grandmother criticizing a friend of Mother's who always called herself a girl, though she had children older than I. "She was a girl when the lake was at Halstead Street!" Gran said testily. Now the Grant Girls and I were no longer girls, I had to admit, but I didn't feel any differently about them or about myself.

I recognized there would be no professional celebration of leave from Columbia, and I harbored, adolescently, I suppose, the idea that this was my Official Send-Off Dinner. The Grant Girls, of course, knew all about the woman who'd hired me for Amherst. Bernadette Lowell, a kind of mother-of-all-literary-feminists, had returned to teaching five years ago after writing books about gender in literature and culture that most of us feel will be studied and remembered long, long after we're gone. She was a heroine to any and all who meant to make sense of societies that reflected the limited destinies of biology and misogyny, and mirror it back in their art. The Grant Girls were suitably impressed and, as supportive friends, pretended to believe that it was only right and just that I should have been chosen to work with Dr. Lowell at Amherst. But I knew it was a complete fluke of great good fortune.

There was a party atmosphere about the evening. We rejected our usual chardonnay, opting instead for Cosmopolitans. I felt like a coed, lifting the martini glass of pale pink liquor, canting like a liquid jewel in the shallow, angled bowl; and, in an uncharacteristically candid gesture, I told them so.

"A coed?" Adele hooted, or was it Laura? "I should think we'd look like socialites! Like Barbara Hutton!"

"Barbara Hutton, that's *so* long before our time! Was that the last moment women were truly sophisticated?" I asked, conjuring photographs of chic hats, diamond bracelets and a zebra-tufted booth at El Morocco. "Was Hutton the last holdout for the diamond bracelet and the martini, before we'd all read that Randolph Scott, not diamond bracelets, stood between Barbara Hutton and Cary Grant—and that the martini, not the money, stood between her and real life?"

The girls looked thoughtful for a moment, or maybe just a little tipsy, missing a beat and masquerading as thoughtful. "What do you think stands between real life, and *us*?" asked Laura, turning directly to me. Suddenly, it seemed, I had no air in my lungs.

"What an *odd* question," exclaimed Adele, as I blindly stumbled toward the path of an appropriate answer. I was grateful for Adele's response. Apparently, I was already pie-eyed. I must have been if I'd even contemplated answering such a query.

And what the hell *was* real life, anyway? My cramped apartment and a job with which I had so little connection I felt no loss in leaving and no need to contact coworkers to share a fond farewell? Or was it a move to an assignment so vague I had to help build its curriculum, or a move to a town with no personal associations and no suitable home? What kind of real life was this?

Then I heard someone say, "*I'm* going to buy this mad, old Victorian heap of a house in Amherst!" I thought I recognized my own voice announcing this with what someone who didn't know me might call "gusto." Indeed, someone else *could* have said it, because until that moment I had no idea I was going to buy the house. Nevertheless, and in what I can only describe as a kind of psychotic stupor, two weeks later I signed the papers. The house was mine.

CHAPTER 2

How to Move Your Life

1. Appraise all belongings and determine what is worth keeping and what is worth moving. Separate them. Figure out how you are going to get rid of all belongings not worth moving. Somehow, this is far more difficult than simply moving them.
2. Arrange for all move-worthy belongings to be packed and delivered to a storage facility on the outskirts of Northampton, Massachusetts.
3. Make a list of everything that needs changing, fixing or updating in the new house and estimate when you might be able to move your belongings into each room as renovated.
4. Rethink the whole idea.
5. List methods of suicide.

If you have ever moved, you understand that people will stay in the most deplorable environments simply to avoid considering things that belonged to the people they no longer are. This is not just a job of hauling heavy belongings; this task confronts memories too painful to lift.

There is the picture of your mother looking beautiful and fragile in a Norell dress, taken the day she told you she would have been happier without children.

In the drawer of your dresser is a handkerchief with the letter *J* embroidered on the corner, lent to you by your grandfather under circumstances you can't quite remember. It was never a beautiful handkerchief, and you may not even be sure that he thought much about you; and yet, it is a tiny piece of him, entrusted to you, and you can't let it go.

And here there is a chunk of lava from a volcanic park in Arizona; ugly, lumpen and impossible to dust within its million tiny crevices. You picked it up after you presented the paper at Arizona State on the "Language of Women in Politics," when you and that photographer went off to Sedona, where he talked to you about harmonic convergence and you got massaged, naked, in the hot sun on the patio of your hotel room. It is impossible to know which of those facts seems more unbelievable, but now you can't very well throw out the piece of lava. It is, like so many of these things you will consider, too close to the bone to discard.

Books with crumbling bindings and socks without mates, earrings missing tiny stones, half of an expensive alligator watch strap with a solid-gold buckle, shoes that are comfortable but too homely to wear in public and shoes that were expensive and sleek but hurt after only ten minutes of standing—all get touched and moved and considered. Underwear bought for a particular dress, binding, with straps in places that pinch, gets held up and inspected and packed in case, just in case you want to wear the dress again. The dress in question is a decade old, with a bodice that may have been cut too low ten years ago when the skin on your breasts was not crepey and your upper arms were toned.

And then there is loose change. What seems like thousands of dollars in pennies and nickels, covered in dust, some with sticky edges and some with black smudges, rests in the bottom of baskets and cups and drawers. If you stop to count, I promise you, it will amount to no more than nineteen dollars; but if you don't, you will remember forever that you tossed out at least a thousand dollars in sticky nickels.

There are photographs of people you don't recognize and photographs of you in ways you don't wish to be remembered, but they each contain elements of places or times you do not wish to forget. There are papers with people's addresses and unfamiliar phone numbers. Who is "Bob," scrawled, presumably in his hand, on the back of a bar napkin carrying a Pennsylvania area code? If you throw this piece of paper away, you will remember, at a moment when fate confronts you like a Bergman reaper on a beach, exactly who Bob is, and you will know for sure that you threw away your one chance at salvation or the number of a great rib joint on the Main Line.

On top of this, the work is hard. The boxes are heavy. No matter how clean you think you are, the things you don't want to see are grimy and dusty and crumbling and old, and that's not the worst of it. Because no matter how difficult it may have been to put these things into the cartons that have become your universe, you will dread, and rightly so, the day you will have to unpack them and go through this exercise all over again.

The day I bought the house, I drove directly from the lawyers' office and opened the door with an old-fashioned skeleton key, presented to me with a flourish at the closing. I stood alone for more than a few moments in the foyer, trying to feel something I assumed would be ownership or relief. When nothing solid or significant came, I set off to explore the house. I opened doors and entered rooms and looked in the closets searching for something—a hat with a feather, a volume of poetry, a letter with a foreign stamp; some quixotic sign sent to me from lives lived within these walls all through the last hundred or so years, assuring me that I'd done the right thing in saving their house and preserving their memories. But there was no message from the great beyond. There was quite a lot of dust and dirt, and moths flew out of an upstairs closet. There was mold in the carpets and a hole that looked to have been eaten by whatever it is that might eat rugs in a runner in a third-floor hallway. But I found no message from the next imagined world.

I ran water in all of the bathrooms to feel its pressure. I flushed all of the sooty toilets and used the one in the room I presumed would be my own bath, with some tissue I found crumbled in my sweater's pocket. The front and back stairs were compared, yet again, to see which of them seemed more rotten or rickety, as I figured I could use one while the other was being refurbished. Alas, it was a grim toss-up, and little I stood on seemed truly safe. The hot water was not yet turned on, but there was great force in the water pressure, the kind of power modern plumbing has all but eliminated in its energy-saving equanimity. The silvered knobs were original and lovely, and the porcelain of the claw-footed bathtubs and pedestal sinks was thick and white, and I could see that with some effort, the surfaces might clean up well, if not beautifully.

I returned downstairs and stood again in the foyer as the late afternoon sun poured in liquid and low through the thick glass of the windows. The effect was as romantic as I'd remembered from my first visit. This is my house, I tried again, with a small but strange and unsettling mix of disbelief, gratitude and fear. I trekked once more through the floors, trying to making mental note of the furniture I had crowded in my apartment and the pieces I still had in storage from my parents' house. A dining table, which had not seen its leaves in decades, might be reintroduced to its companions. A lovely Pembroke breakfast table, whose hinged panels had been forever folded at my bedside, might now take its place as a real table. I walked in circles and wondered where to begin, not knowing how big the pieces I owned might be, not knowing how large the walls I stared at might measure.

Abandoning that exercise as beyond my ken, I picked out a front bedroom as mine and felt the earliest twinges of possession. I might not yet be falling in love, but I might be flirting with the promise of love, the idea of love, the making of a place in my heart for love, though it may have been more a wish than a promise. What the other bedrooms could become remained a mystery, but I returned downstairs and watched the light in the room I now thought of as my office get lower and warmer and never harsh. I anticipated the likely hours I'd spend there and imagined where my desk might sit so that the light would be most appreciated. There were corners full of dust and debris and a few worrying damp patches on the foyer floor that looked newly wet, but I knew we'd address it all, once I could see my things in place.

Arranging for the furniture to be delivered had been as easy as a phone call, and early the next morning I met the moving van in my lumpy driveway. The movers eyed the cracked and broken surface with a skeptical eye toward their tires. We lifted the broken screen away from the front door and set it leaning against the house. The movers were not careful to hide their evaluations of whether the porch steps, not to mention the porch itself, might fail to support the weight of hefty men with full boxes and furniture.

I remembered to bring a carton of cleaning supplies, paper towels and toilet paper, and when one of the movers asked, early in the game, if he might use a bathroom, I directed him to the bath at the top of the stairs and handed him a new, wrapped, roll of toilet paper.

They had only begun to move the cartons into the hall of the first floor when I saw water begin to drip through a seam in the ceiling near the stairs. The surface of the ceiling began to swell to create a pouch like a pregnant cow's. I stood motionless for long minutes, not knowing what to do or how to change the fate unfolding before me. Though everything moved in slow motion, I was only marginally aware that the movers were scrambling around, getting cartons and furniture to safer positions while I stood still, unmoving and dumb, and watched the ceiling break into pieces and the water hit the floor, full of plaster and dirt and brown scum. It crashed like something hard and not liquid. It splashed toward me as if thrown in my face to say, "Wake up and smell the sewage, honey. Absolutely nothing will ever be the same."

My first call was to Donna, who dialed a plumber from her cell phone and met me on the steps of the house an hour later.

"Welcome home," she said, laughing, with just a tinge of "I told you so." My second call was a cleaning crew. The one I found listed in the Massachusetts Yellow Pages as "Disaster Master" seemed perfect on all counts. I moved back into my room at the Lord Jeffrey Inn, and I seriously considered never moving out.

When Disaster Master left the scene of the flood, four days later, the house was as clean as a whistle. The scummy water had been scrubbed away from the downstairs floor and the ceiling patched. Every surface in the bathrooms had been forced into antiseptic cleanliness, as had the kitchen. The walls and floors throughout the house had been swept and wiped and washed and dusted, the rotting carpets had been rolled up and thrown away, and the rooms smelled of disinfectant and soap, rather than mothballs, old musty fireplace soot and mildewed mold. I'd had an exterminator eliminate the wildlife in the walls, attic and basement by means I chose not to explore. But the romance was over.

I no longer had the innocent fantasy that Murphy's Oil Soap might hand me a livable house. For all I knew, all of the plumbing was waiting to explode, the stairs to collapse and the roof to fall in. I knew how to fix none of it. And I knew with a dreadful certainty that once it was fixed, I still wouldn't know how to make this place a home. The house was waiting for me to decide what to do. Cartons were stacked floor to ceiling, tight and fearful against the walls. Whether or not I could see the territory ahead, I knew that Lewis and Clark faced no whiter water than I.

CHAPTER 3

On the second floor of a brick building backing up to a quadrangle, I found my office. Even at first glance, I knew it was perfect. A late-August breeze came in through the casement windows, rustling the leaves and carrying an aroma of apples, though I could see no apple trees. I was only a week away from the start of classes, and my desk should have been overflowing with information on students and curriculum notes to and from Bernadette Lowell; instead, my desk was piled high with books on decorating, restoration, plumbing, paint techniques, gardening, masonry, creating walkways, developing moods through color and pattern, stairways, draperies, stenciling and even a guide to roofing. I'd cleaned out the Home Design section of Amherst Books and found a dozen more titles on Amazon. I wasn't sure of the questions to be asked, but I prayed for answers on each illustrated page. For days on end I had gone through these books in a whirlwind of desperation and excitement, marking pages with yellow Post-its. They stuck out like messy tongues from every book, at every angle, all challenging me to make sense of choices disparate and unrelated, one to the next. If I'd had enough distance to think about my behavior, I might have recognized my inability to leave the House Books at home, on my first day of work, as a tad obsessive.

My secretary was named Fran. Earlier that morning she met me at the door, introduced herself and graciously helped me move those very books from my car into the office, chattering on about my supposedly impressive credentials, as she lugged carton after carton up the stairs. The contrast of Fran to Celeste, my secretary at Columbia, was staggering. Celeste, at two hundred and fifty pounds, did not condescend to pick up so much as a paper clip from the floor. She clearly resented being a secretary and avoided, it seemed to me, discussions about anything except vacation time and the need to protect her decorated nail tips. I fantasized that Celeste was plotting to murder me with a huge hammer she kept at the center of her desk, as visible as a lighted stop sign. Since she'd never replaced a single roll of toilet paper in the office bathroom, I didn't think she was the type to offer help with our department's carpentry. Murder appeared to be the only infraction recognized by the committee at Columbia that dealt with the firing of union staff, and there were times, I found, that I actually looked forward to her impending attempt. At least it would have broken the tension.

Fran Estovan was cut from a different cloth, a witty-looking long-limbed skinny girl with black Mamie Eisenhower bangs and little white sequins on her cotton cardigan. She wore rhinestone-studded cat's-eye glasses, and her arms looked a little rubbery in a way that reminded me of Olive Oyl.

I shared Fran and an office suite with a professor of French literature named Josephine O'Sullivan. Everyone, Fran explained to me, including students, called Dr. O'Sullivan "Josie." Her office sat directly across the foyer from mine, and Fran sat between us at a desk cluttered with family pictures, rubber ducks, bobble-head dolls, a wind-up gorilla toy and pens with tops that looked like daisies and pinwheels.

I could see that Josie had hung café curtains of dotted swiss at her windows, and they fluttered in the breeze. Her desk was the same big, wooden, square institutional issue as mine, dating, I guessed, from about the Second World War, but she'd painted hers a creamy white and rubbed the paint to look worn. The gray-green carpet, installed in all of our offices, was covered with the botanical squares of a needlepoint rug, which, Fran told me, Josie had stitched herself. Her walls were painted pale yellow, and even her desk chair was upholstered in floral linen. It was, perhaps, the most residential, and therefore inappropriate, design scheme I'd ever seen in a professional office, and I was both put off and drawn to it. I was reminded again that I was on new ground. I'd seen nothing like this in our offices at Columbia.

Josie must have gone home at lunchtime because around two o'clock she marched into my office with a white ironstone pitcher of roses, fresh from her garden, apparently intent on welcoming me on my first day at work. She was small and round and very pretty. Everything about her curved up optimistically, from the ends of her dark bobbed hair to the corners of her mouth. Her big, fleshy, deep-peach roses, she announced, were called "Dolly Partons," and she moved stacks of my books to the floor to make room for them.

I'd never so much as sprouted a plant from an avocado pit, so I couldn't imagine how she managed to grow roses. I was unclear as to whether she, herself, had named them "Dolly Parton" because of their resemblance to abundant rosy flesh, or if this was truly the name of the rose. I was frowning, I suppose, pondering this question as well as the very idea of a bustling, chubby little woman in a pink and gold Hermès scarf barging into my office, moving my books and placing uninvited things on my work surface, when she put out her hand to shake mine. "Dr. Harkness, I presume," she said.

"Joy," I answered. She smiled as though this were a small joke. Maybe to you, I thought.

Josie shook my hand like an executive in a boardroom, with a definite downward and masculine single shake, and the casual comment "I'm sure you've already figured out that *I'm* Josie O'Sullivan," and then she invited me to join her family for dinner at their home that very night. I explained that I had far too much to do to take an evening out of my schedule for dinner.

"Like what?" she demanded.

"Well, all kinds of things," I stammered.

"You have to eat . . . ," she pressed. And so, though it clearly was none of her business, I allowed myself to be trapped into listing the things I had to manage just to begin to unpack my belongings. From stairs so rattling and unsteady that all of my furniture remained on the first floor, to plumbing I feared might carry me off to the Ganges, to light fixtures that may never have worked properly and could now, at least in my imagination, burn a house down as I lay in bed, in a substitute and roughly made-up bedroom off the dining room. There was no exaggeration, so it was easy to lay it on thick, in hopes that it would buy me an excuse from the social expectations of being a "suite mate."

"Whoa!" Josie sort of laughed. "Call Teddy Hennessy," she said. "Call him right now. Here, I'll call him for you . . . ," and with that she lifted the receiver of *my* phone, asked the operator for the Hennessy number, dialed and spoke to a woman she called "Maureen." Turning my phone to face *her* and read off my direct number, she asked the woman to have Teddy call me back. "It's a huge project, Maureen," she explained, "and right up Teddy's alley. But he has to begin it immediately, or Joy will have to go somewhere else—and I would *hate* that . . ."

Josie O'freaking Sullivan would *hate* that? *Jesus!* What do *my* house and *my* projects have to do with blasted Josie O'Sullivan? I fumed. "Look," I said, trying not to reveal my gritted teeth, "about dinner—it's more than just the house. I haven't begun to file my course work, and I've got a meeting with Lowell on Friday, and it all has to be done by then—but I appreciate the offer." She looked bereft. "Perhaps we might do it some other time," I offered weakly.

"Oh sure," Josie said. "Many other times. My husband is a travel writer, and the girls and I find we miss him less when he's away if we keep the house full of company. He's in Greece right now for *Town & Country,* on what amounts to a 'scavenger hunt for the ultrarich,' but you'll meet him soon. You'll like him."

Right, I thought, I'll be sure to talk about the ultrarich with him.

Hours after she left, I could still smell her perfume in the air, or maybe it was the flowers. I recognized a faint but deep feeling of nostalgia I attached to that scent. Though I could neither pinpoint the source of the aroma nor the memory it suggested, this sensation, akin to longing, was a feeling to which I was distinctly unaccustomed.

The phone rang after six, as I was about to pack up my gear and head for home. A boyish voice introduced himself as Teddy Hennessy and, without asking whether or not it was convenient for me, announced that he could be at my house around seven that evening. It wasn't a conversation, it was a pronouncement, but I took the bait and didn't argue. I gave him my address, hung up the phone and hastily loaded some design books into an old, leather L.L.Bean tote I'd carried since college. It strained at the cargo.

I drove the ten blocks or so to my house, and entered, turning on what few bulbs hung from the ceiling on cords like ripe fruit. I'd set up my parents' dining room table in, of all places, the dining room. It seemed a novel idea, as it had been used, ends folded, as a console table, pushed against a wall in New York, for nearly twenty years. My two hard-backed chairs were pulled up to the table. My father's wing chair and a shapeless sofa I'd bought at Crate and Barrel about a decade ago sat in the living room like guests at a function who'd not yet met. The wing chair was high on casters and covered in a beautiful crewel, well worn but jewel-colored. The couch was low and the color of a smudge. The light from the ceiling bulb was unforgiving, pointing out their disparity. My bed was in the room off the foyer I'd begun to think of as my office, because I didn't trust the bathroom upstairs and, frankly, I didn't trust the stairs themselves, although Disaster Masters said they thought they were "safe enough." My domestic life had not improved between New York and Amherst, I had to admit. If anything, it was worse. Now, not only did I have a home with no welcome; I had a home that put me, literally, in peril.

I laid the books on the dining table and tried to open them to the marked pages. I was once more caught up in the problems of having highlighted images that seemed to have nothing to do with one another: one porch looked like the entrance to a log cabin, a stairway was distinctly Gustavian, I'd marked neoclassical moldings, loggias from Italian villas, Carpenter Gothic door surrounds, Federal pediments and a kitchen straight out of a farmhouse in Provence.

Clearly, I was in over my head when I noticed that it was twenty after seven, and then twenty to eight, and then ten to nine. At five after nine there was a knock at the door. Standing in the dim light of the porch was a hulking figure who looked like an overgrown child. He wore a baseball cap, shorts and a psychedelic T-shirt that said, EAT, DRINK AND SEE JERRY. Teddy Hennessy walked into my foyer.

I was, I suppose, annoyed at his idea of punctuality, but I was more aware of wanting to cram as much information as possible about the problems of the house and the ideas I had for creating a kind of perfect home into this one meeting, now shortened, I imagined, by his lateness. In my nervousness and haste, I probably blathered on. Teddy didn't say much. He did things like take his penknife and lift moldings away from the walls, while my heart stopped at the idea of vandalizing the house even more. At one point, admittedly near a rather large hole in the wall, he took his fist and pounded an even larger area away, creating a new cloud of dust. "Hey . . . hey, hey!" I cried.

"Just trying to see how brittle the boards are," he muttered. I followed him gingerly up the rickety front staircase and down the rackety back. We inspected the place in the upstairs bath where the plumbing leak seemed to have originated. When I showed him that the water-break in the ceiling had not been directly under the bathroom leak, and asked how that could be, he didn't answer me.

I took him over to the dining table and showed him the Post-it-noted images in hopes that he would make sense of my references, as though revealing a dream to a Jungian and hoping for direction and enlightenment, but none followed. He was as unresponsive a human being as I had ever met. I had no idea whether or not he understood what he was looking at, and, in retrospect, I may have filled what seemed like too much empty space with far too much useless information. He made a few notes on a yellow pad. He drew a few diagrams, but they made no sense to me. He suddenly appeared to call an end to the meeting by walking toward the front door and touching the doorknob.

"Wait a minute!" I put my hand on the door as if to stop it from opening. "Can you *do* this job—I mean, what would you do, how would you handle it? Is this even something you're *capable* of doing? And how much could it cost, and how long would it take? And do you understand any of the ideas in *any* of the books I've shown you? I don't know if you are even *interested* in this house!"

And Teddy said this: "My container is kinda full here."

"What?" I said, completely stumped.

"I'll have to get back to you, man," he said.

He called me "man." Good grief, I thought. And he left. I noticed that he drove an old Subaru station wagon, and while I couldn't see the color of the car clearly in the dark of the driveway, there was a piece of lumber tied to the top and one of the taillights was lit in a perpetual blink. I watched from the porch as the winking car drove away.

I was suddenly hungry and realized I'd had no dinner. I reached to open the cabinet for the box of Special K, and the door pull came off in my hand.

CHAPTER 4

I'm not sure at what age it occurs to you that you are no longer "dating." I'm not even sure that I ever actually "dated" at all. We traveled in packs in high school and college, pairing off for an evening or a weekend, but I was never really invited out alone—one-to-one; never given a high school ring or a fraternity pin. Those things belonged to the generations before mine, I believed. But for a long time, and probably far too long, I had a secret wish: the adolescently romantic idea that there was someone out there for me; someone I hadn't yet met who would ask me on a date and make sense of my life. I harbored the hope, I'm now embarrassed to admit, that like a girl in a Lifetime movie, I would look into someone's eyes and find a reflection of my inner life. But sometime between my teenage years and the first years in New York, that idea had pretty well evaporated. I'd grown up.

It might be noted, at least by me, that the literal presence of a husband neither met nor quelled that fantasy. My husband, nice as he might have been, never was that someone. He never looked close enough to begin to see the girl who'd longed to swim in a more exotic sea, always harboring the hope of leaving the safe haven of Saint Louis for the adventurous coast of Manhattan. My delight in Columbia's offer came as a shock to him. "A bolt from the blue," he said—that alone seemed reason enough to leave him. How can he not understand me? I thought. Has he not read my poems? Though now, whenever I fall across a bit of my own old poetry, I have to admit it's opaque in ways even I can't fathom. I wrote in a form designed to carry expression, ideas and emotions in streamlined, literary, modern gestures that were the fashion of the moment, but the form and even the content, I fear, were designed to obscure the feelings as well as the facts of my real life. Maybe I stopped expecting a man to decipher the code, at about the time I stopped defending the fantasy that I had anything important enough to say. The poetry in my life had stopped figuratively and literally.

Unless you are a hooker or a supermodel, New York, apparently, is not a likely place to meet available men. I don't know why that is, but I know that I am not the only one to have noted the fact. At any rate, I suddenly found myself in Amherst, at an age some might call overripe, attracting possible contenders without any effort on my part. On my third day at school, three of them hovered about the quadrangle as I ferried boxes from car to office, watching me rather openly and apparently discussing me. They were middle-aged, slightly paunchy and one was balding, but they stood like teenagers at a malt shop watching the new girl unpack her Thunderbird. It was embarrassing, to say the least.

Fran smiled and announced at lunch that I was "new meat for the Coyotes," and Josie seemed to get a real kick out of the situation, as she described what I was likely to find. While there certainly were others, she explained, these three fellows traveled as a pack. All were single, all were, she assumed, straight, and all three seemed to get an immediate handle on the new women on campus each September. My arrival at the English Department, she informed me, had its own bit of hoopla, and they were, no doubt, responding to the hype.

"God," I said, "this is awful. This is so humiliating."

"Oh?" Josie's eyebrows shot up. "Are you gay?" she asked—rather brightly, I thought.

"No! Of course not!" I retaliated, bristling.

"Well," she said, somewhat deflated, "there's no 'of course' about it—but if you're not, then just relax and enjoy it. I mean, I haven't been single in twenty-five years and maybe I'm out of touch with the scene, but I think a little attention might be, as Martha Stewart says, 'a good thing.' They're basically harmless—kind of goofy guys, if you ask me. But you might get to share a few good meals, you might see a movie you wouldn't have seen, and—who knows?—you might even make a friend or two." She crossed her ankles; her lime green nub-soled driving shoes matched the green in yet another Hermès scarf. She looked at me hard. "You never know when you might need a friend."

My face was hot from the discussion. Who the hell is Josie O'Sullivan to push herself into everyone's business? I thought. She doesn't know anything about me. But I found myself waiting for the ambush of the Coyotes with equal amounts of anticipation and dread. Truth be told, I also entertained the terrible doubt that came from fearing they might not pounce at all. I might not, I figured, have even looked interesting enough for them to bother checking out. Fran and Josie would both know, and most important, I would know—that no Coyotes had come a-courting. The whole thing created a kind of artificial anxiety that was a ridiculous way, I thought as I unpacked my books and organized them on the heavy oak shelves, to begin my introduction to a new life.

And yet, I couldn't help myself; all through the afternoon I stole quick, surreptitious glances out the window to see if the pack were any-where near, but there was no sign of them. At four o'clock Fran arranged her desk and said good night. Josie had been gone since just after lunch, and I was alone in the suite. I heard no one enter and was on my hands and knees putting heavy reference books—the *Webster's* and the twenty volumes of the *Oxford English,* the *Birmingham Collins Cobuild* and the *Arden Shakespeare*—on low shelves, when I sensed the presence of someone. I turned my head and came face to fabric with a pair of green corduroy trousers leaning on the doorjamb of my office. I looked up and saw a camel jacket and a receding, sandy-hued hairline. Not the best position to meet predators, I thought.

"Hello," said the Coyote.

"Hello," I said. I just stayed on the floor.

"Can I help you up?" he asked.

"No. No thanks. It's my office, and I've chosen to operate from this plane for a while." I thought if I were sharp and not encouraging, I might get him to leave, but he continued to chatter on as though this kind of situation were normal for him. He seemed arrogant right from the begin-ning. He sort of snorted when he laughed, and he looked down his nose at me. Of course, I was on the floor.

I hoped I might turn the moment into a screwball comedy, quick-witted with fast Ben Hecht dialogue, but clearly it was not my element. He made no move to leave, and eventually, I got up; not as gracefully, perhaps, as I might have wished. I got up the way a forty-eight-year-old woman gets up, with a hand on the desk and a hand on my knee.

The Coyote introduced himself as Kevin Betts. He is, he tells me, the Poet in Residence at Amherst—a post, he tells me, that was created for Robert Frost. He stands before me puffed up like the inheritor of the talent of Frost. He tells me that he knows I have published two books of poetry.

Oh God, if there is a God, please, please don't let it be possible that he's read any of my poetry. Not to worry. Kevin Betts wouldn't waste his time reading anyone's poetry but Kevin Betts's—and an occasional Robert Browning, selected for seduction. It was all too clear.

Still, after about fifteen minutes of pointless repartee, I found myself agreeing to have coffee with him at six thirty at a place called Judy's, a place known, I was assured by Kevin Betts, both far and near, for *specialty coffees*. The term chilled me, and yet I agreed to go to Judy's. I agreed to meet Kevin Betts there. I agreed to drink a "specialty coffee." Like a rent-a-wreck on a highway, I was moving into the fast lane of my life.

CHAPTER 5

All right. I drank a coffee called "Java and Jive." It had Amaretto and something else—Strega or heroin or . . . Jesus, I don't know, something deadly and, I'm sure, addictive. Kevin Betts had a coffee fantasy with whipped cream and coconut on it, very like a hot Dairy Queen sundae with everything but the cherry. He got cream on his nose when he tried to take a drink. I felt intoxicated from the first sip, but I hung on and sometime through his endless rendition of his year at Oxford as a Rhodes scholar, I began to come to. He told me the university was abuzz—he used the word *abuzz*—about my arrival. The "Jamesian deconstructionist," he proclaimed, as though I knew what that meant. I mean, I know what it means, but it means nothing.

I announced at seven thirty that I had to go home, that I was renovating my old house and I needed to be there if the contractor called. Kevin proclaimed old houses his forte, his passion, his raison d'être. Could he please come back with me and inspect my house? I remembered the ploys boys used to get upstairs to my apartment eons ago; this one was no less obvious, but Kevin Betts looked soft and out of shape and by now the heroin or the caffeine or the sugar or something was working to revive me and I was certain I could take him, should he try anything. He followed me in his car and pulled into the driveway behind me.

He began to pick the house apart from the moment he opened his car door. The driveway was too near to the porch, he said. The porch had been an add-on, he was sure, because of the way it bisected the door surround. So terribly crass was the porch, he was snorting and resisting touching the wood of the banister as we stepped up to the front door. He entered the foyer and proclaimed the closets on either side of the door to be added, probably in the "terrible nineteen twenties." I loved those closets. I loved the whole idea of those closets. I knew the doors needed to be replaced so that they, at least, matched, but I loved those closets. We went through the rest of the house with Kevin Betts snorting and sneering at every turn. The few times he stopped his monologue to ask what I had in mind in terms of renovation, he rolled his eyes at my answers and I could see he thought the horrible house had taken an even more pathetic turn and had fallen into the hands of an actual cretin.

I was sure that I had proven myself far too unworthy for Kevin Betts when he leaned over and kissed me with a kind of force and power I had forgotten men possess. I briefly considered blackening his eye but found myself returning the kiss and matching the force. He took my jaw in his hands and held the back of my head with fingers much stronger than they'd looked. I put my hands under his sport jacket and ran them up his chubby rib cage to his breast. I squeezed in direct proportion to the force on my head and neck and the force of his mouth on mine. He dropped my head and stepped away. "I can't do this if you're going to try to be dominant," he said, accusingly.

"Excuse me?" I asked.

"I need you to be submissive," he demanded.

"Well, I'm . . . gosh . . . ," I stammered, "I don't know what to say."

"Look," he said, "I think you've said enough. This isn't going to work."

"With whom does this *work*?" I asked, incredulously, wiping my mouth with my hand.

"That's enough," he said. "I don't have to stand here and let you criticize me."

"I'm not, I mean . . . I didn't . . . ," but I let it drop.

I walked him to the door and he seemed to collect himself, but when he got to the door he turned and said with a softer face, almost a smile, "You know what you need?"

Oh God, I thought. He's going to offer to spank me. I looked at him defensively, trying as fast as I could to think of a graceful pass.

"You need Teddy Hennessy," he said. "He could whip this place into shape for you in no time."

"Yeah," I said, swimming through the gray matter of confusion between relief about the spanking and the tidal change to a conversation about my house. "He was here just yesterday, but I'm not sure he even understood this house—"

"He understood all right," Kevin said, wiping his lips with his handkerchief. "Teddy could do this house with his eyes closed. He's the guy for you." And then he left, after kissing me on the cheek as though we'd had the most pleasant of evenings.

This is what dating is like, I thought, this horrible mix of boredom and fear and humiliation and confusion. I vowed that no matter how insistent, intriguing or even seductive the Coyotes might be, I would not go down this path in the forest again.

CHAPTER 6

More than a week passed. No Coyotes approached. Classes were up and running. I had almost learned the names of my students and almost mastered some of the names of some of the faculty, but I was in the upward curve of accommodating the existing Amherst curriculum and marrying it with my own, while finding supply closets and the bursar's office. I'd gotten lost on my way back from the cafeteria more than once, and I was considering, like Hansel or Gretel, leaving a trail of popcorn or marking trees with ribbons. All in all, it was taking me about twice as long as it had at Columbia to do even the simplest things.

I had my first meeting with Bernadette Lowell and the other members of her team. They clearly think I'm a Grand Fromage, and I am torn between wanting to stand on a box, wave my arms around and shout that they have, almost certainly, confused me with someone from another school, and wanting to sit back and smile like the second Mrs. Gioconda because—I may be nuts—I do so want to be part of this wildly ambitious experiment.

Bernadette continues to be an impressive package. A kind of Julia Child of academia, she toots in her Vassar voice, which is both lower and higher than a human voice might be, about the merits of proprietary scholarship. This is not an abstract concept; she means to create a new way of learning, and she means to own it and brand it for Amherst.

She is focused on the fact that humans take in information in a variety of ways and believes that if we, as educators, were less judgmental in our assigning worth to those ways, and more flexible in our delivery systems, we might see a breakthrough in education and a flowering of knowledge the likes of which civilization has not seen since the early days of the Enlightenment.

It would be easy to be sarcastic about this unguarded, audacious passion. I'm so used to sneering that now, when a great idea might have landed, like a chip off a meteor, somewhere near me, I hardly know how to react. But I can see in the faces of those she's calling her Core Team a cautious buy-in to the daring of this dream.

The concept of graduate work managed under her Immersion Technique is the theory that in the general is the specific. We would test this with a plan for the study of Shakespeare, where students would be intensively cross-fertilized with ideas of science and philosophy, art and medicine, music and history, encompassing the whole environment in which Shakespeare would have lived and the world of choices he might have made, given that society. She believes that the results we'll get, in theory and scholarship, from those graduate students will be very different and far richer than the work springing from traditional study.

For this program, Dr. Lowell intends for us to discover a technique in teaching our individual subjects that will hold education together within a larger shared proprietary philosophy. As we expand the program, each period of literature, for instance, will be colored by an understanding of the science, art and ethics of that era. She wants us to consider poetry, psychology and Pascal's *Pensées* in the light of Bach and Braque and Bauhaus. She wants to reset the whole idea of college curriculum. And, audaciously, she wants Amherst to stand for this new initiative; the idea of recasting liberal arts within a nest of classic humanities.

Not that Bernadette thinks this is the best or only way of teaching. Quite the opposite. She is railing against all mediocrity and sameness. And she's already warned us—we will never have seen criticism as we can expect to see with this experiment. The world, she told us, in a matter-of-fact and almost cheerful way, rustling papers as she talked, is full of envy and fear and always standing in wait of a great idea to destroy.

In fact, Bernadette hopes that other institutions will find their own ways of relating information in innovative strands of technique that might suit another student better than our approach. She's looking for all kinds of keys because she believes that there are all kinds of people— and every one of them might be unlocked to greatness or insight or pleasure or creativity if they might only find their way to the institution that could direct them to the root of their own particular genius.

Bernadette cites, for instance, the difference between Asian calli-graphic reading, or *scanned information,* as she calls it, and Western reading comprehension—letters built to create words that stand for sounds that are then assigned to concepts. How dare we, she says, be so glib about labeling some conditions as "learning disabilities" when half the world "reads" information in a completely different and impression-istic way.

Her plan is a long game. It's no accident most of us on her team are younger than she by a generation or more. Lowell wants us in from the beginning and committed to the long reward. She wants us to discover and accommodate the diverse ways in which humans take in informa-tion, eventually breaking the line between Eastern and Western tech-niques of learning and expressing creative thought, without status or rank, so that an individual might follow a system or technique compati-ble to their own nature—to the way they were naturally "wired." She wants the systems to accommodate them rather than the other way around. And then she wants institutions to embrace contrasting learning methods, for clarity, choice, branding, competition and, most of all, fruitful growth, as we help to push the universe forward. Nothing less.

Her message is messianic, and yet there is a humble and innocent approach to her position. Find out how people learn. Find ways to accommodate them.

At the first meeting of her team, we sat simply, in a circle of chairs. Bernadette's papers were messy and ragged around her in loose stacks, and she rattled her big soft tote bags more than once to unearth another example of her train of thought. We, her charges, were, for the most part, silent. If she had her way, there *would* be a new dawn in the whole idea of educational presentation and academic branding, and not one of us could imagine Bernadette not getting her way. No raised voice, no sharp gesture; Bernadette Lowell was a sweet, large, strong woman who looked as though she could prepare a pot of porridge, start a revolution or, all by herself, push away the stone at Jesus' grave.

She introduced the staff and made each little introduction a kind of honor. The quality of the men and women she's chosen over the last few years to create this plan made me almost blush to be sitting in the same room, no less the same circle. Here was Adele Friedman, author and rising star on her own, lured away from Yale by Bernadette two years ago as her first chair, now the head of Amherst's Psychology Department and looking like a pre-Raphaelite heroine, with her dark salt-and-pepper curls billowing around her narrow shoulders and a nineteenth century pin tucked in the high neck of her white wool shirt. Ben Roth, the senior member of the European History Department, was soft spoken and good humored. He wore his hair neat and short around his perfectly proportioned head, and his clothes were country-club polished, a white turtleneck, camelhair blazer and soft gray flannel slacks. Known to be one of the best Renaissance lecturers on the East Coast, he brought a particular air of gentle breeding to the proceedings.

Iris Attas had written her doctoral thesis on the historically changing nature of ethics in medicine. Out of the Philosophy Department, she'd cut a new area of study. She was small and dark and immediately likable, dressed in a chic tweed skirt, woolen tights and clogs. She'd been brought over to our program from Penn. Her husband, Steven, looked like a rich European businessman to me, but to my surprise, he was a professor of comparative philosophy at the University of Massachusetts and was on loan to us. He fiddled with his BlackBerry through most of Bernadette's talk and our subsequent discussion, but when he spoke, he was articulate and supportive in clarifying and solving a few of the points of process that threatened to hamper our ability to act as an efficient team.

Beth Goodman, Elisabeth Long and Alexi Marquette represented the Amherst Drama Department. Marjorie Voorhees was a historian who had made her career in detailing the authenticity of Shakespearian text and reference. Lowell had snagged her from McGill, which was quite a coup. That evening, we were missing a scholar named Horace Horamian, most recently from Temple University, in Philadelphia, where he had integrated a study of the history of mathematics into its math curriculum. Bernadette was excited to introduce him to us, and she called him on her speaker phone. We all said hello, like a class of third graders.

Todd Dixon's background was, perhaps, most parallel to mine. He was a classic English lit guy, but he had a longer history of teaching Shakespeare than I, and about five years ago he'd produced a small book, released to the general public, about how Shakespeare's plots and characters could be seen, recycled, in popular culture. Todd had come to us from Harvard. He was a bit of a wreck in a classically academic way: heavy, bearded, disheveled; his hair was a disaster, his face puffy; his shirt had food stains, and he didn't sit up straight. And there were a few minutes when I thought he might have fallen asleep. But just as I was about to count him out, he snorted loudly and told a story of such relevance, with a delivery so fresh and engaging, one completely forgot his appearance.

Still to be filled: representatives from music and art and applied science. Bernadette was not sure exactly what she was looking for here, and she wanted our help in terms of content and contacts.

I sat next to an elegant older gentleman named Howard Peal, who, I was given to understand, is the classics scholar here and respected throughout his field. He took my arm on the stairs in a gentleman's gesture, though I suspected he was steadying himself as much as allowing me the idea of my status as the newest "lady" in the circle. His long narrow feet were elegant in their polished and tasseled loafers, but the marble of the steps was worn and slick. Well, I thought, begin as you intend to continue; we're all going to have to haul one another up this mountain. And that was, I think, the real point of Bernadette's meeting.

At home, I persisted in sleeping in the study on the first floor, venturing upstairs only to shower—and even then, half expecting the water to stop or the tub to crash to the floor below. Needless to say, I never left conditioner in my hair. I darted back downstairs to towel off and to blow my hair dry. They were not the most relaxing weeks of my life. I heard nothing from Teddy Hennessy, though when I asked around for recommendations, his was the only name that came up. I found myself reluctant to call him, so sure was I that he had no insight for and no interest in this house.

On a Saturday night in mid-September, I was sitting at the dining room table, the surface strewn with short essays from my basic composition class. I was trying to make a connection between each page and each barely recognized, hardly remembered student face. The essays seemed a grim reminder of a generation raised on cable television, YouTube and video games; made up in equal parts of pornography and violence, wrapped in cloaks of banality so alike, one to the other, that I had to keep looking at the stack I'd gone through to make sure I had not already read the essay in hand. This is common. The early work of first-year students rarely sings with originality. Somewhere in the year they begin to find their voice. Somewhere in their last year they begin to exercise a degree of control over that voice, and sometime before they're sixty, if they're very lucky, they decide what it is they really have to say.

I was wearing pajamas, faded blue flannel with pictures of clouds floating everywhere. Over this, an old, rust-colored cashmere cardigan that had been my father's—making it at least twenty-two years old—as that was how long he'd been dead. On my feet were suede and wool slipper socks—stretched out of shape and long worn. My hair was a wreck, with curly bits and renegade wiry strands escaped from a topknot held with a take-out-Chinese chopstick. On the table next to me lay a now empty plastic container that had held a helping of Stouffer's frozen Macaroni and Cheese, a dirty fork, a rumpled section of paper towel and a can of Canfield's Diet Chocolate Fudge Soda. Clearly, this was not a lifestyle vignette I would have chosen to share with the world.

It was after eight when I heard a knock at the door. Standing in shorts and Birkenstocks, though the temperature had dropped to about fifty degrees, was Teddy Hennessy. "What are you doing here?" I asked, not inviting him in. I honestly didn't mean rudeness, but I was so taken aback.

"I came to talk about your house," he said, frowning. "I thought you wanted me to get back to you, and I've been hearing all over town that you were waiting for me to call." He continued to stand on the porch. I continued to stand in the doorway.

"Well, I did expect you to call, not just show up without an appointment. What makes you think I can stop my work to see you?"

"All right," he said through his teeth, as though restraining some deep, long-seeded anger. He took a deep and audible breath. "Do you want me to leave, or do you want me to talk to you about your house?"

"Oh, for God's sake," I said, opening the door for him to enter.

For the next forty-five minutes this boy or this man, chewing a huge wad of gum, dressed in his baseball cap and shorts with a somewhat too small T-shirt straining across his stomach, pointed his fingers at detail after detail, making sense of the original house and adding up the changes, decade after decade. He decreed which of the accretions should stay and which should go, and I found myself agreeing with every decision. This was not a case, he pointed out, of a house that should have stopped in time. And he used the term *embalmed house* in derision, meaning houses that were faithfully restored to their original condition, without regard or respect for their ability to live through and within their times. There were additions made through the years that accommodated central heating and the needs for storage and new appliances that simply made old houses function in this century; but neither, he stressed, was this a house that should lose its original sense of self. His talent for scale and proportion mixed with his deep knowledge of history in both architecture and practical life were impressive enough to make me forget the picture of Garfield on his T-shirt.

When he finished, we had a kind of outline of all the things he felt would need attention, from the roof to the basement, from the driveway to the wallpaper. And within that list, there were things to address immediately, some that could wait, and others that would require more information to ascertain their degree of priority. In total or part, it was enough to make the stouthearted turn and run.

"How much?" I asked meekly.

"Well," he said, "let's see." He took from the pocket of his shorts folded pieces of paper with columns of figures and notes that separated materials from subcontractors' fees and his own hours. I tried to look over his shoulder for a bottom line, but he didn't relinquish the full bundle.

"Not all of *this* has to be done at once," he said, more to himself than to me, ticking things off with a blunt pencil textured with tooth marks. "We can tackle *this* area by area. But some of the stuff *can* be done at the same time, as long as we don't all get in one another's way." He *wasn't* talking to me. He was muttering to himself. "There are things—like the stairs and the plumbing—we've gotta deal with. And we gotta check the roof and the clapboards for rot." Suddenly I was on his radar. He turned to me. "I can bring in the plumbers while we deal with the building and the carpentry. And, as I said, I think we should do some of the simpler things to just make this place more comfortable; so even though you're living in a construction site, it could feel like your life is getting better every day. You know? We don't have to deal with *some* of it, like the driveway—until spring. And we don't have to deal with the top floor—*ever,* I suppose."

He showed me how he had outlined what he imagined the total costs could be, if he found the worst, in terms of the roof and the siding and the pipes and the electrical. And he assumed we would have to do most of it over from scratch. I gulped. But he broke down details in terms I could easily understand. He showed me where he'd need to subcontract for specific trades and what he could do alone. He seemed to know enough about what those tradesmen's budgets should be. The subs would not buy materials, he explained, definitely. They'd tell him what they needed, and *we'd* buy the materials. He'd estimated the total budget on the last handwritten sheet. He told me that he was rarely off by much, that he usually figured a worst-case scenario, so that there should be only pleasant surprises, and as long as we stuck to his plan, he'd honor his fee, even if his time went over his estimate.

The cost was much less than I expected. I exhaled. Beyond this, he suggested that we begin to make decorating decisions on the first floor and gave me a ballpark outline of those options with high and low budgets noted. Again, the costs were less than I would have anticipated. Especially for his time. "But I'm already here," he said. "While I'm waiting for glue to dry or for the lumberyard to deliver or for the roofing guys to fix something, there are all sorts of things I can be doing. I'm not going to charge you twice for that time."

"When can you start?" I asked.

"Monday."

"Monday. Two days from now—Monday? *This* Monday?"

"Yeah," he said, as though surprised at my astonishment. "I expected to start on Monday. That's why I'm here tonight. I finished a job across town this afternoon."

And that's how Teddy Hennessy came to work in my house.

The days grew into weeks. When I left for work in the morning he was already on the job, and in the evening, when I came home, he proudly showed me the progress of each day. On Sundays he took his mother to church, though he often returned in the early afternoon and continued working. Sometimes I made dinner for the two of us, and we'd eat in the kitchen, sitting on stools that pulled up to a makeshift counter he'd fashioned for his paint and his equipment. Sometimes he picked up a pizza or Chinese. Many a night I went to bed to the sound of him scraping paint or sanding a molding or to the swoosh of his brush as it glided across a ceiling or the tread of a stair, with rock music playing on his boom box. No one played, strummed, drummed or sang anything that had been recorded within the last twenty years, and it was nearly always the Who. Sometimes the Grateful Dead, every so often a bit of the Kinks or the Allman Brothers would sneak in, but for the most part, it was the Who, day in and day out, mixed like a memory from my teenage years, with the redolent scent of pot.

CHAPTER 7

I was going to lunch at Josie's house one Saturday in early October. She had worn me down with invitations. Her vagabond husband was off on yet another adventure in upscale travel journalism, and she was planning what she called a "girls' lunch." It would include her girls (Jackie and Lizzie, ages thirteen and nine); her friend Donna Fortunata (by happy coincidence, my realtor); Donna's daughters (who were, I assumed, about the same age as Josie's); and, from our office, Fran and me. I was anticipating the day like a visit to the dentist.

I came out of the bathroom in a terry cloth robe about ten o'clock in the morning and found Teddy at work on the staircase. I tried to step around him, my legs and feet still wet from the shower. "Teddy," I said, "you must listen to that tape of *Tommy* ten times a day." He looked at me, as though to say, "What's your point?"

Clearly, I had no point that could matter to Teddy, so I simply dropped the subject—too late, unfortunately, as he launched into a monologue about the Who that could have been a doctoral thesis. He knew everything about them. He knew about Keith Moon's death and whom he'd offended within the twenty-four hours that led up to his demise. He knew all about the late John Entwistle's heart condition and Pete Townshend's problems with pornography—"a massive mistake, man"—and exactly where Pete happened to be when the police came to call.

Teddy knew how each of Pete's songs was conceived and how many times the band had recorded each song and who else had covered the song and what Pete thought of each artist who'd covered each song.

Townshend was always referred to as "Pete," as though a close personal friend or relative, rather than a celebrity, distanced by culture and money and fame and geography and—let's face it—deliberate actions to remove himself from the crush and spittle of the adoring crowd and—therefore—from Teddy.

One could assume he knew their blood types, their personal physicians and how many times a week they had marital relations or, I suppose in the case of rock musicians, extramarital relations.

I was trapped. My body, still wet from the shower, was making a little puddle on the floor. Teddy rambled on with passion and energy and a level of detail and critical insight I believe I'd missed when writing my Margaret Chase Smith biography; on the other hand, all this information was about the Who.

I finally edged past him and toward my temporary bedroom—soon to be office—in increments so small as to be imperceptible, as though Teddy, mid-Who, noticed anything outside of his encyclopedic elegy. It took him nearly twenty minutes to wind down. I changed and came out of the bedroom-office, a little fearful that he might launch, once more, into Whoville. Instead, Teddy picked up a book that sat atop a stack of books I'd brought home from school.

"Yeats," he said and then recited from memory:

I went out to the hazel wood,
Because a fire was in my head,
And cut and peeled a hazel wand,
And hooked a berry to a thread;
And when white moths were on the wing,
And moth-like stars were flickering out,
I dropped the berry in a stream
And caught a little silver trout.

"Teddy," I said, amazed he would have memorized such a thing, "what is this?"

"Yeats," he answered, frowning at me in disbelief, as though he thought, perhaps, I'd never heard the name. "The poet?"

I drove to Josie's following the directions I'd written on the back of a telephone message sheet; driving while reading off the names of twisting lanes called unlikely things like Dog Tail Corners and Putter's Hill. The roads looked like driveways, and the driveways looked like roads. More than once I turned into what I thought was my "third right" turn only to have it read PRIVATE ROAD just beyond the shrubbery. It amazed me how one could go from the civility of town to the wilds of the backwoods in what seemed like a hundred yards.

Finally, the much-anticipated Putter's Hill was revealed on a small sign, and my little BMW climbed the steep drive to find Josie's house a complete and absolute surprise. Based on the decor of her office, I had, of course, expected a vine-covered cottage; shutters, morning glories and settles at the door. Instead, I found a house out of *Architectural Digest:* a white, gleaming cube with ship's railings and huge windows, cantilevered from a hillside and looking over the valley like the bridge of a great ocean liner. The land at the front of the house was flattened in approach, with formal and justified hedges bordering rose gardens that were in what I assumed to be their last burst of color. A gleaming white gravel path bisected the garden and led to a parking area that was more a courtyard of paved pale stone with a long, low white building at the far side.

I recognized Jackie, the older O'Sullivan girl, from the pictures on her mother's desk. She greeted me with a smile and her hand extended. Her hair was like her mother's, dark and wavy and glossy with health. She wore it long and pulled back away from her pretty face, still round with childhood. I started to introduce myself but stopped, midsentence, as my eyes took control of my brain. The foyer was central to the house. The main room, also central, was two stories high with a huge, mullioned wall of glass. The light and the views were breathtaking. The furniture was a mix of what looked to be museum-quality antiques and Asian pieces of such exquisite simplicity I could only guess at their value. The view of the valley, from the center of the house, directly across from the entrance foyer, opened up just beyond a large sculpture of a running attenuated hare.

To the left of the entry was another vast space with softer seating and a slightly more casual air. It ran directly into the kitchen area, separated from the living area by a long bar, punctuated with red lacquered stools. Josie was at this bar mixing something in the bowl of a fire-engine red mixer that looked like a Buick. I handed over my box of local candy shop truffles and was introduced to Josie's younger daughter, Lizzie, who poured me a drink from a big crystal pitcher. "It's pink lemonade!" she told me excitedly.

Josie laughed and pointed to the smaller pitcher—"Vodka with limes." She gestured with her chin to the lemonade. "To spike the punch, if you know what I mean." Berry, the O'Sullivan fox terrier, lived up to Josie's office stories and jogged in circles around the island, making little yelping noises. The O'Sullivan girls fed him corn chips and guacamole at almost every turn. The family was just how I imagined it would be, but somehow, it was also rather wonderful.

Donna and her brood tumbled in the front door. I met Ava, eight years old, a giggling, blond Xerox copy of her mother, and her sister, a six-year-old, tiny, dark-haired temptress named Marta. Right on their heels was Fran, wearing a vintage Elvis circle-skirt and a sweater trimmed with fluffy pink rabbit fur that both delighted and repulsed all four little girls; and, I must admit, I felt conflicted in exactly the same way. Their arrival brewed a jumble of jackets, bunches of flowers, bottles of wine, hugs, laughter and Berry—yelping, wagging, sniffing and bouncing up and down like a ball on a rubber band.

From the moment of their arrival, the conversation never stopped for a minute. It ran from breeds of dogs everyone loved, to dogs they hated; to foods they loved, to foods they hated—far more of these, I might add; and movies and music and fashion and Barbie dolls, American Girl dolls, baby dolls that looked Asian or black, and back to fashion and on to *High School Musical* and *Hannah Montana*.

I knew very few references. I had little to add, but instead of feeling left out, as I often had in New York when the conversation turned to something about which I had only the scantest knowledge, though it was more likely to be Mahler or strains of DNA, this time I felt included. Josie, well, everyone actually, made eye contact with me and acted as though they had no idea I couldn't keep up my end of the conversation. And instead of being panicked or bored, I'm amazed to report, I was fascinated by the Barbie conversation; riveted to the new language and vocabulary that seemed central to *Hannah Montana* and *Powerpuff Girls,* and while I didn't appreciate Berry humping my foot to no reprimand, his ears were like silk velvet and he eventually tired of sex and jumped up on the loveseat next to me, curling his warm body against my thigh. I stroked his ears and listened to the cacophony of girls and women and the easy exchange that comes from families secure and loving and full of shared support.

For all of the dread associated with the day's outing, I found that I hated to leave Josie's house. I wasn't alone; it was nearly six before Fran mentioned getting home to have dinner with her husband. I learned he was an arborist. "They used to call them tree surgeons," Fran told us, and had us laughing about her mother-in-law, who would talk about Rick, her "surgeon" son, to her friends, most of whom never knew, and never would know, he operated only on trees. Donna's girls needed to get home to be picked up at eight by their father, Donna's ex-husband, who would take them to his parents, their adored and adoring grandparents, for an overnight and a break; and, we learned at the last minute, too late to mine for details, about a date for Donna with a local doctor. The place was teeming with life and lives, and everyone, except for me, of course, was looking forward to an evening that sounded even better than our afternoon. I had papers to review and made my appreciative good-byes.

I gingerly drove down the precarious trail, back into town, and I pulled into my driveway. It was still chockablock with broken and heaved concrete, but somehow everything had changed. The last of the evening light was settling deep and golden. The house had been painted a warm apricot, a color in such contention that I made Teddy promise that he, himself, would pay to have it repainted if, in any way, it resembled a pumpkin. He was so sure of himself that he promised he would do just that.

The first strokes the painter made were shocking, with a color so strong against the primed dull, grayish white, it seemed Crayola-orange. I was certain I should have held to my instinct of painting the house in white or cream. Teddy reminded me, for at least the fourteenth time, that Queen Anne Victorians were designed to take strong color and that once a whole area was painted, the color would settle and mellow. A deep, rich cream trim and porch, instead of the expected white, also helped to soften the overall look. The house had been painted less than a week ago, but I could now barely remember it in its gray, chipped and depressed skin. And much as I had to hand it to Teddy about the color, I had thought it would take some getting used to.

As I pulled into the driveway, I noticed for the first time that the house painters had pulled most of the weeds from the yard, probably to secure their ladders. And now the apricot house sat in front of me, lit like a Néstor Almendros movie, warm and ripe and fresh. The porch steps were even, and the missing Carpenter Gothic details had been replaced so seamlessly one would have thought the house had been cared for lovingly since the turn of the last century. A light shining from the foyer through the old rippled glass of the front door couldn't be seen as the makeshift bulb Teddy had rigged. It looked, instead, as welcoming as a lantern in a storm. The apricot house. *The Apricot House,* I repeated over and over to myself. It seemed so right for this street, for this town. If someone told me that Emily Dickinson, Amherst's most treasured neurotic native, had been the kind of vegetarian who'd eaten only apricots, it all would have made perfect sense.

That night, as I tucked myself into my makeshift bedroom, I couldn't help but replay the events of the day, testing the inkling that I was now welcome to become part of something else. Not that I knew yet, with any clarity, what that "else" might be. But I understood, with some reservation, that this warm cluster of women had invited me into a world that was alive and real. We'd sat all afternoon, doing little but sharing; the women still, the girls sometimes squirming and laughing, and the dog curled and dozing at my side. I realized, at the moment Berry began to snore, that I hadn't felt the warm contact of a living being sleeping against my body for a very long time. The easy, comfortable and entitled way with which he took his place against me had been my experience with neither man nor beast.

CHAPTER 8

I came into the office early on Tuesday morning. My first class didn't begin until after lunch, but the hammering at home was taking its toll. Fran looked like a cat who'd swallowed a canary as she approached my desk. Her rhinestones sparkled. "Guess who called yesterday afternoon?" she teased. I looked at her blankly. "Coyote number two!" she said triumphantly, waving the name and telephone number on a little pink memo sheet with her name on it. I didn't reach for the memo sheet. I didn't change expression. "Aren't you going to call him back?" she asked.

"I'm not," I replied. "Nope."

She placed the memo on my desk and walked away, her hips swaying in cropped capri pants, like a drag queen's parody of a Connie Francis movie. She sort of giggled, looking back over her shoulder, and said, "He'll call again . . ." Very irritating, I thought.

I refused to look at the memo or the name or the number written on it. Instead, I opened my briefcase, took out my papers and began working. About eleven thirty the phone rang. I jumped. Fran buzzed me. It was, indeed, Coyote number two.

"I said you were in," Fran jeered in a singsong.

"Right," I said, glumly. "When do you reach retirement age?" I answered the phone in a businesslike manner, with my name; much like a bank manager might pick up a call from a loan customer, not encouraging or familiar, but not exactly rude either. "Joy Harkness," I said, and the Coyote answered in a smooth voice, "Joy, you don't know me, but I've seen you around campus and I think we should meet."

"Uh-huh?" I said, sounding, I hoped, noncommittal.

"My name is Paul Cavanaugh, and I teach environmental design here at Amherst." He sounded like an announcer on a public-service film: confident, concerned and practiced.

"Uh-huh," I said, as though listening to one of those solicitation calls where you wait for a break in the telemarketer's script that allows you to say, "Please take my name off your list."

"Kevin Betts—actually—gave me your number," he continued and got the rise out of me he might have expected.

"Oh!?"

"Yeah, yeah. He said he thought we'd really get on."

"Really—ahhhhhaaa!" I was just astounded, and I wasn't sure which part astounded me the most; that Kevin would pass my number around, or that Kevin would think I had anything to recommend me to anyone.

"Gee . . . I, um . . ." I know I sounded anything but bright and clever. I was slow and plodding. I was lost and fumbling. I wished to be any-where else, doing anything else. I wished that English were not my first language.

But Paul seemed not to notice that I had yet to utter a sentence made up of real words. He just chugged on like the Little Engine That Could, saying that Kevin told him I loved old houses, he knew I was new to the area and there were so many wonderful places to see and to visit, and blah blah blah, and in fact, he said, there was this little inn he thought I would really enjoy, saying that he'd made a tentative reservation for Fri-day night and he so hoped I could go with him, that it was one of his favorite restaurants, romantic and calm and private—and he hoped that I would let him be among the first to welcome me to this part of the world, and more blah blah blah. And still, I sat on the phone, silent as a stone.

I heard myself say, finally, "Friday night."

"Yes," he said, "Friday night . . . I hope you—"

"*This* Friday night?"

"Yes."

And to my astonishment I said, "Friday night's fine."

What was happening to me? I felt like Howdy Doody with Buffalo Bob pulling the strings. Where, in God's name, was this coming from?

"Why don't I pick you up at seven on Friday?" he asked. "Does that give you enough time to get ready after your classes?"

"Ummm. Ahh, uhm-hummm." I was back to my grunts and noises. What kind of language, I wondered, is this? No matter. Paul Cavanaugh seemed to understand it.

"Great. I'll pick you up at seven. See you then."

Oh no! From somewhere in the back of my brain I knew that it was my turn to talk again as I realized I needed to tell him where I lived, but he'd hung up the phone. Of course he knew where I lived. It came to me, I have to tell you, with a kind of embarrassed twinge: Kevin Betts had obviously told him all he needed to know.

I hurried home on Friday afternoon, darted past Teddy and headed for the shower. I was much more comfortable upstairs these days. The floorboards were secure, and the plumbing had been fixed. Teddy had painted the bathroom a fabulous color in an English paint he'd found called Folly Green. I bought a shower curtain in a Persian print of browns and greens, golden yellows and deep reds, and laid two of my parents' old kilim rugs on the tile floor. Teddy had surprised me, just the day before, by fitting my scrappy old medicine-cabinet mirror with mahogany picture-frame molding, and hanging a set of six vintage textile–patterned prints he'd found at a flea market in a long line down the empty wall. It was my first finished room. He had installed a holder for my hair dryer and shelves with baskets for my soaps and powders, shampoo and conditioner. He had mounted a light fixture in brass and frosted glass over the sink and another coordinated sconce on the wall. It was the nicest room I'd ever lived in. I loved this room, but mostly I loved the freedom from fear of floods and falling through the floor.

Last Sunday we'd moved my bed up the staircase to my real bedroom. And there it sat, a mattress and box spring in search of a headboard; awaiting, with something akin to longing, some color or decoration on the walls, besides spackle, where the removal of the unevenly peeling wallpaper had lifted the plaster. The chipped and dry kickboard moldings were a dozen different shades of mud brown. I peeled my sweater over my head as I walked into the room and found that Teddy had left, on my mother's old candlewick bedspread, a Farrow and Ball paint sample book fanned open with large pages of colors he apparently thought the bedroom should be painted. It was very confusing. There were four greenish-khaki-to-cream colors with names that rivaled nail enamel for inventiveness, if not clarity: Cooking Apple Green, Pale Hound, Fresh Hay and Farrow's Cream. I suspected he wanted me to choose a color from the lot, and then I saw the wallpaper sample. It was a William Morris print, or so it was labeled in the selvedge, with a pattern all curvy and yet geometric at the same time; all of these green and creamy colors were woven through the tendrils.

"Teddy!" I called as I walked back to the top of the stairs, holding my sweater in front of my bra. "These are beautiful—but I don't understand how all of these colors and this pattern could work in one room."

He took his time getting off the ladder at the bottom of the stairs. He didn't turn off the Who or even put down his paintbrush. He came up the stairs slowly, walked past me and into the bedroom and gestured with the paintbrush in his hand. My sweater remained in my hands, covering, or so I intended, my underwear. But the inappropriateness of my dress didn't faze Teddy, nor did it occur to me as I stood, captivated by his analysis of my room.

"Someone removed the high, picture-rail moldings from these walls years ago. We need to put them back. So, imagine you have a kind of molding starting about here"—and he daubed his wet paintbrush on the wall at about shoulder height. "From the molding up and all across the ceiling, I think we should do that Morris print. Right time period for the house and it's, like—your colors." I didn't know I *had* colors. I didn't get to ask him, though, because he went on talking and gesturing. "The molding around the windows and doors and the floor moldings—I thought we should do in that cooking-green color, and then we can create tray moldings, like paneling, along the wall under the rail and detail them in the two cream colors and that greenish Fresh Hay paint. You see, the colors are not that far apart and it will give them dimension, and when the light comes in this room it will be, you know, great." He turned to gesture toward the other wall. "I think you should look for a big, high, Victorian bed with a carved headboard. And I think instead of curtains we might do shutters in the same green."

I was trying to keep up. What I understood I loved, but I was steps behind him in picturing it. My hesitation might have seemed to suggest a bit of negativity and he rushed in.

"Or, if you hate shutters, we *could* do moss velvet draperies with a lace curtain underneath. But, you know, you seem a little more—like—tailored to me than that; you know what I mean?"

"No. I mean . . . yes!" I said. "I mean . . . I love the *idea* of shutters—"

"Well, we could do shutters and lace curtains, too. You know, it's all correct. But do you like the idea of those colors and the moldings? Because I thought I could get going on them while the electrician is here doing the wiring in the stairway."

"I love them," I said, "but I thought *you* thought we should finish downstairs first."

"I know. Yeah. I do think that. But this room is right off the bath-room, and that room looks so great now. And I just think that you should have, like, a nice bedroom. And all it will take is a little paint and a little paper, you know what I mean? A little paneling . . ." His voice trailed off as he looked at the walls. "*Then* we'll move downstairs. In fact, I think I've got colors picked out for the stairway and the foyer. What do you think about painted floors?"

"Painted floors?" I didn't think anything about painted floors. Was I supposed to?

"You know," Teddy said, "don't let me flood you with all this stuff now. I've got to finish painting the base coat before my electric guy gets here tomorrow. He can't work around wet paint—so let me get *back* to it, okay?" He looked accusingly at me, as though I'd been keeping him from his work.

"Of course," I said. "Fine. Absolutely." And anyway, it was time to dress for the dreaded date with Coyote number two.

I don't like clothes that make too much of a statement. I want quiet, comfortable things that don't try to speak for me. I don't want clothes that proclaim, "Look, I've got breasts!" Or, "Can you believe how dra-matic I am?" I just want clothes I don't have to worry about, and most of the time I seem to manage with a good pair of pants, a tailored shirt and a jacket or cardigan sweater. Why, you then might wonder, was I searching my closet for someone else's wardrobe that Friday evening? What did I hope to find as I went through each drawer four and five times? Everything I pulled out looked shapeless and old and depressed.

Whose clothes are these? Whose clothes do I want? I might have asked myself.

At last, I found an old midcalf skirt—older, I fear, than some of my students—that I paired with a pair of boots polished quickly with Neutrogena hand cream. I put on a dark gray turtleneck sweater and pulled the gray and red throw off the back of the couch to use like a stole. Josie had worn a kind of blanket stole last week and I admired it, but what am I coming to, using house blankets as apparel? I put on lipstick and headed downstairs.

Teddy looked up at me as I passed through the stairway and the foyer. "You look different," he said.

"Do I?" I asked.

"You look really different. Are you wearing perfume?" Suddenly I felt embarrassed, like a teenager questioned by a parent before a date. I nearly expected him to direct me to "go upstairs now and wipe that lipstick off your mouth!" I didn't want to admit that I looked any different than the girl who shared his counter, his mac 'n' cheese and a solid discussion about the merits of polyurethane on stair treads.

"I might be," I answered, as though that kind of thing could slip my mind.

I started to walk past him to the front door when it hit me: I had no place to go. I was being picked up at seven, and it was only six forty. I felt suddenly hungry—ravenous, actually—and remembered the stories of Victorian girls, fed whole dinners before an evening out so that they would pick at their food and appear to be the waifs their corsets made them out to be. I wanted to march right into the kitchen and make myself a peanut butter and jelly sandwich. I stood for a minute in the hall, my stomach flipping, my mouth longing for the sticky sweetness of peanut butter. *Okay,* I thought, *that's it.* I walked in and pulled down some Stoned Wheat Thins and took out the peanut butter and blueberry jam. Teddy followed me.

"Oh great," he said. "Snack break—or is this dinner?"

"No," I explained, "I'm on my way to dinner. I have a date." Teddy snapped his head around and looked at me as though I'd said, "I have an eggplant on my head"—as though he understood the words all right, but not the meaning. Or as though the meaning could not possibly be true.

We each ate half a dozen crackers with peanut butter and jam, and

Teddy talked about color in such an effective way I almost forgot I was nervous. Suddenly, there was an assertive knock at the door, which surprised me, so removed was I from my anxiety. I felt my heart lurch. I checked my lipstick in the chrome of the toaster. I had Stoned Wheat Thins crumbs on my lips and peanut butter in my teeth. "Teddy!" I hissed. "Get the door, and tell him that I'll be there in a minute—and keep him in the foyer!"

Teddy gave me a long, cold stare. I was a foreign body to him. I was an alien who'd taken over his pal's identity. I was something he didn't think existed: a middle-aged woman on a date.

I smeared off what remained of my lipstick and ran my tongue over my teeth. Bending down to the toaster's surface, I applied a fresh coat of Revlon's long-wearing color to my mouth. I practiced a smile. I don't ever remember doing anything like that before in my life. Practicing a smile was not something I grew up doing, not something I'd been taught. I was forty-eight years old and smiling into a toaster. Not very promising, I remember thinking as I turned the corner of the kitchen and entered the hall that led to the foyer. I had no idea just how unpromising it was.

Paul Cavanaugh was of medium height. He was dressed in the academic uniform of khakis, a button-down shirt and a corduroy jacket, but all of his clothes seemed to be gray or perhaps a color a little drearier than gray. A kind of pallor-ecru-gray; the color, I remember thinking at the time, of old computers or, I realized with horror, dead people's skin, and his own skin tone, sadly, was a near match for the gray beige of the apparel. Most surprising to me, and it took a while to register, as it was all of the same color: he was actually wearing an ascot. I couldn't remember when I'd last seen an ascot, even on someone's father. Paul Cavanaugh's balding hair had most likely been red when younger but was now also a grayish beige-brown and frizzy with a rough, pot-scrubber texture. To complete the picture, he licked his wet and very red lips incessantly, like a Coyote playing the Wolf while considering the relative merits of tender Riding Hood or her crispy grandmother. If I'm to be anyone in this story, I thought, I'd better be the Woodsman.

Paul Cavanaugh's car smelled of cabbage. I can't imagine he cooked in his car, although I do remember a cookbook some years ago, during the last energy crisis, advising people to heat meals wrapped in foil atop their cars' engine blocks. Truth be told, I had a lot of time to think about food wrapped in foil and cooked in cars, as I was in that car for a very long time. I imagined whole fresh trout with daubs of butter, slices of lemon, a liberal sprinkling of herbs and a flourish of French sea salt. I thought of tender slices of beef braised with a handful of chopped tomatoes, a few kalamata olives, sprigs of rosemary, a dash of port, a grind of pepper and a good dollop of olive oil. The cabbage smell was countered by an imaginary rendition of a smoked pork chop surrounded by grated red and celadon cabbage, studded with raisins, coarse pepper, a julienne of dried apricot and a pinch of caraway—all moistened with a touch of gin. I hardly ever cooked, but apparently the idea of car cooking released my imagination. Or perhaps I was just desperate to think of something other than Paul Cavanaugh.

He introduced the subject of industrial design and the ergonomic aspect of automobiles. I'd already allowed that the loss of real wood inside and running boards or fancy fins outside had made cars virtually indistinguishable to me and therefore completely, absolutely, definitively uninteresting. He must have taken this to mean that I was terribly interested in cars because he talked about them nonstop for nearly forty-five minutes. I said virtually nothing. I know that it was forty-five minutes because every ten minutes or so I looked at my watch and waited for a break in the monologue to ask just how far this charming inn was from Amherst or Northampton. As I thought the charming inn was *in* Amherst or Northampton, the trip itself was beginning to be a great, though not welcome, surprise.

When I finally broke through the car talk to ask where in the *world* this inn was, Paul Cavanaugh said that it was "just up the way here." That's the phrase he used, "just up the way." Half an hour later the peanut butter and crackers had worn off completely and I was ravenous. It was half past eight.

"Paul," I said, "where the hell *is* this place?"

"It's just up *here* . . . ," he said.

"What's that supposed to mean?" I whined. "You said it was 'just up here' half an hour ago. Where is it? What *town*?"

"Lakeville," he answered, somewhat sheepishly, I thought, although perhaps now, in retrospect, I am reading more into it.

"Lakeville, *Connecticut*?!"

"Do you know Lakeville?" He brightened.

"I know where it *is*," I said, "and I know it's nowhere *near* Northampton!"

"I never said it was near Northampton!" he yelped, as though accused of shooting someone's dog.

"You did," I said. "You implied it."

"I certainly did not." And we would have been off and running except that just at this moment we pulled into a driveway and up to a country inn so picturesque it might have been on the cover of a guide-book for New England vacationers.

A valet dressed in eighteenth-century vestments with twenty-first-century sneakers opened my door. As he bent down to help me from the car, I wanted to ask if he could confirm the smell of cabbage, but I refrained.

I was bristling from the latest Coyote exchange and wondering why in the world we had driven so far for dinner. Could the food at such an inn be so much better than anything within ten miles of a university town? I climbed the inn's front steps with Paul Cavanaugh just behind and was greeted by a smiling host who clearly recognized Paul and spread his hands in welcome. "Can we get your bags?" he asked.

"We're just here for dinner," I said, and the look on the face of the host, darting his eyes past mine to Cavanaugh's, told me everything.

"Aren't we?" I asked, standing my ground on the threshold of the inn's front door. "Aren't we here for dinner?"

"Yes, of course," the Coyote began. He took my arm to guide me into the inn, giving the host a "not now" frown.

"Wait just one minute." I stopped in the foyer before entering the dining room. "What's going on here?"

"No need to be upset," said the Coyote in a practiced voice. And he explained to me, the way one might enlighten a three-year-old about the wisdom of training wheels, that he'd thought "the distance was so far, and if dinner went long"—went long? I thought—"we might want to spend the night at the inn."

"Jesus!" I said. "You don't even know me, and you assume that I would spend the *night* with you! What's the matter with you!" He didn't have the decency to look guilty. He cleared his throat and licked his slick red lips, as though gathering energy to deal with a difficult person.

"Let's talk about it over dinner. We're here, and I'm sure you're hungry. I know I am." He looked expectantly toward the dining room. A number of dinner guests looked up to see us standing in the doorway. I don't think they caught much dialogue, but the uneasy crackle of the air between us was loud enough to be heard in the back of the room. I held my head high, about to walk back out to the car, when the aroma of fresh bread hit me. And perhaps I smelled a garlicky roast chicken, and was that grilled lamb? Certainly there was a suggestion of rosemary and cinnamon in the smoky, seductive invitation from the kitchen. Winding all about the savory scents was a sinful, deep promise of something that smelled like devil's food cake or molten chocolate. I was, indeed, a very hungry woman. I allowed Paul Cavanaugh to take hold of my elbow and navigate me into the room and toward a table where a waiter held my chair.

CHAPTER 9

I hate to tell you it was "worth the trip," as the Michelins say, but it was. Diver scallops with little turbans of translucent pancetta; lamb shank—sweet and falling off the bone, with a sauce of tomato, raisins, cinnamon, and maybe there was orange in there—served with orzo studded with coarse mint, pine nuts and diced pear. The wines were sublime, and the dessert—yes, I stayed for dessert—was a pistachio soufflé. Good as anything I've eaten in France. Was it worth the company of Paul Cavanaugh? Well, that may be straining the juicer.

He talked incessantly all through the meal. I remember thinking that he'd spent far too much time in the company of academics, which, for a guy who dealt with the physical science issues of ergonomics, was too bad. I mean, one expects drivel from the Philosophy Department: Are We Here? Or is it simply, Are We? And Lord knows I've pitched a forkful myself in getting through the prerequisites of comparative literature in an Ivy League institution; but, for God's sake, to refer to the "velocity of consumer endorsement in the change of weight in the handles of knives" was exceeded only by his indulgence in the actual and theoretical factors of what constitutes "cut." I blessed the fact that my lamb shank was fork-tender as he dissected the minute differences between blades that slice or tear, divide, incise, pierce, gash, carve, sever, pare or hack. I looked up occasionally to check on a clump of mashed parsnip that clung to his chin, just below his full, vermilion and always wet bottom lip. It remained resolutely in place through dinner and dessert. I don't believe I uttered a word, besides ordering my food. I nodded, I suppose, and I may have said "ummm" now and then, if only to suggest some level of polite behavior.

And when the meal was over, I allowed a smile to our maître d' and asked that he give the chef my compliments. Paul beamed as though he believed all had been forgiven. He stood and took my elbow in a way that was far too familiar. I removed my arm, strode into the foyer like Germaine Greer emasculating the Racquet Club, and asked for my coat. We rode home in silence, of that I am sure. I was keyed up; too angry to fall asleep in the passenger seat and maybe too wary to lose consciousness, though it was nearly one thirty when I got home.

At my insistence I walked to my porch alone, and climbed the stairs. They seemed steeper than they had earlier in the day. Exhaustion hit me like a mallet the moment I entered the house. I crossed the foyer and found Teddy asleep on the living room couch, paint colors, fabric memos and wallpaper samples spread around him like objects in a magpie's nest. His hat lay on a wallpaper book, his head was canted back on the sofa cushion and thundering snores rhythmically filled the air. I leaned down to rouse him and noticed, for the first time, that he had a fringe of the longest, thickest eyelashes I'd ever seen on a man; so lustrous, they were actually glossy. Isn't it a shame, I thought, he couldn't have hair on his head as thick and beautiful as his lashes? Teddy, I guessed, for all his boyish manifestations, must have been hovering around thirty-five, and his hairline was heading behind him quickly in two deep V's. Not that many people saw it. He almost never appeared in public without a baseball cap, and I'd never seen him take his hat off indoors except when he cleaned up after work and washed his face and hands.

As I leaned close to wake him, he smelled like a young boy. It was a scent I'd nearly forgotten. It took me completely by surprise, and I gasped at the recognition: the smell of childhood and my brother, Tim.

Timmy was fourteen when he died; hit by a drunk driver in the parking lot of a Carvel, he lingered in a coma for about a week. They wouldn't let me see him in the hospital; there was a rule about children under twelve visiting. But I knew with certainty that if I had been able to persuade them to let me in, I could have awakened him. And while I know the facts are against me, in some stubborn and defiant way, I still believe I would have.

I'd loved everything about my brother. The way he laughed and the way he looked and the way he smelled—of soap and shampoo and chlorine and little-boy sweat. He was not quite two years older than I, and he was everything to me, a hero and a boyfriend and a protector and a scout. There could be no replacement for him in my life. I wouldn't acknowledge his death to the outside world but held it inside, turning it over and over, like a stone in my pocket, for years. When my mother, tearful, I'm sure, for my psychic future, got beyond her own shock and grief and insisted that I let go in some visible form that might be recognizable, at least to her, I refused and tried even harder to hide the fact that the center of my life had suddenly gone missing. I just took him inside of myself and brought him along through my childhood.

For most of my growing-up years, not a day went by that didn't include Tim. It was just a fact: some part of him completed me. Some part of him took my SATs with me, and some part of him packed my suitcase for college and walked down the aisle with me and signed my mortgage, and then left my husband and headed, finally, to my real life in Manhattan.

He and I had kept alive the promise of my talent in the most unpromising of circumstances, a dull marriage in the American Midwest. But I lost him soon after arriving in New York. I have no memory of including him in my city life or, more to the point, any of the repetitive day-to-day activities that became my maintenance at Columbia. Timmy was not designed for a life of bland routine. And if New York was not exactly tedious, I had found a way to rub all the exotic off of it; to, in fact, create a life exactly the opposite of what I'd hoped New York would bring me.

I never found the sophisticated handle that would have come naturally to Tim. He would have held court at book parties in New York penthouses, talking about having just seen Mailer at some PEN event. He would have had dinner with Harry and Tina, and punched Jonathan Franzen for dissing Oprah, making the point that Dickens worked for money and Thackeray worked for money. Timmy would have taken New York by storm, but I, through an unfortunate mix of shyness and a nature too deliberately intent on the solid and the sure, lost the thread of him while grading papers and grumbling about affirmative action in the teachers' lounge. And here I was today, nearly fifty years old, leaning across this snoring contractor, fifteen years my junior, and breathing in his boyishness, to be pulled back through all those decades like a whirlpool effect in a cheap movie.

I steadied myself and put my hand on his shoulder. "Teddy," I said quietly, "it's nearly two o'clock. Do you want to spend the night on the sofa? Shall I get you a blanket?" He roused himself and looked at me as though he weren't sure who I might be.

"You smell good," he said sleepily.

I almost said, "I could say the same to you," but I didn't. I turned to walk toward the hall closet that held blankets intended for guest rooms not yet addressed. Teddy, on the other hand, stood and apparently pulled himself together, and when I turned, his hat was back on. He explained that he had to get home, that his mother worried if he wasn't in his bed in the morning, and it was far too late to call her about a change of plans. He gingerly stepped around the paint chips and samples and asked if we could make some decisions about them tomorrow, and I agreed. As he opened the door he turned back. "You're home late."

"Yeah," I said. "Yeah, yes."

"How was it?" he asked.

"Quite bad," I answered, hoping he wouldn't ask for details. He didn't. He smiled and sort of waved his signature palm-flat-at-you sign of hello or good-bye, and he was out the door.

CHAPTER 10

I 'd taken to having lunch in the office with Josie and Fran. The fact that I can say this in a way that sounds so easy and natural belies the fact that I'd never had lunch with coworkers until I came to Amherst. At Columbia, each day, I had a tuna salad sandwich on soggy whole-wheat toast, made the night before and stashed in my briefcase to be eaten while working at my desk. It wasn't good, but it saved the stupefying $9.50 charge for a tuna sandwich from the local "gourmet" deli, it encouraged work without interruption, and it allowed me to avoid the mess of including other people in my life.

Here I was in Massachusetts, however, up to my thighs in people. Though I'm reluctant to admit it, the company was somewhat agreeable and the food delicious, but I kept feeling valuable time was leaking away while sitting and listening to campus gossip over lunch. I have to confess that my workload was certainly no less than it had been in New York; it was, with Bernadette's project developing, actually greater. I had no fewer students, I wrote no fewer reports, and everything was getting done as well as it ever had. Perhaps, I had to admit, my work was even somewhat better, more tightly focused.

Josie took control of lunch for the three of us nearly every day. She brought sandwiches, salads and soups made from leftovers so delectable I could only assume the original meals were French-chef quality. We would huddle around the desk in her pretty office, and she would divide the food and pour glasses of iced tea, lemonade, cider or mineral water—all brought out of a picnic hamper authentic enough for a polo match or the opera at Glyndebourne. Each meal was capped with one perfect sweet: an oatmeal cookie, a truffle rolled in cocoa, a pecan praline or a slice of apricot-almond tart. Josie was a wonder. When we would fuss and compliment her, she would shrug her round, plush shoulders and say, good-naturedly, "What's the big deal—three more helpings!" She liked the company, she said, and somewhere during those first months, I believe that I began to like the company, too.

I held for a while a tiny but nasty suspicion that Josie might be culturally retarded or emblematic of a new kind of antifeminist backlash. I had an idea that Phyllis Schlafly could be hiding beneath Josie's desk, what with all the *Ladies' Home Journal* talents that made their way to our office. I was careful to steer clear of political debate for the first few weeks. But it turns out Josie was as resolute a feminist as Kate Millett. Josie's translation of *The Ladies' Paradise* for Viking has made it to the top of most women's studies courses across the United States, not only because of the graceful, sensitive and witty English she crafted from Zola's soap-opera French text, but because of the insight within her accompanying notes. Her interpretation of the semiology embroidered within the minute detail of the literal fashion of nineteenth-century France is as breathtaking and poetic as it is heartbreaking and illuminating about the limits of women in those days—and now. In addition, Josie's family sponsors a major scholarship for women in advanced mathematics here at Amherst; and God help anyone who stands between either of her daughters and their chances to be anything on earth—from president of the United States to dog warden. But happily married she is, and just as skillfully as she leads her students, she bakes her tarts and paints her furniture and braids the hair of her own beloved girls.

Fran and Josie, so well cosseted in their own marriages, took me in like an aging spinster sister who needed placement in the arms of a good man for their own sense of completion and, I presumed, for their own sense of control. The last of the three Coyotes had been, I figured, steered away by the track record of his compatriots, though Josie and Fran remained focused on Coyote speculation as they sifted through memory to bring up the names of single men whose only vital credentials might be breathing and being listed within a telephone directory somewhere in the world. I discouraged this line of talk. I told them in no uncertain terms that I had no deep desire to marry again or to share my life with anyone, and while I'd admittedly been lured by the idea of one last fling, it certainly wasn't worth all the fuss that came along with it.

Still, I suspected that they were gathering a dowry between them: two sheep and a cow, a hundred gold pieces, a yard of books, an acre of good land and twenty dish towels. Any day now, I figured, I would be offered with this bonus to potential husbands on eBay. But the days came and went, and there were no bidders, Internet or otherwise.

The trees lost their leaves, and some days found the Amherst sky beginning to take on that cold, bone-white pallor of New England winters. But each time I turned onto my street, the apricot house drew me down the block, toward its heart. Teddy had the downstairs fireplace working, and it warmed both the rooms and my own heart to come in after work and see the play of light dancing on the walls. He'd found a wallpaper he called anaglyphic—white, thick and pressed into shapes that were vaguely Moorish. He placed this around the living room from floor molding to chair rail and painted the rail and the paper a kind of bluish-grayish-greenish color. "Imagine," he said, "crossing Jasperware blue with Jasperware green." And he told me how, not finding what he wanted, he had decided to mix the color himself. He'd already painted the walls above the chair rail a color between cream and yellow, a kind of manila, vanilla, banana-cream-pie color. The ceiling was tinted a robin's egg blue. If this sounds much more colorful than it was, it's because so little contrast existed in the color values themselves, which were soft and fresh and lovely. The trim on the wood was creamy white. The shade in the hall was the same soft blue-gray-green and a color he had used upstairs, called Fresh Hay, a kind of gentle, golden khaki. The pale blue ceiling prevailed, and the trim was, again, creamy white.

Teddy had taken down the doors and part of the wall in the butler's pantry. The little room was then painted the same high-gloss cream as the trim except for the surface at the back of the shelves, which was painted the blue of the ceiling. He found an old institutional pendant light of frosted glass to hang in the pantry, and we stacked my grandmother's china, my mother's collection of ironstone pitchers and all the crystal glassware—unpacked for the first time since my wedding, twenty-five years before—on those shelves. Every now and then, Teddy would stand a platter flat against the wall or hang a small painting or framed postcard he'd found at a tag sale in a kind of visual punctuation.

The butler's pantry became an art installation, visible from the living room and beautiful with objects I was surprised I could relate to: the platter my parents used for Thanksgiving turkeys, the brown and white transferware pitcher my mother told me had belonged to my great-grandmother. There was a stack of creamy white Wedgwood dinner plates with fluted borders, which looked as pleated as the skirts I wore as a child. Resting on one shelf was a tiny watercolor of an apple, painted by Tim when he was ten. It had hung in my parents' kitchen until I dismantled their house twelve years ago and packed everything away.

For years these things had been more than a bother, hidden in card-board boxes and taking up space in my apartment at the bottom and backs of my limited closets, stacked in my extra bedroom and stored under my bed. More than once I'd considered pulling them out and donating all of the contents to Riverside Church for its annual tag sale, but the sheer chore of unearthing the cartons from behind the snow boots and brooms and the old books and the tool boxes had proved too great, and they were, therefore, preserved through sloth. Now, I couldn't imagine living without them. These treasures, as I was coming to think of them, were taking their place, as though the world might be told about me through exposure to their loveliness and the stories contained within each chip and crackle of patina.

Teddy and I shared dinners of scrambled eggs and toast, or French bread pizzas, or, Teddy's favorite, Hot Pockets. We talked through the meals about design, architecture, music and, to my surprise, about liter-ary themes—like the use of hallucinogenic imagery in the poetry of Yeats and Poe.

We had discussions about the cultural function of art and literature; discussions that were based, because of Teddy's innocence, in a kind of simple logic I'd not experienced in academic discourse since my under-graduate days at Wellesley, when teachers indulged us in some level of conversation about what all of this learning and expression was "for." But neither at Washington nor certainly at Columbia did I ever hear any-one stoop to engage in what would have seemed so adolescent a concept as "intent" in art. Quite the opposite. At a Columbia lecture, I heard a snaggle-toothed and stringy German authoress of an execrable and artificial book about mermaids, of all things, claim that books shouldn't have "ideas." And no one stood up and laughed out loud. No one left the lecture hall, shaking their head in bewilderment or dismay, or in a justified snit that such banal, emotionally false claptrap had invaded academics. The next day in the teachers' lounge, no one snickered about anything, except her greasy hair and her dental challenges. And that "no one" included me.

What became apparent in my conversations with Teddy was my acceptance of a kind of snobbery I thought I'd avoided: the notion that accessible writers and artists were hacks. In my academic club, art had been elevated to the point of empty vapors of pretension, hovering, quite pointedly, over the grubbier aspects of life. This was all designed to float by a restricted pack of club members, tutored to respond appreciatively to classified gestures and code words. Because Teddy's questions were guileless and untainted by even the most fundamental professional conceit, the history of cultural acceptance became a story of the king's new clothes. If the rabble is able to decipher the code, it is no longer, after all, a code at all.

There is a point I often make in class about the influence of French aestheticism on Henry James—who sank from the clear ring of *Washington Square* to the mannered and neurotic obfuscation of *The Golden Bowl* in what were clearly twenty very painful years. After failing to make money by page or stage and living off loans and the gifts of friends, James exhibited a behavior much like the heroines he mocked in his novels, developing his own brand of social climbing and claiming no longer to care for the attentions of the coarse and unworthy bourgeoisie—which is to say, his "readers." Those later books, those in which his own uncomfortable inferiority is played out through the shadows and subterfuge of his convoluted prose, are the harbingers of the hollow and affected literature that has marked much of what the twentieth and twenty-first centuries have accepted as fine.

I have made a living off Henry James. I love his stories and his characters and his searing ambition. My heart breaks for his need to be accepted and comfortable in his own skin. Would that he lived in our time; Henry might have had a chance at happiness with no loss to that critical, clever, compassionate sensibility. But I have been banging on about the issues of clarity and accessibility versus style in his work for most of my tenure. I was full of self-congratulations. In front of Teddy, however, it was different. I was simply embarrassed. I have sipped from the cup of academia. I have written in sentences that ran on for a quarter of an hour, and used words like *exigencies*. I wrote a review in the *New York Review of Books* that claimed to admire the "evanescent holographical mass of a writer's allusion." And so, Teddy asks, essentially—but not in these words, of course—if the purpose of writing is not, in fact, to impress, inspire and illuminate the largest number of people with ideas great enough to change, stimulate or enhance the culture. Is it not, indeed.

Teddy's knowledge of literature and history was spotty. He was almost entirely self-taught and drawn by artistic and intellectual directions I suspected found their inception in the music of the late sixties and the drug use that must have seemed, at the time and for a generation of educated and coddled boomers, necessary for self-examination. As I knew from Josie that Teddy had been born in the midseventies, and not the moment I identified as the epicenter of the Age of Aquarius, I deduced from his stories that his older brother, Joey, and the Deadheads who became Joey's clan, also became Teddy's inspiration. They must have represented for Teddy, as they had for Joe, a benign and nonjudgmental family, and Teddy naturally and intrinsically carried into the next century the mantle of self-indulgent narcissism that had marked the hippie, New-Age baby boomer.

The upside of that youth movement, if you could call it that, included a distinctive and stubborn kind of honor, an unrelenting idea of facing each challenge of the day stripped of the facade of societal decorum to uncover a response that was innate and natural. I recognized the callow nature of this quest even as it went on around me in the sixties, but I also admired the idea of it; and, at least on this aging boy, it seemed devoid of dogma.

It wasn't the New York abrasiveness *masquerading* as honesty I'd found at Columbia—that sneering swagger of a barb, aimed at the very core of hierarchy; juiced, perhaps, by your whiteness, or your femaleness, or your maleness or your *Mayflower* relatives or the fact that you

might be—God forbid—smarter or better educated or even, quite literally on the employment roster, the actual boss of these bozos. No, this
was a benign and generous idea of innocent honesty and exposure.

Teddy's responses were uniquely Teddy. His clothes and his schedule
and his manners were of a form he'd invented. His deep knowledge and
passion for the history of home design was something he'd learned by
taking apart house after house, like a doctor with bodies in a morgue.
The hipbone's connected to the thighbone. "The foyer delivers . . .
like . . . the promise of the home's . . . you know . . . DNA," he pronounced. And each house brought its story and its age to him. He had
innate taste and style. His eye was as sharp and cultivated as a museum
curator's. And it turned out that over the last twenty years, his time off
had been spent doing only two things: attending rock concerts of only a
very few and very specific bands and visiting historical American houses
and the museums that held their original furnishings and decorative arts.

I found it difficult to align the two activities, but that was Teddy. He
was not hesitant to share the stories of his Deadhead days, traveling to
concerts with his brother, Joey, or his grief at the death of Jerry Garcia,
any more than he would have denied me the information about visiting
the home where Teddy Roosevelt had been raised and how he had first
discovered that the colors of Victorian houses were not the muted and
grayed, sepia-rich hues we'd come to identify with the period, but more
often garish colors—bright and bold, because the light in the houses,
between the heavy velvet draperies and the gas lighting, was so dim. He
could bring up references of moldings from the White House to the
home of Harriet Beecher Stowe, which, he informed me, lay in pieces in
a warehouse in Litchfield County, Connecticut, as the town fought about
the cost of resurrecting this piece of history.

He could lead me to deeper understandings of chair rails and treads
of stairs and the work of itinerant muralists. He could explain how the
design choices, which seemed to me to be so arbitrary and vast, were, in
fact, reasonable parts of the culture and their times; some practical and
purely for function, and others for status and rank. His knowledge of
color, paint textures and technique was the stuff of textbooks. And his
eyes would light up when the subject turned to egg tempera or milk-
based paint. A moment later he might delve into the joys of following the

Grateful Dead around the country, eating grilled-cheese sandwiches in parking lots and playing Hacky Sack in circles of fans aged twelve to seventy. He described the dreadlocks of teenage white girls, black toddlers and elderly Jewish men on the Dead Trail as though they were banners of knotted hair, billowing in the freedom of a community based on music, sharing and free love.

"Did *you* experience free love?" I asked.

"Whatsat?" he replied, not to suggest that he didn't know what free love was but, more to the point, that he hadn't heard or didn't understand the question. "Whatsat?" was a typical Teddy response to almost any question that required an answer based on thought. His main defense was to get the ball back in your court. In fact, on the rare occasions he would telephone me, he would begin almost every call with the question, "What's up?" Or, "Wha'sup?" I finally stopped the habit by saying each time, "Teddy, you called me. How about you tell *me* what's up."

I'd never met his mother, but I'd formed an opinion about her. I figured her to be an aging flower child, a wisp of a girl on her way to being geriatric, wearing a granny dress with a waist-length braid of gray, entwined with feathers and flowers. If Teddy were on the far cusp of the hippie movement, I figured her to have been early to the party. A kind of Timothy Leary girlfriend who had tuned in, turned on and dropped out too many times to move on to disco. The fact that no father was mentioned supported my fantasy. A stream of her men, I surmised, had taught Teddy different maintenance skills; and as they moved along, as all rolling stones will do, one could have left Teddy the legacy of plumbing, another of hanging paper, and yet another of working wood. Perhaps his mother was a siren who would attract the craftsman she needed at the moment, throwing the plumber over when the pipes were finally perfect, for the expert on installing a roof. Mrs. Hennessy, as I imagined her, might have been a gold digger who collected home-maintenance expertise instead of diamond bracelets from her Lochinvars. I couldn't figure the churchgoing on Sundays, but as it didn't fit my fantasy, I simply ignored it.

It was with some surprise then, when Teddy invited me to a family gathering, that I realized there was no basis for my imaginings and if I attended, I would certainly see the real Mrs. Hennessy for myself. My first thought, however, was to beg off. The last thing I needed was to meet even more people. Josie, Teddy explained, would be there, and that, at least, gave me a reason for exploring why, in the wide world, I'd been included.

"Maureen Hennessy invited you?" Josie said, her eyebrows arching.

"Well, she seems to have invited me through Teddy. Do you think that Teddy would just invite me on his own?"

"Oh, *God* no." Josie said. "Teddy wouldn't do anything on his own. His mother controls his life. She makes most of his appointments for work, and she keeps him on a tight lead. In fact, she ran his only long-term girlfriend out of town. She doesn't let girls get near Teddy." Josie frowned. "That's why I'm so surprised she invited *you* to their house."

"Josie," I said, "I'm hardly a 'girl,' and I'm certainly not girlfriend material for Teddy Hennessy! I've got to be fifteen years older than he is, and I'm, I'm . . . you know. I'm not . . . girlfriend material!"

Josie laughed. "Well, it's just as likely that his mother *thinks* you might be and wants to check you out!" The image of the easygoing, flower-child, love-the-one-you're-with, dulcimer-playing granny began to evaporate before my eyes.

"What is she like, Josie?" I asked, and I listened as she told me the story of Maureen and Teddy: The oldest boy, Joe, about fourteen years older than Teddy, had been destined, his parents prayed, for the priest-hood. At seventeen they sent him to Saint John's Seminary, over in Brighton, and he dropped out six years later, a year short of his ordina-tion. The parents lashed out at him with an energy born of shame and contempt, and delivered with a force so great that it was thought to have brought a heart attack on the father. Mr. Hennessy retired from his exec-utive position and his corporate insurance career in his early fifties and chose to sit at home, listening to not much more than the beat of his dis-appointed heart.

From the moment of his heart attack, and perhaps motivated by economy as much as concern, Maureen nursed her husband like a mar-tyr, dropping their country club membership, leaving no time for golf or cards or anything else she had come to enjoy for herself. Everyone said she was selfless, but in caring for her husband, she left her boys to care for themselves, without perceiving that Joe felt guilty and humiliated and Teddy was just a kid.

Saddam invaded Kuwait about that time, and Joe enlisted in the army and was sent to the Gulf. He was back within a few months and in and out of veteran's hospitals for a few years with a whole series of vague symptoms: headaches and rashes, fatigue and mood swings. His parents practically spat when they talked about him, as though he were a wastrel.

Josie's father-in-law is some retired bigwig with a connection to the military. He went to the same church in Amherst as Teddy's family and was asked by their priest to talk to the Hennessys. Josie told me that Dan's father sat Mr. and Mrs. Hennessy down and told them about Gulf War Syndrome, the chemicals these kids had been exposed to, brain injuries, shell shock—the whole thing—but they continued to rattle on about Joey's dropping out of Saint John's. Josie said that Mr. O'Sullivan thought the Hennessys were "buck stupid" and "stubborn as mules." She smiled and shrugged and got back to her story.

Joey couldn't hold a job or wouldn't. The only thing he seemed to care about was the Grateful Dead, and he traveled, sometimes for months on end, with the tribe of supporters and fans who found a way to see every concert.

Teddy worshipped Joe, and to his credit, Joey cared for Teddy with an earnestness separate from everything else in his life. When he was in Amherst, he included Teddy in all he did, taking him everywhere from rock concerts to parties to pool halls. Josie thought that Joe had exercised a strong degree of "do what I say, not what I do" discipline with his brother as Teddy's grades in school were high and his mind remained clear.

Josie married Dan O'Sullivan in 1993 and moved to Amherst just about the time Teddy was finishing high school and starting college at the University of Massachusetts. He was young and sweet and interested in art and furniture and found his way, through his mother's church and, therefore, Dan's family, to her studio. Josie had, nearly twenty years ago, while working on her doctorate in French literature, refinished and painted furniture in the style and discipline of the eighteenth century, as her mother had done in the Restoration Department of the Met. She hired Teddy as a weekend assistant and taught the teenager how to strip a finish, and mix colors, and wet-sand between coats of varnish as he helped her to move the heavy furniture up on blocks and down again. She said he was a delight to teach.

One Saturday in 1995, he didn't show up at her studio in the long white building across the court from her house, and he didn't call. Josie rang his home and got no answer. Later that night she had a phone call from her mother-in-law telling her that Teddy's brother, Joe, had been killed in a car accident on the Mass Pike near Boston. Teddy never came back to Josie's studio, and two months later, Mr. Hennessy died.

From that moment on, Josie told me, Maureen Hennessy made Teddy believe that he was the only thing that kept her alive. She persuaded him to leave college to care for her. She used him as a chauffeur and a maintenance man and an escort. And when the pension and inheritance from Mr. Hennessy proved to be inadequate for her lifestyle as a widow who had once again picked up her country club activities, she convinced Teddy that instead of going back to college, he could work as a handyman and contractor in the houses of her friends.

For fifteen years he dismantled and rebuilt kitchens and back stairs, replaced windows and reset gutters, and he read and learned all he could about the houses he worked on and the decoration he loved. He became a one-man historical society as he restored and protected the architectural detail of the houses in town and, in his unassuming way, became an expert on the decorative arts of the last century and a half. Maureen made his appointments and kept his books. And for fifteen years he turned over his earnings to the pool of household income that sustained the home he shared with his mother and the activities in which she chose to participate.

Some years back, and Josie remembered that it must have been close to ten years ago, Teddy became involved with the daughter of one of the deans of the University of Massachusetts. Anne was a senior at Smith, quiet and plain and maybe five or so years younger than Teddy, though Josie's impression was that after Joe's accident, Teddy never appeared to age a day. I understood what she meant. Emotionally, Teddy was right where Joe left him.

Maureen, as the whole town apparently knew and commented upon, managed to wedge herself between Teddy and Anne. She committed Teddy to construction jobs that took him a bit out of town and then planned an accelerated list of evening activities that required his escorting or chauffeuring duties. Church friends, seeing the trend, offered to ferry Maureen, but she declined. Anne sometimes accompanied Teddy and his mother at Teddy's beckoning, always sitting in the backseat, as Maureen complained of carsickness. Maureen countered Anne's determined presence by inviting elderly friends for Teddy to chauffeur to her excursions, allowing no room in the car at all for Anne.

Teddy may have felt himself trapped between his choice of partner and his responsibility to his mother, but he never stood up to what the rest of his community saw as tyranny; though Josie was uncertain whether anyone outside of the family had broached the subject with Maureen or with Teddy.

Maureen never relinquished the myth that Teddy was her link to the outside world and that all her joy in life had died with Joe and his father, save Teddy. Anne could hardly compete with this, and she took off for graduate school in California, never to return to Amherst. No drama, or so it seemed, to the end of the affair—"and more's the pity," said Josie.

As far as Josie knew, Anne had been Teddy's only girlfriend, and Maureen made it her business, since then, to find out as much as possible about any single woman Teddy might come in contact with—from the secretaries at the hardware stores to the customers of his clients "*and their daughters*," said Josie—and to "nip" potential romantic relationships "in the bud," as Josie put it.

I listened to this gossip without a single interruption, question, comment or even gasp. Though my heart lurched more than once, thinking of the bright, sweet boy Teddy must have been. I was quietly packing my material for class when she stopped her story, turned to me and said, "You have to go, you know. You really have to meet her, now."

"It seems to me that I should stay as far away from that situation as I possibly can," I said, remembering the book on James Joyce's Dublin I'd promised to bring to class, and I searched my bookcase for its spine.

"Joy," said Josie, "if Teddy's got a chance at all, it's with you." She looked at my horrified expression and just barreled on. "I'm *not* saying he thinks of you as a girlfriend or ever would. But he obviously cares about you. You talk to him. You listen to him. You've let him have free rein in your house, and he's enjoying the success of that freedom. And I'm saying that you see more of him than anyone else, even more of him, these days, than his mother. You're the one with access to him, and you're the one who can convince him that he's got his light hidden under a pail."

"And I'm the one who is late for class, Josie," I said, spotting the book and pulling it off the shelf, and the subject was closed.

I don't need this family drama, I thought as I walked across campus. I don't need to be put in the position of urging Teddy Hennessy to do anything except finish my house, and I'm *paying* him to finish my house. But I knew that he was, as Josie suggested, putting far more attention and care into this project than he could possibly be paid for. And I also knew that he looked for my approval in more than his contracting skills.

Teddy and I had begun to talk, very tentatively, about the fact that his life skills—his craft and knowledge—could earn him credits toward finishing his bachelor's degree. They could, I suspected, even be put into a form that might earn him part of a master's. He might find himself teaching courses on historical restoration within an art or architecture department of a university. We touched on the subject, but I knew instinctively to tread lightly. There was some deep well of fear or guilt connected with the subject of returning to school.

I was nearly at class when I suddenly realized that Teddy and I had both lost beloved older brothers. I wondered if his loss was somehow connected to what kept Teddy from growing. This insight or question, however, did not at the time appear to have anything to do with me.

CHAPTER 11

On Saturday morning I was sitting in my newly finished home office. My study. My workroom. My retreat. I could hardly believe how peaceful it was. There was a place for everything. Teddy had fashioned a desk from two filing cabinets, a hollow-core door, and some legs. He then had the town fabric shop stitch up a kind of slipcover for the desk out of khaki canvas. He ordered a glass top and underneath the top he randomly placed color copies of pages from a botanical book on ferns. Frankly, I didn't understand the ferns, but he took more of their pages and matted and framed them in a long, low line around the room, and I had to admit, the effect was beautiful. He painted the little room sage green with the same creamy white paint on the trim and wainscoting that ran through the rest of the house. He hung a plain craft-paper window shade on the one long window and painted the shade's bottom hem with an irregular line of daubed-on sage green dots. An old wooden desk chair from a consignment shop was painted green, and a fragment of dark green rug, left over from a client's installation months before, was bound at the carpet store in town. On the far side of the room sat my old bookshelves, now divided into four sections chair-rail high; Teddy screwed them together, added a top and some moldings, and painted them the same color as the wainscoting behind them. Instant built-in bookcases!

There were my books! My precious thesauri, my *Elements of Style* and my rhyming dictionary; the *Columbia Guide to Standard American English* and Mencken's *American Language;* the two great Arthur Quiller-Couches, *On the Art of Writing* and *On the Art of Reading;* Edward Sapir's *Language: An Introduction to the Study of Speech,* Fowler's *King's English* (of course) and Bartlett (obviously) and Simpson's *Contemporary*

Quotations. There is T. S. Eliot, *The Sacred Wood,* and Carl Van Doren, *The American Novel.* Bulfinch and Brewer and Joseph Campbell, and— can you imagine?—Teddy found space for all eighteen volumes of my *Cambridge History of English and American Literature*—perhaps my first investment in writing, after my high school thesaurus.

Upstairs in my bedroom, still stacked on the floor and waiting for just the right bookcase and a moment of inspiration from Teddy, lay the books closest to my heart. Every book by Henry James, every book by John O'Hara, every book by Edith Wharton, Nabokov and Updike. Novels, short stories and plays by Faulkner, O'Brien, O'Neill, O'Casey and Fitzgerald. Books full of the collected essays of Gore Vidal, most all of Truman Capote, all of Willa Cather, some of Flaubert, most of Zola, all of Tolstoy, all of Chekhov, all of Proust and Joyce and Meredith, all the plays of Arthur Miller, most of the plays of Philip Barry and J. M. Barrie, William Inge, Tennessee Williams, nearly all I could get my hands on of Stoppard and Caryl Churchill. There were, of course, my Shakespeares—and my parents' Shakespeares and my grandparents' Shakespeares. There were biographies, auto- and otherwise, in the dozens, from Boswell on Johnson to a ghastly but fascinating Alma Mahler Gropius Werfel I could never make myself throw out. I loved the way biographies on the shelf made your mind bounce around like a pin-ball, based on their proximity to one another: Mary McCarthy to Whittaker Chambers to Anthony Burgess, Matisse to Moss Hart, Leonard Bernstein to Beethoven (or is it the other way around?), Isak Dinesen to Dawn Powell; and most were still in boxes, as were all of the poets. We were thinking of taking the back hall, lining it with bookcases and at the north end, building in a window seat, surrounded top and bottom by books. Absolute heaven.

I heard Teddy come in and go straight to the kitchen, which was his latest target. I kept working on my papers, and at about eleven o'clock Teddy appeared at the door with a mug of tea and some buttered raisin toast on a plate for me.

"So, can you come next Saturday?" Teddy asked, shifting his footing and proffering his snack.

"What's it all about?" I asked. "I mean, what kind of gathering are you planning? Is it a celebration or what?"

"Yeah," Teddy said, as though I would understand what that meant.

"Yeah—what?" I asked, studying him over the rims of my glasses.

"Yeah, it's like a celebration."

"Okay," I said. "I'll bite. What kind of celebration is it?"

"It's kind of complicated," Teddy answered, as though talking to the wall.

"Look," I said, "can you tell me something about this *before* I show up?" Had I agreed to show up? I almost rewound the tape in my head to see if I needed to add a disclaimer.

"Here's the thing," Teddy said. "My father died days before Thanksgiving a few years ago?" He often ended sentences with the uplift of a question to suggest that you might not be following the facts. And he didn't know that I knew that a "few" years ago was fifteen. He continued: "And my mother has not wanted to celebrate Thanksgiving in a, you know, traditional way—ever since. So I drive her to my aunt Nora's church down in Great Barrington, and they feed homeless people on Thanksgiving. So . . . we do a kind of Thanksgiving-feast-thing a few weeks before—so we're not, like, cheated out of the whole turkey and stuffing business." He looked relieved that he'd gotten the premise out in the open.

I know that this is a really judgmental thought, but I can't help it; I thought, Jeez, this is *so* Catholic—this idea that you can take a day and celebrate Thanksgiving but not *call* it Thanksgiving and therefore it's *not* Thanksgiving and you can't be *blamed* for enjoying it.

"Who is invited?" I asked.

And Teddy told me: his aunts—three of his mother's sisters and one of his father's—and some of the folks from his mother's church and, he hastened to add, as though he could read the draw of that crowd on my interest, "your friend Josie O'Sullivan and her husband, Dan, and her girls. You like *them,*" he seemed to implore. "And some other people from the town that we know . . ." He looked off, as though he continued to think and add up names in his head. I could imagine this turning into a laundry list: Mr. Jones from the bank and Herb, the butcher, from Oak Street Market? And Mr. Springer and his wife, from the new IGA. You know? As you drive into town? I wanted to stop this before it started. The whole thing sounded like my idea of hell.

"Okay, okay, Teddy," I said. "I'm not absolutely sure I can spend the whole day, but I'll certainly stop by and—"

I was interrupted. "But my mother will want to set a place for you, and I have to tell her if you're coming for dinner."

Dinner. He was pretty emphatic, and I was just about to decline when I looked at his face. His brows, underneath the peaked brim of his baseball cap, were furrowed. He looked as though my being at his house might be the most important thing in his life at that moment. And so I agreed, but dinner only, not the whole afternoon before, not the whole night after.

"Warn your mother, so she won't think that I'm rude"—or so that she'll know I'm rude beforehand—"that I have a lot of work to do and that I can't stay all day." At least that's what I believe I got across. His shoulders sagged in what I took to be a kind of relief, and he smiled his lopsided grin, absent, for the moment, of the usual fretful expression that accompanied all discourse.

Before either of us moved from our positions, the front doorbell rang. Teddy had rewired the bell, and it sounded Andy Hardy old-fashioned in its deep electronic voice. At the door were three of my students returning a book, and I took it from them. They seemed to want to discuss it more fully, and we talked for a moment, their animation almost infectious. Teddy stood behind me mixing joint compound and staring at the kids at the door. They remained on the porch as we talked. They invited me to go to a lecture with them at the Emily Dickinson house. It sounded interesting, and I asked if they might consider reporting on it to the class next week.

I thought it was a nice little visit. I closed the door and turned back into the room to find Teddy eyeing me as though I were a criminal.

"You didn't invite those kids in," he accused. "They came all the way across town to return your book. Obviously," he said, rolling his eyes, "they could have given you the book in class." He turned to face me fully and said, with real gravity, "They like you. They want to know you better. They wanted you to come to the lecture with them, and you let them stand on your porch. You didn't even invite them in."

"They're students," I said. "I'm their teacher, not their friend."

"You're a *person,*" he said. "You're a person, first. They're *people*— just like you—only not, you know . . . so old."

"Well, thanks," I muttered, shuffling back toward my den, my lair, my cave, my burrow, my roost, my nook, my cranny, my cove, my cubby—my adored office.

I tried to get back to work, but the faces of my students floated up to me from the page, and the criticism in Teddy's voice stung in a way I simply couldn't put aside. He was completely wrong, of course. They were students. It was only a moment anyway, and hardly worth his going off on that kind of harangue. And what he was suggesting was just inappropriate. After all, I thought, I don't know anything about them, personally. But I did. I read their essays and their short stories. I knew a lot about their fears and their dreams. Far more, perhaps, than they'd even meant to share in their purple, self-revealing prose.

I didn't want to be their friend. I simply wanted to be their teacher. But I had to admit, something was changing in the way I believed a powerful educator could impact the lives of students. This must be the influence of Bernadette, so alive with promise about our "calling." Or maybe it was Josie, full of gossip and delight about the personal details and potential of her students, each of whom sounded, in Josie's signature hyperbole, "supremely gifted." Or maybe it was Teddy, who knew his subject so well that he could turn it into a living, breathing reality, not just theory and critique. The idea that he might someday bring his practical, balanced skill and passion to students was seductive and infectious.

If I had begun to daydream about the kind of teacher I hoped Teddy would become, it hadn't, until now, occurred to me that I might try to become a better teacher myself. This was all too confusing.

At any rate, I *certainly* wasn't going to invite students into a work zone, with ladders and spackle and wires sticking out of the walls. Maybe when the house was done. Maybe another time.

CHAPTER 12

On November 6, I drove to Teddy's Imitation Thanksgiving Festival in a kind of stew. The idea of this charade irritated me beyond reason. Finding Harold Ross's birthday listed in my *New Yorker* diary on that same date suggested a more authentic feast day to me than the creation of Faux Thanksgiving. Will there be soy or gluten pressed into the shape of a turkey rather than real turkey? I wondered grimly. Will they have stuffing to eat, or will they hang a piñata of a turkey and batter it into giving up sandwiches?

I was carrying a book of poems by Richard Wilbur for Teddy and an orchid plant for Maureen, wondering if I should be, instead, delivering a horn of plenty and a corn pudding.

The Hennessy house was a large split-level ranch at the edge of a development I would have positioned somewhere between *Leave It to Beaver* and *Bewitched*. There was a walk rimmed with now browning azaleas, but the front door was banked by two large pots of mums in bloom, and the property and the house were meticulously maintained, as one would expect of a home cared for by Teddy Hennessy.

I parked on the side of the road behind many other cars and braced myself as I approached the front door. A woman of indeterminate age answered the doorbell. I mean this quite literally; she looked neither young for seventy-five nor old for sixty. Her hair was unnaturally black and beauty parlor stiff-styled, and her clothes showed her trim figure to an advantage, slim jersey slacks and a knitted ivory tunic with an Aztec pattern at the hem. She wore large gold earrings, coral lipstick, and her hands were carefully manicured. She gave me a lot of time for this level of scrutiny as she stood at the door unsmiling and openly assessing me. There was no warm greeting. There was no sign of welcome. She didn't even move backward to bid me enter but stood her ground.

"You must be Joy," she said flatly.

The fact that this was Maureen Hennessy dawned on me more slowly than I would have wished. I must have looked awkward, managing my handbag, the wrapped book of poems and the orchid plant, but she made no move to help me. I maneuvered the strap of the handbag up my left wrist, switched the book into my left hand and presented the orchid plant with my right. Mrs. Hennessy did not reach for it but stood and watched me as though I were a performing seal. I was momentarily stymied, certain that I had done something wrong. Teddy appeared on the scene, all warm host manners and jovial attendance, dressed for the holiday in jeans and Birkenstocks, a bright yellow T-shirt with a turkey on the back and an orange baseball cap. He reached for the plant. "Oh," he said, "a cymbidium, that's great!"

"It's for your mother," I stammered to him rather than to her. "This is for you"—I offered the wrapped flat, square package of what clearly was a book.

"Oh, great!" Teddy said. "A tie!" It was one of his silly jokes. We'd talked not so long ago about gifts where the contents of the present are telegraphed by the obvious package: the "tie" present, the "ring" present and, in the old days, the "music album present"—and this gift was so obviously a book and not a long and narrow tie that we both laughed. I looked at his mother and her eyes narrowed watching him, though when she saw his head turn toward her, she smiled as though she'd been smiling all along.

Teddy was chattering on about the guests and the food and the fact that it was so warm for early November that everyone had opted to sit outside. Maureen interrupted him. "Booboo," she said, "would you go outside and check the fire on the barbeque?"

"I just did, Ma," Teddy said, smiling at me and barely breaking the pace of his party overview.

"Would you check it now. Please," she asked, if you can imagine a request delivered as a sharp demand. Her rudeness and her manner did not seem to register with him.

"Sure." He touched my arm and promised to return and introduce me to their guests.

"I'll introduce Joy," Maureen said, taking my arm as though we were old and dear friends. I don't like strangers touching me. I don't even like hairdressers or manicurists or doctors or nurses touching me. I've just never been comfortable with it. I certainly didn't like Maureen taking my arm, and I could feel myself stiffen in her grasp.

"Booboo is a good boy," she said as she led me across the foyer toward the first clutch of guests.

I wasn't sure I'd heard correctly the first time, and the second time she used this name I asked, "What did you call him?"

"Didn't he tell you what we call him at home?" she asked, and shook her head as though talking about an errant child. She stopped midfoyer, though the closest guests looked at me with the expectation of an introduction. She lowered her voice. "Well, there are two reasons for the nickname, I s'pose," she said, and explained that Teddy's older brother had loved Yogi Bear and they had promised the name, as in Yogi's sidekick, Booboo Bear, when they explained to him that a baby was on the way.

I laughed and told her that a few years ago, when one of the teachers at Columbia was expecting a new baby, her older son would only accept the possibility of naming the baby Aladdin! I laughed at the memory. Maureen didn't. She was irritated. Intent on telling me the real reason for the name Booboo, I had hampered her timing.

She leaned forward, conspiratorially. In her broad South Boston accent, she explained what a difficult birth she'd had with Joey, Teddy's older brother. "It was," she said with great drama, "the most excruciating, agonizing event in my life. But also, of course, the most glorious. It is what we're here for, after all, and terrible pain is a necessary part of it. It is the cross women bear, like our blessed Mother." It sounded like *Mah thahh,* and it took a moment for me to register just whom she might have been referring to. I hardly knew what to say.

"After . . . that . . ." She paused and looked away, her eyebrows knitting, her lips a stoic line, as though remembering the fires of hell. "I was told," she continued, "that I should not have more children. And we were very careful, if you know what I mean. There was no birth control back

then—not that I think it should be allowed now, mind you." She nodded
her head as though I were in agreement. Where is this going? I thought.

"My husband was a good man, God rest his soul. He was good"—she
sighed—"*and* kind, but he was only flesh, you know. And," she said
sourly, poking me in the ribs with her elbow, "you know men.

"Well," she continued, "I found myself"—she lowered her voice
even more and hissed—"pregnant."

My mind was spinning. I'd met her not four minutes ago. Could she
be telling me this? Teddy had returned and was now at her elbow and
within earshot.

"I was thirty-six, and the whole idea of birth at that advanced age was
very dangerous. I even considered . . . just for a moment, of course"—
she hissed again—"an . . . alternative." There followed another suitable
and dramatic pause. "We knew we didn't want another child and we certainly didn't want to risk my life, but we just couldn't murder a baby. I
mean, how can anyone even think about such a thing!"

I had no clue how to respond to any of this. I was at a Mad Hatter's
Un-Thanksgiving party, and the Queen of Hearts was giving me way too
much information. The idea that anyone considered thirty-six too old to
bear children, the idea of Teddy as unplanned and clearly unwanted, and
the idea of offering all of this information to a total stranger—I was in
fear of saying so many things that could cause a rift so early in a relationship or, more to the point, so early in the day.

But Maureen was not to be dissuaded. She continued, "And because
Booboo is also the word for a *mistake,* the name stuck. He was our little
Booboo! Our little mistake! Isn't it *clever*?"

We both looked at Teddy and found him beaming fondly at his
mother. "Oh," I said, "*clever* isn't the word."

Teddy led me across the living room, introducing me briefly to some
of the members of Mrs. Hennessy's bridge club. They were a pleasant
enough elderly couple, but I prayed he wouldn't leave me with them and
my prayer was answered. After just a moment, he led me out the French
doors to a terrace where as many as fifteen people milled about, some sitting at a round, umbrella-shaded table, others at two picnic tables, while
some sat on benches and on the slate-topped stone wall of the terrace.

Teddy was on a mission and headed like a missile for a group of women sitting at one of the picnic tables. He proudly introduced me to his mother's sisters: Brigid, Frances and Theresa. They scanned me as though I were the dinner entrée.

"Booboo is doin' your house, I heeyah," said one of the sisters, the others nodding.

"Yes!" I said, with as much enthusiasm as I could muster. "And he's doing the most wonderful job."

"His mother says he's very proud of it," said another sister. Teddy was glowing.

"Oh, yes, well . . . yes. He should be proud of it. It's coming along beautifully." And I patted him like a dog that's brought the paper.

"We'd like to see it sometime," announced the third sister, declaring her intention to be invited.

"Oh! Oh, yes, of course. Well, Teddy knows my schedule. You can drop in while I'm at class, and he can show you around." The sisters looked at one another with raised eyebrows. What? Was I supposed to invite them to something social? I don't do social. If Teddy got the nuance, he made no show of it. He was being summoned across the yard by another guest and darted away with a kind of shoot-you hand gesture directed at me.

We stood in silence for what seemed like a month. "What a pretty sweddah," said one of the sisters.

I was grateful she'd broken the ice and swam toward the remark as though it were a life raft. "Oh, *thank* you!" I said with too much verve, I thought, for my personality and for the sweater. "It's one of my favorites."

"Did you get it in New Yawk?" she asked. The other sisters were looking at me as though watching a mouse walk toward the cheese lure. I was uneasy but, for some reason, anxious to please.

"I did. I got it at Saks. They seem to always have the best sweaters around—they must have a great knitwear buyer or something—"

And here came the blade: "Those kinds a' fashions and prices are well beyond *us*," said one sister. "We don't need to spend a lota money tryin' to impress people up heeyah." She looked to her other sisters for reinforcement, and it came, like a Greek chorus: "Oh, no. We don't need to impress people up heeyah."

I could feel my cheeks flush. Why had I ever agreed to come to this stupid, stupid party? And dinner hadn't even begun, for God's sake.

Josie must have arrived moments before the ambush and spotted it from across the terrace. She quickly crossed toward us, and taking my arm with a warm greeting she acknowledged each of the sisters by name and asked if they didn't agree it was an unusually glorious day for November. Oh, they did, they did, thanks be to God. Such a glorious day. And she led me, shell-shocked, away from them.

"So you've met the three witches of Amherst!" She laughed.

"Four, if you count their sister," I added with a scowl.

"Well, of course, but 'the Girls' here have never married and they live together in a cottage that's like walking into a Hallmark card from hell. It's terrifying. Everything that can be is covered with something crocheted or made of lace. They have crocheted cake covers and crocheted edges on their dish towels. They all sleep in the same bedroom—three twin beds lined up against the wall with three matching nightstands that hold three copies of the same lamp and three statues of the Virgin Mary. Talk about horrifying."

Josie led me back across the terrace to a group of people that contained her daughters. There were three adults, a pretty young woman whom I recognized as one of the school librarians, a handsome man in what I guessed to be his midforties or early fifties who looked familiar but I couldn't place him in this environment, and another, slightly shorter man in a Missoni sweater, also handsome, but round and pink and polished. I don't mean *polished* the way my mother used the word— a kind of certification of good manners. I mean *polished* the way a silversmith might use it. Polished like the bottom of a copper pot in Paul Bocuse's kitchen. And I guessed, by the way his arm was wrapped around Lizzie's shoulders, that this was the peripatetic Dan O'Sullivan.

He greeted me with warmth and good humor. He'd heard so much about me, he said, and he generously and seamlessly included me in the story he'd been telling as we approached, about a tourist in a bazaar in Morocco. When all had had their chance to respond, he introduced me to the group; the librarian's name was Beth, the handsome fellow was Will Bradford and he taught psychology at Amherst. Josie stood next to Will and, I thought, deliberately took a step back as the introduction to him was made. She looked at me with a kind of meaning-ful intent.

"I haven't seen you around campus," I said. Josie's eyebrows shot up.

"Then you haven't been looking," he answered. I thought that he was the other half of the librarian couple, but suddenly it came to me: Coy-ote. I looked at Josie with a matching high-eyebrowed recognition, and she smiled, proud that I'd figured it out.

"How are you all connected to the Hennessys?" I asked.

The librarian was a niece through Mr. Hennessy. Dan had grown up in town with the Hennessys as acquaintances of his parents, and with Mr. and Mrs. O'Sullivan Sr. retired to Palm Beach and the other seven O'Sul-livan siblings scattered across the globe, Dan remained the touchstone of the Amherst clan and kept his contacts with those who had long been a part of his family's life. Will was a fraternity brother of Dan's at Dart-mouth and considered him among his closest friends. But Dan's travel schedule didn't allow much socializing in Amherst, and in order to spend time together, they'd brought Will along today.

I had a minute to consider the coincidence and decided that Josie had been behind it from the start. Never mind. At least there was some relief in being away from the witches.

The Thanksgiving meal was served. Maureen Hennessy introduced a priest who looked like a tiny child in oversized ecclesiastical vestments. He couldn't have been taller than five feet, but his voice boomed with a froggy resonance as he blessed the meal and us. There was a buffet of dry, overcooked turkey, tasteless and greasy stuffing, gray green beans in a casserole with some processed onion flakes on top and mashed sweet potatoes with the metallic taste of the tin clinging to its candied sweet-ness, and a crust of emulsified marshmallow hardening on the surface—the kind of food that would have caused my mother to rush away from the gathering in fear of ingesting working-class values. I wondered out loud whether this get-together was Mrs. Hennessy's way of being the first in town to serve seasonal turkey, as everyone knows that within twenty-four hours after Thanksgiving, even the most succulent bird looks like something you'd rather wait a year to sample again.

Will paid attention to me. He was funny and bright and well read and generous and handsome. He admitted to loving contemporary poetry, and I told him about the book I'd brought for Teddy. He knew, of course, the poems of Richard Wilbur, his favorite being one of mine, and the reason I'd chosen the book for Teddy—a bird, trapped in a house, reminds the writer of his teenage daughter, attempting to free herself from the constraints of adolescence and the limits of home. But he also knew the *Candide* translation Wilbur had done for Leonard Bernstein forty years ago and the brilliant translation he'd done of *Tartuffe* about ten years later, in 1963. I knew Will was interested in me. He played to my strong points and interests. And for once, I wasn't *completely* cynical and suspicious.

Will and Dan shared all kinds of yarns about their college years, encouraged by the cheering section of Lizzie and Jackie and Josie, who suggested stories like sweetmeats to be sampled.

"Dad! Dad! Dad!! Tell the one about you and Willy going to the Army-Navy game in Philadelphia in the old convertible with fake noses and glasses on!! Tell the one about the time you fell asleep under the bleachers and Will went on the date for you!!! Tell the one, Dad! Dad!! Tell the one about how you met Mom and Willy liked her, too!!" That's the one I wanted to hear, but it was not destined to happen that day.

Teddy came and sat at our picnic table and began to share information about a house in town he thought should be bought by the historical society. It was the house three doors down from Emily Dickinson's, lived in by her uncle and the scene of some important gatherings, literary and otherwise. It had fallen into disrepair, with floors so shaky Teddy feared falling through, and a staircase that moved underfoot—even, Teddy said, in worse condition than he'd found my stairs. Worse condition, I thought. Is this possible? But clothes remained in closets, and nineteenth-century toys lay untouched in the nursery. It was a beautiful house, he said to me, as everyone else knew it, set back from the road. Teddy was clearly smitten and anxious to get the town started in the process of buying the place. Waiting, he felt, was not an option. Attention was needed soon, before something terrible, like a leak in the roof or a nest of animals, caused damage beyond repair. I felt a twinge of what I might have identified as jealousy, if I'd been more introspective or honest. Teddy was excited about another house. There would be another project after mine. Dan promised to look into pulling together some of the movers and shakers in town, and he and Teddy made a date to meet, there and then.

I took this resolution as a natural and positive break in the festivities and decided to use it as a time to slip away. My good-byes to the O'Sullivans included promises of get-togethers I thought would probably never happen, but when Will Bradford, with his soap opera name and his cashmere sports jacket, asked for my phone number, I knew he would call. I already thought of him as my last Coyote.

Teddy walked me through his house as I aimed to thank his mother for such a—I searched for just the right word: unique, rare, matchless, singular, remarkable, illuminating?—afternoon. We found her in the kitchen in a huddle with her sisters. They looked up at us like children who'd been caught lighting matches, but regained their imperious and intimidating composure within seconds. Teddy seemed completely oblivious to their attitude. He smiled warmly at them and at me. He joked and provoked them, and, in fairness, they did seem to find him adorable. Good for them, I allowed. But my thoughts weren't on Teddy as I walked to my car and drove home; my thoughts were on the Coyote. And when, at half past ten that night, the phone rang, I knew before I answered it that the caller was Will.

CHAPTER 13

William Denning Bradford swept into my life like a storm and took over the emotional landscape, such as there was, to the extent that I had to wonder if there had been any emotional content before him at all.

In a matter of days he was calling to wake me with songs and limericks. He popped by the office to join Josie, Fran and me for lunch. He e-mailed between his classes with brief, goofy messages and forwarded jokes or little endearments that embarrassed me to read and embarrass me now, even more, to repeat. Things like, "I'm going to run across campus and jump all over you like a big brown dog." I was horrified and scared and intrigued and nearly delighted and totally overwhelmed. Nothing like this had ever happened to me.

We met for brunch the morning after the Hennessy party, and from the moment we met on the sidewalk in front of the Pipe and Drum, there didn't appear to be a question or hesitation on his part. It was as though preordained; for Will, we were, from that first day, a couple. Or at least he behaved as though we were. I was flattered, I suppose. But slower to sign on. After all, everything about my life was new.

Will talked from our first evening together about wanting to be married. He talked about how difficult it was to manage the crushes of young girls and still maintain the discipline to teach them and how he thought, if married, he might have a better chance at distance. He said that he thought he'd been passed over a few years ago as head of the department because he remained unmarried. The chance was coming around again. Adele Friedman, the head of the Psychology Department, was resigning to move to Berkeley within the next year. Her husband had been appointed campus architect for the University of California, and she was promised the job of dean, within two years, if she too would move. I knew it was so; we were sad to be losing Adele from the Shakespeare program. Will didn't want to be passed over again. It was time for him to marry. If I struggled with the fact that there wasn't a question of my agreeing or even being asked, I also had to admit that my chances of better offers were probably slim. Do you know when the minister says, "And so it was written . . . ?" That's just how it seemed.

So often, Will says, "success in life is a matter of timing." Here he was, a confirmed bachelor, just coming to the realization that what he wanted now, more than anything, was to be married and settled—and I showed up "out of the ether." It's destiny, he says. What luck, when the universe delivers the very thing you are ready for. "Very Zen," he says.

I must feel the same way, he suggested, kissing my neck. I told him, candidly but kindly I hope, that I'd not been looking for someone to marry. Really, quite the opposite, I think. "And this doesn't seem very *romantic*," I said. "It's more like deciding that there is a job opening you want filled, and taking the first person who walks in the room."

"No," Will said, "it's not like that at all." He shook his shaggy salt-and-pepper hair. "Hasn't it *ever* happened to you? You see something wonderful, that you never knew you wanted, never even thought about before—and suddenly, you know, that's *it*. That's what you want. And you have to have it!" I cast about in my memory bank but could come up with nothing.

"No," I said, "I'm very level. There's nothing unplanned or unexpected that I've ever just decided to go for, out of the blue. I'm not *like* that."

But as the words came out of my mouth, I suddenly thought about my position at Amherst and, for heaven's sake, the house! And now—a dozen things: wallpaper samples and a green-and-chrome toaster that looks like a classic car's grill, a slab of white marble with tan and gray veins that Teddy found at a local stone dealer and thought we'd use as a surface in the guest bath, a heavy Victorian pedestal of carved mahogany that I saw in the window of an antiques shop late one night and sent Teddy down the next morning to buy—no matter what the cost. Hell, I wanted things that three months ago I hadn't even known existed. So I supposed this was what had happened to Will—and me.

He had a kind of William Holden–in–*Sabrina* quality: sure of himself but boyish. Or Paul Newman in *The Long Hot Summer*. Sexy, certainly, but practiced at it. And I suppose that's what made it so powerful. He knew what he was doing. I mean, I'm hardly an expert, but it certainly was different from any other relationship I'd ever had. He was funny and charming. I can't imagine a woman not falling in love with Will. You'd have to be dead. But it seemed almost impossible to believe that Will was in love with me.

He was perfect. He wasn't demanding or cloying. He didn't need to stay at my place every night, but when he did, the sex was tender and fine. He didn't like to be held or touched when he slept, and neither did I. There was a nice, cool band of air between us in the bed. Only very secure people can sleep like that, neither needy nor overly demonstrative. Every now and then one or the other of us might reach across and just touch a thigh or kiss a shoulder. He often placed his foot in such a way that it just touched my leg. I found it very sweet, and I was very grateful.

It was happening so fast. In the first weeks we were together I was, uncharacteristically, never far from tears. I, who had hardly ever cried. I was so overwhelmingly grateful; grateful to God, I suppose, if I'd believed in him, and grateful to Will—in whom I did believe. And there was another surprise: I had no idea that grateful would hurt quite so much. I didn't realize loving would bring up fathomless fear. With all the books I'd read and analyzed and taught and treasured about love and life—how is it that I never really knew falling in love could be so terrible?

Josie, I thought, had her own concerns. Uncharacteristically, she seemed to bite her tongue. I'll admit, I've never been one to read the emotions of others with any clarity, but there was something hanging in the air that I felt she wanted to say and didn't. Finally, after about a week and a half of Will's very attentive behavior, Josie braved the conversation. She twisted the edge of her scarf as though screwing up her courage. "Willy seems to be giving you the rush . . ." She let the end of the sentence just fade.

"What do you *mean*?" I asked, probably blushing, as I'd never had a conversation with a woman about a man, in my life.

"Well, I mean, he is so . . . all over you." I looked at her narrowing eyes and the set of her mouth and was jerked out of my teen-scene foot shuffling by this completely irrational thought: Does she have a thing for Will?

"Listen," I said, "you introduced us. This is *your* thing—"

"I didn't think he'd get serious," she said. "Will is just not like that. He's the kind of guy you can have a good time with and pick up and put down—you know—through the years. A friend. And I didn't think *you* would get serious, *either*. You know, like you *said,* you didn't *want* to get serious." She looked pained. "Will's like a guy to go out with and have fun with and know that he's not going to break your heart and you're not going to break *his*—"

"I don't think so, Josie." I said. "This Coyote seems pretty serious to me."

"'Serious,'" she repeated, her dark eyebrows knitting over her deep green eyes. "What do you *mean*?"

My nagging thought was not dispelled. "Listen, are you—you're not *jealous,* are you?"

"Jealous!" she exploded. "Are you *nuts!*"

Josie huffed and puffed and then quickly and visibly collected herself and continued with a calmer approach. "Look, Will is great. He's fun. But, you know, he's a player. He's a—what do you call it?—a gadfly. You said you didn't *want* a committed, involved relationship. You said it over and *over*. And I thought, *Fine*. He was already interested in who you were—you were *new,* and Will loves 'new.' So I thought, *Wonderful!* You might have a little fling, I mean—sex without commitment is nice, isn't it? I mean—I've been married since the Stone Age—but, you know, I *hear* it's nice . . . easy . . . no strings." She looked helpless. "Most of all, I thought you could become his friend. He *is* fun"—she seemed to plead—"and you are so smart and serious. You have your own thing, you know? And you're so much a cut above his, his . . ." She stumbled. "I mean, he *really* needs a solid, grown-up woman to be his, you know, his *friend,* his *companion*. But not *romantic* . . . not serious—like *that*."

I didn't want to hear it, and so I didn't. What I heard was that Josie, my friend, the friend who'd bullied her way into my life and pulled off bits of my armor, Josie—who'd been married since the Stone Age—*was* possessive of Will. Given Dan's wanderlust, it all made sense.

I'd not cared about many people in my life, and now, goddamn it, I cared about Josie. I saw that she could be hurt by my relationship with Will, so hurt that she'd have said anything; my heart ached for her in a way I don't think I'd felt toward any living person ever before.

"Maybe that's how it was, Josie." I tried to be gentle. "Maybe Will was once happy-go-lucky and gadding about. And maybe I *did* say that I didn't want to get involved with someone—and maybe I meant it at the *time*. But people change," I said. "Look at me," I said, thinking about Amherst and the house and even the very unlikely situation of standing there, as we were, talking about something so personal I could hardly believe it myself. "Look how much I've changed."

Josie looked at me, all right, but she looked at me with so much sadness.

CHAPTER 14

There was a strain at the office. Josie still brought lunch. Will showed up about half the time and ate with us, but there was a level of carefulness that had now appeared in Josie and, to some extent, in Fran. There were looks between the two women—discreet, to be sure. They were not, in any way, behaving badly. They were not catty or rude or intrusive or cold. They were neither passive-aggressive nor aggressive-aggressive. They were just like themselves—just as they would be at lunch if Margaret Thatcher had turned up.

And there was a strain at home. Teddy still labored away, but now his presence seemed an intrusion and I knew he felt it. Will would call while I was cutting the French bread pizza into quarters, and I would have to tell him that I would call him back, or I would leave Teddy eating alone while I left the room to talk to Will. And on the nights we would come in together at eight thirty or nine, intent on bed—or at least on some kissing—Teddy would be there, on his ladder, looking down at us from beneath his cap's brim.

"It's like he's your father," Will said one night. "I feel as though he's always judging me."

"He's not judging you," I said. "He's judging me. I think I was a kind of mother figure for him and we had a sort of rhythm going here with work and meals and approval, and now it's all different."

"Is it all different?" Will asked, raising my chin with his hand like Moondoggie did with Gidget when she got pouty. "Maybe we should do something that makes it all more permanent." He kissed me, and we didn't talk about it or anything else that night.

Will's apartment was on the second floor of an old Federal house just off campus. The house had been divided into six apartments. He had one of the two larger apartments on the top floor. One entered by going down an alley at the right of the house to a doorway with two bells. I'd only been there once. We'd dropped off a large package on our way from school one evening, and I had the distinct feeling that he hadn't wanted me to follow him from the car into the house, but I was curious about the apartment and more curious about feeling that he didn't want me along.

"It's not all spruced up," he said. "I don't want you to think I'm some kind of slob—I've just been dashing in and out since we've been together." I thought that was so dear. Imagine worrying that I would think less of him if his apartment was not in order.

"Don't be silly," I replied. "I don't care how you keep your apartment—I just want to see where you live." He hurried up the narrow stairs to a tiny landing and unlocked the door. One entered directly into the living room. There was a bathroom behind the landing and a large kitchen next to that. A bank of small mullioned windows ran across the back wall of the kitchen and overlooked an untamed yard.

Will threw the packet down on his kitchen table and hurried me out of the apartment. "I want to see your bedroom!" I cried, laughing at the hustle. Will put on a voice like Dudley Do-Right's: "You've seen more than enough, my pretty! Always conniving to see men's bedrooms! You're a randy little wench, aren't you! I know your type!" His grasp was tight on my upper arm, and he was pushing me down the stairs faster than my legs would go.

"Hey! Hey!" I cried, half laughing and half in protest. But I was jostled out to the car, and I stopped laughing as he crossed in front of the car and got in.

"What's this bum's rush thing?" I asked, ready for a full conversation, but he took my face in his hands and kissed me and said he didn't want to waste another moment, he wanted to get me home and properly— well, let's just say that he wanted to get me home. I kissed him, and we held hands, like teenagers, while he drove to my house.

We ate Cornish game hen for my first Amherst Thanksgiving dinner. I used my mother's china and my grandmother's silver and set the dining room table for two. Will made wild rice with sultanas and almonds. I'd forgotten to get whipping cream for the Mrs. Smith pumpkin pie, but except for that, it was the best Thanksgiving I'd ever had. It certainly beat the Chinese takeout I'd had for my last fifteen Thanksgivings, as I attempted to convince myself that having Kung Pao Chicken was my very own tradition. I noted with pride that we sat at the dining table in the dining room. I lit candles. This was my house. This was beginning to be my life. I could learn to love this.

The following Saturday I was scheduled to attend an all-day meeting about the new Shakespeare program. Each team member was to have prepared a brief on how we saw our specialty dovetailing with as many of the other disciplines as possible. For something so revolutionary, there was shockingly little negative debate. I was beginning to see that Bernadette's newer teachers, and I suppose that included me, had been chosen very carefully both to blend and contrast with the more seasoned Amherst staff. If the Shakespeare pilot was only the first part of Bernadette's grand plan, the established staff seemed to understand that the ball had rolled far enough down the hill that they had only two choices: get with the program or be flattened under a sphere of massive willpower.

"A hundred years from now," Bernadette began, "people will study our programs and see that some of what we tried may have been primitive, and a lot of what we did was built on instinct, but all of it was a part of developing something that put learning first. Not teachers. Not systems. Not efficiency. Learning." She looked over the rim of her glasses. "We're going to make mistakes. And we're going to try to correct them, and then we'll make new mistakes."

Todd Dixon leaned forward with a deep smile. "As Beckett says," Todd intoned, "'Fail again. Fail better!'"

We all laughed, and Bernadette applauded. "Exactly!" she said. "That's the spirit."

Iris raised her hand in a sweet, shy gesture—and Bernadette nodded. "The only thing that concerns me," said Iris, "well, not the only thing—but the main thing—is that no one has ever done this. We have no one to look at to see if we're doing it right—if you know what I mean. Just the whole way we need to keep the other teachers informed about our own progress with full classes and with individual students? It's a huge amount of communication, and we don't have any existing procedure to study or follow. And I'm sure that things will fall through the cracks." I think we'd all worried about this. Everyone was nodding and grave.

"No one learns how to do anything of real value," Bernadette said, leveling a gaze at each of us, "if they're afraid of making mistakes. You won't be alone. We'll all be there to make sure that we *all* keep moving forward."

She seemed to consider her words even more carefully. "God knows university life is full of sloth, but none of you . . ." Her voice trailed off; she appeared to be so moved, as she took us in one by one. "You're all so competent and so very conscientious," she said. "So something falls through the cracks. So what? We'll pull it back out. It's far more likely that you won't try something because you are afraid it will fail me or fail our students. But you *can't* fail if you honestly try to move forward. We *learn* from *all* forward motion—if only in contrast—which is just as valuable, and sometimes more so, than success." None of us spoke. There we were, many at the top of our fields, but we sat in a circle around her like docile, well-meaning children who wanted only to excel and to please.

"I know I'm asking a lot," Bernadette continued. "I'm asking you to be your brothers' keeper. I'm asking you to watch out for how their work dovetails with yours and how yours might enhance theirs. And I'm asking for a spirit of cooperation and a level of personal responsibility no school has ever asked of you before. And—in many ways, I believe—that responsibility will also become your reward."

That first Saturday afternoon the whole Core Shakespeare Team worked, against all of my private bets, so efficiently and, I'd have to admit, so happily, that we were finished at four o'clock; hours before we'd anticipated concluding the exercise of divvying up the Bard into interdisciplinary but coordinated doses. Compared to a meeting at Columbia, it seemed a virtual miracle. Bernadette looked at her watch. "I'm amazed and delighted that we're two hours ahead of schedule," she announced. "And—while it's a seductive idea to push on and maintain this good energy, knowing that we have more than a full year's work ahead—I think that we should take this as a good omen and a reward! So, go out into the world and reclaim your weekend!"

It was a cold and rainy evening, but it still felt as though we'd all been set free for an early vacation and the humor was high. I helped Bernadette clean up the meeting room where we'd gathered. Howard Peal, our gentlemanly classics professor, had brought the most wonderful Viennese pastries, made by a little shop he knew in Boston. In a gesture others seemed to recognize as typical of Howard, he'd brought enough for an army, and when we urged him to take the leftovers, he admitted that he had twice the amount of pastries at home, where they might become a very unbalanced but indulgent dinner for Edward Greeling, his physics professor companion; Speedstick, his greyhound; and himself. Bernadette was on one of her endless diets, and after everyone else demurred, I took the bounty with me.

As I drove past the house where Will lived, I looked up at his lighted windows and, in a gesture that owed nothing to my upbringing, I stopped the car, backed up and pulled into his driveway. The thought that I might do something spontaneous and run up his stairs, unbidden and unexpected, with my Viennese treats was so unlike me, I was practically giddy as I made my way down his walkway—as though dropping in unannounced on the man who shared my bed was a daring, bohemian and untamed thing. I imagined his delight at seeing me hours before our planned rendezvous. Of course I imagined, and this is almost always dangerous, that he would have the same reaction I might have if he were to interrupt and surprise me.

I made my way down the long walk at the side of the house and was just about to ring the upstairs bell when the door opened and a UPS man stepped out. He smiled and held the door for me. I didn't bother to ring but walked up the stairs to the small landing. There were only two doors across from each other; to the left was the apartment of Will's neighbor, an older nurse he had mentioned a few times, and to the right was Will's door. He'd hung a large brass *B* in the center. I took a breath, knocked at his door and heard him bellow back in a good-natured way, "Bring it on!"

Will opened the door wearing only boxer shorts. He seemed shocked

to see me at first, and I felt as though he held on to his composure with
effort. "Joy! What are you doing here? You're supposed to be on
campus," he said accusingly, as though he'd found me smoking behind
the gym.

"I got out early—for good behavior," I said. "You're not dressed," I
stated the obvious. "Who did you think *I* was?"

"*Think* you were? What are you talking about?" asked Will.

"What does 'Bring it on' mean?"

"Bring it *on*?" he asked.

"Yeah, through the door—when I knocked—"

"Oh. Nothing. I was answering the *door,* for God's sake."

"It's a funny greeting," I said.

"What?" he said defensively. "My—what would you call it?—'door
etiquette' doesn't pass muster? Is this a big problem for you?" He was
"testy," as my mother used to say.

"No," I said. "No, not at all." I didn't want him annoyed at me.
"Look!" I proffered Howard's box of pastries with a flourish. "I brought
you Viennese sweets! Lots of *schlag*!"

He looked away from the box I was holding. "I'm getting in the
shower," he said with a sour expression. "Go home, and I'll meet you
there later." This visit, to say the least, was not working out the way I had
imagined it would. This surly distracted guy was not the Will I knew.
And where the hell *was* my Will? My Will was charming. My Will was
teasing and sweet and darling.

My Will's evil twin turned me around with his hands on the back of
my shoulders and gave me a soft nudge toward the door. I felt odd and
very uncomfortable and so uncharacteristically young and needy and
queer and confused and rather to blame for the whole damn thing. I
knew better than that, but I didn't *feel* better than that—and I hated
how I felt.

I was just in front of the door, as close as could be, about to reach for
the doorknob, when there was a kind of grating, scraping sound, more
like the scratching of a cat than the knocking of a person. I instinctively
opened the door, and there stood a woman of, I would guess, at least
sixty-five, rather small and dark with a cap of unnaturally dark, short,
shiny hair, wearing what we used to call a negligee. Maybe we still call

them negligees, I hadn't seen one in years; in fact, I'm not sure I'd ever seen one in person. It was black, made of some kind of poly net material, hemmed to the knee and see-through. She was naked underneath. She stood on the landing with the door to the apartment behind her wide open. She looked equally surprised but not nearly horrified enough, I thought, given her apparel.

"Valerie," Will said flatly, "this is Joy. I've told you about Joy." He raised his eyebrows. Valerie considered me as though I were a rump roast in a butcher's case.

"Yes," she said, with a kind of finality, her hand on her hip.

"Joy, this is my neighbor, Valerie." You would have thought this the most normal of all introductions, given his demeanor, although I'd heard him suck in his breath sharply when the door opened.

"The nurse," I said. She nodded.

"Yes," he said. "The nurse. Val, do you need something?" She went from being languid, nearly motionless, to very animated in the blink of an eye.

"I smelled gas," she said brightly. "I thought it was coming from my stove, and then I wondered if it was all over the building—so I thought I'd better check with you first." Clearly this is a lie, I thought. But their behavior was so normal, so even. And she was the most unlikely partner for Will that I just didn't let myself think what I seemed to be thinking.

"I don't smell anything in my apartment," said Will hastily. "But as soon as Joy leaves I'll come over and take a look at your stove."

"Oh, would you do that?" she asked. "That would be great. I'd feel so much better." She turned and walked back to her apartment. Her bottom was flat and wrinkled. Her thighs were dimpled, but her breasts stood out like the pointed conical breasts of a young teen. She looked over her shoulder at me and said, still moving, "Nice to meet you, Joy—"

"Yes," I said, more nodding than speaking, "thanks."

When the door closed I asked Will, "Does she do that often?"

"Do what?"

"Do what?! Come over dressed like a prostitute and ask you for help."

"Well," he said, "her closet doors come off the track, and her drain gets blocked up. But, I don't know. She's alone and she works long hours and she doesn't have much support—and I don't notice what she wears."

"Don't notice what she *wears*?! Are you j*oking*? She was naked!"

"She was not. She was wearing some kind of lounging robe or something."

I was disoriented. I felt, for just a moment, as though I'd actually imagined this creature, but I took a deep breath and got the better of myself.

"Will!" I cried. "She was dressed in Frederick's of Hollywood!"

"Well! I'm so sorry if my neighbors don't meet your refined sense of fashion!" he huffed. "Why don't you just go home to your 'decorator' and pick out a few more paint chips, and maybe the trauma will pass." Again, he urged me down the stairs, shaking his head. "Go home, Joy. I'll be over in a while. I'm taking a shower."

I was going to suggest that I wait for him. "Couldn't I—"

"No! Just go home. I'll be over soon." As he opened the door at the bottom of the stairs and put his arms around my shoulders, he seemed to soften a bit and Evil-Twin Will morphed back into my Will and kissed the top of my head and the tip of my nose. "Just go home now. I'll be over in a little while, and we'll have a nice evening."

He sounded so grown-up and responsible. I felt humiliated in a strange and general way. I had no center to the feeling or the offense. I felt like a yearning and impetuous girl who wanted too much and asked for too much. Was I going to make a fuss over his boxer shorts or her nightgown? Come on. I stood around and talked to Teddy wearing only a towel, and I wouldn't want to have to defend that. I'd expect Will to trust me. And the nurse was clearly too old for Will to be romantically interested. How could I know what clothes she lounged in? Or be critical of his helping her, like a dutiful son, when her life came off its tracks. Was I now going to see *every* woman, no matter how young or old, innocent or inappropriate as a threat to me? Wasn't this what made Teddy's mother so pathetic?

I sat in the car in the driveway for at least five minutes playing the scenes this way and that, a lump in my throat and tears stinging the backs of my eyes. Any blame for Will only made me look weak and neurotic, seeing things in shadows and assuming the worst. As though I didn't trust that I *could* be loved. I should have played this all out in high school. How was it happening now? Damn that Josie—*damn her* for putting these ideas in my head.

CHAPTER 15

Will arrived about two hours after I got home with a spectacular bottle of wine and a book of Seamus Heaney's poems, *Open Ground,* which I'd somehow missed in my collection. Will thought that Heaney's insight about Ireland was the perfect metaphor of psychological revelation about one's parents—their intentions (good and otherwise), their mistakes, confusions, anger and guilt. He intended to use Heaney as an example in his classes, ever the politician, taking his cues from the buzz surrounding Bernadette, and he rattled on and on about literature, poetry and psychology as though I neither taught literature nor had any idea about the psychological weight of the subject. Good grief, I thought for a moment, what does he think literature is? But "Good luck, Will," was all that I said about it.

When there was a break in what I detected to be a somewhat nervous exposition on his part and a far too quiet acquiescence on mine, I began to apologize, halfheartedly perhaps, for my uninvited appearance earlier that afternoon. Truth be told, I was far more sorry to feel so vaguely humiliated than I was sorry for dropping in, but for all kinds of legitimate and illegitimate reasons, I determined that an apology was a good political tactic. Will stopped me, and I was deeply relieved that I did not have to continue an act of contrition I did not, fundamentally or fully, feel. But I did want the incident behind us. I wanted the sweet, warm simple idea of being loved back. I realize now that he didn't interrupt me by saying that I was always welcome in his home, and he never suggested that any blame be assigned to him. But he did take me tight in his arms, and he rocked me back and forth, saying, "Shhh. Shhhh. So it's over now; I'm not angry. Shhhh." And I was grateful that—whatever it was—the *incident* was over. I was past what I was choosing to see as my neurotic response to Josie's interference. I was past it all.

We built a fire and cooked a steak in the fireplace on a grate that Teddy had rigged. And we drank the wine and shared some of the sinfully delicious Viennese pastries, and I barely lifted my head from his shoulder to chew. When we were finished eating, and I made moves to collect the dishes, Will kissed me to get my attention and asked what kind of wedding I wanted. My mouth went dry. This was all too soon. Will argued that he believed we both knew where things were headed, and I had to agree that, while I knew precious little about partnerships, it did seem as though we'd been a couple since we met. He pointed out that we were, neither of us, spring chickens. That's the term he used, *spring chickens,* and I looked at my hands, which had, in the last few years, begun to look like my grandmother's hands; a little stringy where they had been smooth, with freckles collecting into clusters.

"What's the *point* of waiting?" Will asked, showing some agitation that I wasn't getting on board as quickly as he.

"Well, there are so many questions and issues," I stammered.

"Like what? We both work here. We both live here. We're both adults. The legal stuff—I mean, I imagine you have property and family stuff—we can have all that worked out by lawyers pretty fast. And in the meantime, we could be married."

Alas, I was not as corny as Kansas in August, nor starry-eyed, giddy or spinning daydreams in love like a Hammerstein lyric. I did love Will, but I was surely no blushing bride. And anyway, a lifetime ago, I'd had all that: the young suitor who asked my father for my hand, a white satin gown straight out of Camelot, a coronet and the longest, softest veil Saint Louis had ever seen. I had a cascade of calla lilies and a bevy of bridesmaids in green velvet, bell-sleeved dresses, with their hippie-wild, postadolescent hair held back in snoods, woven thick with jasmine. I had a country club wedding that made the society pages of the papers from Saint Louis to Chicago, with detailed reports about the topiary on the terrace and Peter Duchin himself, imported with his orchestra, of course, from New York.

My mother had attended a special Bill Blass appearance at our branch of Neiman Marcus a few months before my wedding. Together, she and Mr. Blass picked out her dress. No dowdy, matronly Mother of the Bride was she. Until she died, this pale green, knife-pleated, silk chiffon dress hung in her closet, where she might see it each time the automatic light responded to the door's movement. Mother would often remember Blass talking about the pale green of the dress as the perfect complement for her light auburn hair. He made her feel, I think, that she was the only woman in America who should have worn that dress. He must have been a genius, because my mother was nobody's fool. But that was long ago, more than twenty-five years ago, and they are all dead now, Blass among them. The community of family friends who surrounded me at that wedding were faded from my memory in almost complete erasure; as I'm sure, if they still lived and breathed, I was from theirs.

"Can't we just *get* married?" I asked. "Do we have to have a wedding?" I'll admit, even before I researched my options, I was more than a little alarmed at the thought of staging a pageant.

"Why of course we have to have a wedding!" Will said, apparently offended again, his eyes narrowing like a small-town spinster's at the suggestion of living in sin.

"But I thought weddings were for parents," I said, remembering the line my father had handed me decades ago, when it was clear my mother had taken over and I'd lost control of mine.

"Weddings," Will answered in a manner that suggested he was explaining alternate-side-of-the-street parking rules to someone who'd never seen a car, "are designed to strengthen a weave of community as it celebrates the shared rituals that remind us of our place on earth and in our shared society. There is a kind of responsibility to it."

"Yes," I said, noting the rigid social scientist in his academic persona. "But they're very personal things too. I don't really *have* a community here—and I—"

"But *I* do." Will was emphatic. "I've lived here my whole adult life. My work is here. My life is here." There was no lightness to his expression. He might have been talking about where his *New York Times* was to be delivered.

"Well, okay," I said a mite sarcastically, "then *you* be the bride. I suppose I should be asking what kind of wedding *you* want."

"Do you think that's *funny?*" Will stated with a nasty bite. "You have absolutely *no* idea what kind of wedding you want."

He looked disgusted.

"Don't be angry at me," I said. I was being reduced again to a whiny girl. I could hardly believe my ears.

"I'm not angry," he said angrily. "I just can't *believe* that you won't take this seriously. There are a lot of women who would be very *happy* to be talking about their wedding."

"Who? Who are they?" I asked.

"What?"

"Who are these women?"

"What?!"

I thought it was a valid question. "Who are they?" meant how different are they from *me*. But I was getting nowhere and I was pissing him off and this was my big romantic wedding proposal night and I could see that I was the one who was spoiling it. I had to get ahold of myself. I had to develop new skills. I had to be someone else, and I had to be someone else pretty damn fast.

"Look, Will." I tried to sound reasonable and calm and caring. "I don't have any living family. I hardly know anyone here. I *really* only know you. And I'm not someone who likes being in the spotlight. I've never been part of a big group, if you know what I mean. I'm not a joiner."

He looked away. "This isn't all about you, Joy. The point of getting married is that it's about both of us. Not just you."

"Right." I took a breath. "I know, of course, you're right." I was losing this fast, and the set of his jaw and a stiffness in his body told me that I was losing him. "Look, you're right. Whatever you want. As long as it's not too much of a performance, you know? Just quiet and modest and simple."

"Okay, then," he said, but it didn't look okay. "I was thinking about January second. It's a Saturday."

January second. Good grief. I felt a little flare of panic in my chest. "Where?"

"Well"—he seemed to be warming up a little—"I thought that we might do it right in town at the Lord Jeffrey." At least this place was comfortable. I liked the Lord Jeffrey. It had a kind of personal resonance for me. I'd stayed there when I was looking for my house and again as I waited for my belongings to arrive from New York, and I moved back in for a few days as Disaster Master worked his magic. I must have shown some level of relaxing into the idea.

He continued, "I thought, a small ceremony followed by a cocktail reception or a lunch. You can wear a pretty suit; maybe something in a cream-colored silk. You know, tailored and classy."

"Classy?" I repeated for clarification.

"Classic," he said impatiently.

"Okay," I said. "Okay, I can do this. But—I hate to shop."

"What kind of woman hates to shop?" he asked dismissively.

This kind, I thought. The kind you want to marry. But he put his arm around my shoulders and said, "I'll go with you. It will be fun." Perhaps it wasn't my kind of fun, but I was willing to suspend disbelief, at least for the moment.

A few days later Will arrived with a beautiful Victorian ring of tiny emeralds and diamonds set in platinum. It fit as though it were made for me, and though I wore no rings and never had, except for the first few months of my long-ago marriage, I thought I could get used to the feeling of this ring on my hand. Still, I took it off and sat it on my appointment book as I worked at my desk.

On some level I must have recognized my discomfort with the concept of the wedding as I was reluctant to share the news with Josie and Fran, but it was obvious I would have to; Will wanted Dan as his best man. Would I have to ask Josie to be an attendant? Did I even need an attendant? Were there any rules at all for a "geriatric wedding," as I referred to it in a dark joke to myself. I looked through the overflowing Bridal section at Amherst Books and found nothing at all to give me direction. Not a book or a single bridal magazine applied to me or my age group. Occasionally, an elderly father or a son "gave away" an apparently older bride, but what a chilling message that phrase, "to give away," seemed to send. And, if a very small segment of the brides displayed seemed shorter, older or thicker than a runway model, the shining white dresses made them look broad as a barn or, at the very least, ill advised and masquerading as a virgin. Talk about mutton dressed as lamb.

Surely, I was not the only over-forty bride in America. Was it really possible that no one had addressed the issues of apparel and etiquette? It was bad enough calling attention to myself; I certainly didn't want to call attention to the fact that I was doing something gauche. I went home and searched the Net for books on the subject of mature weddings, nontraditional weddings, noniconic weddings—and came up dry. I had no mother I might implore for direction; I had no aunt or sister. I didn't want to involve Josie. Finally, in desperation, I dialed my old friend Laura Grant, early enough in the morning to catch her before she left the Brooklyn house for her office at Columbia. She answered on the first ring. I asked after Adele, and almost immediately, and without background or fanfare, I blurted out the wedding news and my confusion about how to proceed.

You would have thought I'd told Laura that I'd won the Nobel Prize; she was as excited as a schoolgirl. Except for the night of the Cosmopolitans, and that had hardly been over the top, I'd never seen a hint of this side of Laura. She hooted and swooned and wanted details I was basically unprepared to deliver. It wasn't that I was withholding information, but most of the romantic detail was simply missing from my story. Will and I had simply met, and it seemed we'd decided from the start that we would be together, and now we were setting the day to make it legal; no more or less than that. For some reason, she seemed to find this even more romantic. "Preordained," she said wistfully; a word I found difficult to fathom in love or life.

Laura, however, was of little help on the etiquette front. She knew of no book or set of rules for older brides, though she suggested that I look it up in Emily Post or one of the general etiquette books. I thought I had a Letitia Baldridge reference somewhere, and Laura remembered, with what I detected as glee, that it was Baldridge who set the etiquette standards at the Kennedy White House.

Perhaps it was more history than gossip, but Washington was Laura's beat. Though the Washington era of the Grant Girls' focus was a hundred years earlier, she rattled on about President Kennedy's nickname for Baldridge and the difficult times "Tish" had in the state-dinner seating of the wives of businessmen, academics and diplomats whom

Kennedy was reputed to have "known." It made me think, for the first time, about the very fine line one draws between history and gossip. After all, the Grant Girls were well respected for work that was, essentially, 150-year-old gossip. It was a revelation to me.

"Thrilled," Laura kept saying. *Thrilled*. It was so romantic. What would I wear? And I closed my eyes and told her, as simply as I could, that I supposed I would find a nice tailored suit somewhere. She sighed. "That sounds nice." Still, it seemed to me that she was suggesting in her sigh that if it were her wedding, she would be cramming her ample form into a traditional, white, princess dress, complete with petticoats, puffed sleeves and a veil perched atop her cottony-beige hair.

"I hope we'll be invited," she said breathlessly. "I can't wait to tell Adele!"

I assured her that I wouldn't get married without them and heard myself fall into the abyss as I said, "After all, you're my closest friends." Holy God. Though when I looked back on it, I meant it. The Grant cousins were my closest friends. I remembered Josie once saying, "More's the pity" as I worried that I wasn't really anyone's best friend. Well, except Will's, of course.

Will chose to sleep over two or three nights a week, though I was never invited to his bed. His workload was heavier, he said, with the Christmas holiday just ahead and tests and assignments due before the break; and with the management of the wedding and the contacts and calls from his friends and associates, he needed to be home. Perfectly understandable, I thought. He's inviting hundreds of folks; I'm inviting two. We talked on the phone each night before bedtime, and the calls felt complete and warm as he asked me to tell him my day, and he commented on every detail with wit and humor and comfort. He told me jokes and talked about the future and the trips we'd take to the lakes of Italy and the pyramids of Egypt. We never talked about him giving up his apartment. We didn't get around to talking about him moving in here. I found myself putting off the conversation and even putting off thinking about where his clothes might go or if he'd have an office in the house. There were, after all, five more bedrooms that Teddy and I had yet to address, and I suppose I just figured that Will would expand into some of those rooms. Certainly it never occurred to me that I would be asked to change a single thing Teddy and I had done. I didn't want it to occur to me. My house had just become familiar.

Will and I fell, almost immediately, into the habit of going out to dinner one or two nights a week; at least once a week we also took in a concert or a lecture or a movie. I found I liked walking into the theater with him, holding his arm, knowing that we would go home together, as it seemed we did on those nights, as though this were normal behavior. And while we had been a couple only for a month, it was one of the comforting parts of our relationship, as though this were something we had gotten used to and took for granted. I had never grasped the luxury of taking something for granted before. I would never again forget it.

On this Wednesday night, this night in question, the temperature was unusually mild for December and there was a light mist in the air, exaggerating the holiday lights into spheres of vapor. My hair was curling up and getting wild. My darling brother, Tim, used to call me "Bozo" on rainy days. Tim, with the smooth, blond hair of a Beach Boy, teased me about my kinky, curly locks, which went horizontal at the slightest hint of dampness. I had on my old trench coat and noticed, as I left the office, that the belt loop had torn and was hanging loose from the top. It was looking creased and rumpled; each dry cleaning had begun to take more out of it, rather than returning the appearance to its former crisp, and I thought, "reportage" impression.

Will and I were talking about Benjamin Britten, as the concert we were heading toward featured his work. We turned the corner and walked in front of the library. Suddenly someone was yelling. I looked around, and the whole world seemed to be moving slowly. A tall, willowy student, a very beautiful girl actually, was standing in front of Will. My arm was still locked in the crook of his. I had taken a step forward and was ahead of both of them and somewhat off kilter, as my balance was thrown back toward Will. She was the angriest person I'd ever seen. I couldn't quite grasp the point she was trying to make, but I noticed, as though through plasma, that a small crowd was gathering. She was yelling about love, it seemed. Love and sex and the rest of her life being for nothing. And she knew about the others.

And, "Does *she* know?" She turned to me. "I bet she *doesn't* know." Who is she talking about? I thought. Me?

"Well, I'm *not* giving you up," she spat. "I'll kill myself first!" She seemed to stagger toward me, her liquid fall of hair moving in slow motion like a curtain of silk. Her lips were pulled back from her white teeth like a snarling dog. "Look at this!" She poked at my arm. "She's horrible," she said, both advancing and recoiling, as though looking at a reptile in a zoo. "She's old, and she's ugly. You"—she turned to Will—"you will regret this the rest of your life. I know it, and you know it!"

I looked at Will and half expected him to shrug his shoulders in good-natured amazement, like one does when one encounters a crazy person on a New York street; as though somehow, in all of their pain, there's something staged for your amusement. But when I really looked at him, the whole thing began to come into focus.

It was too late. I'd already stepped toward her to put my hand on her arm, as one might quiet a child in trouble, but she turned on me, full force, like a wild animal. She threw herself toward me and pushed me with all her strength to the ground. I fell hard and hit my knee and my side and then my cheekbone and my forehead against the two-leveled stone planter that ornamented the library steps. She was cursing like a Shakespearian witch as Will bent over me and helped me to my feet, saying over and over, "Should we call an ambulance? Shouldn't you just stay quiet? Should we get you to a doctor?"

It took more than a moment to shake the haze from my brain, and I looked at the poor, pathetic girl. I remember thinking that I could see she was the kind of girl who'd thrown tantrums as a child and would continue them, addicted to the drama and the release and the attention, all her life until she finally blew herself out. No one of any quality would care to weather the storms she inhabited. She was only eighteen or nineteen, and the chances to get it right were almost certainly close to being over for her, already. She was now crying loudly, like a child separated from her parents in a big-box store, who certainly feels fear but also hopes her directed wails will attract the attention of her target audience.

I looked at Will. He was fumbling to get a handkerchief out of his pants pocket to mop the blood that was running down my face. He approached my cheek with the linen, and I looked him right in the eye. "Go and take care of that girl," I said.

"What about you?" he asked. "Shouldn't we get you—"

"Don't touch me." I pushed away his hand. "Don't touch me." And my voice got very quiet and very calm. "Don't call me. Don't ever try to see me again." I stepped back away from him. "Now go and take care of that girl and get her to a good psychiatrist or something, and do it before she hurts herself or someone else."

I began to walk away and felt a strong pain in my right knee. The pants were torn, but I didn't want to stop to inspect my leg. I mostly wanted to be away from everyone's eyes. I felt humiliated and ugly and horrified at being part of a spectacle. A few of the women approached me, and I took some Kleenex from one of them and thanked her while allowing little conversation. *No, thank you, thanks so much—I don't need anyone to walk with me. No, I don't need a lift home. No, I'm fine. I really am just fine. Thank you so much. Really, very kind of you. Thank you, but no.*

I'm not sure how I walked the ten or twelve blocks home. I remember it only in spotty memory. I passed Teddy's car in the driveway, I suppose, though it didn't register. I let myself in the front door. I think it was unlocked. I stood for a moment in the foyer, realizing that it hurt, almost too much, to take off my raincoat. I wasn't sure why. I heard Teddy's voice and had the feeling that he was coming toward me very fast. And then I don't remember anything until I woke in the living room.

CHAPTER 16

Teddy was washing my face when I opened my eyes. My wrist was scratched, and gravel was embedded in the heel of my right hand, which oozed a kind of watery blood. My ribs hurt so badly it hurt to breathe, and as I moved my leg for greater leverage, I felt, again, the pain in my knee. I cried out involuntarily. Teddy helped me roll up my pants, and we both gasped as we saw the blood-soaked kneesock and the gash above, also full of gravel, in a knee swollen like a ham.

Teddy didn't think there was a cut that warranted stitches, not even the one over my eye, but he did think the knee should be X-rayed, as well as my ribs and my head.

"Teddy," I said, "my head should be examined. No doubt about it. But it's not about this fall."

"This was a fall?" he asked, warily.

"Yeah," I replied. I took the facecloth from his hand and pressed it to the place over my eye where the swelling seemed greatest. He took my sock off, and a long river of blood ran down my leg and onto the new rug. I lay back with my head against the couch, and Teddy ran off to the kitchen to fill baggies with ice for my head and my knee.

Bolstered with towels, we made our way to his Subaru station wagon and the emergency room of Cooley Dickinson Hospital. It was in a part of Northampton I'd not seen, and the emergency room reflected a larger population than the community of Amherst suggested. As I waited, it surprised me to find a drunken or drugged man bleeding profusely from a leg wound with no bandage and no help, sitting next to a little girl whose mother brought her in because she might, or might not, have had a fever. The girl looked just fine to me. Her mother let her sit on the bare floor, coloring in her coloring book, inches from the growing pool of blood. It was ten o'clock at night, and here in Massachusetts a parent thought it a good idea to take a reasonably healthy child to a hospital emergency room to have her temperature taken. It was like being on another planet.

But Teddy had called the triage nurse at the Amherst Health Center, and, as they'd made the arrangements for our arrival at the hospital, we were taken quickly. Three hours later we emerged, through the Santa- and reindeer-decaled doors, more or less as we entered. I'd been poked and prodded and X-rayed, I was coated with antiseptic salve and band-aged, but I was not broken and I didn't need stitches. There was nothing, really, to fix.

Teddy drove me home and got me up the stairs and drew a bath. It was nearly two in the morning, but I didn't question his presence. I didn't ask whether or not he'd called his mother. I didn't apologize for ruining his evening or getting blood on his khaki pants. I went into the bathroom, took the bandages from my knee, got into the hot tub and cried, and when I was finished crying, I got out of the bathtub and arranged fresh gauze and bandages on my knee and put on the blue paja-mas with the fluffy clouds that were hanging on the back of the bath-room door. Teddy had made Ovaltine. Two cups. Clearly, he thought we'd both had a difficult night. I got into bed, and he covered me and sat on the edge of the bed and drank his Ovaltine and then he drank mine.

"So what really happened?" he asked.

"I fell. I told you." The stony look on his face suggested that I should have known better than to lie to the person who'd rolled up my pants, mopped up my blood, spirited me away to a hospital and spent three hours sitting in the waiting room between an old woman with a running nose and a lunatic who claimed he had swallowed an EZ Pass chip.

And then I started to cry, again. "I've made a terrible mistake, and I don't even know yet what's happened or how to talk about it or what I've done," I blubbered. I was flummoxed. It was like swimming in gray and murky water. But I swam toward the idea of a shore. It was less about wanting to keep things to myself and more about needing clarity about what really had happened. I knew, horribly, that Will didn't love me. Probably never had. It was becoming clearer by the second that I had been set up to be a kind of straight man's beard. In fact, if I were honest, Will had never hidden his agenda. He talked about it openly right from the beginning. I walked right in. Like Catherine Sloper in *Washington Square,* I had only wanted to believe in the parts I wanted to believe. It's not that I hadn't understood that marriage might make Will more acceptable to the university, but I hadn't followed the line of thinking to its logical ends: It might also obscure his misdeeds. It might make people believe, even if it were not true, that *if* he had as a partner a serious, respected and respectable grown-up wife, he was less likely to be out tomcatting with students. And if his wife were a matronly academic, might he not look more serious, himself? I felt ugly and old and betrayed and fooled and stupid.

And I faced the awful truth: I didn't have a great love in my life, and this wonderful, unexpected dream of love had been a lie. It was as though I'd found out, in the most terrible way, what I'd known all along: That I was not destined for real happiness, that letting people into your heart was, indeed, too dangerous, that I had no aptitude for human feeling. That I was not worthy of love. That I was, and would always be, alone.

These thoughts tumbled through my head with no connection to my voice until I realized that I'd been saying them all; bumbling, ranting, blithering this drivel with tears streaming down my face. I didn't do this when my marriage broke up, I thought. This must be a kind of breakdown.

I couldn't stop talking. I told Teddy everything: the stories of thinking that Josie was jealous and of the negligeed nurse and of the pastries and the requirement for a public wedding and finally, finally—this horrible push from a spoiled and desolate teenager. Now I saw the whole scene: lying on the sidewalk and looking up at this bucking girl, restrained by strangers who all looked at me with a rich palette of mixed emotions: concern, interest, curiosity, superiority, kindness, empathy, recognition, fear, disgust, pity.

I had only one truly clear emotion of my place in the moment. I was humiliated. I, who had never caused a fuss in public, who had been embarrassed at my father's tears at the funeral of his son—my brother. I was now the kind of woman who'd been part of a scandalous moment on campus; laid low by a younger and clearly more beautiful competitor. There I had lain, in the dust as it were, bloodied and made ridiculous, with my frizzing hair, faded red and streaked with gray, and my hips too wide, and my raincoat rumpled—I could now see that I was ridiculous even before the fall. I felt very, very sorry for myself. And I voiced the worry that everyone on campus knew.

"Knew what?" Teddy asked. "You mean this attack?" By now, he was sitting with his back against the high carved Victorian headboard he'd found at a flea market and had refinished for my bedroom. His arm was around my shoulders, and I was crying into his polar-fleece sweatshirt. I noticed that the tears ran down the front, rather than soaking into the fleece.

"Know . . . you know, *know* . . . know about me. And Will. Know all about this horrible scene. And know—now—that the whole thing is all off."

"What's off?" And I suddenly realized that the only person I'd told about the wedding was Laura Grant. It was the definition of mixed emotions in that, God forbid, I would now have to call Laura Grant, and, thank God, I would have to call no one else. I didn't know whom Will had told, and I didn't want to know.

"We were planning to get married on January second." There, I said it. Teddy held me closer and stroked my hair.

"He was a dork, Joy," he said.

I had just lost what I thought was the love of my life and my one very slim chance for happiness. I was in the arms of someone who used the word *dork*. This is a breakdown. I'm definitely having a breakdown, I thought.

I was more tired than I ever remembered being. A sudden and irresistible urge to sleep came upon me, and it occurred to me, with some fear attached, that sleepiness might be a symptom of a concussion. I was about to say just that, but I sank into the polar-fleece of Teddy's sweatshirt and then everything was dark and the pain stopped.

The bedroom faced east, and though the nights were longer and mornings darker as we faced the shortest day of the year, the sun came through the lace curtains early enough the next morning. I woke with my head hurting, my hand raw and my leg stiff. When I moved my knee, I felt the skin burn on the surface as though I'd ripped a plastic covering that held all my nerve endings. It seemed I'd only moved a fraction of an inch, but it felt monumental. I was lying on my side and facing the window. There was a weight on my hip and a warmth behind my knees. It came to me slowly and surprisingly with little alarm, that I was not alone in the bed. Teddy Hennessy was in bed with me. I struggled to turn, half expecting to see him sleeping in his baseball cap. He was still wearing his sweatshirt, his mouth was open just a bit and he looked like an angel, and it took me completely by surprise. Again, his thick, black lashes fringed against his clean, apple-tinged cheek. His lips were deep pink and perfectly shaped. His skin was luminous; his nose was beautifully formed. How had I not noticed how handsome Teddy was? He seemed, except for his work, such a goofy boy; I certainly had never thought of him as a man. But, in fact, he was one of the most beautiful men I'd ever seen at so very close an inspection. Not that I'd looked at so many up close.

He tightened his grip around me. His breath smelled sweet and clean. He buried his head in my neck, and I felt protected. I felt cared for and not alone. I was unself-conscious in a way I had never been with Will, never been with anyone, before. It must have been the culmination of all the dinners together with fluffernutter sandwiches and French bread pizzas and Teddy rolling in with take-out Chinese or calzones as we discussed the merits of eggshell versus semigloss paint finishes.

It could have been the way he had made such an important difference in my house and in my life, seeing, long before I, that I had some connection to the space in which I lived and that it had a connection to me. It must have been the completely disarming way I could move through my house in a bathrobe or towel and fuzzy slippers and not consider him as a man or an outsider.

In a way, and this was horrible, it was a little bit like the European aristocracy discounting the humanity of their servants, but it had served to break down all of the "other" that I suppose I had always made of people. I had lain in Teddy's arms all night and was now basking in his warmth and the presence of someone who cared about me. Three nights ago I couldn't comfortably lie in the arms of the man I was about to marry.

This is almost certainly a breakdown, I told myself as Teddy opened his eyes, raised his head a bit, and after a long, searching look at my bruised and swollen face, gently kissed my mouth. I didn't pull away.

I know it makes no sense, but he looked like the cleanest boy in the world, like a six-year-old just out of the bath. His cheeks glowed, his hair was soft and shining and he smelled of soap, as he had months before, when he had reminded me of Timmy, and the thought of my brother, here in this intimate moment, brought a whole new wave of emotion that threatened to take me under with no promise of safe return. I'd always fought those feelings, but now I dove toward them—Timmy and Teddy and my breakdown. I deserve this, I thought. *I've been hurt.*

Teddy was gentler and more careful than any man I'd ever been with. He made love as though it meant something serious and sweet. It was different enough so that I could compare, though I'd not had a wealth of experience. I grew up in the sexy seventies and I read *Cosmopolitan,* but I was no more able to "Seduce My Boss" or "Have a Fun Fling with My Best Friend's Husband," as the magazine advised, than I could have flown out the window. And if that "If It Feels Good Do It" groovy moment, which everyone seems to remember with nostalgia, did not seem to hit our neighborhood in Clayton, Missouri, it did not fly into my dorm room at Wellesley either; not, at least, while I was watching.

This was not the easiest first-time experience. My hand was raw, and we had to be careful about our legs, as even a tap against my swollen, bandaged knee threatened to send me howling. Getting out of my flannel pajama bottoms was challenging enough. My head hurt and my ribs were bruised, but I managed to hold Teddy and take him in and it was more comforting than I ever thought sex could be. In fact, it had never before occurred to me that comfort, itself, might be a primary reason for sex.

I knew grief. I'd lived with grief for forty years. I knew very well what it felt like believing that nothing would ever be all right again. But this time, before my grief had a chance to settle in, I was presented with a new way of looking at life. As long as we're breathing, the game's not over, I thought. Why had I never thought about that before?

This new idea of feeling cared for and comfortable and trusting and warm was a startling contrast to how I'd felt with Will, and suddenly, there was no grief at all. Will hadn't been a failure; he'd been an experience. I could hear Bernadette's voice in my head. Will supplied me with the contrast on which to judge this moment. I hadn't wanted a wedding.

I wasn't even sure I had wanted Will in my house. Teddy belonged in the house. He had created the house. If I was going to be honest, the feeling I could most identify just now was relief. I was relieved. I was honestly relieved. Or else, and I figured this just as likely to be the truth, I was in the throws of a really, really big doozy of a breakdown.

CHAPTER 17

We celebrated Christmas on Christmas Eve. Teddy brought me rosemary bath oil and a pale ochre terry cloth robe, perfectly coordinated to the new bathroom. I bought him a Yeats anthology and a book on historic preservation that I later realized he could have written. We had lamb chops for Christmas Eve dinner, and he left at nine to take his mother to Mass with the promise that he'd return in the middle of the night. He did, but was up again within hours, as he needed to take her to another service at sunrise.

When he returned, around three in the afternoon, he had a tiny Christmas tree nailed to a base of raw boards so that it would stand on its own. We placed it on the bureau in the dining room, and I found a star pin of rhinestones that had been my mother's, which we put on the top. We ate French toast and went right to bed. Teddy fell asleep before his head touched the pillow and didn't wake or move until the next morning.

I'd been invited to Josie and Dan's for New Year's Eve. Maureen Hennessy was to be there, and Teddy was included—without, I figured, Josie knowing anything about our new development. It was reasonable to assume Will would be there, but Josie called two days before the party to assure me that Will was out of town and would not be making an appearance at their party. She was matter-of-fact about it, concerned but easygoing. She neither asked questions nor revealed what she'd heard, but her warmth through the call and the way she managed to barely mention Will's name, while letting me know the coast was clear, told me that she knew all she had to know about the end of my very short engagement. She displayed not a hint of gloating or superiority. I felt enormously appreciative of her, and yet, I was not ready to talk about Will or my feelings and I found myself unwilling to share what I saw as the latest evidence of my instability, the change in my relationship with Teddy.

I decided to pass on the party and let Teddy attend to Maureen with no challenges to his responsibilities as her escort. I suppose, to some extent, I was hiding out. I sat at home, reading *Other Voices, Other Rooms* for the twentieth time with *New Year's Rockin' Eve* blaring in the background for company. Is this a beginning or an end? I wondered on this night of reflection about new years and new chances. But everything was new, and it seemed that I had lost the mechanism that decided the relative value of those things. I chose to put the questions away and return to my book.

And so our days went on much as they had before; Teddy sanding and nailing and scraping and building and painting, and me, back and forth from school. While the college wasn't open for classes over the Christmas break, we were allowed access to our own offices, and I used the time to get a little ahead of my students and myself and embark on a project I thought had some real potential.

By the tenth of January, as students and teachers began to return to campus, I found I'd done enough research for Teddy to bring him a full file, pulled from the Internet, about university credit for life experience. There was, in fact, a course at the University of Massachusetts on how to present the life skills one had amassed to qualify for college credit; and this, I figured, was the way to begin.

That evening, I opened the file on the dining room table and called Teddy in. I told him I'd had a brainstorm a few months ago, and I talked about his going back to school and getting a degree. I talked about his teaching. I talked about passing on information to another generation as part of the obligation of a true connoisseur and certainly of a craftsman and a restorer. I could imagine him, and so I said, leading a class on the intricate differences between the Carpenter Gothic detail of Connecticut and the Carpenter Gothic detail of Kansas. I could imagine him dissecting the painting of the sky in various Rufus Porter murals for a class of talented disciples. Most of all, I could so much more easily imagine thinking of him as a teacher or an expert, and not a contractor or a handyman.

I did all the talking, like a lecture in a hall. He nodded once or twice. He looked at the material politely, barely touching a page or two. He didn't lift a thing from the table. He didn't say much. But his usual breezy attitude was almost immediately extinguished by the subject. His jaw was set and tight. He asked no questions and made no attempts to extend any of my theories or expand on my ideas about his future. There was not a shred of malice or rudeness in his manner; he simply appeared to emotionally withdraw. I pushed a little more, and while he remained courteous and respectful of my efforts, gratefully acknowledging my time and care, he made no attempt to embrace the message. Teddy stepped away from the dining room table by walking backward and not turning away from me. As he approached the kitchen to clean his brushes in the sink, he pulled his sweatshirt over his head. His T-shirt read: I'M NOT AFRAID OF THE DARK. I'M AFRAID OF NINJAS IN THE DARK.

The Tuesday after winter term began, Josie called out to me on the pathway, as I was heading to my first class. She scurried over from our building's entrance, wearing only a cardigan and hugging her arms to her body against the cold January morning. Donna Fortunata, she said, would be coming to lunch at the office that day. I thought for a moment that she might be asking me for some privacy, and the concept tumbled out clumsily, as though I were soliciting permission to eat in the cafeteria. Josie looked at me wide-eyed. "I've invited her to have lunch with *us*," she said sternly. "You and Fran—I was hoping you didn't have other plans. She needs her community."

Needs her community? What's this? I wondered. All through my class that morning, my mind floated back to the question of Donna, like an unopened parcel left in an alcove. There it sat, waiting to be inspected, while I discussed Edith Wharton and her attachment to homes and material things. In class I was reminded, once again, that Wharton's first real success was not fiction, but a book about the decorating of homes, written with her wicked, witty walker of a friend, Ogden Codman. Their dogmatic and condescending book retains not a shred of the wit or delight that must have formed the basis of their friendship, but it is clear to me that Codman's presence changed Edith's life forever. He called her Puss, she called him Coddy, and while he gleefully schooled her with examples of the most egregious breaches of style in both dress and decor, affected equally by New York's most socially prominent and insecure, he also pointed to the clean lines of classical buildings, the austerity of pale marble and the inherent beauty of perfectly crafted woodwork. He introduced Edith to the idea of Italian gardens and Palladian architecture. Most of all, he gave her the first framework in which to create homes and a life of studied grace, if not warmth and comfort.

Sadly, Edith never found real warmth and comfort, and I contend that she gave even less to the living, breathing characters around her. Comfort was, for the most part, reserved for those who lived on her pages, and even these doses were parceled out by the eyedropper, and too often rather too late in their own stories.

As I hurried back to our office for lunch, I wondered how much, if at all, Teddy and I reflected the friendship of Edith and Coddy. Still, the thought of Donna remained in the back of my mind, jarred to the forefront the moment I saw her walk through our door, just moments after I'd arrived. She looked haggard and tense. Her hair was pulled back in a low and untidy tail. Her eyes were naked of their usual mascara and were pale and red rimmed. Her mouth was a stiff, straight line, and I suddenly realized that I'd never seen Donna when she wasn't smiling. Josie asked nothing of her, and that gave me my lead. If Josie wasn't asking, I certainly was not going to. All would be revealed on its own, I'd learned from watching Josie. Or not.

Our meal was not simply a reworking of O'Sullivan leftovers, but one clearly planned just for this day. Lunch was, in detail, little frittatas, cooked in individual tart tins, redolent with thyme, their custard enriched with Brie and pancetta, paired with a salad of endive, almonds and grapes. I ate my quotient and then happily ate most of Fran's, who was also a little sallow and quiet through lunch. I moved slightly away from both Fran and Donna when, sometime during the salad, it occurred to me that maybe this malaise Josie had taken for temperament was actually a kind of flu going around campus; but by the time Josie had sliced the wedge of chocolate orange cake into four slivers of tastes for us all, Donna was off and running on her story, and it was no flu.

When Donna stopped to take a breath, Josie would fill in some of the details she thought we wouldn't understand without her editorial input.

"My ex-husband," Donna began, "is a liquor distributor." Josie gave a kind of short nasal laugh with her distinctive raised eyebrows, which suggested, at least to me, an ex-husband who may have had more than a professional interest in his wares.

Donna was not slowed down by Josie's editorializing. "Jordan," she continued, came from "a really good family in Bernardsville, New Jersey. Great people," she said. "But Jordy was a handful."

Josie interrupted again. "Jordan had been 'removed' from about half a dozen colleges—starting with the University of Virginia and ending here in South Amherst at Hampshire."

Donna got us back on track. "Jordan's dad was a liquor importer." Again Josie filled us in on the fact that he handled some of the finest wines in Italy, including the gorgeous Prosecco we'd sampled at Josie's lunch months before. But Donna and Josie alike suggested that his position with the Italian Trade Council, his Episcopalian wife's standing with the movers and shakers of Somerset County's charities and whatever brand of high society they have in New Jersey, paired with the indulgent love of their only son, made it impossible for them to let Jordan slip through the cracks.

"There were *some*," Josie suggested, leading us to believe that she was the "some" in question, "who thought it would have been better for Jordy to hit bottom and face facts."

"Well, his parents weren't going to allow that," said Donna. "And I suppose I'm as much to blame as they are. Together we formed a kind of buffer around him. We hoped we could protect him from the world. But it didn't really work."

"Of course not," argued Josie. "He needed help, for God's sake, not protection."

"Oh, come on, Josie," Fran said. "Are you going to tell me that if one of your girls has a substance problem, you're not going to try and protect her?"

Josie looked thoughtful, but she didn't back down. "I hope I'd have the strength to do the right thing," she said.

"Yeah," said Fran. "Accept the things you can't change, change what you can and have the wisdom to know the difference. That wisdom part is a tall order where your kids are concerned."

"Well, when there's an addiction," Josie said, "you're not really dealing with *your kid,* are you? You're dealing with the *addict*—and that's a different thing."

"Wait a minute," I said—not quite sure whether I could even ask such a thing. "Was Jordan an addict or an alcoholic?"

Fran answered, but all three laughed. "That's like asking, 'Was he in Beijing or China'—you know?"

No, I didn't know, but I was trying to follow. Josie got back on the bus with a rant about Jordan's parents and their unwillingness to deal with the reality of their son's issues.

"Listen," Donna continued, "it was so much more complicated. And I take a lot of the responsibility here. I didn't tell his parents about his 'anger issues.'"

"What do you mean . . . anger?" I asked. I came from a home where no one raised a voice, no less a hand. The violence of movies and literature were purely entertainment for me.

Donna spoke in a surprisingly matter-of-fact way about how Jordan had thrown a chair, in a pique of temper, through an apartment window, narrowly missing a pedestrian on the street, five floors below. It had happened before their wedding, and it frightened her.

"Well, I would think *so*!" I exclaimed, and everyone turned to look at *me*, for a moment, and then Donna returned to the story.

"Jordy promised he wouldn't misbehave, but, you know"—she glanced down at her hands—"he just couldn't keep his promise. When he would get angry, he'd move his fingers in this really specific way—like his fingers would get kind of rigid but bent. And his wrists would get stiff in this way that made his hands tip up." We must have all looked confused because Donna pulled her elbows close to her body with her arms straight at her side and she tipped her hands up, palms parallel to the floor, with the fingers bent, as though she were about to play the piano. It was strange body language, but it immediately conveyed tension.

"So," she continued when she felt we'd all understood the visual, "I'd see this strange hand thing—and I'd start to feel kind of sick to my stomach. After a while, he'd screw his hands into fists and walk through the house kind of pacing, as though he were looking for something, and I'd go around trying to find a way to defuse the bomb I knew was going to go off. I mean, I'd straighten every room, I'd look everywhere—making sure that nothing was out of place. I'd hang up my coat or make sure I'd moved my slippers away from the side of the bed—you know—anything could set him off when he was in one of those moods."

"Didn't you tell him to *stop* it?" I asked, expecting all of them to look at me again, as though I were naive, but Josie and Fran looked to Donna, just as I did, for an answer.

"Well," she said, "sure I did. I tried everything I could. I pleaded with him, and I told him how it hurt me. And I scolded him, and I threatened to leave. But he'd cry and beg me not to—and tell me that I was the only one he trusted, and that this feeling could only come out in a place where he felt safe—and he felt safe with me. He loved me." I couldn't tell whether Donna was overcome with emotion or just numb, but she got very quiet and cold when she told us that he'd put his head in her lap and cry and beg her not to leave him.

I did notice that Donna's own hands were shaking a little bit as she recounted one of Jordan's tantrums while driving to his parents' house in New Jersey. "I don't remember what actually set him off to begin with, you know—even before we got into the car. We were already late for dinner, and he thought that was going to be an 'issue' with his parents, and we kept getting behind really slow drivers in massively heavy traffic. *And* it was pouring—I mean cats and dogs. Jordy was really heating up about being late and about the traffic, and then we heard this metallic kind of clanking in the front of the car and it began to lose power. He managed to get us into the slow lane and then onto the shoulder of the road, with cars honking and almost hitting us and, you know, guys shaking their fists and yelling out their windows—like we'd broken down just to piss them off—it was pretty scary."

But once they were safe on the shoulder of the road, Jordan started screaming like a banshee. She told us that he rocked back and forth on the steering wheel so hard that he pulled it right out of its housing. "I mean, there he was," she said, "with the Saab's broken steering wheel in his hands, screaming and swearing."

We were a transfixed audience as Donna told us how she got out of the car, frightened and crying horizontal tears—"like," she said, "Betty Boop in a cartoon"—and she described how she had walked down this dark New Jersey highway in the rain, toward some kind of safety in an unknown landscape. Jordan got out of the car and followed her along the verge, with trucks rolling by at breakneck speeds, hitting their horns and sending up grit-studded showers of oily spray. He begged her, crying even more dramatically than she, to forgive him once again, and she did. Watching her tell us was, literally, heart wrenching.

"Tell them about the last time," urged Josie. "The time you left."

Donna straightened her shoulders and explained that when she was pregnant with their first daughter, Jordan promised to get his anger under control. For more than two years he held to that vow, but she could see the toll it took, especially when he drank, though now that she thought of it, sometimes even more when he deliberately didn't drink; the long walks in the night, the veins that throbbed at the side of his temples, the rigid upturned gesture of his fists.

"Two months after Marta was born," she said, "and Ava was just about two years old, Jordan came home from work in a fit. Nothing was right. Work was demeaning. His boss was a fool. This was no life. He was far too valuable, he said, to put up with nonsense from his coworkers."

He went into the kitchen and took long draughts right from the freezer's vodka bottle. Donna followed him and was, she admitted, reproving and a little harsh. She stood at the kitchen door holding Ava.

Jordan responded to her criticism by turning around and hitting her in the face so hard that she lost a tooth.

"And then I did the strangest thing," she said. "I put the tooth into the pocket of my pajama pants, I walked into the bathroom with my frightened, crying baby in my arms and I managed to wrap the tooth in a wet cotton ball so that they might be able to reinsert it at the hospital— which they did." She smiled a fake smile and pointed at the front tooth on the right, which now seemed a little lopsided to me. I wondered if it had looked like that even before the incident.

"I picked up a clean towel and put it around my neck, to catch the blood spilling from my nose and mouth, I put my car keys into my pocket. I picked Marta out of the crib and, wearing only a T-shirt, pajama bottoms and flip-flops, I carried two crying babies out to the car."

Donna remembered most of the incident in detail, and she told us how she calmly strapped the squirming girls into their car seats and drove herself to the emergency room. She remembered not panicking; her thoughts about the drive and the hospital were crystal clear in memory. But she remembered nothing about Jordan after the punch. Did he say anything to her when he saw the blood streaming from her nose and mouth? Did he say anything when she took their children from the house? Did he offer to drive her to the hospital? She remembered nothing. When she tried to tell the doctors or describe the situation to her parents and in-laws, she had no memory of Jordan beyond the hit itself.

"Can you remember now—now that it's all so long ago?" asked Fran.

She could not. She stayed overnight in the hospital, with the girls tucked into a cot next to her hospital bed. And she never again went back to that house.

After the incident, Jordan's parents were, apparently, wonderful to her and to the girls, as were Donna's own parents. They formed a kind of phalanx around her and staked her to a charming house right in Amherst, where she'd gone to school. They supported her as she got her real estate license, and though she did well financially, they still insisted on adding to the girls' education fund and paying for their summer camps and special treats. Jordan communicated with her through his parents, and after a year or so, they developed a reasonably calm and steady relationship. He never asked for more than was offered. All his fatherly activities were shared with his parents or managed by and with Donna in Amherst. She never again saw his anger flare. There had been no arguments about his arrangements in seeing the girls, and so it had gone, without discomfort or incident, for a bit more than five years.

"Wow," Fran said. "That's some story."

"But it's not really over, is it?" asked Josie, putting her hand on Donna's knee and leveling a kind of glare at Fran and at me like, Wait until you hear this.

Donna had begun to date a radiologist from just outside Northampton, and it was looking to all like a serious relationship. The girls liked him, and in October they spent a weekend together on Cape Cod.

"So," Donna continued, "when Marta and Ava told their father about the weekend, Jordan became unhinged. There were these long rambling phone calls about who I saw or who I was allowed to see and who his kids were allowed to spent time with. It was really out of hand. And I'd try to stay kind and sympathetic and tell him that he'd always be the kids' dad—and it would seem to settle down and I'd hang up. And then he'd call back—right away—yelling again."

Donna and the girls had invited the radiologist for Thanksgiving dinner when her parents drove up from Baltimore.

"I really didn't want to tell the girls *not* to tell their father things. I mean, they're little kids." Donna shrugged. "What could be worse than getting in the middle of some grown-up's issue and being afraid of what you can tell one parent or the other. I just won't do that."

When Jordan heard about Thanksgiving, the whole thing cranked up a notch. Although the yelling had all but stopped, Donna felt that the calls were even worse. "Creepier" is how Donna put it. And she was certain Jordan was watching, or stalking, her. She had no evidence, but he knew too much about where she had gone each day.

"He'll call around dinnertime and ask me where I've been, and I'll tell him the truth—that I showed a house over on Taylor or I met a potential buyer for coffee—and before I can say *anything* about them, Jordan will say something like, 'Did you go to the Black Sheep?'—and of course I *did*—so I ask him, 'How did you *know* that,' and he says, like, 'Know *what*?' And he says something like he was *just guessing* that I'd take a client to the Black Sheep. But it's too weird." She shook her head. "It's *creepy,* you know? I'm sure he's watching me. And . . . I'm kind of afraid of him."

She saw a strange car parked for hours with someone in the driver's seat, just across from her house, two nights ago, and it drove away when she came out of the house to investigate. Fran asked if she recognized the car as Jordan's, and Donna said that she didn't recognize the car at all. In fact, she told us that Jordan always has a pretty flashy car and this just looked like an *ordinary* car—"a Camry or something" was how Donna described it. "But he could have *rented* it," she suggested. It seemed a little far-fetched to me, a paranoid turn in her reaction.

"Yeah," Donna said, looking at me, perhaps reading my body language, "you're right. *Obviously,* it could have been a coincidence. At this point I could be just adding things up wrong. But what if I'm not?"

Josie suggested that Donna call the police to get a restraining order against Jordan.

"How can I do that?" asked Donna. "I can't even convince *you* that it's his car. And he's made no specific threats. And it's been years since he displayed any *overt* violent behavior, and I really do not want the girls to know what he *did* in the past—especially if it *stays* in the past."

Josie brought up calling Jordan's parents, but while Donna agreed that their intervention might be of some help, they were now well over seventy years old, and bringing them news that could upset them was the last thing she wished to do. Josie and Fran made suggestions from tapping the phone to installing cameras around the house. To what end? we asked. Did Donna really believe that Jordan would hurt any of them? She shook her head and began to cry, and Josie put her arms around her, and Fran held her hand until she'd cried herself out. It was obvious to me that this wasn't the first time she'd cried about Jordan.

I had little to add. It was like the plot of a grand novel. At the center were two little girls, protected from the truth about their father by their loving and concerned mother, who looked, in her pressed jeans and tiny cashmere sweater set, barely older than they.

That night, at home, I was thinking that I had never before been privy to the problems of acquaintances. Well, that's not completely accurate. In a school like Columbia, other people's problems are the lifeblood of one's social life. There isn't really sharing and there certainly isn't a shoulder to cry on, but there is, in the strangest way, a kind of welcome distraction in the problems of others. You don't hear about them directly. You hear about them in passing, in the lounge. You hear another bit as you wait for coffee in the morning or in the hall before department meetings.

No one comes to you and asks, "What should I do? My daughter is ill." No, you hear that her daughter is dying, and then you hear speculation on whether or not she will be able to manage her classes or finish her book. You hear the teachers who will try to take advantage of the situation. You hear the administrators worry about their own standing, if they allow too much slack in the responsibilities of their teachers. You hear far too many people opine as to the worthiness, or lack thereof, of the manuscript that has been put aside, the value and success rates of the many treatments for cancer and the mental state and general well-being of the woman at the center of the drama. Dates of death are bandied about like odds on a daily double.

I was musing about this when I realized, with a kind of catch, that it was just possible that only I had been left out of the fold at Columbia. Others may have been consulted. Others may have felt more connected to the problems and the people. It was indeed possible, I now had to admit, that no one had come to me to ask, "What should I do?" but *had* gone to someone else. In fact, Donna was not really coming to me, either. She was coming to Josie. I just happened to be there.

CHAPTER 18

I don't know what I expected of Teddy. I suppose I thought he would be enthusiastic about going back to school and that he would bring all kinds of materials to the dining room table to match up with the columns and courses outlined in the section about life skills and credit. He did not. I left the folders and pamphlets sitting on the table for a week, and then I packed them all into a large envelope and put it in the deep middle drawer of my grandfather's highboy, which now stood in the charming papered alcove created by the front stairway.

We had begun to tackle the design of the hall upstairs, and Teddy was building a window seat, surrounded by bookcases. Between the walls and the ceiling, he added corbels, which he'd squirreled away years ago, after picking them up on a demolition job. These curved brackets with their scrolled acanthus pattern gave the space an architectural definition, suggesting a kind of private reading nook within the hallway. Teddy had installed a brass swing-arm lamp on the wall and asked me to help choose the shade. He'd brought home four different possibilities that I thought looked just the same. I could tell that Teddy was frustrated and discouraged with me, and then, suddenly, I could see that he had an idea.

He tore out of the house without a word, just the hand gesture of a single finger, suggesting a kind of "one minute" shorthand. He returned about twenty minutes later with a bolt of vintage fabric and unfurled it with a flourish. A sky-blue linen ground sprouted roses of cream and green and a soft cocoa brown.

I loved it, but I wasn't sure what it was. It looked like fabric from the nineteenth century, and it looked like fabric from the 1940s—all at once. And I told Teddy so.

"Yes! Exactly." He seemed proud of me. "It's Aunt Elizabeth's house!" Teddy said with huge excitement. "Aunt Elizabeth's house from *Bringing Up Baby*. Remember? It's a late-thirties Hollywood idea of classic New England. I often, you know . . . think of that house as . . . what"—Teddy looked around as though I'd help him finish the sentence, but I had no idea where he was going—"kind of . . . you know . . . inspiration for *this* house. It's this country house and comfortable and not pretentious—but it's smart and you can *see* that books and ideas live there. And it's just what I think this house should be. You know?"

Yes, I thought I knew *just* what he meant—although I could barely remember Baby, the leopard, never mind Aunt Elizabeth. But I was proud too, in a crazy kind of way, that I was—sort of—able to place the period of the fabric. And I was pleased that he thought of this house as a civilized home of ideas and letters. That's just how I thought of it.

Teddy put the sample down where a cushion would be and then wrapped one of the lampshades in the print. Charming. Perfect.

"We'll paint the trim cream and the interior walls this same soft blue." He touched the blue ground of the fabric. "It's a bit darker than your blue downstairs but still within the family. And we'll do cushions of cream and green and brown with green piping—unless I can find a little check of these colors. That would be *great luck,* but who knows?" He was all fired up with excitement and went downstairs, like a happy camper, to consult his precious paint-chip guide.

I wasn't always quite sure what to make of Teddy. I know that my father, were he alive, would view such a scene and pronounce Teddy Hennessy a little "light in the loafers"; but I knew that this wasn't true, either.

We made dinner together. I concocted a kind of stir-fry, with bok choy, mushrooms, broccoli, scallions and chicken in a teriyaki sauce that Teddy had shopped for, delivered and chopped after downloading a Martha Stewart Quick Cook segment he'd seen on television as he sanded the ceiling in the back hall. He made brown rice with scallions, ginger, cashews and dried cranberries. He'd brought bottles of Chinese beer back from one of his mother's church-bingo destinations earlier that week.

He never mentioned what he told her about us, and true to form, I never asked. During the week he ran Maureen-duty intermittently, breaking his work pattern through the day and into the early evening, but I was so busy at school I hardly noticed. Sundays were still, significantly, her day with Teddy. Between getting up near dawn to drive her to church and then ferrying her around for the afternoon, he was rarely back at my home before six. He never complained. In fact, he never really talked about his mother at all.

Making dinner, reading aloud, humming along with the Who and looking at paint chips and fabric swatches and samples of woodwork and hardware and cabinet pulls and hinges and faucets; nothing in my life so far had prepared me for this. Everything was, dare I say it, fun. Everything was easy. And Teddy seemed to always be touching me, from a poke in the ribs to holding my hand or stroking my hair, and instead of being put off by it, I was finding it wonderful. In fact, I was finding it necessary. The smallest things—the way I washed my face, the process I used in making the bed—it all seemed to amuse and delight him. And I admit, a lighthearted, teasing, silly childlike relationship had emerged that was part of a personality I didn't know I had. Never had I, and certainly not in an adult relationship, created devil horns and a mustache out of shampoo suds. Never before had I tried to sing while gargling. Now we had morning opera gargling contests. I was the contender with my gargled rendition of the "Triumphal March" from *Aida*. But Teddy was clearly in the lead with his "Bohemian Rhapsody," sung as though Freddy Mercury had his mouth full of suds.

Nearly every night was the same. I would work, we would eat something simple, I might work a little more and catch Jon Stewart or Stephen Colbert on TV before falling into a lulling kind of lovemaking with Teddy, and then we'd sleep in each other's arms. It was too good to be true. It was glass jarred and hermetically sealed. I met no one else, except at work. No one called me at home. We saw no one together, and no one, to the best of my knowledge, knew about our relationship.

But on a Sunday night, as we were entering the second week in January, the phone rang at just a bit after eleven. I have no living relatives, so there is no angst attached to the ringing of a phone in the night. One look at Teddy's face told me the world was not the same for him.

I answered, and a nearly hysterical voice met mine. It took me long moments to ascertain that it was Donna Fortunata and that she was in some kind of trouble. Jordan was somewhere near and threatening. She had not only her girls in the house but Josie and Dan's girls as well, as the O'Sullivans had driven to New York for the weekend and were due back in town very late. She had tried Dan's cell phone and, not getting through, supposed that they were on the part of the trip, through Connecticut, that has no cell service. She thought I might have another cell number for Josie, but I didn't. It was clear she needed some help from someone.

I knew very well that six months ago I would have signed off, without a shred of guilt, legitimately sorry that I didn't have Josie's number. This time, I heard myself say, "Stay put. I'll be right over," realizing almost immediately that I had no idea how to find Donna's house. I had the presence of mind to put Teddy on the line. He asked for a few landmarks, knew where to find her, and was sliding into his blue jeans before I was even out of bed.

I filled Teddy in on the Jordan story as we drove. We found a white house of classic 1940s styling, set back from the road on a long, manicured lawn, much like the houses in my parents' neighborhood in Saint Louis. Donna's car was in the driveway, and there was another car, a standard sedan, parked at the curb. The lights were ablaze from every floor, but all seemed quiet. We knocked at the door. No answer. We knocked again. No answer. Teddy tried the door; it opened and we walked right in. I was steps behind him as we announced ourselves to no response. There seemed to be no one on the ground floor, and we began to walk up the stairs when we heard a kind of thumping sound, then a pounding at a door and man's voice I assumed to be Jordan's insisting that someone come out. At first I thought he was yelling at Donna, and then as we climbed the stairs I heard more clearly, "You are *my* daughters! You listen to *me*! You come *out*, you hear?" He pounded heavily again on a door.

Small voices answered, "Go away, Dad . . . go away, you are scaring us! Just go away, please—please . . . No, Daddy, no . . . Dad, please . . . we'll call you tomorrow . . . Go to Grandpa's. Talk to Grandpa." Their voices overlapped. They were terrified, no doubt, but also solicitous to Jordan.

Teddy and I walked up the staircase and turned on the landing of the second floor, moving toward the third, where the yelling and pounding was coming from, when something caught my eye in a dim light down the hall. There, on the floor, a sock, maybe—or a kind of ball—in a light pink color made me look again, and I stepped toward it. Deeper into the hall I could see that it was Donna's hand, attached, thankfully, to Donna. She was lying on the floor of her room, one arm extended out into the corridor. I ran toward her and turned her over. One side of her face was crashed in, the bones were flattened and blood ran from her matted hair and her nose and her mouth like a river.

Long ago, when I first moved to New York, there was a hit-and-run accident on Riverside Drive. A nice man, whom I knew only by sight, had been hit by a car. I recognized his dog, pacing at the edge of the crowd, and picked up her leash and walked her into the gathering to deposit her with the police who were dealing with the incident and interviewing onlookers. My neighbor's face was smashed. His cheekbone was splintered. I recognized his green duffle coat, but there was no easy way, in the red confusion of his face, for me to discern what remained of him and what was missing.

"This is his dog," I told the policewoman who was writing up the episode. No, I didn't know where he lived, though I knew it was somewhere in the neighborhood as I saw him walking his elderly clumber spaniel nearly every morning and every night, regardless of the time I left or the time I came home. I didn't even know if he lived north or south of my block. I looked down at the dog, who was straining to get to her owner. My hands began to shake. I could answer no more questions.

"Perhaps it has a tag with a phone number," the policewoman surmised, gesturing with her chin toward the dog.

"Yes." I wasn't sure if she expected me to look at the dog's collar, but I handed her the leash, stumbled away and vomited in the mesh garbage pail at the corner. My hands were trembling right up to the elbow, knowing I had not asked the question—Is he alive?

Donna's face was no better than the dog walker's, only I knew it more intimately. I knew the crinkles her eyes made when she laughed and the little crooked half smile she gave when she thought that something was ironic. And she thought most things were ironic. I looked at the bloodstained carpet and actually wondered how anyone could ever clean *this*? And then I heard Jordan, or at least I figured it was Jordan, turn on

Teddy. It seemed that Teddy had lured him away from the girls' door and Jordan lunged, still holding the golf club that he must have used to hit Donna. I ran to the bottom of the stairs to the third floor and caught sight of the golf club slicing through the air and Teddy dodging it, moving quickly and gracefully, like a small wiry boy, rather than the solid and sturdy adult I knew him to be. Teddy kept on talking. I couldn't hear all he was saying, but he used Jordan's name gently, over and over in his attempts to secure some kind of rational response.

I picked up the phone at the bottom of the stairs, expecting Hitchcock details, like no dial tone. There was, of course, a dial tone, and I rang 911 and requested, with shaking voice, police assistance and an ambulance; and I told a soft-spoken man about Donna and that the assailant was still in the house and threatening everyone. I told him about the little girls locked in the room, and he asked if I thought they were safe. I said that they were, for the time being. He asked if Donna was conscious. I said no. He asked if she were alive. I answered him, shocked at the question, that yes, I certainly *thought* she was, but in fact, I didn't know.

I asked him to hurry. To get off the phone. How long would we have to talk about this before he would come in an ambulance with some police?

"Please. Please. No more questions," I said, my heart beating in my ears, "just *get* here."

"Everything was dispatched as soon as we had your address," the kind man told me. "You should hear sirens any second now."

I didn't want to watch Teddy and Jordan. I didn't want to go back to Donna to find out if she were dead. I wanted to run from the house, and on my way down the stairs I told myself that the police and the ambulance would need someone to wave them into the driveway, lead them into the house and up to the problem. I pictured myself standing outside in the cool air, watching out for them and then just walking away down the street, once I knew that help had arrived. I stopped, on the stairs, completely paralyzed for what seemed like long minutes but that must have been only seconds, at which point I suppose I came to my senses and ran back to Donna, felt her pulse and found it to be strong. I put a pillow under her head and immediately remembered that head and neck injuries should not be moved until medical help is on hand. *Too late. Too late. Oh, God.*

"Donna! I'm sorry. I'm so sorry." I said. "Can you hear me!" No response. But I heard sirens, and they sounded very far away.

I ran upstairs to Teddy and found Jordan cornered near a window. He was no longer brandishing the club, and Teddy was speaking to him calmly and evenly about handing it over.

I've had to give the following rendition of events to the police and to both sets of lawyers, and I now remember it as something told to me, rather than something I lived through. Perhaps that's the danger of telling the most heartfelt details of your life: they no longer can be yours alone. At any rate, this is what I've told them, and this is what I believe to be true:

I approached Jordan, and he looked at me and put his left hand into his pocket, waving the golf club once more with his right hand, out in front of him like a sword. The head of the club was red and matted with something that looked like dried weeds or straw, which I much later realized (or was told by the police) was scalp and hair. Jordan took something out of his pocket, turned ever so slightly, and the sheer muslin curtains were on fire. We never saw the lighter; we barely saw his hand. But I clearly heard the sounds of the sirens on the street as Jordan broke the window with his body and leaped through it.

I am clear, however, about this fact: rather like a horse at a circus, the sight of a man jumping through a window is made even more dramatic when he jumps through flames.

The sound of the glass must have caused the girls to look out their window because I could hear one or both of them screaming, "Daddy! Daddy!! No! No! No!" The naked desperation, the fear and love and loss in their voices simply tore my heart apart.

Teddy pulled the curtains down from their pole and stamped on them until the fire went out. He told me to get water to pour over the charred fabric, and I went looking for a bathroom. By the time I got back with a water-filled wastepaper basket, the police were filling the house. Within minutes the girls had come out of their room. Donna was being looked after by paramedics, and a policewoman was clearly keeping the girls away from her while taking their statements.

Teddy and I gave all the information we could. Jordan, it seems, was not dead; he'd landed in holly bushes and was badly bruised and very scratched. I think I knew that night that his knee may have been dislocated. I happened to see that they got Jordan into an ambulance, which sped away as they worked to stabilize Donna on the floor of her mauve and lavender bedroom. Are they taking them to the same hospital? I wondered.

The two sets of girls were momentarily confusing to the police, and as detectives and forensic specialists arrived prepared to measure, mark and take bits of physical evidence, the relationships of the children to Donna and Jordan had to be retold again and again. The police kept coming to me to explain their actions, as, no doubt, I looked to be the oldest at the scene. I was made to understand that the activities growing around us, and some of the forensic tests under way, were necessary, if Donna should die. *If Donna should die.* It didn't seem possible.

Eventually, all four girls stood in the living room with us, as the paramedics passed through the foyer with Donna on a stretcher. Marta and Ava called out and tried to move toward her, but a heavy policewoman put her hands on their shoulders to restrain them and, I suppose, to comfort them. "We shouldn't get in the way of the doctors," she said. "We want your momma to get right to the hospital real fast so that they can get her better and home to you."

Marta was crying, and Ava was holding back tears. Ava was trying to sound adult and reasonable. "I want to tell my mommy that I love her. I want to tell her that I'll take care of Marta and that she shouldn't worry." The policewoman looked at me and closed her eyes. She put her hand on Ava's head and stroked her hair.

"She knows all that, darlin'," she said. "I promise, anyone'd look at you'd know that."

I kept calling the O'Sullivan house, and still there was no answer. I didn't have Dan's cell phone number, and neither Lizzie nor Jackie could remember it. At one thirty the police told us we could take the girls home with us or they could put them in a hospital room overnight. I weighed the relative merits of tranquilizers and medical observation over the trauma of going to a hospital after an incident like this, but it was Teddy who said, with certainty, "We'll take them home to Josie and Dan's, and we'll stay with them until the O'Sullivans get home."

We gave the O'Sullivan address and home phone number to the police, and we bundled the four quiet girls into Teddy's Subaru and drove them up to Josie's house. When we got there, the house was locked tight. Jackie and Lizzie were so thrown by the events of the night, they were nearly senseless and couldn't remember where a spare key might be hidden. We were practically out of the long driveway when Jackie remembered a key hidden in a magnetized box on the back of the metal hinges of the studio gate. We pulled back in, the key was there, the door unlocked and we tumbled into the cool white foyer of the house. None of the girls wanted to go to bed, and they didn't want to be separated from one another or from us. We pulled blankets from the bedrooms and put *Clueless* on the large plasma-screen TV. Teddy had each of the Fortunata girls lying in his arms, and he stroked their hair.

I sat between the O'Sullivan girls. I was surprised to miss Berry, who was boarding at his vet's home with her Pomeranian for the weekend. Lizzie said the Pomeranian was Berry's girlfriend. I wasn't sure what to make of that news. Jackie put her head on my shoulder, and Lizzie put her head in my lap. I scratched her arm, just the way she asked me to, for what seemed like hours. I began to nod off during the second hour of *Clueless,* when the sound of the door opening and Josie's ringing voice woke me. "What the heck is going *on* here!" she asked, rather good-naturedly, given what looked like an ad hoc school-night pajama party at three in the morning. Teddy got up and took Dan and Josie back into the foyer, and they all emerged ashen and shaken. Dan took his girls in his arms, and Josie took Ava and Marta and just held them, and within seconds everyone was crying.

They put all the girls to bed and put the kettle on for tea. Dan called the hospital to find that Donna was in intensive care, in critical but stable condition. Jordan was in police custody on another floor of the same hospital. His knee would require surgery. Dan and Josie seemed to have access to all kinds of information at all kinds of hours, beyond what a normal citizen or even a family member might get. I wondered how connected they could be, that hospital records were opened for them in the middle of the night over the phone.

I had a full day of teaching the next day. Dan was scheduled to cover a new shared-private-jet service to the Caribbean, but he was certain that he could reschedule. Teddy had a historical society meeting at four that he would cancel and he'd promised his mother a ride to her bridge game, but he knew that he could arrange the local taxi service for her. Josie would call her TA and have her cover her classes. It took me a while to figure that we were covering the bases, from watching the girls to monitoring the hospital care of Donna. "Well," I said, "I finish at four. I can be here sometime after four."

"That's great," said Josie generously, never suggesting that I should change a bit of my schedule as had everyone else. I supposed she'd assumed Teddy had still been working on my house when Donna's call had come in. I was grateful she'd not asked. And it was only midday on Monday that I realized I was the only one of the four adults who had made no concession to the crisis beyond last night.

CHAPTER 19

Josie called the office with every detail of our team vigil worked out: Be at the hospital at five o'clock, Fran reported, to take over for Josie, who would go home to fix supper for everyone. Fran would take over from me at eight, and Dan would go to the hospital at nine to sit with Donna until midnight. Josie would drive back at midnight and stay the night.

Donna had not awakened, and Josie and Dan did not want her to wake without someone close to her in the room. Donna's parents were due to arrive from Florida this evening, and Josie was hoping that they would visit her first thing in the morning rather than drive to the hospital, in their apprehension and exhaustion, directly off the plane that night. I had no doubt that Josie's suggestions would be followed.

"Good grief," I said, "she's like Patton." Fran laughed weakly in acknowledgment but offered no other explanation. She'd worked with Josie, after all, for years.

I followed my instructions and drove to the hospital, found my way to the main entrance and was sent to the intensive-care floor. Josie saw me step off the elevator and came out of Donna's glass cubicle to greet me; she seemed tired but bright. She reported that Donna had squeezed her hand, and the doctors confirmed some weak response. While this was good news, there was, still, no waking her. Josie told me that it was also important for *me* to hold Donna's hand and to stroke her skin and to talk to her. "Talk to her about anything," she said. "Talk to her about yourself . . ."

Oh, God. I began to panic. Stroke her skin? I'm not good at this. I'm not one to talk to someone awake, no less comatose. Josie needed me to be responsible, but I wanted to say to her, Lizzie and Jackie would be far better at this than I—you can't trust me to do this right. But Josie hugged me, apparently unaware that I was frozen to my spot. She dashed back into the fishbowl of a room, kissing Donna on the forehead and promising to return.

"Goulash at the house," she directed as she made her way past me in the hall. "It will be warm and waiting for you, when Fran arrives to take your place at eight," she said with a smile—warm but commanding, clear-eyed and charismatic, like Joan of Arc. I could imagine legions of men, pious or superstitious, gullible or reasonable, believers and nonbelievers, lining up behind her and marching, like lemmings, right off a cliff.

I stood outside Donna's room for minutes. A nurse asked me if I needed anything. No, I said. I was fine. She looked at me as though a little amused, as though *my* being "fine" was not high on her agenda there in the ICU. A large X-ray machine was being wheeled into an adjacent compartment, and the orderly needed me to move out of the way, out of the hall; and so, finally, I had to go into Donna's terrarium of a room. Her face was bandaged across one eye, over her forehead and down to her throat. There were drains coming out of the bandages near her ear, filling vials with translucent, pale pink fluid. I sat in the only seat in Donna's room, an aqua leatherette side chair with wood trim. It was so homely, I knew it would appear in a chic midcentury boutique in Tribeca, sometime in the next few years, priced at thousands of dollars.

I took out my book, *The Age of Innocence,* with my notes scribbled in the margins. One of my classes, planned for next semester, an expansion of my Gilded Age curriculum at Columbia, was on the American experience in Europe within the sensibilities of Henry James and Edith Wharton. I looked at their American characters, treading water in the England and Europe of their stories, and planned to compare those elements with the lives the writers had led before their European defections, as I sometimes saw it. The snipings to and about each other, and the vivid and sometimes bitchy letters between them about their cultures on both sides of the Atlantic, formed the beginnings of my idea that the two of them were stitched up in a kind of "insecurity blanket" that blamed the young, naive and fragile social system of America for most of their personal failings. God knows, beyond their considerable talents, there were enough examples of their own individual failings to fill more than a few volumes; but in that way that sometimes seems like divine intervention, their collective genius took the clay of self-pity and defended sensibility and molded it into true art.

Even with a book I loved, my reading was sluggish and studded with nagging guilt. The same paragraph came before my eyes two, three, four times. I was absorbing nothing.

"Listen, Donna . . ." My voice sounded false and shrill. I looked for some kind of response. Nothing. "I'm sure Josie's told you that the girls are fine and safe, except that Ava now wants all the Chanel clothes that blond girl wears in *Clueless*—so you need to get up and sell a couple of big houses fast." I was talking like a greeting card.

I knew it made no sense, but I barreled on. My heart was pounding. "Look, Donna, I know you must *think* that you can't live through this, but you can. You really need to try. The girls need you so. Would you believe it if we brought them *here* to *you*? We can do that, you know. Dan and Josie can arrange anything—apparently . . . You just *can't* give up." I felt a presence behind me, turned to look through the glass, and saw that a nurse was, indeed, looking at me. She knew that Donna couldn't hear me. I must have looked like the fool I felt myself to be. I stopped talking to Donna and returned again to my book, but I kept thinking of Josie and letting people down and not following instructions.

"Okay. Right . . . Donna," I said, "I have to find something to talk to you about, and I feel like an ass here. Can you hear my voice? It doesn't sound at all natural, does it? I'm going to find something to talk to you about." My eyes searched the room and found it anonymous with only white towels and paper incontinence pads stacked on the surface of the sink. In a flash a psychoanalyst would have a field day with, I immediately thought of a bridal trousseau, and it reminded me that only eleven days ago I was supposed to have married. What a strange few weeks I'd had. But the last thing I wanted to do was admit my failures to Donna. Not alive or dead.

Then I remembered a lesson I'd taught in first-year cultural studies nearly thirty years ago in Saint Louis. "I'm going to tell you about New Year celebrations, because we just had New Year's a few days ago. Can you remember that?" I waited a moment for a reply and then continued, as I do when teaching and the class seems to be elsewhere. "Okay," I said, "here we go. New Year celebrations go back at least four thousand years. In ancient Egypt the Nile flooded every autumn, and the silt it left allowed farmers to grow their crops. So autumn, and the time of the flood, indicated to them the start of a new year—the beginning of the 'matter' that allowed their way of life, in other words.

"Babylonians, on the other hand, celebrated *their* New Year in the spring when the plants showed signs of rebirth and the fields were ready to be plowed. Babylonians started the whole idea of New Year's resolutions when they made solemn promises to return borrowed farm equipment." I was warming up. I knew how to lecture, after all. "I know," I said. "It's bizarre that our ideas of resolving to get more exercise or to stop smoking come from a Babylonian vowing to return a plow. I'm thinking of borrowing someone's weed whacker just for continuity." I looked at Donna for encouragement or recognition. None were forthcoming; still I forged ahead.

"The Greeks paraded a baby in a basket in their New Year ceremonies to represent the spirit of renewal and fertility—and, of course, today, we continue to use a baby to represent the birth of the new year . . . Okay." I took a breath. "Japanese hang banners of straw across their doors to bring happiness and luck. I have no idea why *straw*—I suppose it's a reference to fields and growth and crops—but they also make sure that, as the clock turns to midnight, they are laughing to ensure the year starts out on a happy note and, as my mother would say, 'Begin as you mean to continue.'"

I looked at her lying there, so still and unmoving, her lovely face broken into pieces under the bandage. "Please tell me that when the clock struck midnight, you were laughing, Donna," I touched her hand. It felt cold, but I touched her hand and then I held it for a moment. I can do this, I thought.

I was about to launch into the New Year's Day annual Polar Bear Club Swim, a tradition clearly for lunatics, in the icy Atlantic waters of Coney Island, the freezing cold of Lake Michigan in Chicago and off the coast of Vancouver in the frigid Pacific, when suddenly I looked down and really saw her as Donna, not some body lying in a bed, designed to add to my general discomfort on earth. Was this, I wondered, what Timmy had looked like, as he lay in the hospital? Had he been bandaged? I didn't picture him that way. I remember asking my father if Tim had already eaten his ice cream when the car hit him. I remember Dad telling me that he didn't know. I leaned forward. I thought I might rouse her if I could only connect.

"Donna," I said. "It's Joy. I'm here." I felt tears sting the backs of my eyes. I waited for long moments. "I don't know *how* to talk about myself," I said. "I never have."

I looked up and saw Teddy watching me from the other side of the glass wall. He smiled. He wore a gray wool vest open over a white T-shirt that said, I'D RATHER BE WHALING. It was one of his favorites, with the picture of a happy-faced whale, unadvised, it would seem, of his fate. Teddy's baseball cap was from the Lenox Volunteer Fire Department. I waved. He went to the nurses' station, and I watched him talk to the pretty red-haired nurse. She nodded, disappeared and returned with a folding chair. Teddy brought it into Donna's room and sat down. "Donna," he said, looking at her, "wassup?"

He kissed the top of my head and filled me in on some news. Josie had managed to track down the radiologist Donna had been seeing. His name was Dr. Catsup. I laughed, in spite of myself. "You're thinking "Anticipation"—aren't you!" Teddy asked with a wicked grin. I shook my head, chuckling.

"Any-hoo," Teddy went on, "Catsup is a real nice guy. He just drove me over here from Josie and Dan's. He's down in administration checking to see which of his cronies are here at this joint. He works out of some hospital in Great Barrington or Stockbridge or someplace . . . So. Yeah." Teddy took a breath. "He wants to spend the night here. Naturally, he had to fight Josie tooth and nail to get her to give up her spot next to Donna's bed all night." I smiled at the thought of their confrontation. "I'm not kidding," Teddy said. "I thought he was going to have to kill her." Teddy allowed a wry smile.

"She was talking about the facial reconstruction stuff this morning on the phone," I said. "I think she'd like to be the one to operate, don't you? I mean, hold the scalpel and everything—"

"Yeah," he said. "Whether Donna needs it or not." He was quiet for a minute. He looked at the floor. "You know that Donna had a thing with Will, don't you?"

"No," I said. I felt like the beat of my heart slowed down. "I didn't know . . . that . . . ?"

Teddy didn't seem to want to say more. "You better ask Josie to tell you the details. I don't really know them. It was a few years ago. I don't think he, like, broke her heart or anything. They weren't going out long, but she found him *shtupping* . . . I think it was . . . her nanny . . . in a car parked in her own driveway. It was really cheesy."

"Teddy, why didn't you tell me this?" I asked as though I'd been betrayed.

He looked up from the floor and right into my eyes. "I had a kind of vested interest—know what I mean? Ya know? I mean, I didn't want you to think that I'd tell you that kind of thing because I liked you . . . you know . . . liked you . . . in *that* way."

And, though massively inappropriate, with someone lying just inches away and in real jeopardy, I actually felt sorry for *myself*. I didn't even miss having Will in my life, but Josie's warning came back to me like a slap in the face. Teddy saw me look at Donna, and he took my hand, the way one takes the hand of a child who might misbehave. I think he understood, better than I, how confused I was about Will.

Dr. Catsup arrived as if on cue. We stood. Teddy leaned over Donna's bed and bellowed into her ear, "Donna! Donna! Someone's here to see you? It's your doctor friend!" Catsup seemed to wince. I know I did.

"She's in a coma," I said, tugging the sleeve of Teddy's T-shirt, "she's not deaf."

"Actually," Catsup responded kindly, "it sometimes helps to have an increase of volume—especially if everyone has been talking in soft tones all day." He took her hand, and he kissed the cheek that was not covered by bandages. He was a little guy with a tight beard and terrier eyebrows over brilliant blue eyes, made larger by his wire-rimmed glasses. He brought her hand up to his own cheek and held it there as he took the chair I'd been sitting in and settled it close to her bedside. He shook my hand and introduced himself. When the red-haired nurse brought Donna's chart for him to review, there were four of us crammed into the tiny glass room.

"We should leave," I said to Teddy.

Catsup turned from the chart and thanked us. "You never really know when you're going to need real friends—but when you do and they step up to the plate like the two of you did last night . . ." He stopped and closed his eyes, searching for words. "I just hope there is some way we can pay you back. Something we can do for you."

He looked back at Donna. He looked at her for what seemed like a very long time. We didn't move. He spoke quietly. "I knew how much I admired her and how pretty she was and how much fun she could be. I knew we got along well. I just didn't know until today that I couldn't live without her."

Teddy put his hand on Catsup's shoulder and left it there for a good long moment. "Call us, man," he said. "Call us if you need anything. And let us know if there's any change. Okay?" Catsup put his hand over Teddy's and nodded. And Teddy seemed to give his shoulder one more squeeze as he said, "Hey, it's gonna be okay, man."

CHAPTER 20

T
eddy drove us back to Josie's in my car. We walked in together, and Ava and Marta immediately clambered up his legs and into his arms. Teddy had spent the day with them, building mobiles out of balsa wood with the optimistic idea that they might be moved to Donna's hospital room when, or if, she made it out of the ICU. Teddy threw the girls merrily around his side and shoulders like sacks of potatoes, and they giggled and squealed. I marveled at his ability to keep them behaving like normal children in the face of the most abnormal circumstances.

Josie, true to her word, had made goulash, and the aroma filled the house. I realized just how hungry I was as Jackie and Lizzie led me over to the kitchen counter and Josie shoveled a huge serving of the creamy, pinkish stew over noodles she'd kept warm in a steamer. She sprinkled it all with a handful of fresh, chopped parsley.

"Is there enough for seconds?" asked Teddy.

"You bet" was her answer, and she reached for another bowl. Teddy came over to the counter and put his arm around my shoulder. I saw Josie register the gesture and could feel myself stiffen.

Donna's parents had just left, having eaten dinner with Catsup and their granddaughters, and were on their way to the Lord Jeffrey. Josie did not want to let them enter Donna's house until the blood had been cleaned from the carpet and the window fixed. She'd spent the longest time on the phone with the police trying to get clearance to "tidy the crime scene," with little progress.

"Until Donna is out of the woods, the police, apparently, can't afford to treat this lightly," said Josie.

"What do you mean?" asked Teddy.

Josie looked older and more far more tired than I'd ever seen her look before. Her mouth lost all of its softness as she answered. "I mean . . . ," she whispered, and held the pause for emphasis, "if Donna dies and Jordan is charged with manslaughter, and *he* turns around and says that *Joy* hit Donna on the head with the golf club and *you* tossed him out a window, there had better be a lot of evidence to prove that it's not true." Teddy's mouth dropped. My heart stopped. I was no longer hungry.

She looked at us and rolled her eyes. "Hey, listen," she said, "this is not likely. I'm sort of kidding. Hmmft." She snorted and shook her head. "It is much more likely that he will claim she threatened him and he defended himself. I mean . . . a golf club isn't a standard weapon. And look, the girls were there, and they saw some of it and heard most of it." Josie took a long breath and sighed. "But they're *little girls*. No one wants to put them in a witness box. I mean . . . court. Can you imagine? Even Jackie. And she's practically grown up—but Jesus God, I don't want her in . . ." Josie looked away from us and collected herself. "Well, let's just hope they find enough evidence so that this is an open-and-shut case. To hell with the cleanup. We'll just keep Donna's parents out of the house."

Teddy put his arms around me from behind, and again Josie took it all in. She was too tired to comment but not too tired to notice.

In short, Donna did not die but woke the next day, cloudy and broken but mostly intact, and Jordan did not claim anything but the whole truth. He'd feared losing her and the children. For disguise, he rented a car. He stalked her, he called her and then he went to see her. He thought he'd talk sense into her. He entered the house with his golf club, though he didn't remember taking it in from his car. And when he failed to make her understand how the family could again be happy together, he got angry and hit her with his club and he nearly killed her. Everyone agreed that at last Jordan might get the help he'd seemed to need for so long. While the story itself was resolved within days, the situation was far from perfect. Donna was going to require several operations and months of therapy, news that we accepted with both relief and dismay.

Josie and Teddy and Julia, the O'Sullivan housekeeper, and I were put on duty, ferrying the four girls to and from school, dance lessons, music lessons, after-school sports and the hospital. Josie carried most of the weight, as the girls moved into her house and prepared to live there for the six to eight weeks the doctors suggested Donna would be in the hospital. Allen Catsup became a regular fixture in our lives, joining us for dinners, showing up to watch the girls' indoor sports games or calling at the last minute to head me off at the pass and let me know that he could pick up Marta or Ava at school and get them to their mother at the hospital.

Most nights we all had dinner together, usually at Josie and Dan's; although Catsup took us out for pizza one night—eight of us. Sitting around a table, the kids made yucky noises and vomit gestures at all the pizza toppings the adults suggested. "The man who finally discovers how to make macaroni-and-cheese pizza," Josie suggested, "is headed for riches beyond Bill Gates."

I had, for the first time since I'd left Saint Louis, a routine that accommodated someone else's schedule. The fact that I hadn't made the schedule and was powerless to do anything but hold on, as though to a runaway horse, was another matter. My life was suddenly no longer my own, and I wasn't sure I could track the date when I'd lost control. Was it the night of Donna's phone call? Was it the afternoon Josie walked in with the roses? Was it the day I placed a bid on the old house? Surely, this was not the life I'd come to know as mine, but no one surrounding me here in Massachusetts knew any better. I clung to the belief that when Donna was well, my life would return to normal.

As much as I was part of the crowd, there was less time than ever for private conversation. We all had our parts to play. When Josie handed out assignments, we acquiesced to a man, but one: Fran had a whopper of an excuse. Over the holidays she'd found that she was, at long last, pregnant; by the second week of January she was feeling miserable. Unable to hold down food and barely able to manage swallowing water, her doctor had inserted an IV port and she took in bags of fluid at home to keep herself nourished and hydrated. She looked terrible and felt terrible but was, she explained, thrilled. Absolutely thrilled. "Better you than me," I said under my breath when her meeting with Josie and me in our office was wrapping up.

"No kidding," Josie said flatly.

We had a temporary secretary-assistant named Denise, who had returned to school in her forties to get her master's in art history. She was a strange bird, almost attractive in a hard and urban way that "seemed to have flown a little too close to the scalpel," as Josie put it. Her nose was a ski jump and pointy thin at the end, her eyes set too narrowly together. She spoke with an odd, affected accent, and I wondered if, perhaps, she was from Europe originally. Josie laughed and laughed and claimed to have answered the phone one afternoon and found Denise's mother on the other end. "Pure Bronx," she assured me. But Denise picked up our phones with a lock-jawed, fast-paced "O'Sullivan-Haaahkness"—like a very snooty law firm. Josie got it from the grapevine that many of the callers simply hung up when they didn't hear the familiar "*Good* morning!" of Fran's chirpy welcome. Josie corrected Denise, but it seemed to have made no difference.

Denise kept an expensive-looking can of sandalwood room spray on her desk, and as soon as a human being walked by, she aggressively sprayed their wake. I'm betting that each of us who passed her desk in those first days wondered, if only for a moment, if we were emitting offensive odors, along with our dark thoughts, when we passed her desk. And though neither Josie nor I had seen her file a single document, type a line or change a copy machine's cartridge, she carried with her a kind of haughty censure that was easier to accept than to analyze. Josie and I were, indeed, spun in a dervish fit of extracurricular activity that revolved around little girls and their changing schedules and their incomprehensible needs and hospitals and doctors and family meals, and all manner of things that had nothing to do with our work.

Bernadette was as interested and supportive about this problem as she was about all things, professional *and* personal. "This is life," she said. I remained in awe. Arguably the world's leading authority on women's studies, she found time to write and lecture all over the country and still teach the occasional class, "just to keep my hand in," she'd say with a laugh. She considered all of the students of Amherst *her* students, and they approached her everywhere—from the paths crossing campus to the ladies' room. It was becoming clear that she considered Amherst her art form, superseding even her writing. And even the president of the university seemed to be in her employ. And still, with the tightrope she was braiding, and about to raise with us upon it, she remained a steady commissioner with time for us and all her charges. If she had but a moment, she filled it with value. She was the kind of teacher you could pray they might still make, and the kind of teacher, I was just beginning to discover, I hoped I might become.

Josie called her with the news when the problem with Donna began. Lowell had known Josie for years and clearly adored her, and she promised to help us keep the administrative part of our lives together as we kept the domestic elements of Donna's life together.

"This is what women do," Bernadette said to me as I apologized to her yet again for my schedule changes and the limits on my time. "This is what women have done all through history."

"When my mother was dying," she said, "I had a regiment of women around the two of us that could have fought off—I don't know—Hannibal, or any warrior in the book . . . except Death, I suppose."

She told me how these women took turns sitting with her mother, reading to her, grooming her and cooking their food. How they made sure to come in teams, so that no caretaker was alone, never allowing the strain of being with someone dying and someone mourning to become overwhelming.

"This went on for months," she told me. "I never had to think about how we would manage. It was orchestrated by women," Bernadette said, "just as it always has been. Just as it always will be, I suppose. That's what we do."

I looked at this internationally renowned feminist, with her published collections of writings and all her many honors, and I expanded my ideas about the reasons I admired her. This isn't what I thought feminism was about, years ago, but it seemed I was changing my opinions about a lot of things.

Some weeks after Denise's arrival, Bernadette left a voice-mail message for me saying that she'd dropped off a large folder at my office. It was full of information about a Shakespeare summer program in Toronto, and she wanted my reaction. I couldn't find it anywhere. I looked in the in-box and the out-box; I looked over and under my desk. I looked on Josie's desk, although it wasn't her department. I looked on Fran's desk, which had become, clearly, Denise's desk.

The photographs of Fran's nieces were gone, as was her rubber devil-duck, her postcards of truck stops and the pencils with the streamers and flower tops stuck in the mug from Niagara Falls. The desktop now held, among other things, photographs of apparently glamorous people in expensive and ornate frames, a set of valuable-looking pens in a fluted Victorian rosewood pen holder, an orange ostrich-skin notebook, an eyeglass case with a Prada logo, an antique ivory bangle, a silver napkin ring, a porcelain tray with what looked to be a royal crest, recognizably blue Smythson note stationery, a small silver Cartier desk clock, an oval tin with two Fragonard-like lovers printed on it and something called "Bonbons à L'Anis" inside.

There was no room on the desk for the missing folder, and yet, without moving her things too much, I tried to look. And where was our chic assistant? It was twenty to ten, and she was to have been in place at her desk at nine. When she walked in—diamond earrings gleaming, flannel slacks perfectly cuffed over lizard loafers, a soft cabled cashmere sweater coordinated with a cream-and-gray-patterned pashmina shawl—she looked at me as though I were *her* assistant.

"Why are you touching my desk?" she demanded.

"Actually, it's not your desk, Denise," I said. "It's Fran's desk, and I can't find an important envelope from Dr. Lowell."

She leveled me with an icy stare. "My name," she said, her tiny eyes narrowing, "is not De-neece—as you persist in pronouncing it, but Den-eeeze. Den-eeeze."

I was tired. I had ferried around little girls, and sat at the bedside of someone who might have been dying, and I was having an affair with my handyman, and I was a little behind in my work and a little panicky about it, and my secretary was pregnant and throwing up, and my office mate was now my commanding officer, and I wasn't getting married, and I think that, as Teddy might say, my "container was full."

"Den-eeeze," I said, carefully. "You're fired."

CHAPTER 21

You don't fire someone like Denise without applause. To date, it was the most popular thing I'd done at Amherst, and she'd only worked for us for three weeks. I figured that she had to have pissed off roughly five people an hour over those three weeks, given the response. I called Bernadette, somewhat sheepishly, as I had no idea whether I, indeed, had the authority to fire someone and even less of a clue as to finding a replacement for our replacement. She bellowed with laughter.

"I couldn't imagine her ever working out," she admitted. "The only reason she lasted as long as she did was that Josie has been so absent from the office." Bernadette chuckled.

"You think that Josie is harder to get along with than I?" I stammered.

"Oh, my dear." Bernadette could barely speak, she was laughing so hard. "There is no comparison. Josie insists on full engagement. Nothing less. Can you imagine Denise or Den-eeeze—or whatever the hell her name was—standing up to Josie's interrogation? There's no 'there' there—if you know what I mean." She laughed and laughed. I could imagine her flesh shaking, breasts free from her soft shoulders, the skin under her chin with a life of its own. "You did the right thing, my dear. 'Den-eeez, Den-eeez'"—she said it twice, thrilled, I suppose, by the way it sounded in her mouth—"'you're fired!!!' I love it. I love it."

"But what do we do about—"

"I'll call Madeleine right now. It might be a student for a few weeks until she can line up a real temp. But that's okay, isn't it? You expect Fran back, don't you?"

I didn't know what to say. I'd seen far too many women take their paid maternity leave, causing everyone to fill in and hold their jobs open for them, and then not return to work after all. It seemed a horrible twist on what we'd all fought for. On the other hand, where was the feminist movement on child care? How did we expect women or families to make these terrible choices of careers over children's well-being with no help from their community or support from their society? We'd failed, by the way, across the board. This wasn't about class; affluent women had many of the same terrible dilemmas as working-class women, and without child-care solutions on every level, how would we ever hope to lift families out of poverty? And why was it always the *woman's* problem, as though each one of them invented the dilemma alone? My way of dealing with the situation was to avoid it. No children. No home life. I was focused. I advanced my career and did not waver. Still . . . much as I had to face the fact that we had fought for choice and options, when someone took an option so different from the path I'd chosen, I was always a little judgmental.

Bernadette pulled me into the conversation, a little brusquely. "Joy! Are you there?"

"Oh God, yes. I was just, I was . . . I don't know where I was." I shook my head as though Bernadette could see it through the phone. "Fran is, I think—I mean, I *believe*—Fran . . . ummm . . . She's coming *back*. But the real *point* is that she is six months or so away from *having* this baby. *This* isn't her maternity leave. This is *illness*, I guess. And the nausea could be over tomorrow, or it could go on and on—no one seems to know. The doctor says she's healthy in every other way, so . . . we just don't know."

Bernadette had a good sense of humanity but an acute sense of scheduling, and it was suddenly clear that her allotted time for this phone call was over. "Well, give her my love and tell her to keep her chin up. I'll have someone at your office tomorrow morning, dear," she said. "I'm looking at your roster, right now. You have a class at ten tomorrow. Could you meet someone at the office at, let's say . . . nine fifteen and get them set up?"

I agreed to the nine-fifteen meeting. She promised to have another copy of the Shakespeare material delivered, as I'd never found her envelope, and we signed off.

That evening, sitting around the O'Sullivan table, shelling fresh edamame beans, Josie told us the story of Bernadette Lowell. There were, of course, all of the facts everyone knew about: her academic history, the issue of her having been president of Fairmont College, the women's college to the University of Pennsylvania, and the lawsuit that she filed against Penn when the two schools were merged in 1973.

"I remember that lawsuit," I said. "It was a huge story. Was this before she wrote *Women's Work?*"

No, Josie told us. She'd done *Women's Work* as her doctoral thesis and then re-created it for commercial release in the early seventies; but it came out just before the brouhaha about her position at Penn. Some think, Josie told us, that the book, and its success, was why she'd not been picked for the president's job.

Not only had Bernadette *not* been chosen as the president of Penn; she had not, in fact, even been *considered* by the board to replace the retiring president of the university, though her credentials were finer, many believed, than any of the male candidates, including the fellow who got the job. She very publicly sued and very publicly lost.

With the fledgling feminist movement pitted against the traditional right guard, each branch of the media covered, dissected, anticipated, analyzed and soapboxed every aspect of the case. It became the academic equivalent of the Bobby Riggs–Margaret Smith Court tennis match, and as Bernadette's academic and professional writings had focused on the worth of women's work, it was an ironic and humiliating twist to her career.

"The trial details were in the paper every day. Gosh, I remember thinking that the suit itself was so important," I said. "It seemed as though the whole idea of women playing in a man's world was being judged."

"Exactly. I remember it, too," said Catsup. "Man, oh man—it *was* a huge deal. So *that's* who Dr. Lowell is. I never put the two things together before. No wonder everyone was so excited when she came here." He shook his head, remembering something else. "But wasn't there something—didn't she get kidnapped or something?"

"Well, not kidnapped, but she did go into—sort of—self-imposed exile, I guess you'd call it," Josie went on. After she lost her case, she literally disappeared. The press looked everywhere. It didn't seem likely she could just up and vanish. But for years no one seemed to know where to find her, except her agent and maybe her publisher—because she kept writing. Three years after she left the scene, she published *Feminine Tense* and then two years later, *Hen's Feet*. Can you imagine, volumes on gender issues in literature—and they *both* became best sellers?"

"They *should* have been," I said. "They're the most important books on semiology and gender positioning in literature and popular culture ever *written*, don't *you* think?" I looked at Josie, and she nodded. "They're certainly among the things that convinced me to go into academics."

"I *know* about them, of course," said Catsup, "but I've never read them."

"They're unusually deep and original. And they're edgy and kind of angry, but not unreasonable," said Josie. "A lot of people talk about how important they are—and some folks note how beautifully written—but no one *ever* mentions that they're also incredibly *witty*. Or am I the only one who sees this?"

"I *know*," I said. "You're *right*—*no* one ever talks about how funny her books are! You read a passage that takes your breath away, it's so moving and so clear, and then suddenly, you're laughing out loud. Why is that—that no one ever mentions it?"

"Because you can't be important *and* witty in academics," said Dan flatly. "And you certainly can't be funny and taken *seriously,* if you're a woman—not *anywhere*, but *certainly* not in academics."

"Asinine," said Josie.

"That's stupid," said Catsup.

"Ridiculous!" I said.

"Of *course* it is," said Dan. "Damn stupid. But true."

Lowell's books broke all the boundaries of academic versus popular nonfiction. And they did it without interviews or book signings or television appearances. There were only the growing rumblings about where and why she went into seclusion to write what looked as though they might be the most important books on the subject of how and why a culture assigns and assesses human behavior and worth. The mystery itself acted like a lure. Reporters and students alike sought her out, and for years they wrote about searching for her—but to no avail. She was, Josie recounted, for a good long time the Salinger of women's literature.

And then, as if by wizardry, Bernadette reappeared, after more than a decade, to teach at Amherst and U Mass, publishing articles confronting the ways we educate and the positioning of educational institutions. She was as provocative and brilliant as ever, and her clever, distinctive, witty voice was back in the public conversation as though she'd never been away. Twelve years missing and then back in the saddle with no public explanation; we all asked what that could mean. But Josie knew. Josie always knew.

"Bernadette," Josie continued, "moved to a cottage in the wild or woods somewhere, so out of the way that the likelihood of being spotted seemed remote." She took a long pause and lowered her voice. "Here's the thing. She cut off her hair, she dressed like a man, and being so tall and big-boned, she apparently pulled it off. For more than a decade she was accepted as a man, albeit a man who kept to himself."

Josie told us that Bernadette found that being guarded, somewhat limited in language and display, made her masculinity more believable. I found this especially intriguing, the idea that using fewer words and smaller emotion expressed a more masculine point of view.

And, according to Josie, Bernadette wrote a book about her experience. Josie read some of the chapters, but, sworn to secrecy, she has never discussed them. We wondered why Bernadette was waiting to publish this memoir, and Josie assumed that within the parts she *hadn't* read, there must be something so incendiary that it had to wait until either something changed or, Josie suggested, someone actually died.

"*Who?*" We pushed for details. "What else do you know?" "What kind of person would she be protecting?" "What kind of secret?" "A woman or man with whom she'd had a *relationship*?" The questions were overlapping, pouring from Teddy and Catsup and Dan and me into a puddle at Josie's lap. Dan then remembered the story of a European diplomat, stationed in China in the fifties, who discovered, twenty years into *his* intimate and sexual relationship, that the woman in his bed and dreams was not only a spy but a man.

"Oh, I don't *know*!" Josie laughed, as though we'd been tickling her into giving up more information. "I really don't. It may not be either. Maybe she's grown beyond the subject of gender. Maybe she wants to be known for her *new* passion—the changes she's making in the way we approach education.

"Or maybe she's afraid the press will latch onto a subject as provocative as 'transgender' and she won't get the *chance* to talk about education. I mean, she knows more than any of us about what the culture is likely to do with a hot subject. So . . . it's possible that she's just put it all away."

Catsup, Dan and I preferred to think there was a great dark secret. Teddy said that he wasn't sure he could ever look at Bernadette again in the same way. As usual, he said what we were all thinking. Our supposed sophistication would mask the prurient interest we displayed only in that room, only among this tight, intimate group of friends.

I considered Bernadette—so motherly, so gentle; always on a diet that never seemed to work. Dressed in skirts or supple pants with pretty jewelry and scarves in watercolors like plum and periwinkle, lavender and pink, Bernadette talked easily, smiled easily and had that lovely and infectious laugh that would cause the whole room to laugh with her. What could Bernadette do that would make me believe that she was a man? It was simply unthinkable. And yet, I have to say, I loved the legend that I now placed around her. I loved the intrigue and sense of heightened awareness. And most of all, I loved the drama of the story.

We humans are, after all, lying in wait for the next great story. I know. Literature is my game. I hand the playing cards to the next generations: Emma Bovary and Jay Gatsby, Hester Prynne and Othello, Medea, Newland Archer and Daisy Miller—their stories are what carry me back into the classroom each day; they are the reason I get out of bed. The thing I might not really wish to look at is that their stories may have been so compelling, they allowed me to put off creating my own. As the joke goes, "When Mozart was your age, he'd been dead for thirteen years."

Josie was a first-rate storyteller in the old narrative tradition. She held the history of our tribe (chosen or born) in her hands, and thinking of herself as an outsider, she had a kind of distance from the story itself. Dan was, of course, the writer, but Josie turned fact into legend the way great itinerant storytellers once did, face-to-face, holding us in a kind of albumen of attention that made the distant television, the music of

National Public Radio, the padding of Berry's feet or his insistence on a treat from the table fade behind a translucent barrier of rapt attention. We sat there, her audience, drinking in the facts and accepting the opinions. Catsup and Dan, when he was around, and sometimes the girls and Teddy and me; we would snap the bottoms of asparagus, chop the herbs, pulverize anchovies or whip the egg whites into stiff peaks as she told her stories. We shoveled pasta into our mouths and mopped up sauces with crusty bread. We drank down her words with our wine and our lemonade, our iced teas and our Dark 'n' Stormies. We had no place we would rather be than caught in Josie's web, learning more about the intimate world around us through the details she'd collected, like a Victorian naturalist with a table of specimen spiders pinned to cards. There she had them, annotated and marked: all the working parts of all the people who touched our lives.

Though I could do nothing about it, I knew she was trying to concoct her own story about me. She'll have some job to do there, I thought. I had no story, or, at least, none that I could see. But my vantage point was, perhaps, too close to the shore to see that I had, at last, begun to swim toward my own life.

CHAPTER 22

There is a thin line between prompting and nagging. I'm not at all sure I understand those boundaries, but Teddy finally attended a seminar and visited the offices of an adviser who led classes on assembling academic credit for life work as part of one's acceptance back into academia. And if it wasn't entirely of his own accord, it was encouraged entirely for his own good. Or so I believed.

I knew that I was on thin ground in doing so, but I brought up the subject over the O'Sullivan kitchen counter one night when the entire cabal was in attendance. Just as I hoped, they jumped into the fray, asking questions, giving advice, suggesting possibilities, delivering boundless enthusiasm and forming a kind of battalion that I hoped would carry Teddy through to the end. Catsup, especially, seemed taken with the idea, and he and Dan offered to vet Teddy's résumé and affirm its assertions within the format and concepts given by the adviser. When the possible credits had been assessed, Teddy would need to take an admissions test. This, the group figured, was about eight weeks off, and they immediately formed the idea of a study group that would tutor him through the process. I watched Teddy become round-eyed, like a frightened boy on an inner tube caught in an offshore current. *Good,* I thought. *Good.*

That night we drove home in relative quiet. I wondered if the shoe would drop. Teddy went to the fridge and poured himself a beer, offering me one by tipping the bottle midair with his eyebrows raised. No, I thought not. Teddy drank the beer in a single guzzle and then came up behind me, grabbed me and bit the back of my neck in a way that was aggressive and full of teeth and tongue. His body was hot, and his breath was damp on my neck. He felt like a stranger. As incredible as it seemed,

I was almost frightened of Teddy. I pulled out of his grasp and turned quickly to confront him. He was sweating and disheveled and hazy-eyed. He looked angry at first, waved his hands in a gesture of loose dismissal, and then he looked suddenly beaten and ashamed. He took two steps back from me.

"Teddy," I began, and I shifted my weight to approach him. He put his fingers to my lips as though to stop me from talking.

"I'm just *me,*" he said with a frown and a shrug. "I yam what I yam." Teddy pointed at the picture of Popeye, dancing where a pocket on the T-shirt might be. I thought there were tears in his eyes as he turned away.

Within that first week, Teddy's study group took over for me like water rushing into a flood zone. I no longer had to nag or urge or cheerlead, though cheerlead, I suppose, I continued to do. And while I saw that he twisted and turned, on more than one occasion he had trouble getting out of the assigned positions; Catsup and Dan held him to a higher authority with a male-bonded, team-player mentality that did not seem inappropriate.

Josie asked him one night, as we sat around the newspaper-covered counter, hitting crabs with hammers and picking out the meat, if his mother wasn't pleased that he was going back to school. Teddy looked embarrassed. He said that she wasn't all that enthusiastic.

"You're kidding." I leaped in. "What's the *matter* with her?"

Teddy turned to me with narrowed eyes. "You don't know anything about her. You never ask one thing about how she is, or what *she* thinks about how much time I spend with you. You've probably never even given *a moment's thought* to what she goes through."

"But Teddy," I said. "You see her almost every day. You spend all of Sunday with her. You have dinner with her a few times a week. That's much more time than most grown children spend with their parents. It wouldn't occur to me—you're right—it *wouldn't* occur to me to expect that anything would be wrong. And she knows how we've all formed a kind of support system for Donna and the girls." I could hear myself sort of bleating, like a goat. It was very unattractive.

"She's alone in the house every night. How do you think that makes her feel?" Teddy asked accusingly.

Catsup simply got up and left the table, Dan opened his eyes in a kind of cartoon look of surprise and Josie grimaced and shook her head. There was silence. Loud and angry silence. Josie got up and came around behind Teddy. She put her hand on the shoulder of his purple tie-dyed T-shirt.

"Teddy," she said gently, "it's normal for a man to go out in the world and find his *own* family, his *own* people to love. That's what parents are supposed to do: they're supposed to build strong wings so that children can—safely and beautifully—fly away." She took a long time thinking of the next thing to say. "I'm sure she's proud of you and what you're trying to do. I know I would be, if you were my son."

Teddy looked down at the floor. "No. She's not happy about any of this," he said. "She doesn't understand why I have *any* interest in going to school, and, frankly, I'm not so sure why I'm doing it either."

Everyone spoke at once, voices falling all over one another, full of support and good intentions. Teddy stopped the cacophony by raising his hand and saying, "Look, I'll tell you what I told her; I'm going through this exercise, but we don't even know if I can pass the admissions test. We don't know if anything I've done for the last twenty years will count for anything." Everyone began to protest, and he held up his hand again. "We don't *know*. And even if it *does* count— and I'm not saying it will—*until* I take the admissions test, we don't know if I can get in." Again the voices were raised in encouragement. "Look! Look"—his voice got wearier and older and more seriously considered—"if I can't even pass the test, we don't need to put any more energy into this argument. Let's just take one thing at a time." The marijuana leaf design on the back of his shirt said it all to me: Let's not put too much energy into this. Let's think about it tomorrow. But maybe that was just my interpretation of the moment. Maybe I wanted him to have it out with Maureen for my own reasons. Maybe his way was better.

That night he was distant. He slept with his back to me. But I rested my head in the hollow between his shoulder blades in a space that always felt as though it had been carved from a mold of the side of my face. A perfect fit. Positive and negative space was one of Teddy's favorite subjects, and in that bed I imagined myself as in life, another part in the jigsawed puzzle of his story.

CHAPTER 23

Some days were simple. I would finish a class and actually run to my car, drive too fast to the elementary school, pick up Josie's girls and Donna's girls at the main entrance at 3:15, drive them to the O'Sullivan house, leave them with Julia, Josie's housekeeper, turn around to get back to my own desk to try and complete my work before evening. I didn't mind those days too much.

Some days were more complicated. I minded them more. Ava had ballet lessons at 3:45 on Tuesdays in a studio just off the green, and Jackie had squash club at the gym on campus at exactly the same time. Marta had after-school art classes, which let her out at 4:30, and Lizzie had a 4:00 trumpet lesson with a Hampshire student on their campus. Lizzie's lesson was over at 5:30. Ava's ballet lesson was over at 5:15. Jackie's squash practice let out at 5:00.

On Thursdays, Ava had jazz class in town, and Marta had piano lessons on the O'Sullivan piano; Jackie had squash matches somewhere in the region but was let out of school early and had to make it to the bus at the community center by 3:00 and be picked up again at the community center at 6:00, and Lizzie had chorus after school and needed to be picked up at 4:30.

Teddy and Josie and I sat down early in the process and divided this list based on our class schedules and the logistics of ferrying children in opposite directions at exactly the same time. We had to face the fact that not only did we have Marta's and Ava's school, lessons and clubs to deal with, we had the overflow of the O'Sullivan girls' busy lives, which Donna, with her far more flexible schedule, had helped Josie carry for years. Dan was contracted for pieces months in advance, but he cut back as much as possible to be home most weekends and arranged his deadlines to spend at least part of the weeks ahead at home. We created a big wall chart with the girls' schedules and our responsibilities. God help the one who let a small girl wait alone on a sidewalk in the dark and cold of an Amherst, Massachusetts, winter night. My suggestion that their activities might be curtailed in this time of crisis was barely acknowledged, let alone seriously advanced.

When they weren't in an after-school activity, one of us might take Ava or Marta, or both, to the hospital to see Donna. Catsup usually caught up with us there. Josie tried to keep Julia through dinnertime, and together they made sure that every member of the ragtag tribe were fed by seven. I was back at home, usually with Teddy in tow, around nine. The coursework, the grading of papers, the planned lectures all happened between nine thirty and eight the next morning. The weekend schedules were managed by Josie, Dan and Catsup, and Teddy and I were relieved of our child-related duties until Monday came around again.

It was very early, no more than seven, on a cold Saturday morning on the last weekend of January, when I got a call from a frantic Josie. Mrs. Granger, their regular sitter, had just phoned to report a stomach virus, and had to cancel her weekend's stay. Catsup had his once-a-month weekend duty at the hospital. Dan was away at an American Express conference for travel writers. Josie had not been able to get out of a long-booked panel at Duke University on the semiotic detail within Flaubert, of which she was an expert, and Julia, the housekeeper, had a phone that rang but did not answer. Could I stay with the girls for the weekend?

Teddy had left to fetch his mother for some event or other just minutes before Josie rang, and I was staring at a stack of papers to grade and a lecture laid out in cards, with references all placed along my bookcase, ready for work. So no, I could not very easily stay with the girls at Josie's, but perhaps the girls could come here. I hung up the phone and felt my breath catch. How would I ever finish my work and entertain four little girls, cook for them and clean up after them, not for hours but for days? All the spit in my mouth dried up.

I called the Hennessy house, and Maureen answered. "Yes," she said, as though she had thorns on her tongue, "Teddy has just come in *this minute*." There was an air of "can't you give him a moment out of your claws?" in her voice. And then she thought of a better idea: "He *has* just come from *your* house, hasn't he?" hoping perhaps, against hope, that he hadn't, and that she'd illuminated a problem between us.

"Yes, yes," I said impatiently, "but something's come up with the O'Sullivan girls and the Fortunata girls, and I need his help."

"*I* need Teddy this afternoon," Maureen said, as though the subject were closed for discussion. But Teddy materialized, took the phone from her and promised to be back at my place within the hour.

The girls arrived before nine, all giggles and big eyes. Josie, brilliant Josie, had packed their favorite peanut butter, sour cherry jam, white bread and a box of chocolate wafer cookies—which, they hinted, was planned for a great surprise. There was a little plastic bag of white powder, which I assumed was something other than cocaine, some boxes of different sizes and a tiny bottle of brown liquid with Spanish on the label. There were bags of M&M's and taco chips and a jar of disgusting-looking orange cheese dip. I was assured that it was delicious when heated in the microwave. I could only imagine.

Teddy's arrival was no less anticipated than Santa's, and he did not disappoint. He brought buckets of paint and stencils and rags and stenciling brushes and foam applicators and drop cloths. He took all of this up to the attic, which was empty but illuminated by three bulbs that hung from the rafters. He'd had an idea to turn this room into a kind of playroom for kids for some time, and now he had the manpower. I'd been asking, "What kids?" for what seemed like months. Now, here they were.

We dressed the girls in old T-shirts of mine, which hung on them like dresses. As every surface would be painted, there was not much danger in giving them the job of first coating the walls with a light, spring green. Jackie began painting trim in pale yellow. I went downstairs to grade papers, and when I looked up, an hour and a half had gone by. I made peanut butter, sliced apple and bacon sandwiches on white toast, just as my grandfather had done for me a thousand years ago. I cut them into triangles and took a platter to the attic with a pitcher of lemonade. Already the change was remarkable. This dark, pitched room with the tiny window in the eave was becoming bright and inviting. Little girls, none taller than five feet, had done all of this with one brilliant magician.

They all showed me how, after their next coat of paint, they would begin to lay out the stencils of pop-art flowers that would float between the beams and maybe—there were many opinions about this—float across some of the walls. Teddy looked completely happy. *Tommy* was playing on his portable tape player, and Jackie and Ava were dancing the swim to "Pinball Wizard."

The attic was finished by two o'clock. Only the floor was left to paint on another weekend. There were flowers scattered all over the walls in a very sweet and haphazard manner. On one wall, in the darkest corner and rather close to the floor, Teddy had them sign their work and date it. As one last touch, he applied the roller to the palm of each of their right hands and had them add their handprints just over their names.

"When you are, like, thirty," he said, "and Joy is"—he stumbled and mumbled—"seventy- or eighty-something, you will come back to this room and remember, like, *this day* and what it was like to be a kid and paint a wall and have grown-ups who really liked you and listened to you and took you around with them." Immediately I thought of Teddy and his brother, Joe. I could feel a lump rising in my throat.

"And," said Lizzie, in that breathlessly excited way of hers, "we can put our hands on the wall and see how much we've grown!"

"Exactly," said Teddy.

He ate a peanut butter sandwich or two or three and cleaned up the paint cans, wrapping the brushes in Saran wrap until he could properly clean them later, and he took off to pick up his mother. He promised to be back at seven thirty with the biggest pizza pies in Massachusetts, and we all stood on the porch and waved good-bye as his Subaru pulled out of the driveway and tooted a "shave-and-a-haircut" signal as it rolled away toward town, the taillight still winking a one-eyed farewell.

His absence was palpable. There was a huge, dark hole in the air without him. I'd never missed him as much. In fact, hold that idea—I'd never missed him at all, before this moment. Perhaps, it occurred to me as I registered this new feeling in the wake of his presence, I'd never missed anyone since I'd lost Tim.

"Can I have more lemonade?" asked Marta, tugging the hem of my cardigan, and there was no time for reflection. I was left with four little girls, and I was on my own.

"Okay," I said, searching for suitable subjects to discuss, "who likes Jane Austen?" This was met with complete silence.

Jackie, the oldest and most sophisticated of the girls, looked at me with furrowed brow, as though she couldn't quite remember. "*Who* is she?"

"An author," I began but stopped almost immediately as her eyebrows grew together in a deep frown. She was hoping for a Hannah Montana type or at least one of the Powerpuff Girls. "No," I said, "never mind. How about *Little Women*?" Marta and Ava hadn't a clue. Jackie and Lizzie wrinkled their noses. "How about Beatrix Potter—and *Peter Rabbit*?"

"That's for babies," said Ava, in a way that was so condescending it wasn't even dismissive; but rather, given to me as instruction from an imperious eight-year-old.

"Okay," I said, nearly giving up. As I walked around the bookcase that enclosed the window seat at the far end of my second-floor landing, my eyes spotted a book in the area I'd reserved for my childhood favorites. It was a relatively new book, but short enough so that I thought I might get through it in a weekend. I knew it would read like a charm. "Up to the bathroom on the third floor, everyone takes a bath and gets the paint out of their hair. Jackie is in charge. When you are clean and dry and dressed, meet me back down here for a kind of performance."

"Performance! Like a play?"

"Like a show?"

"A performance is a performance," I said, sounding, I hoped, mysterious.

I went back down to grading my papers, and when more than an hour had passed and the squealing and squeaking and thumping and splashing and yelling had quieted down with Jackie's voice, "I am the boss!" dominating, I read the label on the orange cheese jar and put it in the microwave until it bubbled. Then I used the "serving suggestion" and spread the Tostado chips on the largest platter I could find and poured the orange glop in ribbons all over the chips.

I was standing with book and platter in hand at the window seat when the girls appeared. They were dressed just fine, I suppose, if one can accept that little girls now all dress like little hookers, but their hair, to a girl, was beyond reason; wet in places and dried in others and sticking up and out and paint tinged and frizzed and tangled. "What's wrong with your hair?" I asked.

"We can't get the knots out," offered Jackie and then launched into the horrible truth that I didn't have a special kind of defrizz, detangling agent they claimed to need. I figured that Josie would know what to do when she came home on Sunday night. She would, no doubt, pour this "frizz-off" or "knot-out" liquid all over their heads, and they would, once again, have the hair of little princesses. Not my corridor, I thought.

They sat on the window seat. I brought the green velvet chair out of my bedroom and set it facing them. I placed the floor lamp over my right shoulder. I opened the book.

"Wait! I thought this was a performance!" This from Lizzie, with wails from the others, as though they'd been duped.

"*You* wait," I said. "We'll have an hour of this and see if you don't think it is a performance." I launched into *Jim Hawkins and the Curse of Treasure Island*, written in an eighteenth-century style as a sequel to Stevenson's nineteenth-century *Treasure Island*. I'd come across this book in England a few years ago, and fascinated as I am with the study of language and style, opened it and found myself swept away from the first page.

It was a hunch. If you'd asked these girls if they were interested in pirates and treasure hunts and adventure, they would surely have pouted their lips, shaken their damp, messy and tangled heads and refused any performance that didn't involve a girl with visible breasts and a bare midriff gyrating to a song with sex in the lyrics. I knew little enough about their age group as a target audience, but I get them in the classroom when they are a scant six to ten years older and there's not all that much emotional growth. I can't say I didn't hesitate, but I went with my first instinct and launched into *Jim Hawkins* and they were transfixed. Once again I was reminded, as if I'd ever forget: do not rule out girls from adventure stories. Adventure is human, after all, not male; but most important, their delighted involvement in the romance of the characters and the horror of the gore made me promise myself to not rule out girls from anything.

I read for a swashbuckling hour and a half with a promise of another hour before bed, and the finale tomorrow afternoon. Their eyes were like saucers, and I led them, dazed, into the bedroom, where they sat quietly on my bed and watched Eva Gabor in *Green Acres* on Nickelodeon TV while I finished grading my students' papers.

We had a bit more than an hour to wait for Teddy's return, and they were still talking in their version of a glamour-girl-Gabor-Hungarian accent when Jackie asked if we might prepare the cake, the ingredients of which Josie had packed. A cake? I feared the worst. I didn't know how to bake a cake.

I had what I considered a dream kitchen. It might not make the pages of *Architectural Digest,* but it felt right, it worked well and, most of all, it looked as though it were indigenous to the house. Horizontal tiles, in that manila vanilla color Teddy had used so well through all of the rooms, backed the spaces between the cabinets and the counters. Against all odds, we'd saved the old kitchen cabinets, painted them butter yellow and soft green, and then distressed and waxed the surfaces to a gentle and gracefully aging glow. We replaced the knobs with old-fashioned pulls, and Teddy lined the insides of the cabinets with bits of vintage wallpaper, none matching, but all in the family of our melon and squash colors, enlightened with touches of sky blue. We'd created a chorus line of vintage pitchers along the tops of the cabinets in a collection that was growing by the week. The counters were pale green granite, and Teddy had the stoneyard carve a drainboard into the surface near the sink, which had been cleaned up beyond recognition. Floors were the original wood, stripped, sanded and now painted in diamonds of cream and green. And as one very personal but, I thought, brilliant touch, Teddy had installed an extra counter under the wide windows, to act like a breakfast bar, because we'd gotten so used to sitting there, sharing our meals and planning the details of the house, when it was nothing more than makeshift boards on tall sawhorses. The facelift, successful in spite of so many devastating odds, would have made an aging movie star jealous.

But ask anyone who's ever whipped up a soufflé; a great-looking kitchen does not a baker make. And while Teddy had managed to stock the cabinets with all kinds of things I had no idea I'd needed, I was pretty sure there were no cake pans.

Like a little mother, Jackie shepherded us into the kitchen. Out of the fridge came a container of heavy cream, out of a canvas bag came the bottle with the Spanish label (Mexican vanilla), and a little plastic bag of white powdered sugar Josie had portioned off, and out of a box came an electric hand mixer. Josie doesn't think I own a mixer, I thought. Well, she was right. There was a moment, however, when it looked as though I might not even have a bowl large enough to beat the cream.

In the bag with the peanut butter and white bread there had been a box of chocolate cookies that Jackie had warned me was for a project later in the day. These now materialized, and the cream was whipped with much splattering of counters and backsplashes and navy pullovers and faces and hair.

The cake was made like a log: cookies on their sides, sandwiching layers of vanilla-flavored whipped cream. Jackie was in charge the whole way and slathered whipped cream all over the outside of the cookie log.

"Do you have a pastry bag," she asked, "with a star nozzle?"

"I don't even know what a pastry bag is," I admitted. Jackie looked at me as though I were a poor, pathetic, rough thing, brought in from the streets; Heathcliff, perhaps.

"That's all right." She sighed as she slathered. "We can do it this way, it's almost as good." She instructed me to empty a place in the freezer that could accommodate this cake on the plate, just as it was. I followed instructions and went over to try and move enough boxes of frozen Le Sueur peas and Teddy's Hot Pockets and Stouffer's Macaroni and Cheese and Dove Bar miniatures away from one of the shelves to make room for Jackie's cake. I wound up taking out the ice cube container, turning off the ice cube maker and putting the plastic container outside the back door, where it was even colder than the freezer. I did stop to wonder, If it's that cold, why we would not put the cookie log on the porch? There was no reasonable answer, but Jackie told me to clear a shelf in the freezer, and this is what I did.

When I returned to the scene of the cake, I found four little girls, smeared and spattered with whipped cream from ear to ear and beyond. It was up their nostrils and in their already considerably matted hair and down their necks and on their hands and up their arms to their elbows. Around them was every possible kind of mess: lofts of powder and spatters of cream and cookie crumbs and sticky puddles. There were bowls and spoons and plates and glasses all covered with spatters and sticky goo as well, although I don't think we used all these items in the making of the cake. Every surface, from the kitchen floor to the cabinet doors, was implicated. The toaster had billows of whipped cream running down into the slotted heating elements, and I wondered if it should simply be thrown away.

The cake was put into the freezer with much disappointment over the fact that I had no dark chocolate to "curl" for the surface. I was so out of my depth that I didn't ask how, in God's name, they might get chocolate to curl.

When the cake was safely installed in the ice cube area of the freezer, I turned back to look at the girls and considered, very seriously, running away. Should I begin by cleaning them or cleaning the kitchen?

Teddy came in about twenty minutes later, and most of the kitchen was mopped up, if not whistle clean. What could go in a dishwasher was already there. Little girls, they were quick to inform me, cannot go in a dishwasher. I had a big tea towel that I kept dunking into warm water, and I applied this to every surface of every girl, be it cotton or wool, skin or hair.

Teddy looked surprised. "What's the matter with your hair?" he asked the girls. They once again lit into my cream-rinse deficiency, and Teddy looked at me with a clear intention to telegraph the message "You're not going to leave them like this, are you?" I just looked back, wide-eyed and innocent, though I could see that there were now bits of cream and crumbs embedded in the knotted clumps of their hair. Never mind. Hair isn't the most important thing in life, I thought.

Teddy's pizzas were wonderful. He knew everything kids like, and yet they were interesting enough for me to enjoy. Jackie tested the icebox cake and pronounced it perfect, and six of us ate the whole cake with big glasses of milk. I'll need my cholesterol checked after this weekend, I thought. I almost hated to admit how good the cake was.

The girls wanted to sleep in the new attic room, but moving the beds upstairs was not in the cards. I'd made up the twin beds in two of the guest rooms on the third floor, but Teddy's idea to keep the girls all together was to push the beds of one room close and make them up crossways, so that the vertical length was used as width. It worked well enough. All four girls were tucked in a line. At first we thought they would chatter and jump and get in and out of bed all night, but that phase lasted only about fifteen minutes. They'd been so busy through the day that sleep hit them all at once, and there was soon silence from the guest room on the third floor.

When we climbed the stairs to look in on them a few hours later, I found them sleeping next to one another like little fish in a tin of sardines. I happened to glance into the guest bathroom. I closed and opened my eyes twice. At first I thought they had taken tiles off the walls, so significant did the damage appear, but it turned out to be only towels and dirt and paint smears and bathmats and water and washcloths and more bars of soap than I knew we had, and tipped, opened and puddling shampoo bottles and a soaking-wet slipper of mine that was beyond the shape of anything that had ever been a slipper.

The hair dryer was plugged into the socket near the medicine cabinet, but it was sitting on the wet floor next to the radiator, its cord tangled in a hand towel. Teddy lectured me on leaving the girls in a water-soluble bathroom with a hair dryer plugged into an outlet, and when he laid out the possible dangers I was mortified and shaken.

"It's all right," Teddy said. "Nothing happened. But let's not forget this." And he unplugged the dryer and removed it from the bathroom.

It took us over an hour to clean up the mess, and when we were done we looked in on the girls once more, snuffling and snorting in their sleep, more like little bears than little humans. We descended the stairs with our arms around each other and we went to bed. Tired as we were, we talked and kissed and stroked and made love and talked some more and kissed again and again until the dawn. I kept thinking that I might be dreaming, but when I opened my eyes, there he was, looking back at me and smiling.

When the first suggestion of light filled the sky, Teddy sprang out of bed and into his clothes. I could see the little vertical wrinkle, near his right eyebrow, that always seemed to come back when he was worried or put on the spot. He stuck his cap on his head, gave me a quick peck on the nose and tumbled noisily down the stairs to get his mother to her first Mass of the day. I had always been asleep when he left on Sunday mornings. This was the first time I really understood how early he was expected and how much tension he carried home to her, what commitment he honored and what a hold she had on her son. I lay in bed and thought about all the things I'd missed in a life that had not included a sense of family, of children and a husband who was also a father.

It's embarrassing to admit, but I could barely remember my husband, Paul. I'd never taken his last name; nothing was monogrammed; I'd never put my paycheck into a joint checking account; we'd never talked about having children. The biggest fight we'd had was over the fact that I didn't want a dog. And now I could hardly call up his face or remember how tall he was or how he kissed or even how he hoped his life would turn out. The actual fact of an ex-husband was undeniable, but the living, emotional truth of having had a husband seemed to have passed me by completely. Though I hadn't let myself think much about Will, I suddenly saw that I'd had a narrow escape. I had been about to play out the same piece of theater with Will that I lived through as a young wife. Saved, I was, by a kick in the pants.

I'm not sure I'd ever understood what it could mean to share my life with someone. Maybe I didn't fully understand it yet. But at least on that morning, in my bed at dawn, it seemed an openly stated question, at last; a recognized possibility that I could, at least, imagine, if only as a goal to work toward, or, in full command of my options, reject. One can't, after all, take credit for rejecting something one doesn't really know exists. I'd spent a lifetime giving myself credit for things I never deserved.

CHAPTER 24

By Sunday evening, the girls and I were tuckered out. We had walked in the morning—they, wrapped in woolen scarves, sweaters and shawls of mine, like peasants fleeing Cossacks across the tundra, through the frosty wood and down to the brook by Groff Park to see if it might be frozen. It was. We'd had lunch at one spot in town and ice cream cones at another. The patrons took some notice of their hair, I thought, and Lizzie, whose hair was the most visibly tortured, wrapped my scarf around her head. We played a game to see who might spot a license plate from the most far-flung state, and I failed as an arbiter, unsure as to whether Arkansas was farther away from Massachusetts than Wisconsin.

We came home, and I finished reading *Jim Hawkins,* with one of the most swaggering, blustering, bloody sword battles of all time. They applauded and cheered at the finale, and professed the same surprise at the book's romantic end that I remembered feeling.

Jackie sat at the dining room table, trying to illustrate Georgian dress, using an old reference book on eighteenth-century fashion I found stashed in an unpacked carton in my room. Ava and Lizzie staged a battle with "swords" of Indian corn "repurposed" from a Thanksgiving centerpiece Teddy had brought a lifetime ago. They jumped on the couch and the chairs and the hassock and ran through the house waving their arms and making threatening, stabbing gestures with their corn. Marta was unusually quiet, and I sat down next to her. She put her head in my lap and fell asleep almost on contact. I couldn't raise my voice or get up to work on my lecture or turn on the television or stop the corn kernels from flying through the air and becoming ground into the rug by little feet. I surprised myself by wanting the moment to last. I didn't want to wake her. I liked the warm, moist head, snuggled in my lap. I liked that her little hand held on to the beaded chain of my glasses, even through sleep. I liked the snuffling noises and found them more charming and distracting than I ever would have imagined, and I patted her knotted and matted Rastafarian hair as gently as possible.

With some whispering, all three older girls eventually brought me the remote control, and I switched on the television, where, to my great relief, *Legally Blonde* was playing on one of the cable channels. I'd never seen the movie and I'd now missed at least a third, but the girls knew the film by heart. Having watched it a few times a year all through their lives, they filled me in on the infinite detail of Elle Woods at Harvard Law School. And so we sat from about four o'clock until nearly six, when Marta woke, Elle won her court case, ditched her boyfriend and dressed her dog for graduation. Suddenly all of the girls got hungry at once, and it was time to think about dinner.

Though tempted, I knew better than to serve take-out pizza two nights in a row. There was no way it would stay a secret, and I figured the hair was going to be enough of an issue. Jackie and I took to the kitchen, unearthed a box of spaghetti, and she found a jar of tomato sauce on the bottom shelf of the pantry. I found some cheddar cheese—not Parmesan, I know—but we grated it into a mound and we cooked a package of the frozen peas and mixed them into the sauce. By now, all the girls were in the kitchen, standing on chairs, stirring the pot with the sauce and watching the spaghetti boil and roll around and around. I heard a car pull into the driveway and knew it must be Teddy. I felt a flush of excitement, felt my face get warm, and though I knew it was adolescent, I did, sort of, embrace the feeling. The girls noticed the change and looked expectant. There was a knock at the door and a ring of the doorbell. Teddy wouldn't knock or buzz, I thought, moving through the hall with a sauce-stained tea towel in my hand, and before I could get to the foyer, Allen Catsup walked in.

We all sat down to dinner. While they were not yet a family, Marta was already Catsup's girl; she snuggled on his lap, and he fed her from his plate. That's a dangerous habit to begin, I thought. Ava looked across the table at him, and if I expected a note of hostility or jealousy, none appeared, though she watched him with a kind of detached interest. Catsup began to stroke Marta's hair and, coming up with a hand full of sticky knots, looked at me with curiosity.

"Yes, I know," I said.

"Their hair . . ." He looked from girl to girl and began to chuckle. "What happened to—"

He was interrupted by Jackie, now bored with her own discourse on my being cosmetically challenged. Her rolling eyes and deep sighs suggested that she'd been explaining away their hair to the media for days. Hadn't anyone been paying attention?

After dinner, Catsup was led by the hands up the stairs to tour the attic, referred to now as "our room" by the girls. They told him the kind of decorating details they'd specified to Teddy. He was amused, as was I. He helped me pack their things and gather the mixer, the remains of the vanilla and the peanut butter to take back to the O'Sullivans'.

Then Catsup turned and stood at the door to the kitchen with one hand slightly raised and his eyebrows high above his eyeglass frames. His neck stretched to its full length, and he seemed to want to create a kind of dramatic gesture. I saw the girls look from one to the other in a side-ways kind of glance that suggested they thought he looked a little queer—in the nonhomosexual sense, you understand. I thought so too. He cleared his throat, and when he was certain that he had our attention, he told us, with exclamation points in his delivery, that Donna was mak-ing progress faster than any of her doctors had anticipated. The girls whooped and applauded. We turned out to be the audience he'd hoped to find.

"Will she be home soon?" they asked, and he nodded and announced that in two weeks' time, he would begin a month's leave of absence from his hospital and that he would bring Donna home by Valentine's Day and move into their house to care for her. Everyone would be home together. It was wonderful news, we all agreed. He picked squealing Marta up in his arms, and the other girls jumped up and down, clapping and hugging Ava. Marta put her head deep into his shoulder, her nose tucked into his neck; his beard came down across her eyes, and she closed them.

When he talked about Donna a kind of flush came over him. He looked at Ava and held Marta as though they were what we knew them to be, an extension of the woman he loved. I don't think that I had ever recognized someone as being deeply in love before. Not up close. I don't remember my parents kissing or even holding hands, and after Tim's death they scarcely seemed to look at each other in any loving or meaningful way; not that I noticed, anyway.

My time in New York hadn't exposed me to people who let you see their most intimate or ardent inner lives. I do remember thinking that life at Columbia was devoid of people of goodwill and benevolence. And I remember thinking that they must have had their kind and sweet human emotions removed before they took their jobs, or perhaps the pressures of their academic careers bred it out of them. Here in Amherst, in contrast, every day seemed to bring another heart onto another sleeve.

I walked them all out to Catsup's car. Ava and Lizzie had their arms around my waist, and they tried to match my steps down the path, though my legs were twice as long. It was unwieldy and frost-licked, and I feared we all might topple on the cracked concrete, dangerously uneven and heaved out of alignment from countless frosty winters and no care. At the car, each girl hugged me with youthful enthusiasm and called out thanks as she climbed into the backseat. Marta, still in Catsup's arms, reached out and took my face in her chubby hands and held my cheeks for a moment before she launched a kiss toward my face. The contact of her warm, sticky fingers, the grave gray eyes studying mine, the quiet composure she seemed to exude as she said a good-bye that meant to total the events of the last two days and to thank me for all of it, added up to a moment that seemed close to joy for me. I stepped back, my eyes stinging, embarrassed by the feeling, and unsure how to respond. If Catsup noticed, he was too much of a gentleman to say, and he brushed my cheek with his lips. "Thank Teddy for us, will you?" he said, as he buckled the seat belt around Marta, whose eyes were already heavy in anticipation of the movement of the car. I turned and noticed, as I climbed up the steps to the porch, that my house looked warm and welcoming. The rooms were lit, glowing from within; the colors they reflected were soft and inviting. There was life in this house, and I was a part of it.

I worked on my lecture for about two hours and was nodding off in my desk chair, but didn't want to go up to bed alone, I wanted to wait for Teddy. He didn't come; he didn't call. I slept on the sofa all night, kept company by a TCM marathon of Astaire and Rogers films from which I floated in and out of the plots and dance routines. It was a fitful night.

The next day, as my schedule instructed, I picked up the girls after school and drove them to Josie's. Their hair looked normal, and not one of us chose to raise the subject again. As I pulled into the driveway, I saw Teddy's car parked next to Dan's pea-green jeep. The dining room table was spread with papers, and Dan and Teddy hovered over it, deep in discussion. I stood for a full minute before they acknowledged me. They were both rather animated and seemed pleased to see me. To my surprise, Teddy's life-work résumé was scheduled for assessment the very next day. He and Dan were nearly ready for the presentation. They'd worked on it last night when Dan got home. I suppose I was encouraged and relieved, and yet I also felt an undeniable pang of something less affirmative. I had been left out of this process and excluded from the most benign information about Teddy's schedule. I was hurt in a way I couldn't identify and fearful that the abrasion might show before I could explain the feelings to myself and know what to do with them, so rather than stay for dinner, I chose to get myself out of the danger zone. Before I could get the car door open, I felt that pain that precedes tears, in the back of my throat, and I drove home with a CD of *The Mikado* turned up to a volume that might have been heard back in Nagasaki.

I went to bed almost immediately. I was tired from my weekend as den mother to little girls, tired from the stress of facing skills I had never considered, no less mastered. I was tired from all the emotions raised by the presence of their needs and exhausted from confronting the limits I had placed on my own life and the possibility that those limits might be altered.

There had been waves of fear and excitement, and now I was sure I had misread the whole message. Teddy was not there for me, and I was not enough for him. I had only been teased with the promise of real life. I would never again have that kind of moment—walking down the stairs in a house we both belonged in—arms around each other, to face a night of pure communion, if not, dare I say it, love.

Teddy came in late that night. I'd been in bed for hours, lying in the dark, fearful that he would come to sleep in my house and just as fearful that he would not. I heard his car pull in the driveway. I heard him walk through the kitchen and up the stairs. I quickly closed my eyes as I felt him come near the room. He bustled about, surrounded by the sounds of water running and the soft landings of clothes and shoes. He came to bed with a waft of that sweet, soapy cleanliness that always seemed to be about him, and held me from behind, kissing my shoulder and almost immediately falling into a rhythmic snore. Tears ran down my face and puddled around my nose before soaking the pillow. I didn't know why I was crying. I didn't know what to wish for. I wanted something to stop or something to begin. I wanted to feel more. I wanted to feel much less. I wanted to go back to being me, and I feared, with the greatest dread of my life, that I might do just that.

CHAPTER 25

The following afternoon, Bernadette and the rest of our crew began the specific task of narrowing the material we would use to launch the New Way, as I'd begun to think of the Immersion Technique, next fall. The mission and the curriculum would have to be printed in the catalog in just eight weeks, and the noose was tightening. Adele Friedman, the psychology chair, approached me.

"Joy," she said tentatively, "I hope it's not inappropriate to mention how very sorry I was to hear about you and Will."

Inappropriate or not, her comment was so vague I didn't know whether she meant that she was sorry to hear that we'd ever been together, or sorry about the Crazy Girl incident, or sorry that we were not going to be married. Maybe she meant it all, because I certainly was sorry about every bit of it.

Will's name hadn't come up in polite conversation for months. I felt an odd tightening in my chest as I heard it spoken, and I wasn't sure what a proper response might be. I kind of shuffled my feet, looking for inspiration.

"Of course, I don't know you well," she continued, "but I just feel I should tell you that even if you *had* married"—she sort of coughed or gulped and put her hand to her throat in a Victorian gesture—"he wouldn't have gotten my job. I mean, your breaking off the relationship hasn't cost him a promotion . . . and I thought . . . you know . . . if that gave you *any* concern, that I should make sure you understood that there was far too much history—far too many *issues* in Will's past, that we couldn't risk, however brilliant he might be, making him head of the department."

While I had come to believe that Will had, in fact, cast me in the role of matron-wife for his career, I'd given no thought as to what might happen to him after the incident and the broken engagement, the details of which were surely known through his department and across most of the faculty on campus. I blushed, I suppose, because Adele was suggesting a finer, more sympathetic or compassionate nature than I apparently had.

"Does he know?" I asked.

Adele, nervously fingering a silver pin that looked like a grand feather perched on her shoulder, seemed surprised. "Of *course*. And he's leaving Amherst—which is *much* the best thing—to go teach at some community college out in Idaho." I grimaced involuntarily, wrinkling my nose like a twelve-year-old, and Adele grimaced in just the same way, and her eyes were large and round, and we just stood there for a moment and looked at each other.

The room was filling, and folks were talking in raised voices about some of the material found, copied and distributed by many of the chairs to the team. It was all no less exciting five months into the work than it had been in September when we began. Bernadette had taken the Cambridge model, braided with a high degree of narrowly focused disciplines, reshaped it to her own huge vision and then broke it into pieces like a Frank Gehry building, poised to take off in flight—matching our individual strengths: language, poetry, psychology, philosophy, history, science, math, art and drama, in a way that was so fresh and yet so logical, one wondered why it had not been done before. At the same time I knew perfectly well why it had not been done before. This part of our task required generosity, insight, trust, cooperation, a balanced mix of self-confidence and an absence of ego and grace under pressure. Needless to say, I believed I had no skills to recommend me for such a project, though others on the team seemed oblivious to this and were responsive to my ideas as they shared their own.

Bernadette admitted to me months ago that she was very concerned about one of our department heads. Howard Peal, our oldest team member, had not been handpicked by Bernadette, as he was very much installed at the college and it had been her practice to first invite existing chairs to join her team. To her surprise, he accepted. Howard was the country's leading authority on the preclassical Greeks, having written, more than twenty years ago, the *Odyssey* textbook that had become the standard at most universities. He was well over seventy, Shakespeare was not his true passion, and Bernadette feared that roping him into an area not of his field, and forcing him to enter into a whole new way of presenting material, might prove too much for him. But Howard surprised us all. He felt the success of our Shakespeare effort would mean the chance for him to expand this kind of teaching to Homer and Virgil. Which was precisely Bernadette's point. He'd even talked about creating textbooks to guide the process for other institutions. I thought that each week he looked younger and more spry, and he brought great energy to our meetings.

As we left Bernadette's conference room, Howard took my elbow, like a suitor from an earlier age. "I've been hearing such wonderful things about you," he said. "You've really put yourself out for Donna and her girls." I must have looked surprised. Howard smiled. "My Edward is Allen Catsup's uncle. Allen's mother is Edward's sister, Ellen." He walked close to me and held on to my arm. "You know," he said, "it's very hard to come into a community from the outside and become important to people who have their own full dramas playing out. You have to be very brave to just put your head down and enter the traffic of other lives."

"Josie is really the one . . . ," I said. "She just swept me up like a whirlwind and made me part of her solution. I can't really take any credit."

"Isn't that girl something?" he said. "You're right—a whirlwind. A force of nature. She'll be president of Amherst someday, is my bet. When her girls are grown, you'll see Josie take off. Already started. And she's got Dan behind her and his parents and"—he lowered his voice—"their connections, and their money."

I must have looked clueless because Howard went on conspiratorially, "You know who *Dad* is, don't you?" I didn't. "Secretary of State . . ." he began as though teasing it out.

"Secretary of State O'Sullivan! Of course!"

"And Grandaddy was ambassador to France under Truman and Great-Grandaddy was the first Catholic president of Cornell, and on and on. And Josie's family is no small deal . . ."

I thought he would go on forever with the lineage gossip, but we were now next to my car. "Can I drive you home, Howard?" I asked.

"Yes, yes you can. That would be lovely. It's quite chilly, isn't it?"

It isn't, I thought; in fact it was mild enough for me to throw my coat in the back of the car. Still, Howard wanted a lift.

"But my point is, my dear . . . ," he said, once in the car and buckled into his seat belt. And after admonishing me for not wearing my damn belt and forcing me to put it on, at least while in the car with him, he continued, "My point is that others can open the door for you, others can even push you over the threshold, but only you can take up the challenge and commit yourself to doing something with all your heart."

I wasn't doing this with all my heart. And I was so sorry to admit, if only to myself, that I'd been secretly counting the days until Catsup moved himself into the Fortunata house and I could get on with my life. Howard mistook my regret for humility.

"Now, now," he clucked, "I can see you're one of those girls who can't take a compliment." I waved my hands above the steering wheel in a helpless gesture. "Tell me about this beau of yours," he said, changing direction.

My eyes opened wide. I know I blushed. Howard knew about Teddy. Oh, dear God. "Teddy. Teddy Hennessy. He . . . he, umm. He—"

"Teddy Hennessy, yes," he said, "we know Teddy, dear. He refurbished our kitchen. Teddy found us wonderful old chestnut cabinets—easily a hundred years old—from a farmhouse that was being demolished down around Stockbridge. I think his mother goes to church somewhere down there, and he haunts the salvage places and befriends the demolition workers. He's a wonder, our Teddy." I was quiet. I just drove and stared ahead. "I hear that you've talked him into going back and finishing college."

"I think that Catsup . . . um . . . Allen, that is . . . and Dan . . . have *really* been the forces behind getting him this far. They've just been wonderful to him."

"You don't like to take credit for things, do you?" Howard turned as much as he could in his seat belt to look at me. "I'm told that you are very much the reason for this study, and Allen tells me that Teddy's a real diamond in the making. Of course, we always knew it. Edward just adores him." He looked at me as though he were considering how much he could say. "You know," he ventured forth, "you should put together a study group to get him through his entrance exams—"

"Howard," I said, "I can't ask that of people—"

"We're not *people*," he interrupted.

"I know . . . and thank you. Of course . . . But the thing is, it's not really my place to ask for help for Teddy, and besides, we don't even know if they're going to accept Teddy's life experience toward enough credits that will make him believe he won't have to start all over *again*—and that meeting was today—and—"

"I know all about that meeting, dear." Howard looked at me over his eyeglass frames, which seemed to move up and down on his nose depending on what kind of theatrical impression he wanted to make. "Dan went with him. Do I need to say more?"

I was driving slowly around the square when an SUV with black windows lurched out of a parking space in front of the Lord Jeffrey and nearly plowed into us. Howard made a snakelike hiss and threw his head back. "You see? You see *now* why seat belts are important? You could have had a whiplash!"

I didn't tell him that the seat belts might have kept our heads out of the front window glass, but that I wouldn't count on them to keep my head from wobbling all over the damn place if we were hit by a frigging SUV. Never mind. I said, "Right. Seat belts."

"Joy," he said when he'd composed himself, "Teddy is going to face calculus and probability or statistics along with Shakespeare and some kind of science—at least chemistry. I don't know if they'll waive the second language—"

"He actually speaks Spanish pretty well," I admitted. "His demolition guys and some of his masons speak Spanish, and I've heard him talk to them on the phone—"

"Lord knows what kind of Spanish *that* is." Howard rolled his eyes. "But it's a start. I can do a lot of the classics, you know. Not that you can't, of course, but sometimes it's easier learning from someone with whom you're not emotionally involved. And, of course Edward will do the math—*and* it turns out he's a whiz at chemistry. He could be a chemistry professor—if he weren't head of the Math Department. Keeps up on everything, you know—"

"Howard, this is very generous of you . . . but we can't—"

"We're teachers. We're teachers, and we teach. It's what we do.

Here's a young man we care about. We all see that his light is under a bushel basket, or"—he smiled and paused—"in Teddy's case, under a drop cloth." Howard chuckled at his little joke. "You know . . . we turn these kids out into the world, and we don't really know what we've done for them—or for the world. Few of them touch us. We try to let them in, but they have their own lives and it's very rare that any of them love what we love. Very rare. It's a most unusual kid, these days, who actually cares to make Ovid or Homer his area of study. But we *do* know Teddy, and we like him, and we can see the difference we might make in his life. And— he has so much talent. He found us those wonderful cabinets . . ."

By now we were in front of Howard's house. Set back a bit from the homes on either side, there was a shallow porch, and floor-to-ceiling windows on the first floor with curtains pulled back gracefully, through which one could see a parlor in high Victorian dress. The bones of a formal front garden determined the entry, the boxwood, ever green and full, even in winter, surrounded a thumbprint of a wintered-over rose garden, centered with a pale and slender obelisk. In the streetlight I couldn't tell if it was painted wood or stone, but it looked like Howard, linear, angular, narrower at the top and standing sentry over all he held dear.

"Howard, I'll talk to Teddy and we'll let you know—but either way, it is a most generous offer. Most generous."

"There is the family you're born with, my dear—and then there is the family you *choose*. You have come here and you have chosen to *join* a family, and you have behaved brilliantly. And it is not your place to thank." Howard struggled with his seat belt for so long that I got out and walked around the car and opened his door and pushed the little red button on the side of the plastic form. Seat belts were a new idea when they went into this car, and the belt snapped back like a cartoon. Howard looked terrorized again, and I gave him *my* arm, this time, and walked him to the door. "Won't you come in for some sherry?" he asked, patting my hand.

"Howard, you sound like an old George Cukor movie." I laughed. "Does anyone still drink sherry?"

He looked dramatically wounded and peered at me through the thickest part of his spectacles. "Edward and I drink a glass of sherry every night before we dine."

"I'd love to, Howard, some other time," I said, holding his hand. "Please ask me again." And I honestly meant it. "Teddy's assessment was today. I want to get home to him."

"Of course you do," he said. "Now don't be proud. Tell him what we talked about."

CHAPTER 26

Teddy was standing in the foyer as I walked in. He did not smile in greeting, and his eyes seemed red-rimmed. My heart sank.

"I'm late," I said. "I'm so sorry. I drove Howard home. Our meeting went very well. Very well." He said nothing.

I filled in the silence with bits about the Shakespeare program, distracting and procrastinating. Teddy shifted from one foot to the other. He looked like someone who wanted to say something and like someone who didn't want to say a thing. When I finally ran out of steam, I just stopped talking and stood in the foyer quietly and waited. Nothing came.

"Was it so terrible?" I asked at last, walking into the living room. I picked up my aunt Helen's creamware pitcher, intending to bring it to the kitchen. The flowers from the weekend were wilted, and the water smelled like a tramp's breath. Teddy shook his head no. He looked down at his work boots. They had bright yellow laces I hadn't seen before. I supposed he must have bought them for the interview today. Except for his shoes, I figured that he'd been dressed by Dan. He was wearing a dark green turtleneck and a tweed sport jacket. "You look terribly nice. It's a lovely sports jacket," I offered.

"It's Joe's," he said.

"Joe's," I repeated. "I don't know who—"

"My brother Joe's," Teddy explained very quietly. "Dan said I should have a sports jacket, and I thought Joe woulda wanted me to wear this." And then, more silence. My heart ached. He'd held on to his brother's jacket for nearly fifteen years.

"Oh, Teddy, I'm so sorry. Didn't they take *any* of your background seriously? Won't they give you credit for *any of it*?" It seemed so unlikely that he could have come up with a complete loss, when his knowledge of buildings and design was so vast. "At least they must—"

"They took it all seriously. I mean, they granted enough credits. I can probably get a BFA in less than two years if I stay in design and go to classes three days a week. I mean, I think Dan pulled a few strings." He kept looking down at his shoes or the floor. He was mumbling. "And I still gotta take the entrance exam, and that's not gonna be any piece a cake."

"But Teddy!" I said, nearly leaping out of my skin with joy, "this is wonderful! What is the *problem*? You look as though you lost your lunch money—this is great news, isn't it?" I started to walk toward the kitchen with the pitcher.

"It's not great news," he said, dismissively, following me. "It's fucking lousy news. Do you know how expensive it is to *go* to school? And if I don't work those three days a week, do you know how much money I lose?"

"Well," I said, "well . . ." I hadn't thought this through. Should I be offering to pay for school? I struggled. As a professor, I was pretty sure that I could get a family discount or something. Would Teddy have to be family? Would I have to marry Teddy? Or adopt him? This conversation was all in my head, of course. I said none of it to Teddy. I turned at the entrance to the kitchen and I must have looked stricken, but Teddy hardly seemed to notice.

"I have responsibilities," he said.

"Your mother—" I began, but was interrupted as he lunged forward, his eyes narrowed.

"Every time you talk about her, you make her sound like some kinda witch."

"Minor change in the first letter," I mumbled under my breath.

"You *see*? You think this is *funny*. You think that she's someone you can ridicule! You think you're so much better than she is!!"

"That's ridiculous!" I answered. "I don't even *know* your mother!"

He was very wound up, and little spitballs were forming in the corners of his mouth. He flung his arms around a little wildly. I stepped back from him, but he was just getting started. He was careening toward me.

"Unlike *you,* she has a *real* life. She had a husband and children she cared for—when they were sick and when they were *dying!*" His eyes narrowed. "She has a *cat*—she goes to *church*—and people *count* on her. She's given her *whole life* to other people—"

"Teddy, I'm not *criticizing* your mother," I said, stepping back again, and then I tripped. I don't know how it happened, I just lost my balance and went crashing back, my hand knocking into the wall, and the pitcher was broken into pieces.

Teddy seemed to come to with the sound of a breaking antique. It was like a fire alarm for him. The possible ruin of something more than a hundred years old left him flushed and protective. He gently gathered the pitcher's parts and was moving them, this way and that, like a Humpty Dumpty Rubik's puzzle, to see if he could make them fit back together again.

Teddy let himself be distracted by the thing he knew how to do, and I leaned over the counter in the kitchen and watched him carefully glue Aunt Helen back together. One spot at the center of what would now have to be the back was irreparable. The tiny pieces turned to powder as Teddy lifted them from the floor. But the base of the handle and the breaks in the front were now just hairlines, like memories of a disaster— a cloud over an expression that reminds us there has been, in fact, a past.

It was as though the pitcher made the decision for us to say no more until the wound had healed, and I sat in the kitchen quietly as Teddy made me soup; or, to be more specific, "doctored me up" some soup. It was his own invention: a sautéed onion, a large can of Progresso Chica-rina soup, whatever vegetable he might find in the fridge—this time it was a bag of coarsely chopped baby spinach—a handful of angel-hair pasta, some beer, a dash of Tabasco, a squeeze of lime, a grating of fresh ginger, some cayenne stirred in and coarse black pepper sprinkled over the top. It may sound like garbage, but it tastes divine.

We sat at the counter, using dish towels as napkins, and Teddy apolo-gized for yelling. "No," I said. "I didn't mean to make you angry. But I really *wasn't* criticizing your mother, it's just that"—I took one look at his face and decided to change direction. "Teddy, there are all kinds of things you could do—or we could do." I gulped and waited to see if he had any reaction to my including myself. He didn't. "There are student loans, of course, and there's the possibility of not taking it all so fast. Maybe doing one and a half days at the school . . . and . . ."

Teddy looked down at his near-empty bowl. He spoke so quietly. "I've already found what I'm good at. Some people try their whole lives to find that out, you know? I'm good at *this*." He gestured to everything around us.

"Teddy, you *are,*" I said, "you are good at this. But you could be so much more. You could save buildings and write about what makes a building worth saving so that others could go on with your work. You could inspire kids to go into preservation design. You could help to inform landmark committees on some of the design decisions you grapple with every day—like the fact that very few old buildings *are* pure and that many of the changes they carry are *valid* for the lives they've led through the development of industry and culture. You could write the book on this whole subject. You have it all in you. I listen to the things you know and feel about houses, and I just want the whole *world* to hear you. Do you understand?"

Teddy looked at me as though he knew exactly what I meant and it wasn't a meaning he chose to embrace. He looked helpless. The peak of his cap covered his eyes when he lowered his chin, and I had to screw my neck down below my shoulders to look into his face. His nose was red, and his lips were full and scarlet.

"Teddy," I said, and put my face along his arm. His sweater was soft and warm. I wanted to comfort him, but I couldn't find the window to his discomfort. I couldn't see in.

He seemed to change the subject slightly. "I'll never pass the entrance exams anyway," he said. "We don't need to even have this conversation. And if I'm a handyman all my life, won't it be good enough for—"

"But you won't be," I interrupted. "There's no reason for that. We can put a team together to help you get through those stupid exams. It doesn't have to be so hard. We can do it together." Teddy looked helpless and lost. Why wasn't this comforting him? "You have so many friends here who want the best for you," I started again. "They—"

"Yeah," he said. "I did their houses. I put in their stairs and I fixed their kitchens and I changed their toilets, and they all liked me just fine. They didn't think—"

"They didn't *think*. That's the point!" I said. "Now they've thought about it, and they all agree that you deserve something better. At least a chance."

He stood and put the dishes in the dishwasher, wiped down the counters with deliberate focus, went into the other room and returned with his down vest and the rubber-banded stack of the afternoon's mail.

"Are you leaving?" I asked. "We're still talking about your going back to school—"

"We're not still talking about it," he said morosely. "I have to go home and talk to my mother."

I settled into my wing chair, a folder of résumés on my lap, as Bernadette had asked for my input on Adele's replacement in the Shakespeare project. I read the résumé of a man named Cameron Lethridge at least three times, but his information kept turning to fog. I could think only of Teddy and was wondering whether his mother was being supportive of his wonderful news. In all honesty, I was imagining exactly how, at this very moment, she was poisoning our plan. It was hard not to think of her as the wicked stepmother, with Teddy slumbering in a mother-induced coma that might keep him her boy forever.

CHAPTER 27

We were nearing Valentine's Day, the day Catsup was to bring Donna home. That Josie had a plan for this was no surprise; that Catsup managed to put the brakes on her was. As originally O'Sullivan-planned, the day might have rivaled a presidential inauguration, with banners, bands and a ticker-tape parade. Catsup nixed the crowds, even suggesting that Donna's parents and in-laws allow a few days of grace before their arrival in Amherst. He was gentle but firm. He and Josie would tend to the hospital transfer and Dan, Teddy and I would stay at the O'Sullivans and help the Fortunata girls to pack their things. When we heard from Josie that Donna was installed, safe and comfortable, I would drive Marta and Ava back to their own home, at last. A good plan, I thought. Josie still had a starring role, even if it did not include choruses and fireworks.

Our duties had continued until that day. We had gathered around the O'Sullivan dinner table nearly every evening for more than a month. Howard and Josie had rallied the troops for Teddy, and each afternoon he would meet with one of their team for tutoring: Howard's partner, Edward, for math and science; Josie for "refinement" of his Spanish; Howard for classics and Western civilization; even Bernadette insisted on being a part of his general English tutoring, though I suspected she wanted a guinea pig for some of her theories. They seemed to be enjoying themselves. Hardly a day would go by that one wouldn't stop me somewhere on campus to announce that Teddy was a wonderful student. "A natural synthesizer of fact" is what Edward told Howard and Howard told me.

Teddy had taken on more projects to create a cushion that might allow him time for school. And now he worked both earlier and later hours to make up for the time he spent in his tutored classes; but he continued, with part of each afternoon, to run errands for his mother or to ferry her to card clubs, social visits and churches. Since everything from news about Iraqi bombs to the death of a celebrity chef would send her, frantically, off to Mass, this was not always something easily scheduled. I thought she must sense his nearing a change in his own life, as the interruptions and demands from her seemed more frequent and more insistent.

He met us at Josie's, after having had dinner with his mother, every night that ferrying duties allowed. Dinner with Maureen was, he reminded us, at five o'clock, and he always ate a second dinner with us, as he had with me, around seven or seven thirty. Still, he was looking worn and worried. He began to go back to his jobs after dinner and would show up at my house near midnight, weary and troubled.

The Sunday before Valentine's Day I invited the O'Sullivan and Fortunata girls over to my house to make valentines. Teddy found the time and energy to buy paper punches in the shapes of hearts and circles, sheets of white, red and pink craft paper and blank cards and envelopes. He added a package of white paper doilies from the supermarket, glue sticks and a couple of black marking pens.

The girls and I sat on the brightly painted floor of the new attic room on big yellow and green Marimekko pillows, circa 1970, which Teddy found in the Salvation Army Thrift Store. I'd cooked a frozen pizza with the addition of some fresh red peppers and some extra Monterey Jack cheese that Teddy had left in the fridge after his quesadilla lunch earlier in the week. We put chocolate milk, ice cream and ice cubes in the blender and whipped up something like thick shakes. The girls picked off the roasted red peppers but finished the pie in record time.

There were some greasy finger marks on a few valentines, but by and large they were very pretty. Jackie made a card that was refined and disciplined with small hearts of pink that formed a perfect circle in the center of a large red square. Inside, she cut a little square of pink and secured it with tiny red hearts in each corner and wrote, "To my parents on a day that celebrates love. Your girl, Jackie." She then managed to line her envelope in red paper studded with white dots. I thought it was brilliant.

Ava made a garden with heart flowers of red with white circle centers and pink heart petals and addressed it to "Dr Catsup and Mommy."

Marta needed help. We all punched out hearts for her and helped her paste them on her card. She wrote her name, MARTA, in big scrawled letters on the back.

Lizzie pasted a lot of hearts on the front, all sizes and colors on top of one another in a way that was dimensional and textural, if lacking in any clear design. Inside she repeated some of the pasted hearts upon hearts and then wrote, "to my parents—from your LOVE Child, Lizzie." I decided not to tackle the job of explaining why *love child* might not be the most appropriate endearment.

I made a card for Teddy with a minute red heart on the front and a teeny pink square inside with minuscule hand printing that said, "Please be my professor." I smiled and put it into a red envelope.

We went downstairs and watched a DVD of Drew Barrymore as Cinderella and Anjelica Huston as a terribly wicked stepmother. Jackie brought microwave popcorn, and I don't think I was alone in having a wonderful day. I was truly sorry when it was time to get them home.

No one had paid the slightest attention to the weather outside, but as we left, it was raining like a monsoon in a movie and I had only one umbrella. I took the girls one by one to the car and finally made it in myself and faced the idea of driving up those pitched and pockmarked roads to Josie's house.

In New York you are almost never aware of weather. When it is humid and hot you may feel the heat long enough to complain bitterly between air-conditioned offices, air-conditioned restaurants and even air-conditioned subways. When it rains, there can be downpours significant enough that you can't easily get a taxi; or the bus is crowded and damp; or your slacks get wet when you walk three blocks between the subway and home. A few times a year it seems so cold that your lungs hurt when you breathe on your way from one warm enclosure to another, and the snow piles high on corners so that you must walk around the mounds to navigate the sidewalks. But unless you're the cab driver or the bus driver, you're not responsible for driving in any of it. In Massachusetts everyone drives everywhere in everything. Snow up to the hubcaps? No problem. No visibility? Don't be such a wimp.

I was responsible for four little girls, but I pointed my Beemer out onto the street and bent down to look out of the one spot under the

windshield wipers that stayed somewhat clear from streaking and fog-
ging, and we headed up the side of what always felt to me like a road to a
mine shaft on a mountain—to the O'Sullivan house.

When we got there, remarkably safe and sound and damp, Josie was
in a state. That morning at church, Maureen had cornered Josie and Dan
and began to ask about Teddy and school. Dan had chatted on, oblivious
to Josie's daggered looks or the troubled waters he was stirring with the
oar of his news. Maureen's turn came, and she lit into a monologue about
me, saying that I was behind the treachery, that Teddy did not need this
kind of disappointment. He would never get through school, and this
would destroy him. She said that he'd been fragile from the time of Joe's
death and she'd spent her life trying to protect him and shield him from
the pain of his own limitations. How dare I step into a family situation
about which I knew nothing

Josie defended me and defended Teddy. Dan told Maureen what a
wonderful student Teddy had turned out to be. Maureen would hear
none of it. They were saved by Dan's parents, up from Palm Beach for a
few days, who saw the distress on the face of their child and hurried
across the congregation hall to his side. Josie said Maureen looked intimidated and practically fawned in the presence of the senior O'Sullivans. I
could easily imagine all four O'Sullivans using charm, power and status
to their advantage in ways that were almost instinctive and practiced
without much forethought. It was just one of their many valuable cards,
and I was only beginning to enjoy watching them play their hands,
relieved that their gifts were, to date, never aimed against me.

But here, in the luxury of their living room, on the deep cream, raw
silk cushions of their furniture and surrounded by their Asian art, they
apologized repeatedly and sincerely and would not be consoled.

"I can't imagine this isn't going to hurt Teddy," Josie said, with Dan
nodding.

"We've been talking about it all afternoon," added Dan. "We were
going to call you, but we figured you had your hands full with the girls—
and we knew we'd see you here. And we didn't think either of us should
call Teddy, over there. Do you?" Dan was clearly agitated, rattling on and
talking without taking a breath. I was just numb. Was it possible that
Maureen *believed* Teddy was, in fact, too damaged to finish school and

get his degree? Did she say things like that to him? I had to stop, think and remind *myself* to breathe.

"First of all," I said, as my own fog cleared, "*you* didn't do anything wrong."

"I did!" Dan gestured wildly and practically knocked over a lamp that looked like a Giacometti sculpture with a kind of lit pod at the top. He threw himself forward and stabilized the lamp as Josie sort of screamed a raw but soft screech only the two of us could hear. "Don't you understand? I blew his cover!"

"He didn't know," Josie said to me, defending Dan and touching his arm in a comforting gesture. "He didn't realize that Maureen was such a problem." Josie then turned on Dan: "Where *were* you that night we all sort of landed on Teddy about school? Don't you *remember*—he said that his mother—"

"I do remember *now*—I told you earlier—*now* I do! But when I was standing there, I *didn't*! I just *blew* it. I wasn't thinking. I wasn't paying attention!"

"I actually think you were doing the cooking that night—but *Jeez, Dan* . . . to miss this—"

"I *know* . . . I—"

I stepped in again: "Look! Look! Stop this! You told this woman the truth. You gave her accurate information, and now you're beating yourself up about it. This problem is between Teddy and his mother, not between *you* and his mother." I stood up and took over the pacing from Dan.

"You've been a fantastic friend to him, Dan. You and Catsup . . . and Josie . . . and *everyone* . . . Howard and Edward . . . You can't possibly think you haven't done the best by him." I shook my head. "But listen, listen. The point is, he's *not* a child. He's thirty-four years old. There are things we can help him with, and there are things we can't. And *maybe* it's not even our business, have you thought of that?"

Josie didn't think that *anything* wasn't her business, so she was pretty quiet for a good thirty seconds. Dan just looked down at his priceless Tibetan rug. I knew they both felt terrible. I felt terrible, but what can you do?

Josie put her hands together in that here-is-the-steeple thing that she does when she really has an idea cooking. "I think that you should go to see his mother."

"What!?!" Dan and I said it together and almost in the same intonation.

Josie continued without stopping for more reflection, ours or hers. "I think that you should appeal to her, woman to woman. You both love Teddy. You both want the best for him. I think that you should go and let her know that he's safe and talented and smart, and that he *won't* be hurt, and he *isn't* weak, and there are people who love him, and a woman who can share her life with him and give him his own home and the support he must have lost at the death of his brother and his father."

"But Jo," I said, "the problem *wasn't* the death of his brother or his father, was it? The problem was the selfishness of his mother. That's how I see it—isn't that how you explained it to me?"

"Yeahhh," she drawled. "But what woman would ever admit such an awful thing—even to herself?" She lifted an eyebrow and looked shrewd. "If you put it *this* way to her, she has to come on board as an ally."

Dan looked at her as though she were the smartest woman who'd ever lived. I didn't doubt it, but she was trusting someone to be persuasive and cunning and charming and open enough to talk about feelings—and the person she was trusting to do this was me. Maybe Josie's not so smart after all.

"I don't think that I could persuade her—"

"Of course you can!" Josie was adamant. "You have love on your side."

CHAPTER 28

T eddy didn't come to my house that night, and I didn't hear from
him at all through the day on Monday. When I got home I found
no note but only a lumber bill on the bookshelf that I was reasonably
sure I had neither seen before nor paid, and I figured I must owe him
money for supplies, if not labor. It wasn't the reason, but it was one more
excuse to call Teddy. Not that I needed an excuse, of course, but, it
seems, I did need motivation. I could think of nothing that put me off
more than the possibility of speaking to Maureen Hennessy.

It was seven o'clock in the evening; the likeliest time to find him
home, I figured. I dialed. The phone rang. I prayed to the telephone
gods to let Teddy pick it up, and for once they listened. I could hear the
Kinks in the background.

"Teddy," I said, "it's Joy."

"Yeah! Oh my, yeah . . . well, man . . . yeah. Good to hear from you!"
he said, as though speaking to a slightly deaf old cousin in town from
some faraway land. It was extremely queer, this exchange full of hearty
"how are you" tones. Good to *hear* from you? Now, let me see, am I confusing you with someone who had my legs up on his shoulders just three
nights ago, *damn it*?! Of course, I didn't say this.

"Teddy," I said instead, "what's going on?"

"Oh—yeah??" Teddy answered.

"What do you mean, 'Yeah'? Teddy! I haven't seen you since sometime before dawn on Sunday morning. I haven't heard from you. I know
you've been at the house, there are things moved around and there's a
bill from the lumberyard—"

"Oh, don't worry about that—" Teddy started.

"I'm not worried about it. I'm worried about *you*. And I'm worried about us, and I'm worried about me. And I miss you. I don't know how to sleep without you. I don't know what to have for dinner. Where *are* you?" It was so much more than I intended to say. It was more than I knew I felt.

"Yes," Teddy said in that same strange, false voice. "I see. Okay, dude, why don't I stop by then."

"When—now? Can you come now?"

"I could come by tonight. Yeah, certainly. Right."

"What is going *on*! Is your mother there? Are you talking like this because your mother is there? Teddy, that's ridiculous. You're a grown-up man, for God's sake. What are you doing?"

"Right. I understand. Okay, man, I'll see you in a little while." And Teddy hung up the phone.

I stared at the receiver in my hand. This is weird. This is *weird,* I said to myself. What am I doing here? My heart was pounding in my ears. It's like I have a teenage boyfriend, and we're sneaking around behind his parents' back.

The phone rang almost as soon as I hung it up. I assumed it was Teddy, with some explanation of his behavior, but it was one of my students; a particularly bright girl named Rachel who'd been ignited by my idea of James's and Wharton's shared syndrome of an American inferiority complex. Rachel had begun an ambitious project of analyzing the letters between Henry and Edith from a psychoanalytic point of view, in tandem with her sister, who was a psychiatric resident at Mass General, and their mother, who was a Park Avenue analyst. This kind of behavior, bringing outsiders—and family members at that—into our class work, and moving beyond the course of study, was something I would have always discouraged in the past, but this girl was different. Or this time or place might have been different. I have to admit, I found myself taking new positions on a lot of things these days. I was just coming to the idea that "different" might be all I could get to at the moment, in an effort to clarify the events of the life I found myself living.

Rachel's mother had found a vintage published thesis on the letters of James and Wharton that she thought was full of insight as well as what she believed to be new information on their lives. Rachel suggested that we review the material, and if her mother was right, we might want to have it copied for next semester's class. She was calling from the car as she drove toward town and thought she might drop the package at my home on her way back to campus. I figured it would take a moment, with some pleasantries at the door, and as she was within blocks, it could all be accomplished before Teddy even pulled into the driveway. I agreed and scurried toward the stairs to change my shirt and braid my hair.

I was halfway up the stairs when the doorbell rang. Could she be here this quickly? My socks slipped on the step as I turned on my heels and hurtled down, slipping through the foyer and crashing into the front door. "My, my!" I heard through the door. "Is everything all right in there?!" I opened the door, and standing on my porch were Howard, Edward and a giant greyhound, wearing a pastel yellow and baby blue mohair sweater.

They arrived full of courtly manners, introducing the dog as Speed-stick and apologizing for not calling, but proffering a large box, held out in front of Howard like a pillow with a crown. "We saw this in Boston at our favorite bakery, and we just felt," Howard announced, "with Valen-tine's Day tomorrow, that our favorite couples should be celebrated!" Speedstick walked past me with no greeting, headed directly into the living room and began sniffing the radiator with what looked to be intent.

"He's not going to . . . you know," I said, shaking my head and eyeing the dog suspiciously.

"Oh, no!" Edward and Howard spoke together and were clearly aghast at my suggestion that Speedstick might behave like a dog. Speed-stick was, instead, behaving like a badly disciplined preteen as he ignored me and made his way around the living room, disappearing into the pantry and the kitchen.

Lights of a car pulling into my driveway did not suggest to Edward or Howard that they might hurry along. Edward, instead, spoke in his slow and methodical way about how they'd found their way to the Viennese bakery, after visiting friends in Boston, who were both orthodontists and who had just adopted their own rescue greyhound. The story went on and on and ended up with the two of them in the bakery indulging themselves and buying treats for Josie and Dan, Donna and Catsup and Teddy and me. Oh, Jesus, I thought. Couples. All the while, Howard meandered through the living room and pantry, wearing his heavy coat, holding the bakery box before him but taking in every detail.

"What a beautiful renovation," he said. "That's our Teddy, isn't it?"

"Our Teddy," yes, I thought, and my eyes caught a figure coming up the porch steps. Was it Our Teddy? No, it was Rachel. I tried to press by Edward and stand at the door in such a way that she would just hand over the material, but she spotted Edward and he, her, and there was a whole damned reunion in the foyer. I hadn't realized it was going to be "Our Rachel."

"Oh, my goodness, oh, my! How wonderful to see you!" and kisses and hugs. "Rachel, here, was my best probability student in her first year here at Amherst. I wanted her to stay in mathematics and sciences, but no. No. You're getting her in literature; I just have to accept it." He hugged her. "Rachel's father," he explained, inclining his head toward me, "is a microbiologist at . . . Rockefeller, isn't it?"

Rachel answered that he was still at Rockefeller, but he'd just completed some kind of software program for what sounded like a gene-screening thing, the explanation of which went on for what seemed like hours. I hardly understood a word she said. Edward, on the other hand, hung on every syllable and asked questions equal to the impenetrable subject.

Howard and his box came around the corner of the foyer after, I suppose, inspecting the whole first floor. "Rachel!" he boomed. "How wonderful! I didn't know you were a friend of Joy's!"

No, I wanted to say, *not a friend.* "Rachel is my *student,*" I said, and Howard interrupted, "Yes! Wonderful. Wonderful. I haven't seen you since long before Christmas. How are your parents?"

Howard turned to me. "Rachel's mother is a psychiatrist, and her father is a . . . biologist, isn't it?"

"Yes, Howard," Edward said, with exaggerated weariness. "Joy knows *all* about them."

"Oh, you *know* them! Aren't they just the most divine couple?"

"No. I—no."

Rachel launched into the very exciting news about her father and his gene business, and Howard clucked and said—and I must admit I was pleased to hear it—that he didn't understand a word of what she'd just explained, and Rachel and Edward laughed, and Edward said, shaking his head, "Oh, Howard," as though to say, Don't be silly, of course you understood, who wouldn't?

They led Rachel into my living room, asking her about her mother and someone named Alice—perhaps her sister, I guessed, more than a few paces behind. As we walked into the living room, there on the couch, on his back with his legs in the air and his head on the needle-point pillow my mother had stitched, was Speedstick. Lying, stretched out, he took up the entire sofa. No one made a move to suggest that this was inappropriate, and no one asked the dog to give up the most comfortable seat in the house. Rachel sat on the upholstered bench, Edward in the deep, pale-blue chair and Howard in the stiff, wood-framed, crewel-covered, wing-backed chair, with the pastry shop box balanced on his knees. Everyone still wore their coats. I crossed the room to relieve Howard of his package and had just taken it from him when the door opened and Teddy walked in. He looked surprised to find what must have seemed a small party going on. Everyone stood except Speedstick, who turned his head toward the door and finding it had been opened by neither celebrity nor rabbit, turned his nose away with a condescending sniff. Howard and Edward greeted Teddy with great warmth and introduced him to Rachel. I greeted Teddy with the box.

"Open the box! You can open it—now that Teddy's here," Howard suggested with a sly grin. "It's a Valentine's present—for the two of you!" he offered brightly to Teddy. In the box was a white mountain of crisp meringue, all jagged edged, oozing with crème anglaise, and fes-tooned with strawberries, raspberries, red currants and little vampire-inspired rivulets of bloodred syrup. We must have looked puzzled, though it was only partially due to the contents of the box.

"It's a Pavlova!!!" Howard and Edward both bellowed as though it were a winning Bingo number.

"Let me get some plates, and we can all share it," I offered in an uncharacteristic gesture of hostess manners.

"No!" exclaimed Howard, clearly agitated at the offer and my inabil-ity to grasp his intent. "This is your Valentine's dessert! Save it for tomorrow night! Now, Teddy," he said, lowering his voice and taking Teddy's arm, "all you need is a bouquet of roses and a good bottle of champagne."

I took the box into the kitchen and tried to fit it into a shelf in the fridge, which required much moving about of jam jars, Teddy's favorite pickles and jars of mustard in every guise. When I returned to the living room, Edward was recounting to Rachel the tutoring escapades of Teddy for his college entrance exam. It was, according to Edward's report, going swimmingly. Teddy was a model student.

Teddy stood in the middle of the living room wearing a T-shirt with an illustration of a small brown man in a huge orange Mexican sombrero, with the caption PANCHO WELCOMES AMIGOS TO SOB. Whether the shirt had shrunk or was always too small was unclear, but Our Teddy needed a shave, seemed a little dazed and, to my mind, not at all like central casting's idea of a model student.

Speedstick must have done something rude because Rachel was laughing and fanning the air around the dog with my copy of *Camera Lucida*. Howard looked embarrassed, and Edward suddenly stood up.

"We should be going," he said. "You must have things to discuss with Rachel, and we're taking up all of your time." Rachel stood as well. I took Edward's arm and walked him to the door, as he seemed the most likely to move the crowd along. "We've already been to the O'Sullivans', and we'll drop a Pavlova over at Donna's house. She comes home tomorrow; I'm sure you know, of course."

I smiled and nodded that we did. I'd met Josie over lunch that afternoon, and we'd filled Donna's fridge with all the delicacies we could find at our local gourmet shop, C'est Cheese. Edward was going to have a real mathematical problem on his hands with that refrigerator. "It was so kind of you to think of us," I said. "I'm sure we'll enjoy the cake."

"Pavlova!" Howard corrected. "Like the dancer—as light on the tongue as the dancer was on her feet!"

"Yes, of course. Pavlova. Lovely." I said. "That's great. That's great. Thanks so much." They were nearly at the car when they realized that Speedstick remained behind, snoring on the couch. Edward made a kind of whistle between his teeth, and Speedstick bounded, true to his name, from the couch, past me and through the door to the car, in what appeared to be one single, graceful move. Bits of mohair fluff floated through the air in his wake, and he landed safely in the backseat of their Lexus and laid his head on the sill of its open window.

"Speedstick is saying good-bye to you kids!" Howard called as he lowered himself, with considerably more effort than had his dog, into the car.

"Right," I said. "So long! So long, Speedstick." Jesus, I'm talking to a dog, I thought. I'm waving to a goddamned dog. Teddy stood next to me, waving as well, with Rachel next to him, hand raised and fingers wagging. Speedstick opened his mouth and made a kind of yawning yowl followed by mild little yelps; he obviously meant them as a good-bye statement, but he looked bored, through half-lidded eyes, as if pressed into performance by preening parents. They pulled out of my driveway in a maneuver that barely missed sideswiping Rachel's car. Teddy, I saw, had parked on the far side of the street.

As we walked toward the living room and through the foyer, I noticed a slightly sour scent of pot wafting off Teddy, and I wondered if anyone else had picked up on it. Rachel headed toward the bench, sat down, pulled a large yellow envelope out of her tote bag and began to riffle through reams of papers, as though she had hours to spend in their organization. I cut her off, suggesting that she leave with me the things I could read on my own, and that we make an appointment to meet in my office, perhaps on Friday. I told her that we had a round of temporary secretaries but they were perfectly capable of understanding my appointment calendar and setting a time for a meeting. This was only partially true, but it worked in getting her moving toward the door. It still took a while for Rachel to find the pieces she thought I could read on my own, and far more explanation than I'd hoped for in clarifying the difference. Teddy lurked about in the background. He went into the kitchen and came back with a bottle of beer and Triscuits, which he ate directly from the box.

Rachel was finally and blessedly gone, and I turned to Teddy. His eyes were red and a little glassy. He sat down on the sofa he'd found for sixty dollars at a tag sale and had recovered in a stripe of green and blue with checkered welting and insets of a cream-and-green-flowered print set around the soft, boxed sides of the cushions. It looked as though it had come to me straight from the 1930s, and I loved it.

The couch was covered with drifts of mohair from Speedstick's sweater, but Teddy sat down without brushing them aside. He took a half-smoked joint from the pocket of his T-shirt and a plastic lighter from the pocket of his jeans. In the time we'd been together, or to clarify, in the time in which we'd been intimate, he'd never lit a joint in front of me. I would sometimes come in during the day and find him on a ladder plastering, painting, sanding or doing some other mind-numbing and repetitive task with the music blasting and a cloud of fragrant smoke around him, but I had never actually seen him with a joint. I wondered now if he had put it out when he heard my car in the driveway, but it wasn't something I had thought about at the time. I rather liked the smell as it reminded me of my youth, but I didn't smoke pot or anything else, and he never offered me a toke or a drag or a puff or whatever it's called these days.

He was on his second beer in fifteen minutes. We went through considerable quantities of beer, and our red wine intake was so prodigious I'd come to stocking it in cases, something I'd never done before. If pressed, I'd have to admit that I drank no more with Teddy than I always had, which was very little, so the wine and the beer consumption was nearly all, though not exclusively, his. Lights had never gone on in my head about his drinking or pot smoking until this moment, but I'd never seen him glassy-eyed before. I'd never seen this posture or seen him unshaven. Teddy was the cleanest boy I'd ever known, remarkable, I used to think, for a construction worker; he was, instead, clean as a surgeon.

I sat across from him, pulling the bench to the other side of the coffee table. He held the cracker box close and continued to shovel Triscuits into his mouth, with bits and flakes of shredded wheat scattering down like snow, to land on the round hump of his belly where Pancho appeared to be standing.

"Wassup?" he asked.

I looked at him stunned into silence; my eyes widened, my mouth felt slack. "You're asking *me* what's up?" I finally managed. He said nothing. He looked into the quickly emptying cracker box and moved the waxy paper with a rustling, crinkling sound that seemed amplified, like candy wrappers in the theater. "Teddy, you've been gone for days with no contact. And we're a kind of *couple,* don't you think? And . . . and, in this house, anyway, we have a kind of life together. And then you're gone, and I suddenly feel that I don't know *what* we are. I don't know what my rights are about calling you or what my expectations should be."

His dark brown eyes, a color as rich as chocolate, fresh as earth, met mine. "A *'kind of'* couple," he said, mocking. "A *'kind of'* life together. You said it; as long as we're in this house."

"I don't know what you mean," I said, stumbling. "I mean, I know I said 'in this house,' but we're together at Josie's—and for months now, we've been sort of operating out in the open, I guess you'd call it . . . together . . . like a . . . a . . . couple. I mean, look at Edward and Howard—they see us as a couple; they brought that cake thing for us. Not for *me*—for *us.*"

"No," he said. "You said it—a *'kind of life'* together—"

"Teddy," I said, "what are you asking for?" I was beginning to get exasperated. "You eat two dinners because you go home and have dinner with your mother almost every night. Have you moved your things out of her house? Have you made any kind of real decision about how to handle her?"

"This isn't about my *mother.* You always think it's about my mother, and it's about *you.*"

"It's *not* about me, Teddy. It is about your mother and you and your dead brother and your dead father and her hold on you that keeps you forever her child."

"I'll *always* be her child!" he snarled. "You don't know *anything* about families! You never even *wanted* kids. You have no idea of what having a child means. You have no idea the kind of bond between a mother and a child. You—*Jesus!*—you walk away from a marriage, and you never talk to your husband again? You walk away from Saint Louis, and you only go home for your parents' *funerals*? You walk away from New York, and you don't even have friends who come to visit—you don't have a friend who even calls you at *home*? You don't let your students get close to you? You won't have a goddamned *pet*, for God's sake!! If Donna hadn't had this fucking mess, you wouldn't even have the life you're *living!*" His hands were flailing around, and he was spitting a little when he talked. "Don't you *get* it? You have a life full of people because a girl, a *nice* girl you hardly knew, almost got killed—and *you* just want her to come home so's you can get back to your *old stupid* life!"

I could hear his mother behind the discourse. "Teddy, that's not really fair. I've been part of this team. I've done my best." He looked out the window, away from me. "And anyway, what does that have to do with us?"

"You want *me* to be a *teacher*? You think your life is something I'd want to *copy*? Are you fucking *kidding*? You didn't know even what *wainscoting* was, for fuck's sake. You have no *practical* skills at *all*. All you *do* is drop names of old *dead* guys! *Jeez!* You're such an intellectual *snob,* I don't know who you're *talking* about half the time! *Coddy and Puss . . .* ? Like I'm supposed to *know*? *Jesus!* Tart-*toof*? Tart-fucking-*toof*? *Who*?" He took a long step back from me. "I mean, who the fuck are you trying to *impress*—because there's no one else *in* this house with you but *me—get it*?"

I was stunned. I was more than a little hurt. But I said nothing.

Teddy must have blown himself out like a storm because as soon as he'd vented, he looked suddenly deflated.

"I'm like a project," he said. "I'm like something you have to make better and improve—like I improved your house. Except this house was a mess before I did the work, and I'm *not* a shit guy. I'm not like someone with loose floorboards."

I smiled at the idea of Teddy as a house. "I don't want you better for me," I said. "I want you better for *you*."

"I don't need to be better for me. I like what I do. I don't need to be more."

"Teddy," I said, trying very consciously and deliberately to stay out of the name-dropping minefield I obviously inhabited, "everybody needs to be more. Everybody needs to find out how much more they can be. *I* think that's our *mission*. If there's any reason at all we're alive—isn't it to find out how much we can be and find the courage to try to be all those things in the time we've got here? Isn't that what you do with a house? Don't you find out how far you can push a house into a kind of *perfect* thing—its history and its function and its bones and its personality and its time? Isn't that what you really believe about houses? Can't you believe that about people?"

"Do you really think that *you* try to be all you can be?" he asked accusingly, his forehead tightening.

I hesitated. This conversation was now without intellectual armor. I was standing on new ground here; basic and plain and unguarded. The clever use of words would fail me. I'd memorized, analyzed and taught literary references and philosophical theories, never truly considering their private applications. I might use them to win an argument, but not, necessarily, to find the truth in a moment that begged a kind of authenticity and simplicity that I hardly knew how to invite, much less encourage.

"No," I said. "You're right. I've done a spectacular job at insulating myself from an inner life that allowed any real growth. It's all been on the outside. No one has come in—until you."

Teddy looked at me, and tears ran down his cheeks. "I don't want to have to be something else to be good enough for you," he said.

"No," I said. "That's not it. Can't you see how everyone is on your side? How everyone sees that school can only make you stronger and happier and more fulfilled? Why would you"—and then the phone rang.

Maureen was on the line, and she sounded terrible; kind of croaking and weak. I handed the phone to Teddy, and the color drained from his face. He stood up and seemed to run in circles, looking for his flannel-lined jean jacket.

"What's going on?" I asked, alarmed, of course.

"My mother," he said. "The ambulance—the ambulance is on its way. I have to meet it at the hospital."

"I'll drive," I said.

"No. No need. I'll call you later."

"You're not driving," I insisted, grabbing my jacket from the peg and my bag from the hall chair. I took his hand. We bounded down the stairs, not bothering to lock the door. I opened my car door. "I'll drive." I wanted to avoid an argument about driving and drinking and drugs. I wanted to feel stable and solid and sorted out. I knew that this might be an emotional roller coaster more challenging even than the last six months. Was I up to it? This time my eyes were open. I was walking toward the fire, not running away.

CHAPTER 29

The now very familiar route to the Cooley Dickinson Hospital seemed to go faster than ever before. As we approached the driveway, the ambulance bearing Maureen was just pulling into the emergency entrance. I let Teddy out and went to find a place to park. By the time I got into the reception area, he and his mother were both behind the swinging metal doors. I asked the triage nurse if I could go inside, and she took the pen—slowly—from her mouth, lifted her eyes—slowly—from her *Soap Opera Digest* and asked if I were a relative. When I said that I wasn't, she lowered her eyes back to her book and pointed her pen toward the waiting area.

Twenty minutes later I was still sitting there. The nurse was now taking information from a girl in her midtwenties, costumed in Goth regalia, who complained of a pain in her stomach. When the nurse bent her head to the Goth girl's file, I slipped by the triage desk and through the swinging doors. I wandered along the emergency room corridor, looking in all of the alcoves created by curtains of blue and gray, and saw a handful of men and women hooked up to IVs and one man's naked bottom hanging off the edge of a bed. He was groaning pretty loudly, and no one was paying the least attention. A group of young doctors and nurses stood entertaining one another with stories at a tall station on the other side of the hall. I approached and asked where I might find Maureen Hennessy or her son. Maureen, I was told, was upstairs being X-rayed, and her son was in the bed marked 14. A bed? I thought. What's this? They didn't ask who I was. I walked down the narrow corridor and found Teddy, pasty-faced and damp with sweat on a hospital bed with an IV hooked up to his arm.

"What the hell happened to you?" I asked.

Teddy looked up with heavy eyelids. He blushed deep and red. He or someone else had taken his cap off, and his hair had deep, damp ridges at the sides. He explained that they'd gotten his mother into the room and had begun to take her clothes off roughly, handing them to him as they worked. She was complaining of terrible chest pains, apparently writhing with crippling pain. They were pulling at her clothes and trying to get her out of her bra, and she was gasping for breath and sort of screaming at the same time.

"Gasping *and* screaming," I clarified. "At the same time?" Teddy certainly missed any suggestion of sarcasm in my voice, and I decided that was for the best.

They led a big, metal machine on wheels, with wires coming out of it, toward Maureen, and Teddy recalled that he thought it looked kind of scary. And then suddenly, he realized, that while he could see the lips of the doctors and nurses moving and he could see his mother's lips moving, he could hear nothing. He leaned toward one of the nurses and touched her arm.

"I'm deaf," he remembered telling her. It took her a moment to give him her attention. "We've got one going down here!" he heard through his deafness, as she called to her team. He saw a nurse leave the side of his mother, and the two of them caught Teddy before he hit the floor. The next thing he knew, he was lying on the hospital bed next to his mother's. She was now completely naked, and two doctors were gluing pads on her chest, connected to the machine. Teddy didn't want to look at her. She continued to cry out but also had long bits of exposition to share with them. She was, eventually, dressed in a gown, covered with a sheet, wheeled upstairs for more tests, and Teddy remained in the room.

I asked how he felt, and he confessed, unable to meet my eyes, "Queasy and embarrassed."

He also told me that a doctor had just been in to see him. His blood pressure was a little low, but he was fine. I asked if he'd told them about the pot or the beer, and he said no. They told him that this kind of thing was common among family members of emergency room patients. He'd been praying, he admitted, that while he was lying there, his mother was not already dead.

No, they said, not at all. They explained to him that his mother's heart rate and EKG were normal and her blood pressure was normal, and they thought that perhaps she had nothing more than a little gas, though they would check for gallbladder disease. They were doing X-rays now, and they would keep her for at least two hours until the blood work was returned from the lab.

He sat up carefully and threw his legs over the side of the bed. I held his hand for a few minutes, saying nothing. Teddy looked at the floor. When I asked if there wasn't something I might get for him, he told me that he was thirsty. I gave him a tiny cup of water from the sink next to his bed but remembered a soda machine near the nurses' station.

As he was still hooked up to the IV, I walked back down the hall and asked if he were allowed any soda. The folks at the nurses' station assured me that he could have anything he wanted, and pointed me toward the Coke machine. One nurse looked at her watch and said that his IV must be empty by now. She explained to me that the IV was just a saline drip, and that it was simply a precaution against dehydration in any trauma patient.

"You know"—she softly laughed as she accompanied me back to his bed, making a Groucho Marx cigar gesture as she walked—"it couldn't hoit."

I gave Teddy the Coke, opening the can and pouring some into the tiny plastic cup that came out of the dispenser next to the sink, as the nurse pulled the IV from his arm.

"Your mother's a piece a work," she said, winking.

"What do you mean?" he asked innocently, and maybe a little defensively.

She backed off. "Well, I mean . . . you know, she's a very strong gal, that mother a yours."

Teddy brightened as though she'd meant this as a compliment, though I rather doubted she had.

"What's wrong with her?" I asked.

"Hmmm. Has she had something in her life that's bothered her recently?"

Teddy's face reddened. He looked like a poster child for guilt. "Could this attack be brought on by something . . . umm . . . like, upsetting?" he asked.

The nurse's name tag read KIMBERLY UTZ RN, and she looked hard at Teddy and took her time thinking before she spoke.

"Her symptoms seemed acute but contradictory. And the severe pain appeared to come and go. Her color was good; the color of her nails and her lips and her gums was all very normal. And . . . the answers she gave us about her history and her symptoms were somewhat different from doctor to doctor. Her vocalization was, shall we say, extreme—and not at all what we usually see in patients experiencing cardiac episodes." Then the nurse looked at me and said. "And when she was out of her son's sphere"—she turned her gaze back to Teddy—"and out of your earshot, she stopped moaning and she began to give the doctors orders."

I looked at the floor and bit the inside of my lip to keep from smiling.

"What are you saying?" Teddy demanded. "Are you saying that she wasn't in *pain*? Are you saying that she was faking and that there is *nothing* wrong with my mother?" He was becoming agitated.

"I'm not. I'm not. We're doing tests. We're trying to find out if there is anything *physically* wrong with your mother. Sometimes symptoms of serious things really do come and go. And sometimes people are so upset and disoriented that they give answers that seem kind of mixed up. I'm just explaining to you why her symptoms and her behavior don't point to any clear diagnosis."

"Doesn't the aortic nerve run alongside the gallbladder?" I asked. "Couldn't a gallbladder attack bring on an episode of arrhythmia, for instance? Or shortness of breath or even pain?"

"Well . . ." She thought for a minute and apparently decided not to give me a full lesson in anatomy there in the emergency room. "But there was no sign of arrhythmia on her EKG and no tenderness around the gallbladder. But"—she brightened—"the X-rays and the blood workup will give us some more information."

Teddy looked puzzled and desolate. I asked to use the ladies' room, and she began to direct me and then said that as she had to go in that direction, she'd show me the way. As we walked from the room and down the hall, Kimberly Utz looked at me with a long, hard, leveling stare. "She's not your mother-in-law, is she?"

"No." I said. "No. *Jeepers.*" I made a kind of shiver gesture, I guess, because Kimberly Utz put her hand on my arm.

"She's playing that poor guy like a harp," she said. "You should have heard her go on about his fainting spell. No wonder he fainted." She shook her head. "Everything she did in that room was directed at him. She never looked at us." Kimberly Utz started laughing. "And when *he* went under, it seemed like she didn't want to answer us or say anything important that he couldn't hear."

I used the tiny bathroom with the specimen cups on the tank of the toilet and made my way back to Teddy. He was sitting, as I'd left him, on the bed with his legs over the side.

"What do you think, pal," I said. "Your mother is going to be upstairs for tests for a while, and they won't let her leave for at least an hour—until they have results. Should we go to that all-night diner down the road and get ourselves some green eggs and ham?"

"I don't know. I mean, I don't know if we should leave—"

"Teddy, we can't do anything here. I don't think they'll let us go upstairs where the X-rays and tests are done—especially when you fainted at the sight of the EKG machine." I was hoping to get a laugh or a smile out of him, but there was none available. "Let's ask the nurses and the doctors. If they think we'll be of help or be able to see her, we'll stay here. How about that?"

He picked up his jean jacket from the chair, found his cap, fallen under the bed, and put it on. We walked out to the nurses' station, and Kimberly was standing there with two other nurses and an Indian doctor who looked young enough to have a lemonade stand. They urged us to go out to eat, telling Teddy that they'd decided to do a GI series and it could easily take more than an hour, depending on the cases ahead of us. The Indian doctor asked us, with a laugh, to bring "samples" back from the diner.

"Why do you think they want to do a GI series?" Teddy asked me as we eased ourselves into the jade green leatherette booth at the diner. "What do they suspect is wrong?" He looked worried and almost panicked.

"I think they're just ruling stuff out," I said. "Deciding what it's not is just as important as deciding what it is, don't you think?"

"I guess so," Teddy said.

Because he was so upset, he only ordered the Milk Man's Early Bird

Breakfast instead of the Lumberjack's Breakfast Special. The fact that milk is no longer delivered to our door before dawn suddenly made sense to me. The Milk Men are dead. Four eggs, ham, bacon, hash browns, two flapjacks, a corn muffin with butter and jam, and coffee with cream. I started to point out to Teddy that I hadn't seen any lumberjacks either, as it's the breakfast described above with the addition of a twelve-ounce, chicken-fried steak. But I held my tongue and let him enjoy his food.

I had a bowl of oatmeal and a cup of tea. Teddy ate in relative silence. I pushed the idea of suggesting that his mother was simply faking it one way and then the other inside my mouth. I couldn't make it come out, and I couldn't swallow it. I couldn't think of any way to make it sound anything less than evil and manipulative. The truth was right there with us, sitting large in the middle of the booth on the Formica table with the sugar dispenser and the salt with the rice grains. I knew I had to avoid it, so I nervously told Teddy a story about how my mother hated hot cereal and how we'd never had it at home and I hadn't tasted it until I got to Wellesley. I told him how I so fell in love with oatmeal that I asked Frederick Jamesborough Beckan III, a rugby player from Cornell, who clearly had a nicer place in mind, to take me, instead, to a diner on our first date, so that I could eat oatmeal. FJB3 told me that I was the cheapest date he'd ever hosted, and it became a kind of joke with us. I was, literally, his "cheap date."

Teddy looked up at me but didn't crack a smile. Finally he said, "Your mother *never* made you oatmeal? My mother makes me oatmeal every Sunday morning between Masses, all winter long. All winter."

How are you going to compete with that? I thought.

CHAPTER 30

The time was a quarter past twelve. Officially it was Valentine's Day. We went back to the hospital carrying six portions of French fries, three chocolate ice cream sodas, two Cherry Coke floats and two Brown Cows. Teddy had also grabbed two Whitman Samplers with big red bows and little glittery hearts on wires that had been displayed near the cashier. One was for the staff, he explained, and one was for his mother. The idea of giving her a box of candies with nuts and creams after what might have been a gallbladder attack seemed like fuzzy logic at best, but I said nothing.

We walked in and sailed past the triage nurse, as though we owned the hospital. I didn't even make eye contact. Maureen was being pushed down the hall in a wheelchair just as we came through the corridor. Our arms were full of boxes holding upright cups and cones of fries. The bag of chocolates dangled from Teddy's wrist. He smiled at his mother, and she glared at us.

"Where have you been!" she demanded.

Teddy looked stricken. "Ma," he said, "have you been down here long?"

The doctor interceded, reading the scene. "No, no. We're just bringing your mother back this very minute. Your timing is excellent."

"You left me waitin' up there in a very cold hall," Maureen complained, "for at least twenty minutes. Someone was to come and get me. I asked for my son, and no one came. I was very cold!"

The doctor looked at his watch and said with some kindness directed at Teddy, "The test was over just about seven minutes ago."

"Was not," said Maureen. "I know how long you left me sittin' there.

I'm not an idiot." She looked disgusted, like someone who couldn't bear the sight of any of us.

Teddy and I stood motionless, eyes wide, mouths slack, like kids about to be spanked. Kimberly Utz came around from behind the desk and broke the silence with forced good humor.

"Are these for us? How wonderful! Tell me what we have here." She addressed us in a practiced, careful singsong voice, as though speaking to the children we must have been imitating.

I snapped out of my stupor and made sure I spoke in my college-professor voice, deep, resonant and directive—about junk food.

"Fries, obviously. Brown Cows," I said. "Chocolate ice cream sodas, two Cherry Coke floats. We thought there were six of you—at least that's what we counted when we left. And we figured, one extra, in case we counted wrong."

But the labels didn't seem to add up to what we ordered. We pulled off the lids and could see that one chocolate soda was labeled incorrectly as a Brown Cow. Problem solved. This took a good amount of time and distracted me long enough from Maureen Hennessy until the idea of strangling her, in full view of people capable of saving her life, passed.

The French fries were gobbled up by the crew with what we used to call, as kids, "yummy noises." The main attraction was the distribution of the drinks, as the staff negotiated for their favorites. Maureen was getting fidgety, not being the center of attention, and Teddy was looking lost once more.

If I didn't already know it, it was now obvious to me, that at one o'clock in the morning, when you've been on duty since six o'clock in the evening, French fries and ice cream take on an almost transcendental importance. The staff was lost in the treats. Their patients might have burst spontaneously into flame, and I'm not sure they would have taken any heed.

I held on to my professor's voice. "Okay," I said. "What is happening here, with Mrs. Hennessy?" They looked up, fries poking out of their lips like snaggle teeth. The Indian doctor had a ring of vanilla cream around his mouth. "Mrs. Hennessy can go home," he said, turning back to his Brown Cow. Funny, I thought, the Indian doctor is drinking a Brown Cow.

"But what has happened? What do we need to know to care for her?" As if on cue, they raised their eyes to give me level stares, held them for a moment, as if fraught with meaning, and then dropped them back to their fries and drinks. "Guys?" I was dropping the professor stuff and pleading now.

The Indian doctor, Rajiv, took pity on me and stopped eating long enough to explain. "Mrs. Hennessy experienced an episode of pain for which we can find no origin. Her vital signs are good. In fact, they are excellent. Her blood work is good; there is no sign of infection or any raised numbers in her white count. Her enzyme work is perfectly normal. Her gallbladder is not, apparently, inflamed. Her heart is sound. Her lungs are clear. The X-rays showed us no abnormalities. Her GI series was perfectly normal, in fact, excellent for a woman of her age."

He looked at her chart as he continued, "She might have had a bad reaction to something she ate, causing some gas to expand in her GI tract and give her discomfort, but we could get no direction from her about the possibility of any food that might not have agreed with her." He smiled at me and then smiled at Maureen, who looked away again.

"She is in no apparent danger and she doesn't need to stay here in the hospital, but you should watch for symptoms, and if the pains return, I think she should see a gastroenterologist. He may be able to pinpoint something we can't easily see. We can make recommendations for doctors who specialize in this field."

Maureen looked at him through narrowed, angry eyes. "We don't need your recommendations," she said curtly. "Just because you weren't smart enough to figure it out with all your fancy equipment and your pokin' and proddin'." I rolled my eyes, and Rajiv and Kimberly smiled. But Teddy saw me do it, and he looked at me through a cloud of storms.

Kimberly Utz offered the information that Maureen's clothes were still in the treatment area where we'd been, and she began to push Maureen toward that alcove while suggesting that Teddy might want to get the car and that I could help Maureen dress. I was going to suggest that I get the car, but I could see that Teddy did not want to deal with dressing his mother and I couldn't blame him.

As we entered the curtained zone, Maureen saw her handbag, sitting on the chair. "Jesus, Mary and Joseph," she said, turning to Teddy. "Did you just leave my bag here for all and some to take? What's the *matter* with you! Do you ever *think*? Where is your head! Anyone could just take the bag—just sittin' there—for God's sake! Look in the bag, look in the bag—have they taken my wallet?" Kimberly Utz looked at me, her eyes widening. "Count the cash. Count it. There was more than fifty dollars in there. *Count* it!" Teddy did so and found nearly eighty dollars.

"Perhaps someone came in and added some cash," I offered. No response.

"Get the car." She dismissed Teddy like a potentate shooing away a serf. Kimberly Utz helped Maureen out of the wheelchair, and I found her bra and her panties and her pantyhose and held them out to her. She snatched them out of my hand and put them on the bed. Someone had buttoned the cardigan sweater, or maybe she'd brought it buttoned, as a hedge against the cold. I figured she would need it tonight, and unbuttoning it gave me something to do. She put on her navy slacks and a white turtleneck with ladybugs on the folded collar. I had her navy and red cardigan nearly unbuttoned.

Kimberly Utz left us alone to go and prepare the discharge papers. Maureen was sitting on the beige vinyl chair, tying her shoes, and turned away from me when she began to speak. I could barely hear her and had to lean down, crouching on my heels, near her chair. "I know that I put too much pressure on Teddy. He's been everything to me," she said, "a husband and a son and a maintenance man and a chauffeur. I know that I've kept him from having a normal life." I waited. To my surprise she said, "I know that I have been very unfair to him."

She offered no excuse. *Wait* a minute, I thought. This is a breakthrough. I teach literature. I knew how often, after a brush with mortality, a character sees how wrong she's been. It seemed kind of quick, though. If there had been a moment of soul searching or revelation between the gasping for breath and the insight, it was lost on me. But maybe this is the way these kinds of things happen in real life. I only knew these moments from books.

I put my hand on her arm. Her face was still turned down toward her shoe and away from me. "I think your seeing this so clearly is wonderful," I said. "It's a breakthrough. Real change can't happen until you recognize the mistake. That's a great first step." I tried to be kind and supportive instead of buying into her idea of beating herself up. Apparently I was wrong.

"Where did you get the idea"—she turned to me, her face red from her position and her attitude—"that I had any intention of changin' it?" She looked right into my eyes.

I could feel my mouth open. I could think of nothing to say.

Teddy came back into the hospital with the Whitman Sampler. The little wired glitter hearts danced above the bow like fruit flies. As Maureen was being wheeled past the desk by the orderly, she eyed the box of chocolates for which Kimberly Utz and company were thanking us, and she looked up at Teddy accusingly. "You bought Valentine candy for *them*—and not your own mother?"

"I got some for you, Ma!" Teddy said, good-naturedly. "It's in the car. Could I forget my best girl?"

The orderly rolled Maureen out to the parking lot, steered her to the backseat and opened the door. Maureen stood up emphatically from the wheelchair and walked around behind him, opened the front passenger door and got in. Teddy was already in my driver's seat. I stood for a moment at the passenger side of the car and then got into the backseat.

"I'll get you home, Ma," Teddy said, "and then I'll take Joy back to her house."

"No," said Maureen. "I shouldn't be alone after this. You heard the doctor. We need to watch for symptoms."

"But this is Joy's car, Ma—"

"Well, that wasn't very bright of you, was it? How did you think I was goin' to get home?"

"We were just concerned with getting to the hospital quickly," I tossed in, hoping to avoid the subject of Teddy's drinking or smoking pot. Maureen ignored me.

"Where is your car?" she asked. Teddy told her that it was parked at my house, and Maureen engineered a plan that had us taking my car home, with the two of them changing cars and heading back to the Hennessy house.

"But your house is on the way home from the hospital," I said. "Shouldn't we get you home and comfortable?"

"We'll change cars," Maureen said. "It's not a big problem. I only wish you'd thought about it first."

CHAPTER 31

Valentine's Day went according to plan, if your plans had been drawn by Rube Goldberg. The amount of coordination required was almost beyond human, but at a quarter to five in the afternoon, only fifteen minutes off schedule, I stood in Josie's kitchen with Dan, and the phone call came in telling us that indeed the coast was clear for the two Fortunata girls to return home. Lizzie and Jackie wanted to come with us. They wanted to hold on to their extended family, they wanted to see Donna, and, let's face it, they wanted to be part of the festivities; they were their mother's daughters, after all. But Dan's common sense prevailed, and we packed my car to the windows with an impossible cache of totes and books and dolls and stuffed animals and sleeping bags and favorite pillows and paper sacks full of art and craft projects. Josie had taken the lion's share of the girls' clean clothes and materials back to the house days before and installed it all in closets and drawers. My load, I understood, was merely the overflow.

Donna was sitting up on the living room couch, wearing a tiny pink velour warm-up suit, which the girls squealed and branded as "Juicy Couture" or something equally amusing. She looked tired but very happy. Her hair was newly short and a little darker than I remembered it being. A cane was perched on the ottoman. Catsup and I emptied the car in a hundred or so trips, and I have to say he looked up to the challenge ahead; sprightly as a bridegroom with energy to spare. He'll need it, I thought.

We found the Valentine cards with near hysteria, amid the bags and clutter, and presented them to an appreciative audience. I was offered a comfortable seat and a drink, but knew that I should not postpone the beginning of their life together by one more moment. Marta and Ava were on the couch with their mother, like kittens with a mother cat. Ava's head was on Donna's knee, and Donna was scratching Marta's arm. The girls got up and hugged and kissed me in a polite and proper way, turning back quickly to join their mother. My protests notwithstanding, Allen walked me to my car but could barely take his eyes off the front door of Donna's house as he deposited me into the driver's seat. He was back up the steps of their landing and into the living room before I'd even put the car in gear. I left the Catsup-Fortunata family holding on to one another, as they say, "for dear life."

I started to drive to Josie's, but it made no sense. My time there was finished, at least in regard to this family crisis. I turned the car around and headed home. My house was quiet. If Teddy had been there, he'd left no lights on. There was nothing in the fridge except bags of coffee, jars of mustards and pickles, a six-pack of beer and the big white box with the meringue Pavlova. I called Josie, as promised, and gave her the rundown: the girls were home, safe and sound, and all was well at Donna's.

I changed from my school clothes into a pair of corduroy pants, a big turtleneck sweater and topsiders and headed out to the Stop and Shop. On the way, I approached the road that led to Teddy's house. I turned onto it and let the car take me to the Hennessys', pretending it was the car's doing, not mine. My hands got hot on the steering wheel as I made the decision to drop in, uninvited. I pulled onto their street remembering the day I stopped at Will's the afternoon of the Viennese pastries. I blushed when I thought of my naïveté. I blushed when I thought of my own humiliation at finally adding up all of the pieces. And, as though it were in the same column, I blushed when I thought of my performing such a forward act as "just dropping in" on anyone. History suggested that spontaneous gestures were not my strong point; still, I parked in front of the Hennessy house and waited until my courage was high enough to walk to the door. If I hadn't been so nervous, I might have realized that Teddy's Subaru wasn't parked in the driveway.

Maureen answered the door and stood there, just as she had done when I'd first met her, the day of her faux Thanksgiving. She looked remarkably well for a woman who'd survived a self-described "near-death attack" only the night before. She was wearing a beige tunic sweater with little fringe balls at the hem, white knit pants and gray suede moccasins. Her makeup was brightly applied, and she wore a pin of white and gray pearls at her shoulder. I didn't let her keep me standing on the front step but edged past into the living room, where an ironing board was set up and a television tuned to an old broadcast of *The Hollywood Squares* on the Nostalgia Network.

Maureen stood for a moment in the middle of the room, recognizing that she'd lost some control. I didn't speak. Without being invited, I sat on one of two upholstered blue chairs facing the ironing board. The other chair held a languid cat with brown stripes. The cat rolled over on its spine, its head dropped backward over the seat cushion, and it looked at me upside down, as Ingrid Bergman spies Cary Grant in *Notorious*. The laugh track from *Hollywood Squares* howled.

A pile of ironed clothes was balanced on the seat of a wooden chair, and a basket at the end of the board held wrinkled garments due to be pressed into submission by Maureen. She returned to the board and picked up the television's remote control, switching on the mute button but leaving the picture, so that through my visit, close-ups of Rose Marie, Robert Goulet and Paul Lynde punctuated every emotional note.

I asked her how she felt and told her that she looked well. In fact, she looked annoyed and attended to the ironing of Teddy's Happy Face boxer shorts with an intense concentration, grim enough to suggest the manufacturing of land mines. She said nothing. Rather than sit in silence and reluctant to jump headlong into the subject of Teddy, I made another attempt at neutral small talk. I complimented her on her pin.

"Joan Rivers" was all she offered, and she said the name like a curse. I had no idea what she meant or what the connection between a comedienne and Maureen might be. I was going to ask if it was possible that Joan Rivers had given the pin to Maureen, when another idea occurred to me.

"That's a pretty cat you have there," I said, leaning over to pet its fur and moving my hand away just in time to avoid the hissing, full claw attack.

"That's my Pussy," she said without irony.

"Ahh-ha," I responded, deciding there was no safe haven along the trail my thoughts were traveling.

I was out of tricks. I took a deep breath. I cleared my throat. I tried to think of myself as someone who was comfortable with human emotion and fully prepared to confront a difficult subject that was not based on scholarship or intellectual pretension. I climbed up the tower of disclosure and leaped.

"Maureen," I said, "I've come to talk about Teddy. It's time we had some understanding about this." I had my full professor's voice on again, and it was working fine—resonant and solid—but my hands were trembling as though I'd had a dozen cups of espresso. I grasped my left wrist with my right hand and steadied myself.

"Teddy is an artist locked in the body of a handyman," I began. "He has an enormous gift, and he should share that gift with as many people as he can touch. If he can get his master's and teach and write, he'll have a chance to serve on landmark boards, to supervise restoration projects and to influence hundreds of students to *see* the world of restored-residential architecture and its management as *he* does—a living thing—*based* in history but informed and enhanced by progress and technology."

That was it. That was my speech. I'd been thinking about saying this to Maureen for days, maybe months, and now I'd said it. And somewhere inside of me, I'd expected her to be bowled over and to capitulate and say, "Well, I see your very good point and I endorse it," but I saw nothing like that on her face. Quite the opposite. Her mouth was a tight, flat line. She didn't acknowledge my presence but looked only at her ironing. I was plumb out of ideas when I remembered Josie's strategy.

"Maureen," I said, "I know you love Teddy, and I know you want what you think is best for him. I can only imagine what a mother might want for her child, but—"

I'd barely gotten the thought from my lips when she turned on me, spewing her words like splinters from a chipper, and everything Teddy had said in anger to me became clear. "How would *you* know anything about what a *mother* feels?" she said. "You have no track record, my dear. You are not exactly a mother's dream for her boy, y'know. You haven't been able to make a go of a single human relationship, far as I can see. Teddy tells me you weren't even close to your own parents! I have no illusions about your ability to care for or about my son." She looked at me as though I were someone caught stealing a loaf of bread. Maureen

Hennessy set her jaw in a most aggressive way. "You're too old," she spat, "to have your own child . . . and you want mine, but . . . you're not . . . goin' ta get him."

I looked at the baby-blue wall-to-wall carpet, looked at the yawning cat, looked at Paul Lynde, and I opened my mouth and found myself talking from a hollow place of honesty and damage. It was unfamiliar territory, this confessional, but I told her how lost I'd been and that Teddy had shown me how to live in my own house and, therefore, in my own skin. He'd been kind and generous, sharing his gifts in ways that were gentle and yet insistent on my growth. I talked about myself to her—a stranger and an enemy—with an openness I'd attempted only once before with one other person, her own son. I was laid out. She said nothing, but she didn't interrupt and she didn't stop sprinkling the clothes and pressing out their wrinkles and folding them next to one another.

I talked about Teddy. He had been the adult, not the child, in so much he had given to me. Teddy was not a boy, I said. No amount of wishing that he could go back would make him a child again. But no amount of hoping he could move ahead on this trail would work without the support of those of us who cared enough about him to help to light the way. "He's trapped," I said. "He can't move ahead, and he can't go back." If she loved him, wouldn't she help him to grow up? Didn't she know that she wouldn't be around forever—and that someday, sooner or later, his chances to grow and thrive might have passed?

Tears were running down my face. I made no attempt to stop them. I looked up and saw what I'd hoped to see: tears in her eyes.

But she said, "What about me? What about *my* chances?"

I was completely unprepared.

"I moved here with my family from Ireland in 1942," she said, turning off the iron and carefully placing it on its metal rack. "I was five years old. My father caught tuberculosis on the ship. He was almost dead by the time we got to Boston. My mother was in service on Brattle Street. We lived in the back room of a cousin's apartment—no windows, no fresh air. My sisters and my father and me in one filthy room, my father dyin' in bits, day by day. Finally dead, to be found by my sisters and me one morning; his chin covered with blood, his body stinking. Our cousins wouldn't touch him, and they wouldn't touch us. They made us sit in the room with him all day until the undertakers came, wearin' 'ker-chiefs tied 'round their faces. We had to be looked at by doctors before we could leave the room. We had no wake, and we attended no funeral Mass for my father. We just waited in the room for five days. They left food outside the door. We were supposed to thank them for that."

Her accent moved from South Boston to Irish as she spoke. She closed her eyes and paused, clearly in pain. I opened my mouth to speak to her, and I made an odd involuntary little squeak—not a word exactly, but the intent of a word. Certainly not comfort, but the intent of com-fort. She raised her hand to stop me.

"My mother worked as a maid for a family in Cambridge and only came to see us on Sundays. Theresa acted as our mother. She was only eleven years old. She dressed me each morning and sent me and Brigid and Frances to school and picked us up after to walk us home. I never had a new pair of shoes. I had to fit my feet into their hand-me-down, broken old shoes, and it ruined my feet. I still have pain." She turned her ankle around as if to illustrate the point, but all I could see was a slender foot in a gray suede moccasin.

"Soon as I was old enough, twelve or thirteen, all of us girls, we was sent out to work as maids together in a big house on Newbury Street. We lied about our age. We scrubbed the steps a rich people—people like you—people with education and heads full a ideas. And the people like you didn't even see us down on our knees on your stairs. We went home on weekends to the same dirty room, now all full a women—to sleep, five of us in two beds, and cook dinner on a hot plate and carry our dishes down the hall to our cousin's slop sink. We would find ourselves wishin' to be off again on Monday mornin', back in the homes of employers who barely knew our names, back to cleanin' their shoes and washin' out their underwear and scrubbin' the filth off of their sheets.

"We had the church on Sunday, and that's all we had. But we saved our money, and we all saved it the same—and by the time I was nineteen we'd saved enough to buy a little house in South Boston. We rented the first floor out as an apartment, and we lived on the second floor. We still worked, but we had a place of our own to come home to. I had a room of my own. I met my husband, and he went to college at night. Everyone was so proud that I would marry a college-educated man. I finally thought that somethin' would go right for me. I finally thought I might get to be happy. So John moves into our house, we take the apartment on the first floor, and he gets a job with Boston Life—but he was moody and strange, John was. Kept it all inside. He never really got me. Never really saw me, I don't think. I don't know what that man wanted, but it wasn't me.

"Joey was born—miserable birth—but *never* was a baby more loved. He had me and John and Theresa and Brigid and Frances and my blessed mother to love him. But soon after he was born, my mother comes down with the cancer, and for six years I nurse her and try to care for my little baby at the same time. Everyone else is gone for the week or out for the day, and I'm trapped with a cryin' child and a dyin' old woman."

Melodrama on paper barely wounds; a paper cut rather than a stab in the gut. How is it then that pathos in real life, brimming with self-pity, can be so affecting? I could see her scrubbing the stairs with the Aunts, the little girls who would grow up to become the Witches of Amherst. My heart ached for her. And she was the sister who'd made it.

"And then I'm pregnant with Teddy, and John is growin' in his job, and they want to transfer him here to Amherst, and we see our way out of the house. We just walk away from it, leave it to the girls; don't take a penny for what we've put in. For a few years it looked as though it might be all right. The insurance company stakes us for the mortgage and pays the dues to the country club, and I can finally have some nice things and Joe is growin' up a fine boy, smart and good—and finally—old enough to go to the seminary. What we planned all along. And then he comes home! Just like that. He says he doesn't like it. Like it? *Like it?* Who gets what they like in this life? we says. Who do you think you are to like it or not? says his father. And everybody knows, and our life is one big disgrace. Our glory lost. Nothin' but shame he brought on us."

Maureen stepped out around the ironing board into the center of the living room, and I wondered if the tale was over, but she picked up the Pyrex measuring jug from the ironing board and began to water the plants on the windowsill as she spoke. She never looked at me. "And John, one night, gets his self in an uproar. Joey is damned disrespectful, and his father—he just explodes. All the years of holdin' it in, all the years of drinkin' his self to sleep and not talkin' about what he's think-in'—it all comes out like an explosion of somethin' rotten. And he's fumin' about his family and his life in front of us and how much he hates everything and how this son a his, this one hope—is nothin' but shite!'"

I realized that none of Maureen's rant was, exactly, directed at me. She was just talking as though she were in a bubble. And she sat down on the sofa, exhausted from the performance or the memory. "And Joey leaves, and John sits down and pours his self a drink, and I turn on the television, and John says to me, 'I don't feel so good.' And I look at him, and he's gray. Gray like death. And he says his chest hurts, and he puts his hand up to his chest and says the pain is bad. So I call the hospital and we take him there, and they pull him through, but he's never the same. He doesn't want to go back to work. He doesn't want to go to church or play golf. He just wants to sit there and show us all how we've let him down."

And then Maureen looked at me. "So I guess you know the rest. Joey goes to the army and comes back, and he's kilt in a car accident. John finally passes—though he'd been dead for years. But"—she looks at me hard—"I'd been their servant. I cooked their meals and I scrubbed their floors, like they was the rich people I worked for. And they hardly knew my name. John didn't talk to me. Joey didn't talk to me. Only Teddy. Only Teddy would come in and tell me how was school. Or where he went with Joey. He brought me things he made in woodworking class. He brought me candlesticks—I still have them here." She looked around the room to see if they were close enough to point out. Apparently not. But it didn't seem to register with her that this was the first moment she'd uttered Teddy's name, beyond the mention of her pregnancy.

"He's a fragile boy," she said. "He never got over his brother's death. He clings to me, and I know how to care for him. I manage his business, I keep his books and pay his bills and do his taxes. I cook his favorite things. I keep his room."

She looked angry now. "You can't promise to do those things for him. You have your *own* life. A life that has never had room for anyone else but your own selfish self. You buy yourself foreign cars and books and a big house. You have the money to spend on whatever you want; you hire Teddy and then look down on him, like bein' a handyman and a carpenter isn't good enough for you. You hired him. He was good enough for that, wasn't he?"

We both heard the car pull into the driveway. My eyes were long dry, but Maureen's cheeks were still damp and her eyes were swollen and red. She stood up. I shuffled through my bag for a handkerchief to pass to her, but she rejected it, turned away and looked at the door. Teddy came in full of smiles, saw Maureen and his face turned hard. She burst into tears and ran from the room.

"What did you *say* to her!" he demanded. I sputtered something inane. "She's not well," he said. "You know that! What were you *thinking*?!" He did that odd, fast walk-around-the-room-caged-animal-walk thing he sometimes did when he was very excited or agitated. His face was red. He looked down the hall toward her bedroom. "You better leave," he said.

"Teddy," I started, "I was just—"

"Just *leave* and let me deal with this. I'll call you. I'll call you, man."

He called me "man" and he bustled me to the door, and I was out on the front step before I knew what hit me. I drove home, walked into the kitchen, opened the fridge, took out the box and threw the Pavlova into the garbage.

CHAPTER 32

I woke the next morning to a telephone ring and hoped, in some half-conscious way, that it might be Teddy. I'd obviously slept fitfully as the covers were in a knot around my shoulders, and I pushed them aside in one huge clot to get to the phone before the voice mail clicked in. Through the handset, a woman babbled in a rushed and giddy way. It took a moment to clear my mind and a moment more to register, through my sleepy haze, that the voice was, indeed, familiar but the attitude and content were alien, when suddenly I identified my old friend from New York, Laura Grant.

"Hold on a minute, Laura," I said. "Hold on. Could you start again—from the beginning?"

She laughed. "Oh, I *know*." She was breathless. "I know how excited I am and I know it makes almost no sense, but it *is* exciting. It is. And I think you really were the beginning of it all . . ."

I was officially lost. "Okay," I allowed, in that conditional way, as if I were waiting to hear something I understood.

"No, no," she said, clearly getting herself under control. "I'll start at the *very* beginning. It's the only way it will make sense." She took a good long breath. "Adele and I speak every few years, at *least*—whenever we have an important paper published—at an annual conference of Civil War historians. We've been doing this for almost thirty years. And for almost all of that time, I've had a correspondence with a man—a history teacher from a small college in Pennsylvania, near Chadds Ford. He would send me a paper he'd read that he thought Adele and I should see. Or he'd write a review of a book—and sometimes not a new book—just his own personal take on a book he thought we should know. I'd hear from him maybe twice a year. And I would send *him* things that I thought *he* would appreciate. And I would see him—not every time, but *most* of the time—when we went to those conferences. Once a year—for more than twenty-five years . . ."

Laura was babbling along as fast as her lips would travel, and her story seemed to be going down a long, circuitous road that, if not dangerous, was certainly not the most direct route to the point. It was a little like following my mother's stories. I remembered how she would take off on a tangent, and we'd be running after her, trying to follow her line of thought. "Peggy," my father would say, huffing and harrumphing, "get this train back on the track!" But I didn't interrupt Laura; I just let her steam on.

"Sometimes he would come to New York," Laura continued, "and we'd talk on the phone or meet for lunch, and I'd invite Adele to come along with us. Once he came up to the city with his class—and they stayed at the Gramercy Park Hotel, and I met him for breakfast at the National Arts Club.

"He—Charlie, that's his name, Charlie—was married, I think *very* happily, to another teacher, and he had two children—a son and a daughter—and they both became doctors. Through the years I heard all about them—all through their high schools and colleges and medical schools. So, I suppose you could say that we had a *kind* of personal relationship, but we were professional friends. I don't think I ever let myself think of him as a *man,* if you know what I mean. Not *romantically,* you know. He was a *friend,* and I *liked* him. I shook his *hand* when I saw him. We were two professionals, after all, not man and woman. I have *many* male friends—well, I would, as a historian. But the truth was—though I wouldn't admit it to myself—that through the years, when I knew I would be seeing him or when I would see *his* handwriting on an envelope, my heart would, sort of, race. Adele knew. She called him my 'suitor,' and I would always laugh and say she was crazy!"

"Laura," I said, "are you telling me what I think you're telling me?"

"Now don't interrupt," she commanded. "I'm telling you the whole story—just like I said I would. This man—his name is Charles, Charlie Lantzman—started to e-mail me a few years ago, when we all first got into e-mail. And the *relationship* wasn't any different, I thought. It was just that the contact was more *frequent.*

"But something happened this Christmas, when you called to say that you were getting married. And, Joy, I don't bring this up to hurt you or remind you of something lost. You know that, dear, don't you?"

"Oh yes, Laura," I said. "Of course. But . . . go on . . . really . . ."

She was still out of breath and talking like a teenager. "Well, I found myself writing to him about your dilemma, what one should do and where one would find information about a wedding if one were not *young*—just as you posed it. And I told him how excited I was for you and how unlikely it was that anyone would find love at our age. I mean, I know that you are younger, but I told him how, upon hearing your news, *I felt* newly young and full of hope—for the first time in a long time. Writing this to him—or anyone—was *most* unlike me. It was not like me at *all*. And *he* wrote back this incredible letter about the death of his wife *four years* ago. Four *years*! I was his friend, and I hadn't even *known*.

"He wrote that he'd been so depressed, and that he visited her grave every day until just this past October, when it was, he said, as though he woke from a dream—and decided that he needed to choose *life* and be a part of the living world.

"He wrote to me that he *knew* his wife would want him to live. If the tables were turned, he said, he would want her to do the same. And suddenly he was comfortable and optimistic—after years of depression. He was over the grieving. He knew that he was *still* alive and there were things to do and places to go—and, he said, he was going to go to them all!"

She sighed, took another deep breath and continued. "I had *just* finished reading his letter when the phone rang—and it was Charlie! I could hardly *speak* to him. I was nervous and shy with a man I'd known for near on thirty years!

"He asked if he could come up to New York and take me to dinner, and I said yes! I said *yes*, Joy! And I *didn't* bring Adele along. I bought new *shoes*. Pretty, sling-backed, *high-heeled* shoes!"

I couldn't imagine Laura wearing anything as impractical as sling-backed heels. And I'd certainly never thought of Laura as having any-thing that even resembled sex appeal. This was a stunning story.

"We went to dinner at the Four Seasons—can you imagine that?" She was now at a pitched peak, I thought, but there was more to come. "And he came back up to New York the next weekend and the *next*. And then we were walking around Rockefeller Plaza this past Sunday—in the rain—and it was right before Valentine's Day. You know, don't you, that Valentine's Day was yesterday? I mean, there were years when it would go by and *I* wouldn't take *any* notice." She didn't wait for my answer.

"Anyway . . . He took a box out of his pocket, and in it was a ruby ring with diamonds! Diamonds! And he said—and this is *exactly* what he said—'I'd like you to marry me and I'd like you to accept this ring as an engagement ring, but if you won't or you can't, then I hope you will still accept this ring as a Valentine's present.' That's what he said!

"And I must have been in shock because *I* said, 'But Charlie, Valentine's Day isn't until *Tuesday*!' And *he* said, 'I've taken a room at the Waldorf and I'm *staying* until Tuesday, and I hope you will stay with me.' And Joy, I *did*! I stayed there, and he's *still here*—and we're getting married on Saturday!"

"What? *This* Saturday?"

"Yes—at Saint Bartholomew's on Park Avenue. And I want you there. Actually, I'm hoping you'll be my bridesmaid. Adele will be my maid of honor, of course. You don't have to wear a bridesmaid's dress or anything *fussy*—but please, Joy, can you come?"

"Of course," I said. "Of course!" And I was happy for her. Really thrilled. I was delighted.

"I'm wearing a Carolina Herrera cream-colored, silk-chiffon dress. Knee length," Laura said, as though she said things like this all the time.

I was astounded. "You *are*?"

"Yes. Charlie took me to Bergdorf Goodman. Have you ever been in there? Do you know how much those dresses *cost*? It's incredible. But he says he has more than enough money, and after all, this is my one and only wedding gown! Adele is wearing a dress and jacket. It's a kind of olive green silk. I thought she should find something a little brighter, but it's quite pretty and she'll certainly be able to wear it other places. You know how *careful* she is, though God knows why—she has a fortune stashed away from our grandparents—*and* our aunt and uncle, and she has the first *dollar* she ever made."

I ignored that. "Do you want me to wear something *particular*?" I asked, hoping against hope that she'd suggest something in gray flannel.

"Oh yes!" she answered, and my heart sank. "Something *pretty* and not black or gray or navy. Do you own anything that's not black or gray or navy? I couldn't *think* of anything you'd ever worn in a *real* color!"

"I'll find something," I said, "don't worry. This is wonderful news. Now just tell me where to be and when."

She shared the plans. We were to meet at the Waldorf at noon and change our clothes and walk across the street to Saint Bartholomew's at two thirty. The wedding would be at three o'clock, and then we'd all go back to the Waldorf for a cocktail buffet in one of the small reception rooms.

"You've decided all of this since Sunday? You made these plans this fast? You found a dress and a florist and a church and a hotel that could accommodate you with no notice?"

"Yes, of course. This is *New York,*" she said, as though people do things like this all the time in New York.

My head was a jumble. I was wondering what I could wear to the wedding and whether I really had to shop. But I *knew* I had to shop; there was no way around this. I remembered Will promising to pick out my wedding outfit. Would he have known how to dress me? Did I have any style at all? I was thinking of Donna in her tiny warm-up suits and Catsup in his heathery tweeds, Bernadette in her soft watercolors and vintage prints and Dan and Josie in their jewel-colored cashmere sweaters and their Hermès and Missoni scarves. They all had clothes that represented them, clothes that looked like them. I had clothes that were comfortable and didn't show stains. Maybe these *were* the clothes that fit my personality, I thought glumly.

I needed new skills. So I pretended that my life was an upcoming lecture and that this was something I needed to know how to pull into line. Remarkably, it worked. First things first: reserve a room for Saturday night in New York. I called the Waldorf, expecting to be met with a fully booked hotel at this late notice, but when I mentioned the Grant-Lantzman wedding, I was given a room without hesitation on the same floor as "the bride."

I called Bernadette to see if I could move our meeting from Friday, as it was the only time on my calendar I could shop. I alluded to yet one more personal responsibility and apologized. Bernadette wanted to know everything, and I hesitated telling her that I was postponing professional responsibilities in order to make time for clothes shopping. But the truth won out, and Bernadette whooped at the news. She, in fact, knew the Grant Girls—more by reputation than friendship—and she was delighted. There was an outlet center, she said, not too far away in Vermont. She would take me there on Friday, and we could talk about Wharton and James and Shakespeare in the car. "There's no reason why we can't do everything," she said, calling it a field trip.

Thursday was a blur. I had a full day of classes, and I was still playing catch-up for the time I'd lost meeting the changing needs of the Fortunata crisis. But on this Thursday, and it seemed forever more, I was free to reenter my life. Things were supposed to return to normal now.

Josie was back in her office, at least theoretically. I hadn't seen her all day. Martine was our assistant-of-the-week. She had considerably fewer piercings than Anita, the heavy-breasted Bohemian we'd had the week before, whose ill-considered, cleavage-baring, V-necked top revealed the tattooed tail of some exotic creature who'd fallen into the gulch.

Anita had confided in Josie that along with her eyebrow, her tongue and her lower lip, her clitoris had been pierced, and Josie could hardly wait to spread the word. "Why do you think anyone would do that?" Josie asked us at dinner that night.

"How, in God's name," I asked, "did this come up in conversation?" Dan nearly choked on his snow peas.

"What's a critoris?" asked Lizzie, and Jackie looked as though she were actually going to pass out.

"I'll tell you later," she said to Lizzie under her breath.

We never did decide the function of the clit-piercing, though Dan seemed to have some ideas he was going to share with Josie later that night and Catsup said that at the hospital he was seeing a lot of sexual piercing on the most middle-class, normal-looking folks. I decided that Philip Barry's line from *The Philadelphia Story* was the one to hold on to: "The time to make your mind up about people is never."

So, though I have to admit that I *wondered* if Martine, a sweet little blonde with what looked like a bull's lead in her nose, also had a chain-link fence in her pants, I was determined to keep the subject out of our conversation. She offered not a hint and proved to be efficient and cheerful, two characteristics I'd begun to believe were mutually exclusive in office assistants.

There was no call from Teddy, but it wasn't until I was home and sitting at my dining room table that it really hit me. I had spent almost no time in this house by myself. Teddy had been here, for the most part, at some point nearly every day. Our evening meals and our weekend breaks had been shared since the beginning of the school year, when we were nothing more than handyman-carpenter and homeowner. They continued as we became friends, and since the fall of Will, I'd had few nights on my own, and they were understood to be exceptions. Teddy and I had come to this kind of arrangement without ever talking about it. And now I knew that if I didn't take the next steps carefully, I could lose Teddy. I thought, maybe too egotistically, even Teddy could lose Teddy if I wasn't careful.

I had a folder of papers to grade, and the work went quickly and well. The students were bright, and they wrote with feeling and some skill, surprisingly better, I thought, than had my students at Columbia. Then again, between here and Columbia, as I'd begun to accept, everything was different. I was different. The world looked different here.

Had I really understood how the world had become unlike everything before? How much of it was internal and how much was outside of myself? I longed for some clarity and wished someone would invent one of those Day Star programs for human life. The disembodied voice, which sounds to me like a spy named Ursula, tells you not only to "take the next left" but to "trust the next person" and "avoid the man in the plaid jacket."

CHAPTER 33

I ate a banana for dinner. Without Teddy here, will I fall back into my old patterns? I wondered. There were nights in New York when I would lie in bed and think, Did I eat today? Of course those times were balanced by the times I would order a pizza and eat the whole thing all by myself.

In New York you don't realize the toll of the hike across campus, the windy run to the subway and the long walk to Riverside. You don't count the four flights to your apartment as exercise. Here in Massachusetts, everyone drives everywhere and complains bitterly if their car is parked more than twenty feet from the door of their destination. My thighs were soft for the first time in adult memory. My rump was spreading beyond my slacks, and I didn't much like it. So I ate a banana for dinner.

I was sleeping badly. Nothing in the room was comfortable. The bed was too hard or too soft. The covers were too heavy or I was too cold, and I could feel the wrinkling of the sheets underneath my suddenly oversensitive skin. The light from the streetlamp, even through the lace curtain, was too bright, and when the velvet draperies were drawn, it was so dark and airless I thought there might be no oxygen in the room.

Bernadette's call woke me at eight thirty, as a reminder—or warning—that she would pick me up in an hour. I rolled out of the bed and staggered, red-eyed, to the bathroom and began my set of ritual tasks: from brushing my teeth right to left, front to back, and scrubbing my tongue in a way that always made me gag and always made Teddy laugh, to washing my hair with Kiehl's Shampoo and working the lather up to an unrealistic froth before I would believe that my hair was really clean, to the end of the shower rinse—with freezing-cold water—a part of the ceremony that sent Teddy flying out of the shower, out of the bathroom and nearly out of the house.

Now, apparently, it was all to be done, once more, on my own. There was no one to laugh at me. No one to stick my scrubbed tongue toward and say, "Gltheee hohwww cgleeee?"—which is what it sounds like when you say this to someone with your tongue out. My morning rituals, so newly made sweet, now had no smile included, with Teddy gone. Still, hair—washed, dried and braided—and the rest of me squeaky clean, and dressed in a pair of navy flannel slacks, blue oxford shirt and navy cardigan, I was ready for Bernadette; ready for our discussion about Shakespeare and our plans for Henry James and Edith Wharton, and even ready, I hoped, for shopping in Vermont.

Bernadette was wearing a lavender boiled-wool jacket with a pale pink turtleneck and soft, gray wool slacks. The pink-and-blue scarf, knotted around her neck, was Hermès, she told me, a Christmas present from Josie. And her big cream shearling coat was thrown on the backseat of her white Volvo station wagon. The drive was amazing. Not only were we traveling through some of the most beautiful countryside in the world but the day was perfect—crystal-clear with a bright blue sky. Sunlight glimmered off snow-capped roofs, and fields glowed bright and white with shadows of periwinkle and platinum, while Bernadette talked with delight about our Shakespeare program. When we were finally all clogging along in time to this interdisciplinary dance, she said, the students would feel Shakespeare vital and alive in every part of his or her experience: how to read it, how to speak it, how to act it and, most of all, why we should care. Its glorious import would be made alive within its time and relevant in the present day.

It was a gutsy platform, no doubt about it, in an academic atmosphere designed to keep out the Philistines. As it was our job—our paid professions, to be exact—to educate the Philistines, it would seem the idea of enforcing their distance from us and the subjects we hoped to impart would have been counterintuitive. But it now looked, more than ever, as though Bernadette might have begun to break the code.

As we drove, I settled in to talk about American literature, my Henry James and her Willa Cather. Of course, she was one of America's great Cather authorities, and while I'd always thought of Cather as the Great

Plains antithesis of James's and Wharton's European awareness, Bernadette corrected me. We were talking about the passage of the plow in the setting sun that had become Cather's best-remembered image, and how influenced she had been by the French stylists, when we turned off the highway and drove toward the town of Manchester, Vermont. The sun, bright on the crest of a pine-topped hill, sitting above a classic, white-steepled town green, would not have been outside Willa Cather's interest or imagination. Bernadette suggested a place beyond the main street where we could go for what she promised would be "a scrumptious Italian sandwich," and she was, of course, right. My stomach was jumping, full of provolone, pesto, tomato and salami, when we pulled into the parking lot behind the Armani outlet, though I know I was queasy from my proximity to fashion, not food.

As I stood on the hushed floor of the Armani store, somber, dim and concrete as any place of meditation, surrounded by yards and yards of sleeves, skirts and slacks in gray and taupe, beige and sand, and stone and sage and khaki, I must have looked as helpless as I felt. Bernadette and a saleswoman took me in hand, and they put outfits together in ways I could not have done for myself; jackets over dresses, pants and tops with scarves. I stood and looked at the things they'd chosen, and I could hear Teddy say to me, paint sample book in hand, "*These* are your colors." Everything they'd picked was cream and manila, soft green, soft blue, pale yellow, ochre and taupe.

I went into the dressing room and emerged from the curtain in outfit after outfit, like a puppet in a Punch and Judy show. Bernadette sat on a stone-colored tuffet and performed the thumbs-up and thumbs-down routine like a husband. We narrowed the field to two outfits. The first was a grayed-green wool crepe dress with a high round neck and cut-in shoulders. There was a matching jacket that had, instead of lapels, a kind of supple, undulating length of fabric that softly fell from the neck, the inside of each wave revealing a sky blue of double-sided drape. Its competitor was made up of separates; soft, buttery-textured wool crepe pants in a pale blond taupe, with full legs, slightly wider at the hem than the knee. There was a small and beautifully cut V at the hem of each pant leg, allowing a perfect drape over the shoe, or so said my salesperson, who was relieved to find me, at five foot seven, longer in the leg than most women my height, since the pant length couldn't easily be altered. The slacks were topped with a heavy silk tunic in a paler green than the dress and jacket, and a huge challis stole of sky blue, green and taupe in a loose geometric print. The jacket from the dress worked with the tunic and slacks as well, and Bernadette urged me to buy them all. Though clearly marked at less than half the original retail cost, the discounted prices were still far more than I'd ever spent on clothing. I balked at buying both outfits, but Bernadette would hear none of it.

"Are you putting a child through school? Are you paying off old gambling debts? Do you have a mother in an old-age home in *Monaco*?"

I laughed—of course not—but still protested. Bernadette persisted. She took my arm and asked the salesperson if we could have a moment alone. I felt myself stiffen. She looked at me hard and said, "I know that I'm walking on sacred ground here, but I'm going to tell you that I've had a lot of time to think about these things and I—now this is just me— but I don't think we're going to a better place. This is all the heaven we get, and if we don't make the best of it, then shame on us."

"Bernadette," I said firmly. "I don't believe that heaven can be found in a *shopping* bag, and I'm not interested in fashion. I just need an outfit to wear to a wedding on Saturday. I don't really need anything else. I just don't have that kind of lifestyle."

"What kind of lifestyle would that be," she asked, challenging me, her head tilted like the RCA dog.

"You know, that dressing up and looking pretty lifestyle," I said. "I'm not, you know, a 'girly' kind of woman. You know what I mean." And I blushed because I remembered, with a start, the thing I wasn't supposed to know: the legend of Bernadette, as told by Josie. Of Bernadette, in a cabin in the woods, living like a man.

"You think it's beneath you—don't you?—to care about clothes and your hair and your home—"

"No." I said no, maybe a little hesitantly, but I meant no. And maybe for the first time. Certainly my house, my home, had become something deep and comforting to me, far beyond what I'd ever expected to find or feel in an unprofessional world, or a world outside of ideas, of letters and literature.

"This isn't about fashion," she said, making those little quote signs with her fingers around the word *fashion*. "This is about style." She frowned and looked down at the distinctive sapphire and diamond ring she always wore.

"Where would your beloved Henry James be without style? Who is Daisy Miller without understanding the difference between the candy of Schenectady and the art on the walls of Florence? And where would *Wharton* be—her decorating book, her house in Lenox, her infinite notes on architecture and gardens and, most of all, the way she allowed the *detail* of dress or the affectation of fashion to *literally* act as character traits. All the literature you love—all the art—this is *all* style." She took a long look at me. "You're not afraid of it at all on the page. Why does it frighten you so in the flesh?"

I'm sure I looked confused. She sat back down on the ottoman, made room for me to sit next to her and continued, "I'm *not* saying that happiness lies in an Armani shopping bag. Certainly not. But here's what I am saying; you arrived at Amherst the saddest damn woman I'd ever seen—and one of the most talented."

I must have looked surprised. "Saddest?" was all I could say.

"Your work at Columbia was wonderful," she said. "The original Gilded Age curriculum you put together there was outstanding. I know Anna Gage, your department head, I know her well, and I know you had no help in crafting any of that work. Far from it.

"The books you included of James and Wharton—surrounded by the nonfiction texts—were nothing short of brilliant. This work you've begun here on James and Wharton and their hiding behind masks of style and manners *is* clever and original and scrappy. But it's also insightful and human and probably very close to the truth. And"—she rolled her eyes heavenward—"the Margaret Chase Smith biography . . ."

Oh, dear God, I thought, where's the bolt of lightning? Just take me now.

"That biography is far, *far* better than the reviews suggested." She looked at me hard. "You don't *know* that, do you? It's gutsy and witty and grumpy and irritable"—she laughed, more to herself than to me— "just like Margaret Chase Smith. And it was a *wonderful* first biography—a wonderful *biography,* actually. But you don't know how good you are. You haven't really met the Joy Harkness I know is in there."

"Listen, thanks," I said, waving my arm in a dismissive gesture and wanting to move her off the subject, but she continued.

"The pants or the dress—or the two thousand dollars this all adds up to—is not exactly the point. But it's not off the point either. Unless I'm missing my guess, you don't have any real financial worries, do you?" I shook my head no. She nodded. "And I know your salary, because I'm the one who gave it to you." I started to speak but she stopped me.

"Bear with me a minute," she said firmly, and no one would have done otherwise. "It's time you started taking care of yourself. It's time for you to protect that talent and that brain and celebrate what you've got; because if you don't, the output isn't going to be there with the kind of quality and authority and, yes, *style* that—frankly—I've paid for. I *need* you to be the best you can be. You're one of the key players on *my* team, and I need greatness from every one of you." I'm sure my mouth fell open.

"Men say that style is frivolous—clothes are frivolous, homes and hair styles and gossip and entertaining are all frivolous—but most men tend to live one-dimensional lives. They have wives who take care of the homes and the clothes and the entertaining for them. Women bring the detail of humanity into their lives. Haven't you ever noticed that when a wife dies, a man either remarries right away or dies himself, while women go on as widows for decades. That's how frivolous these things are, Joy. Style is the texture of the world."

Bernadette hesitated and then clearly decided to go all the way. "Teddy began to do that for you"—she touched my hand—"to open you up to your own life—like a wife—and now you have to do it for yourself. You have to look in the mirror and like what you see, just as if you were looking at someone you loved. You have to learn to celebrate that person and bolster her and indulge her and encourage her—just as if she were your lover or your child. No more hiding.

"I know, New York must have been rough," she said. "But . . . but this is a brand-new chance."

I wished that I could just cheerfully embrace this new way of looking at the world. But if I couldn't, I did the one positive thing I knew how to do at the moment: I followed directions.

There were flat, sling-back shoes in the same taupe of the pants with a little band of light blue around the low vamp, and a pair of mid-heeled, impossibly pointy-toed pumps in soft sage green. I bought them both. I bought another scarf in a gossamer woven pale-blue blend of silk and cashmere, and a sweater set in pale apple green trimmed with peach. I bought a big cashmere cardigan in a color between ochre and pumpkin with a pale yellow turtleneck of tissue-weight cashmere to wear underneath, and I thought again of Teddy. On the way out the door I saw a small, tailored handbag in a pebbled sage green, a few shades darker than the dress. Bernadette went to get the car, and I dashed back inside to my salesperson and bought the bag as well as an extravagant long stole of deep plumb wool crepe, trimmed with a band of cornflower blue suede.

I pulled the stole out of the shopping bag and handed it to Bernadette as she dropped me at my door. She protested, and I told her that this was the smallest thank-you for one of the largest days of my life.

I carried the shopping bags into the house, sat in my father's wing chair and cried until I didn't think there could possibly be any liquid left in my body.

CHAPTER 34

My room at the Waldorf was nice. This was a little disappointing. I'd wanted more of a story, a little over-the-top illustration of high-end entitlement that might illustrate the difference between real people and—well—"people who stay at the Waldorf." But the room wasn't going to give it to me. It was, instead, a tasteful, spacious, pale gray room with blue silk taffeta draperies. The carpet was cream and gray; the bathroom was large and comfortably old-fashioned with an old porcelain tub deep enough to drown in, if the wedding festivities proved too much. There was a queen-sized bed topped by a neoclassical headboard, painted a distressed white, and the now ubiquitous television armoire, also creamy white and painted with faded blue-gray vines and flowers, as though it held an authentic Gustavian TV.

The walls were studded with black-and-white classical prints, beautifully matted and framed in gold-leafed wood, carved to look like bamboo. The prints were simply hung on the wall, rather than bolted down, as they had been in every hotel I'd visited in France last year. The painting over my bed in Lyon had been huge—at least six feet by five feet—a gruesome depiction of the beheaded and gourmet-plattered John the Baptist, with a hefty *I Dream of Jeannie*–dressed Salome by his side. It had been conspicuously and gracelessly bolted, outside of the frame, directly to the wall. As though anyone could have fit that painting under their coat or into their suitcase. As though anyone would ever have *wanted* that painting.

There was nothing of such questionable taste in this room at the Waldorf, but for the first time in any hotel room, I noticed the finer things: the moldings and the trim and the color of the carpet and the break of the drapery panel at the floor. I could see that each panel *was* at least two and a half times the width of the window, and I smiled thinking that Teddy would have approved.

I'd left home especially early that morning, fearing traffic and, I suppose, fearing that if I didn't start early I might not start at all. The clerks at the front desk seemed momentarily flummoxed by my presence and my hope to check in early, at nine in the morning. The room was empty, they reported, but they'd not finished making it up. And so the Waldorf treated me to breakfast in the lounge off the lobby, and while I ate, a bellhop took my suitcase to the room and the maid hung my clothes in the closet. I was not used to this treatment.

I decided to use my extra time to soak in the deep old tub and was just getting undressed when there was a knock at the door. A porter brought a pitcher of lemonade, a plate of warm cookies and a bottle of vodka.

"I didn't order these," I said. He handed me a note: *Joy—Refresh, renew and calm down! There will be a hair and makeup person here, in room 414, at noon, to help us all get ready. So please join us and use his services! He's a gift to us from Adele!—Can you believe it?* It was signed, *Laura.*

At a quarter to twelve I was dressed. My hair was dry. I was ready to put on my makeup, as usual, and braid my hair, as usual—and I stopped. There was a professional here. I poured myself a lemonade, added a dollop of vodka, and I picked on a cookie—orange with macadamia nuts. I looked in the mirror at myself, wearing my new Armani dress and jacket, and felt betwixt and between, like a teenager wearing her mother's clothes. I sighed and padded down the hall to room 414, carrying the pointy-toed shoes that I found pinched with each step. I would learn the price of beauty, but I would learn it a little later, I determined.

The door to room 414 was answered by a good-natured Adele, whose makeup had just been done, she told me, by Theo Something-or-other. She looked different, very different. She looked lovely. There was nothing about her that resembled an apricot poodle anymore. Theo had taken her cotton candy hair and cut it short and styled it close to her head. The little rows of cheese-puffed hair were gone. In their place was the smooth cap of a pixie cut. She'd changed her glasses to golden oval frames, and Theo had made her makeup soft with corals and peach. Her olive green silk dress and jacket were just fine; in fact they were perfect. Flattering and classic. She wore a beautiful necklace of twisted beads, in coral, quartz, pearl and topaz, that Laura had given her to commemorate the day. I was admiring it when I heard Laura coming into the living room of the suite from the bedroom. We hugged each other, and I stepped back to look at her. She was wearing a slip and her hair was in hot rollers, but her makeup was almost done and her eyes were amazing. Theo had shaped her brows, and she wore eyeliner and lipstick, and she had cheekbones. This guy was a genius. I followed Laura into the bedroom and sat on the bed as Theo finished Laura's makeup, eyeing me with suspicion.

We laughed about how the three of us had rarely worn makeup at all, but Adele piped in about her Jungle Red lipstick, Theo pointing out that the wrong makeup was just as bad as no makeup at all. Theo looked directly at me when he clearly teased us as a group, asking if we really believed that we were so beautiful, we didn't *need* to wear makeup.

"It's not *that*," I sniffed. "It's that we've had other things we valued. The contents of a person's head rather than the contents of their makeup bag." I have to admit, I was a little condescending, a little snotty, and neither Laura nor Adele laughed with me.

"And you can't have both?" asked the beautiful blond young man wielding the makeup brush, and looking as though he'd stepped right out of a Handsome Prince casting call. "You *really* believe that mascara jeopardizes your intellectual standing?"

I thought about Bernadette in her pale pink lipstick and Josie with her three-hundred-dollar haircuts. I would have said, last year at this time, that yes, I thought an interest in mascara might very well jeopardize my intellectual positioning or my academic standing or even the way I thought about myself. Or, even more important, the way I *didn't* think about myself. But this was not last year at this time. This was now.

It was as though I'd gone to another planet where everything was familiar but different. I was sitting in a room with two of the most respected historians in the United States as they had their faces painted, and I was watching them emerge like middle-aged butterflies from cocoons.

Laura gave *me* a present: a jewelry box in Bergdorf Goodman wrap.

Inside were earrings, large drops of peridot and pearl. They were wonderful.

"How did you know the color would be so right?" I asked, referring to my dress.

"I know your colors," Laura answered, as though everyone knew but me.

Theo pulled the hot rollers out of Laura's hair and ran his hands through the short beige curls with some gel or mousse. He directed her hair up and away from her face, sleek at the sides and soft at the top. Suddenly, she looked like Celeste Holm in *All About Eve*. How had I never seen this before? And her eyes were turquoise. New contacts, she told me proudly.

Theo Giza was a doctoral candidate at Brooklyn College, one of Adele's best students, earning his way through school by working at some tony Fifty-seventh Street salon. He was bright and funny and talked about beauty and culture and natural law in such a way that I wondered how I'd *ever* thought this subject was frivolous or trivial.

Beauty, he said, was just a fact of life and one that played an inordinate part in the division of the spoils. Fair? Maybe not. Certainly not. But it is what it is, he said, and he was insightful enough to suggest that in this culture, women were already playing with one hand tied behind their backs.

"How many women," he asked, "are CEOs of 'Fortune 500' companies?"

"There *was* that Hewlett Packard gal," Adele said. Laura remembered that the number of women was somewhere between ten and twelve.

"Twelve out of five hundred," Theo said making his point. "And in the 'Fortune 50'?" asked Theo. None of us knew. "One," he announced. "Women make up just under fifty percent of the workforce, and you are represented at the chief executive's level in the top fifty companies in the United States to the tune of *one*." We looked desolate. Just the way we felt.

"Why," he asked, "when you *know* you are not going to be judged on a level playing field, would you ever dream that you could afford to let go of any advantages you *can* control?" He put down his long-tailed comb and looked at me through my reflection in the mirror. "Your *first* job," he said, "is to protect yourself from being made irrelevant. It may not be fair. You may not be judged by the *right* criteria—okay, I get it—but that's what you've got to work with. That's the straw you've drawn—born into *this* culture at this particular time. I'm not saying you need to be a supermodel. I'm just saying, in this economy, in this moment in time—and even leaving sexist issues aside—can *anyone* afford *not* to be presenting the best possible picture of themselves?"

"Hear, hear!" said Laura, getting up to make way for me at the vanity seat. Aptly named, I thought.

Theo pulled open my loose braid and ran his hands through my wavy hair a few times. The white hair at my hairline looked, remarkably, like highlights, and I was often stopped and asked where I'd had my hair colored. "God," I used to say, as a bit of a poke at both the commercial beauty scene and religion. "God is my hair colorist." And then one day, when a woman responded with an unsettling delight that suggested an absence of irony, it occurred to me that I might be seen as a fundamentalist Bible-thumping beauty fanatic, and I stopped giving that answer to strangers on the street.

Theo put some kind of magic gel in his hands and ran it through my hair, which suddenly became manageable and silky. He pulled it back more sleekly than I wore it, and wrapped a tiny auburn-colored elastic around the ponytail. He then wove and secured the tail into a loose figure eight with soft, curling tendrils deliberately designed to look as though they'd escaped through will of nature.

He turned his attention to my eyes, which he left rather light—just a hint of brown shadow and brown mascara; though, whatever his magic, they looked wider and brighter than my real eyes. My lips were colored a deep brown-pink, a color I would never have picked, but I had to admit it was flattering. My cheeks were brightened with what looked like shocking pink powder in the compact but became just a rosy glow on my skin. Theo slipped my new drop earrings into my ears.

I looked pretty. I was pretty. I hadn't thought that I'd looked pretty since the day of my wedding, when I gazed into the mirror and saw a twenty-two-year-old Camelot princess looking back. But that was a pageant, and I was playing a part. And I figured, and rightly so, that I could hardly go around town trailing yards of veil from a little coronet on my head. This time there was no crown, and I was not twenty-two years old. I was now older than my mother had been at my wedding, and it was only the second time in my life I ever registered feeling pretty.

I hardly knew what to say, except thank you—to Theo and to Adele. I turned to thank Laura and saw her step into her dress, smooth the slip underneath and zip up the closure at the side. She took my breath away. Laura wasn't young and she wasn't trim and she didn't know Gucci from Pucci, but she didn't look foolish or dressed in any way that diminished her. She was Dr. Laura Hotchkiss Grant, Ivy League professor, international lecturer, author, one of America's most treasured historians, soon to be Mrs. Charles Lantzman, and she looked confident and important, and she looked just beautiful.

CHAPTER 35

We formed a little cluster, Laura, Adele, the nervous Saint Bart's wedding coordinator and me, standing behind a door just off the chapel. We'd been given our bouquets—all of green: orchids and tendril vines and tiny artichokes and berries. Laura's had cream and blush roses added to the greens. Bach was being played by organ and cello, and I could see the pews were nearly filled. I began to recognize faces from Columbia, and my stomach started to knot.

I saw the minister, a pretty, kind-looking woman with soft brown hair, take her place at the altar and nod to a nice-looking man—I would guess he was in his late sixties—wearing a dark suit and a pale green boutonniere. I saw him rise from the front row with a younger bearded man, probably his son, and stand in front of the minister. The organ music changed to the heraldic alert before the wedding march, and with the familiar notes of Henry Purcell, I stepped out of the door and walked toward the bride's side of the altar followed by Adele and then Laura. Watching the face of Charles Lantzman as he saw Laura come toward him was all the evidence I needed to know that bliss exists here on earth, even if we only get to hold it in moments.

The ceremony seemed to pass quickly, but it was lovely and personal while still being traditional. Adele and Laura's niece, a chorus member of the Metropolitan Opera, sang a lovely Italian aria *antica*, with piano and cello. Laura and Charlie seemed poised and comfortable, they exchanged rings, kissed, and the minister pronounced them man and wife. Charlie turned and, still holding Laura's hand, hugged his son. The two men each put their heads on the other's shoulders for just a fraction of a second in a moment of intimate sweetness. Everyone stood and

cheered and applauded in what I thought was an uncharacteristic gesture of spontaneity, given the church and the academic background of
the congregation. But it thrilled me, and unexpectedly so.

We hurried across the street to the Waldorf, where there were tea
sandwiches and petit fours on tiered epergnes and champagne passed by
white-coated waiters who all looked like rosy-cheeked schoolboys. The
flowers were huge and lush, in all colors of green, from nearly white to
chartreuse, spruce and deep forest. They were scaled like something
from the lobby of the Metropolitan Museum, and the air was heady with
the scent of lilies. I was into my third glass of champagne after being
approached by far too many Columbia colleagues who made reference
to the fact that I looked so very different; as though a designer label
altered everything. I had a little lipstick on, I gruffly pointed out, as I
managed to put most of them off; and then I saw Harry Fox.

I remembered that the Grant Girls had done an award-winning
piece about Lincoln for Harry when he was editor in chief of *Empire,*
the men's magazine with undeniably literary pretensions. In fairness, only
the *New Yorker* had won more magazine awards, but Harry's magazine
had a fashion section and profiles of pretty women—actresses and ballet
dancers they tried to make sound like intellectuals. When Condé Nast
bought *Empire,* Harry Fox came to Columbia and was thought to be the
heir apparent as dean of journalism. But I'd just heard, earlier in the week
and via the Amherst grapevine, that Columbia was bringing in a
woman—a South American editor-journalist—in a move that smacked
more of politics than of common sense. It must have knocked the
wind out of Harry, but he looked great. Tall and confident, the pink-
dotted pocket-handkerchief a flourish of style, his white cuffs and collar in contrast to the deep blue stripe of his shirt and, as ever, pink socks.

Harry sidled up to me with two glasses of champagne. "I see your
glass is empty," he said, handing me the flute in his right hand.

"I'm amazed there's any left for the rest of you," I answered, taking
the glass. "I haven't been temperate."

"Tempered?" Harry asked, his brow furrowed. He leaned closer to me.

"Temperate. Temperate," I said, repeating myself. "As in temperance
movement. Prohibition. Mothers Against Drunk Professors."

"Ahhh," Harry sighed. "I see." He looked at me more closely. "How are you, Joy? Amherst looks good on you."

I laughed. "Oh yes," I said. "It's the stress-free environment. You get out of the city, and you just can't imagine how quiet life is. I just sit on the porch in a rocker and listen to the crickets."

"How much of my leg are you pulling?" he asked.

"Not too much," I said. "Some."

"But seriously," he said. "You look like someone who's had a month at a spa or a session with a guru—or is this where we talk about Botox or the new face cream you're using?"

"Harry!" I laughed. "You're downright metrosexual! You should have stayed with Condé Nast. You could have been the next Anna Wintour!"

He winced. "Seriously, are you liking Massachusetts?"

"I am," I answered. "I am. Yes. It was the best possible move I could have made. I'm doing my best work. It's a great environment."

Like a stripper, I knew my routine, how much to reveal and when to cover up again. This was my moment for a diverting wisecrack. To my great surprise, I caught sight of myself. I changed my ways. I took a new path. I told him the truth.

"I bought a house. A real honest-to-goodness home, and I think it's making me grow up. And you know, Harry, it's all right. All of a sudden I seem to be part of life, and it's full of messy details and real-life adventures—and terrors and kindnesses—from all sorts of unexpected places." I couldn't look into his eyes, I was afraid I would cry or burst into flame or—God knows what I was afraid of. I looked at the knot in his beautiful tie.

"I went to Massachusetts to hide out, I think, up in the boonies, but instead, I've come out of hiding. Amazing."

He looked at me as though he were puzzled.

"It *is* amazing," he said. He looked sober, in the truest sense of the word. "I suppose coming of age," he said, "can happen at any age."

"I'm sure it's an inappropriate time and an inappropriate place to talk about this," I said, my eyes studying his craggy, lived-in face, "but I hear *you've* just been through the wringer."

"Well, I don't know anymore what's inappropriate," he answered. "I'm trying to find a good way to look at it. I could stay and teach at

Columbia, of course, but I really don't want to stay there now. And then, that leaves the whole wide world. But funnily enough, I'm not all that excited about facing the whole wide world. I thought I had my life planned out very neatly."

He looked at his big hands and studied his fingernails and shifted his weight. This wasn't the cocky journalist-man-about-town I used to know. I liked this version of Harry better.

"Would you like to go and get a real dinner, instead of these girly sandwiches?" he asked, holding a tiny shrimp-salad-crust-cut-off morsel, with his pinky raised.

"Well, I'm of two minds," I said. "My favorite food in the world is the tea sandwich, but I'd have to eat two hundred thousand of them to soak up the champagne I've already had, and I'm not sure I'll live that long. So, yes. I'd love to have dinner with you."

We made our rounds, hugging people, promising to call, taking cell-phone numbers. I was struck by how open and friendly so many of the Columbia folks seemed to be. It must be the environment of the wedding, I thought. It didn't occur to me that it might be me.

I left the Grant Girls in good company, surrounded by the Lantzman family: Charlie's granddaughters, tall and dark, like their handsome parents, his daughter with her arm around Laura's shoulders, his son, Brian, a specialist in infectious disease, deep in conversation with Adele about a scarlet fever epidemic around the time of the Civil War. Laura was inclined, just slightly, against Charlie, as though she'd always stood in the lee of his somewhat curved, evidently comforting body; so natural and right did they seem together.

Harry and I had dinner at a Greek restaurant just off Lexington Avenue. The fish he ordered for the two of us was cooked in a salt crust with rosemary and was nothing short of perfect. Rather than walk back toward the Waldorf, we decided to stroll north on Park, west on Fifty-seventh Street and then north onto Madison. We walked up the avenue, talking about our lives, our childhoods and mostly our work with its wins and losses, while looking into shop windows and commenting on the goods: the leather shoes from England and Italy, art glass from Sweden, marbleized papers from Siena. We considered the mannequins in the windows of designers' shops. Harry was partial to Valentino; he pointed out a suit in the window, a jacket of bittersweet orange, banded with black lace, over black lace pants and a black lace shell, scalloped at the neck. This, he thought, he'd pick out for me.

"Oh really," I said. "At those prices you'd have to pay for it too, I'm afraid—so you better watch what you wish for!"

"It's too bad you didn't bring this up a week or so ago," he answered, "when it looked as though I were still gainfully employed. I would have agreed."

"Ahhhh . . . timing," I said, "is everything."

The strange part of this story is that, like Laura with Charlie, and even with his suggestion of paying for designer clothes, I wasn't thinking about Harry as a date or even a potential date. I thought of us like two old warhorses, sharing stories of battles and conflict. The novelty of opening up to a friend was enough. Harry was a colleague turning into a friend, and I remembered Josie telling me, long ago now, that I could use a few friends. Well, I was beginning to have them. Maybe I was beginning to deserve them.

As we walked, Harry told me that he'd tried for years to ask me out, but that I was "resistant."

"That's ridiculous," I said. "There was nothing to resist. You never asked me out."

"Well," he said, "I tried. I asked you if you had a boyfriend or a woman friend or someone you lived with—"

"You *never* did. You never asked me those things," I said indignantly.

"I did so. Well, maybe I didn't ask you that directly, but I asked all kinds of questions that would have led to those answers, and you refused to tell me."

"I did *not*. I never heard you ask those questions." What is he talking about? I wondered.

"And I tried to find out from others if you lived with someone or were married to someone. No one seemed to know. You were never around school on weekends; you never made friends with anyone or took anyone to your home. No one ever saw you with a date—man or woman. Someone I talked to thought that you had a husband somewhere in the Midwest, where you came from."

"Saint Louis," I said.

"Well, I don't know whether or not they even knew enough to name it as Saint Louis," he said, "but the idea was that you must be going somewhere else with someone, because you sure weren't here. There was some speculation for a while that you might be gay and involved with Adele."

"Adele who?" I searched the Rolodex in my brain for lesbians at Columbia named Adele.

"Adele Grant!" Harry exclaimed.

"Adele *Grant*? Adele isn't gay. Adele isn't a lesbian. I've known Adele for twenty years."

Harry looked at me as though I were mad. "Of course Adele Grant is gay," he said. "She makes no secret about it."

"Jesus," I said. "Where have I been?" Wasn't this weekend the proof that Laura and Adele were my closest friends? How would I not know something as elemental as this, and even more important, how was it that others could know? Was I so blind, or was I not to be trusted? Could I not rely on my own instincts or memories? I was hurt and embarrassed and flummoxed all at once. Maybe it was the champagne, but my head couldn't hold all of this. I remembered Teddy's expression: my container was full. I returned to the safer—or was it?—conversation about me.

"But while we're on the subject," I picked up, "how could you be asking me out? I thought you were married to—or living with or something—that, that . . . that . . . you know . . . that, that . . . model."

Harry laughed out loud. "Oh no! She'd die if she heard you say that. She's not a model; she's a *news* presenter—and we're not married."

"A *what*?" I asked.

"She's a sometime news presenter, and for the last two years or so, she's had a talk show about women's issues. On Fox. During the day. You're not home watching television," he said. "You wouldn't know it."

"Women's issues? You mean—like menopause?" I asked.

"Well, I suppose," he said.

"And *men*ses and *men*tally unbalanced behavior and *men*daciousness and . . . could it be that this show is—all too often—about *men*?"

Harry was laughing. "You've seen it!"

"No, but shows about women's issues are almost always about men. 'Can't live with 'em, can't shoot 'em.'"

"And *your* men issues?" he asked.

"You mean my *people* issues," I corrected him. "I've had *quite* a year." And it all came out. I told him about Donna, and I told him about Will, and I told him about Teddy, and I told him about Teddy's mother. It may have been an abridged version, but I left out little of the detail and none of the humiliation. Harry asked what I was going to do about Teddy and I told him that I didn't know.

Harry and I stopped walking at Seventy-ninth Street because all of a sudden the champagne must have worn off, and my feet were like two screaming toothaches. In the taxi I slipped off my shoes, and Harry offered to rub my feet.

"I don't think I want my feet rubbed by the boyfriend of a model-slash-talk-show-host, if you don't mind," I said, straight as that.

Harry smiled and said that would be fair enough, except that he wasn't her boyfriend anymore.

"Are you sure?" I asked.

"Pretty sure," Harry answered.

"Give me a call when you're really sure."

"You bet," Harry said, kissing my nose as I got out of the cab.

CHAPTER 36

Driving all the way home from Manhattan the next morning, I thought about Teddy. I thought about his kindness and his sweet nature. I thought about his talent, and I thought about his mother. I was sure she'd done whatever she could to discredit Joey in his eyes, and while I knew it hadn't worked, I also bet that it laid enough doubt so that nothing she said had ever left Teddy's heart.

Could I do this to him? Could I take his mother, the one person in whose life he felt he'd made such an important difference, and destroy that belief? This was my dilemma: if I told him the truth about his mother, to save him, I could destroy the one thing he believed was absolutely true.

I knew what I had to do, and I didn't like it.

I called Teddy's on Sunday night. There was no answer. I left a message on their machine. No call was returned. I called Teddy on Monday night. Maureen answered. "Maureen," I said, "it's Joy. How are you?"

"Teddy's not here," she said with as much venom as she could muster.

"Would you ask him to call me? I have some things I need to discuss with him." I managed it all in a pleasant enough voice, as though I were completely unaware of her attitude toward me. She just put down the receiver. No call was returned.

I phoned again on Tuesday night, and Maureen answered again. She must have changed her card-playing habits, I thought. For weeks she'd needed him to ferry her around to her bridge clubs night after night. I went through the same routine: I told her that I'd not heard from Teddy, she was silent, that I needed to speak to him, she was silent, and that I was asking her, please, *please,* to have him give me a call. She grunted or sighed a good-bye. I prefer to think of it as a grunt, but that might just be my take. At any rate, there was no return call.

On Wednesday I rang again, this time earlier, around four thirty. Maureen answered.

"Listen, Maureen, I'm going to call every night until Teddy calls me back, and if he doesn't call me back soon, I'm going to come over and park my car in your driveway until I can see him. And if that doesn't work, I'm going to get all of my friends to call and come by with me until we shame you into giving Teddy my message or telling us where we can find him." I realize that this had the psychopathic quality of combining a teenage slasher movie with the mafia, but short of a horse's head in the bed, it was all I could think to use as a threat. Her fear of the O'Sullivans alone should make her cave in to my demands, I figured.

I called Josie and asked if I could come around and talk to her and Dan. Of course they extended the welcome. "Come for dinner," they said, and I was delighted to do so.

It was good to sit at the O'Sullivan table again. It had only been a week or so since I'd been there, but it felt like months to me. They filled me in on the Fortunata clan, and I told them about the Grant wedding in New York, pulled off without a hitch in less than a week. "Shotgun wedding?" asked Dan.

"Hardly," I answered. "The bride is sixty-one." Lizzie and Jackie looked shocked, as though no one that old could possibly be a bride. "Get used to it," I said.

The girls went off to their rooms to do their homework, and we settled down to talk about Teddy. Josie poured tea, and we moved onto the red leather couches in their kitchen-den. Dan lit the gas fire in the hearth, and the light of it held us in a small pocket of glowing warmth that I recognized as a good approximation of their gentle friendship.

I brought them up to date on the Hennessy activities, as far as I knew them, since their run-in with Maureen in church, two weeks ago. They laughed until they cried at the story of the hospital. They especially loved the part where Teddy fainted and Maureen refused to speak to the doctors until he regained consciousness.

"I can see it! I can see it all!" said Josie, laughing. And they loved her accusing him of giving Valentine's candy to the hospital staff and not to her. But when I told them his answer to her, they both stopped laughing.

"So he called *her* his 'best girl'?" asked Dan. "In front of *you?*"

"He did."

"And he had *no* box of Valentine's candy for you," Josie clarified.

"Well, I wouldn't *want* a box of—"

"That's not the point."

"No. I know."

I backtracked and told them Maureen's comments about recognizing that she was unfair to Teddy and her line about having no *intention* of stopping her behavior. They looked aghast, as I knew they would.

And then I told them about my visit on Valentine's Day, in my plan to take their advice. Though Josie was already shaking her head as my story began to unfold.

"I'm so sorry; I'm *so* sorry" was all that Josie kept saying.

"Don't bother. It's just as well that we know what we're up against," I said. Maureen would never let go, I explained. Teddy was paying for some wrongs that started long before he was invited onto this planet.

"The biggest problem is," I continued, "at least as I see it—if he isn't made to understand that he's not responsible for his mother's happiness or unhappiness, he has no chance of determining his own fate. But, the paradox is that even if I could break that trust and uncover the truth, I think his whole sense of self-worth could be in jeopardy. He *sees* himself as her protector, and he's proud of himself for doing the job as well as he has. Remember, there's no other relationship here. Not really. When push comes to shove, I get in the backseat."

"Well, that's what a shrink would do, isn't it?" asked Dan. "Wouldn't they get him to see that his life is a lie? Wouldn't they get him to break the pattern?"

"They might," I said. "But they'd get *him* to break it—not me. *He'd* be there, asking for help. *He'd* want direction. And they'd work long and hard to get him to a point where he could accept the truth. I mean, the world would be great—wouldn't it?—if we could just all go to shrinks and sit down and tell them the story of our lives in fifteen minutes, and they'd tell us, 'Get over your mother' or 'That death of your brother's—it wasn't your fault. Get on with your life!' And we'd give them two thousand bucks, and that would be that. I mean, we carry around these bodies that we think we're using for protection or warmth, and it turns out they're just *literally* dead weight." Was I listening to myself?

I thought of Charlie Lantzman and the adored wife he'd loved and lost, and the difficult time he had in putting the past behind him. But I'd seen, with my own eyes, the wonderful bonus he'd earned in doing so.

"Sometimes you have to work *really* hard to choose life," I said, "and it has to be *your* choice."

Josie looked as though she might cry. Josie hated to lose at anything: traffic tickets, monopoly, Go Fish, growing roses on the harsh hillside of a Massachusetts mountain. Josie wasn't going to let life get the better of her.

"But his mother has taken his choice away," she said with a sigh.

"I know," I agreed. "And I know that this could sound harsh, but plenty of people have made the right choice with less help than Teddy's had. He had his brother, Joe—who tried to show him what was important. And he had all of us in his corner—all of us who've cared about him and put ourselves on the line for him. I don't know that we're really prepared to step into the fray any more than we've done."

"I am," Josie said brightly.

"Well, the thing is," I tried to explain, "I mean, the thing here—"

"You mean," Dan interrupted, "that you're not." He said it. I was grateful. I wasn't sure I could have.

"Look. One of the things his mother said to me was that she takes care of him. She pays his vendors and reconciles his books and his banking and his laundry. She accused me of not being capable of taking care of him because I had my own life. And my first thought was, No, we've been—essentially—living together since December and, in many ways, for months before that. But I was kidding myself. I don't wash his shirts. I don't deal with the repair costs on his car. I don't keep his receipts and put together his tax stuff. I don't count on him to put money into a joint account so I can pay the electric bill. This hasn't been real life.

"His mother keeps him on a leash. She makes him fetch and give her his paw a hundred times a day, just to remind him of his place, and let's face it, it's a place that makes him comfortable. I'm not prepared to be his mother. It's going to be hard enough for me to trust someone as a partner. I don't think I could actually fulfill two roles at the same time. And who knows what kind of shape he'd be in if he *really* understood how she'd used him and how little regard she has for him?"

"But what about Teddy?" Josie asked desperately. "What will *happen* to him?"

"I don't know. But I've got to tell him that I can't go on being his girl-friend, and it's not about the fact that he's a handyman. Well, in a way it is, but it's not the whole story. And I'll tell him that I'm still behind him and I'll let him make his choices."

"Well, I just think—" Josie started, and Dan interrupted her.

"No, Joy's right. We can't take on Teddy's whole life. Even if we could, I don't think we have the right to force something on him, and Joy is pointing out that he isn't asking for our help. We all just surrounded him and hoped we could pull him along with the current until he realized he was swimming on his own. But he's not even asking to get *wet* here."

"First, I have to find a way to get to him. Maureen is *not*—I'm *sure*—passing on my messages." I told them about my threat to bring my friends over. We laughed, but Dan picked up the phone.

"What's their number?" he asked and dialed as I told him.

"Maureen. Dan O'Sullivan. Yes! Oh, she's fine. Ahhh. Right. They're fine too—should be back up here in a few weeks. Time for Easter. I will. No, I will. Absolutely. Now, Maureen, I'm sitting here with Joy Hark-ness, and I understand that she's been trying to get hold of Teddy all week. Well, then—since Sunday night. Right. Where *is* Teddy? Yeah—and what time will he be home? Okay. I want you to have Teddy call Joy as soon as he gets home. Will you do that for me? Whether he wants to or not. I want you to promise that you'll make sure Teddy calls Joy—because this is important—okay, Maureen? Okay, thanks. I will. I will. Same to you. Okay, bye. Bye. That's right. Bye now."

"Oooh," I said to Dan. "You're good. You're really good."

We decided that I should get home quickly as Teddy was expected any minute, according to Maureen, and I drove home with my CD of Patsy Cline singing "Crazy," a lump in my throat holding back tears.

There's no doubt that I've cried more this year than in the past twenty combined. I'm still not ruling out my breakdown theory. Teddy told me, when I ran it by him, that muscles have to break down before they can grow bigger and stronger. Maybe that was what was happening to my psyche. I liked his take on it, but let's face it, Teddy isn't exactly Bruno Bettelheim. Of course, from what I read, even Bruno Bettelheim wasn't Bruno Bettelheim.

I sat in the living room and waited for the phone to ring, and when it did, finally, two hours later, I was still sitting there, quietly, contemplating my life and, as they say, my navel. At any rate, I was zoned, and the ring of the phone lifted me two feet off the couch. Perhaps I sounded winded when I picked up the receiver because Teddy sounded genuinely concerned when he asked if I was all right. I was about to throw it back at him, and I stopped.

"I'm fine. I'm okay, anyway. But Teddy, we have to talk. Can you come over?"

It was clear he hadn't gotten my messages, and while I sensed that he was sorry about it, I didn't hear any frustration or anger directed at his mother. He certainly wasn't as cross as I would have been had someone kept messages from me, but his reactions weren't like mine, and that detail was as abundantly clear in this call as in all my recent thoughts. He agreed to come by the house, and we set the date for the following evening.

Twenty-four hours. It seemed so far away. I wanted it over now. All through the next afternoon the hours sluggishly moved forward until four thirty, and then suddenly, at four thirty, there was not enough time. I would never be ready. Yesterday I knew my part backward and forward; today I had no idea what to say. I wasn't sure what note or tone to hit. And I wasn't at all sure, no matter *what* direction I chose, that I was about to do the right thing. Teddy had his blind spots and his difficult moments, but for the most part, he was a dear and sweet companion. Bernadette was right. Teddy was right. I would never have *had* this house—this home and this life—without him. Insofar as it went, we'd been happy together in this house. We ran our part of the Fortunata team well. I'd seen *much* worse marriages than the partnership of Teddy and me.

Marriages. Marriages—was I thinking about a *marriage*? What *was* I thinking about? Would I marry someone who let his mother ride in the front seat of the car? More to the point, would I marry someone who would let me ride in the *back*? Now, Joy, I said to myself, don't be petty. Where she rides is hardly the issue. I was up and down, and for the next three hours the inside of my head ran like a movie with a soundtrack that had come off of its sprockets and was no longer synced to the action.

At last, Teddy's car pulled into the driveway. He was two hours and twenty minutes late. I was relieved, annoyed and panicked in the same moment. He hesitated at the front door, as though he were going to ring the bell, but I saw him change his mind and just walk in.

It had been a beautiful day; the snow had melted back from the sidewalks and revealed impossibly green grass underneath. The sky was blue as a children's book. Still, it wasn't yet March, and Teddy walked into the house wearing his Birkenstock sandals; the bare white skin of his feet looked vulnerable, to my eye at least. He took off his fleece-lined jacket and left on his baseball cap. It was faded red, with crossed oars and a typeface proclaiming the name of a sculling team from Philadelphia.

"Wassup?" Teddy asked, sitting down heavily in the wing chair. The beginning wasn't promising.

"Would you like a beer or something?" I asked. "I bought some of those little hot-dog appetizers you like so much."

"Weenie wraps," he said, unsmiling. And while he turned down the hot dogs, he gave me a thumbs-up on the beer. I went into the kitchen and pulled the beer bottle from the fridge and was looking for an opener when he came in behind me. He hit the edge of the cap on the side of the stone counter in that way I never could seem to master. I reached for a glass, and he put his hand up and said, "Comes in a glass—remember?" I smiled, and with this, finally, he smiled just a little.

I poured myself a short glass of Pigs' Nose Scotch. My favorite. We sat at the counter in the kitchen, and it was almost like old times. Old times, just two weeks ago. But I decided it was time to tackle the subject at hand. I took a long breath and prepared to jump. Before I could get a word out, he said, "Nice lipstick." It was the brownish-pink one Theo had given me for the wedding. I almost lost my nerve. That's what a compliment can do for me, I fear. And it wasn't much of a compliment. But I steadied myself and took aim.

"Teddy, I know how hard this has been for you. You've felt so pulled between your mother and me, and I know you want to be loyal to both of us." He looked down at his feet. Maybe they were cold. "There are so many things I want to address here. So many things I want to make sure you are clear about. First of all, I'm not upset with you. Not with anything you've done."

He took a sharp and audible breath. "Upset with *me?*" he shot back. "*You* come in *her* house, *without* being invited, and you *insult* and *browbeat* my mother until she *cries*—and *you're* worried that I think *you* are upset with *me?*"

"Teddy, it wasn't like that." I talked fast and I tried to explain that I had hoped she and I could talk about his going to school, but that it was clear the whole subject upset her. I had really tried my best to calm and soothe her, but there was no way she wanted to hear anything about the subject from me. I was so *very* sorry it had caused her any distress. It hadn't been my intent to hurt her—*the old bitch*, I thought but didn't say and, apparently, I didn't let it show on my face.

Teddy was mollified, I think, by my somewhat obsequious apology. At any rate, there was no place for him to go emotionally. I had taken the air out of his angry tires, so to speak. He relaxed on the barstool and drank his beer. In a way, I almost thought that he was under the impression that everything was going to be fine and we'd be back together now that I'd "learned my lesson."

I started again. "Look, Teddy, I'm incredibly fond of you. In my own way, I love you and I appreciate all kinds of things you've done for me—so many things I don't think you even know you've done. You've been the best friend I've ever had, and I'll love you always for it. I don't need you to go to college or to be a professor or to be anything but what you are right now—I *don't* need it for me. I really believe that *you* would be happier and more fulfilled, but if it's *not* what you want, then I don't want it *either*."

"It's not that I don't *want* it," he broke in. "It's that it's all so *hard* . . . and . . ."

"I know, I know," I said, putting my hand on his arm. "I really do understand. But I want you to know that if you feel you want to try—I'm here and Josie and Dan and Catsup and Edward and Howard and Bernadette—we're all in your corner for you. Remember what Edward said: We're the family you can *choose*. But we're not here to browbeat you, Teddy. We're only here to help. And from this point on, you call the shots. If you want us, you just have to ask, and we'll be there to help in any way we can."

Teddy looked so relieved, it seemed as though every muscle relaxed. I thought he was going to melt into a puddle at my feet.

"There is one more thing, though," I said. "I can't go on being your"—I searched for any other word—"girlfriend." I couldn't see his reaction, under his hat. "It's so clear that your mother is desperately unhappy about this, and it's put *you* in a difficult position, and therefore, it's put *me* in a difficult position."

He lifted his head and thrust his chin out. He seemed for a moment to be defiant. I almost thought he was going to say, "To hell with my mother!" but instead he just looked back down at his sandals and furrowed his brow.

"I don't want to go through the details," I said, "because I know that you are going to want to address each of them, or try to solve them, and I know you *can't*. At least you can't with things as they are. So let's not deal with the disappointments on either side."

"Wait a minute," Teddy said, squinting a little at his feet. "Are you breaking *up* with me? Are you blowing me *off*?"

"I wouldn't look at it that way," I said. "There's no point in looking at it that way. You came into my life, and you opened up all the doors and windows, and you made me look at myself in a new way. And you made me a house in my image. And it is exactly right. Every choice you made is exactly right for me. You'll always be here and you'll *always* be welcome here . . . but . . . . I've been thinking that it's possible we mostly had this house in common, not each other." I let that thought sink into both Teddy's consciousness and my own. "*And* I think it's likely, and a very good thing, that there will be *another* house—not mine—and you'll give yourself over to it and create *another* miracle. And I need to let you go and do that."

"But it doesn't mean letting *me* go," Teddy said, guilelessly.

"It does. It does." I nodded my head and tried for the right words. "Look, Teddy, you are tied to your mother in a way I can't compete with, and her discomfort is not going to go away. And you're not going to be okay with that, are you?" He shook his head. "And you're tied to your work in a way I don't *want* to compete with—for your sake *and* for mine." His head was bowed, and, once more, I could hardly see his face for the brim of his hat.

"This doesn't have to be so very sad." I touched his cheek, but I just couldn't say all I felt. *It is sad. It's sad for me that I won't sleep next to you anymore and put my face against that place in your back that feels as though it had been carved out of you for me. It's sad that I won't have you here if I come home with a wonderful idea or full of some terrible fear or loss. It's sad that you won't see the house move through the seasons and get more beautiful with age and use. You've been the only one in my life to ever share these kinds of things, and now I'm going to lose you and it is very, very sad.* But I couldn't say any of this. I didn't know how to say it and still let him go.

Teddy hugged me for a good long time. His head was on my shoulder. He didn't ask for more. I couldn't read whether he was full of remorse or nostalgia, or just holding on to the comfort as long as it lasted, or if he was thinking about what his next move might be. I tried to prepare myself for the possible plea of a continuance. Perhaps I was trying to give myself the strength to say no, if I were presented with the fact that an imperfect relationship might be better than no relationship at all.

And then he sat up. "Maybe I'll get a dog," he said.

"What?"

"Maybe I'll, you know, get a dog."

I can't say I wasn't shocked, but I really tried not to be offended, as I struggled to find the best possible way to process this. In a way, it was in line with his approach to challenges, I tried to tell myself; he so rarely expressed remorse or major discouragement. He just rolled along to the next thing. It was how he navigated Life with Mother.

"Good," I said, maybe a tad flatly, "that's a good idea. A dog."

I walked him to the door with my arm around his waist. He grabbed his jean jacket and carried it out. On the porch he kissed me, sweetly and wistfully—or so I interpreted the kiss.

"Will you go with me?" he asked, still holding me close.

"Where?"

"To pick out the *dog*," he said.

"Oh. Oh, sure. Sure, I'll go with you. I mean, it's my replacement, right. I should give it a few tips."

As he walked down the steps, I saw on the back of his heather gray T-shirt an Edward Gorey ink sketch of a flying blackbird.

CHAPTER 37

We met at the dog shelter three Saturdays later. Teddy had phoned the place to say that he wanted an older dog, calm and already house trained. Was that what he thought of me? He'd had a call from the shelter about a dog whose owner had died. The dog was five years old and perfectly trained. Maybe "too trained," the dog adoption official had suggested to Teddy.

"What do you think he meant by 'too trained'?" I asked Teddy as we sat in the visitors' area on red molded fiberglass chairs, waiting, I assumed, to be called in to view the dogs. I could hear barking in all different voices from behind the Sheetrock wall.

A door opened, and a round man with a comb-over hairdo and a sweet, kind face walked through, holding a leash attached to a slim, long-legged, short-haired hound of spotted brown and white. The dog was handsome, but he held his glossy dark brown head low and looked at us from under his brow, with a kind of distrusting concern.

Teddy introduced himself to the comb-over as Teddy Hennessy, and introduced me by saying, "This is my friend" and pointing his thumb at me. The round guy introduced himself as George. "We talked on the phone," he reminded Teddy. He indicated the dog with a twist of his head. "He's incredible," he said. "German shorthaired pointer. Musta been trained by Nazis."

"Whoa! That's a little harsh," I said, as Teddy knelt down on one knee to let the dog see and then smell his hand and to rub the dog's neck. But the dog took a slight step backward and rather deliberately looked away as Teddy petted him.

"He doesn't like to be petted," the fellow said, more to Teddy than to me. "He doesn't much like to be touched. He doesn't growl or bite or show his teeth or anything; he's not aggressive in any way—and not sub-missive either, really. He's kind of above it all. He just turns his head away from you, and you know he doesn't like it. But he's real smart—real smart, he's trained, and he takes voice commands as fast as can be, as though he thinks there's a firing squad in the next room. He sits—"

When George said the word *sit*, the speckled dog sat. All three of us ooohed, on cue. We're all trained, I thought. But the dog didn't look at any of us.

"He hasn't soiled his pen. He eats his food. And not a peep outa him. All the other dogs whine and yelp—they're scared to be here, they're lonely and their routines are gone and—geez, they're just scared. It's pathetic, and your heart goes out to them. This fella, I don't know, it's almost more pathetic. He won't say anything, no barking, no whining; he won't look any of us in the eye, and he must be hurting. His owner died last week. My theory is the guy must have been real sick for a long time and he needed a dog who could work on voice commands. This breed is supposed to be real owner-loyal." George stopped and stroked the dog's head, though the dog paid the attention no heed. "The fact that you wanted to take him to work with you every day was what made me think you'd be good for each other, you know? But it could take some time for him to see you as his. Know what I mean? Don't get, you know . . . dis-couraged." He looked at the dog, who looked depressed. "I don't know any more than that." The dog's bobbed tail hung down. His ears hung down. He looked actually, literally, humanly depressed.

"Do you know the dog's name?" I asked.

"Oh, yeah, of course," George said. "He's called Henry. His owner was named Larry James—taught statistics or something at U Mass—maybe you knew him?"

"Good grief!" I laughed, and the dog looked up at George and then at me.

"You knew the guy?" George asked.

"No," I answered, "it's just that Henry James is my subject . . . you know . . . my primary focus of study. That's all. I mean, nothing's wrong."

"Well, so! Maybe he's meant to be your dog!" said George kind of cheerily.

"No," I answered.

"No!" said Teddy, at exactly the same time. "He's for *me*."

Teddy filled out the paperwork. Henry was already neutered, so there was no charge for that, but Teddy gave the shelter two hundred dollars to continue its spaying and adoption work. He and George were becoming good buddies. I sat on the fiberglass chair as they talked about the shelter. Henry James sat next to me, looking off toward the wall, like an autistic child.

We went out to Teddy's car, and he opened the back and told Henry to jump in, and Henry did exactly as told. Teddy asked Henry to sit down and Henry did so, but there was no tail wagging and no sign of wanting approval. Teddy had a great-looking dog bed of brown-and-cream tattersall in the back of his car, with a sky blue, cream and brown plaid Pendleton blanket folded next to it. And there were two matching brown-glazed Rockingham bowls, sturdy and deep like casseroles, almost certainly not intended for dog bowls, but perfectly formed for such.

"You've been shopping," I said, picking up one of the bowls.

"Aren't they cool?" said Teddy. "I found them over in Sheffield yesterday. They were sort of expensive—I mean they're old—probably eighteen eighty, but I figured, what the heck? They're exactly right. And brown-and-white-speckled dog . . . brown-speckled bowls . . . you know . . ."

"I know." I smiled at his sense of detail. "Well," I said, "it does look as though you found the perfect replacement for me—literary references and all."

"Yeah," Teddy said, "he's not *exactly* a replacement," and I thought he was going to correct my idea that he would be silly enough to think that a human relationship could be no more important than one with a pet, but I was wrong.

"It's even *more* than that," Teddy elaborated. "He's afraid of contact. Just like you were." That was much more insight than I expected from Teddy, and it hit me behind the knees. I couldn't speak. I looked away, just like the dog.

"I've got to go," I said, a lump rising in my throat. Teddy kissed me on the cheek. "Good luck to you—both," I said. "He's a very lucky dog."

Teddy smiled his sweet smile, chin down, eyes up under the brim of his Boston Red Sox cap and made the shooting gesture with his hand to say good-bye. I watched them pull out of the parking lot. Henry James looked out the back window, the saddest dog I'd ever seen.

That was Saturday. The next Thursday was a big day. Fran came back to work. Because we hadn't seen her since January, the sight of her was both welcome and shocking; she was both smaller and larger. She'd lost a lot of weight during the three months we'd missed her, but her little tummy was prominent and displayed in a figure-hugging T-shirt with a little drawstring under her newly pronounced bust. Her hair was shorter, bobbed square just above her ears, and she looked remarkably well for someone only days off nine weeks of intravenous feeding. Fran's nausea had passed at the five-month mark, as if by wizardry. She reported that she woke up one morning and knew immediately that the problem was completely gone. She felt terrific.

Josie brought a wonderful orange cake, which she knew Fran loved, and we had a great lunch together, filling her in on all the things she'd missed. When I heard the stories coming out of our mouths, I could hardly believe that we'd lived through all of this in just a bit short of four months. The Den-eeze story was as much of a comedy hit as the Jordan story was horror. She laughed and cried, as they used to say in old movie trailers. But through it all, Fran kept looking at me and looking at me.

"You're the most changed. More changed than I," she said, and Josie nodded her head in agreement.

"What do you mean?" I asked.

"You talk! You really join in. You seem happy to be here and happy to see me! I didn't think you *liked* me. But then, I didn't think you really liked anyone. You're, like, totally different than when I left. And you *look* different, too."

I was wearing the Armani sweater set with Laura's pearl and peridot earrings. I wore things like that a lot now, but I was sort of embarrassed to have it pointed out, and I began to change the subject when the phone rang. It was Teddy.

He asked if he could come over after work. He sounded like someone in distress. "Of course," I said. "Anytime." And he said that he'd be at my house around seven.

I got home just minutes before his car pulled in the driveway, and I saw him get out and open the back door for Henry. No leash. The two of them walked up the front steps, Teddy walked in and Henry waited. "Come on, boy," he said, and the dog came in. Henry James then waited to be told where to stand or sit. He looked at Teddy like a pitcher watches the catcher to see which pitch to throw. Teddy indicated a place on the rug, and Henry walked over and waited to be told to sit. "You can lie down there, Henry," Teddy said. And so he did.

Teddy told his story. Maureen hated Henry James. She didn't like the idea of a dog in the house. She thought dogs were dirty. She thought any dog would upset her cat, and I noticed that Teddy was careful to not call the cat by name. Teddy had promised Maureen that she would love this dog once it was home, and he promised that he would keep it clean and wash its feet before it entered the house. He'd done all of that. The cat took no notice of the dog, nor did the dog care a whit about the cat. He kept Henry with him all day, as he'd planned, and as soon as they returned home the dog stayed in Teddy's room—in fact, in his bed. Still, Maureen complained. She worried that there wouldn't be enough room in the car for her friends now that the dog rode shotgun with Teddy. She worried that Teddy might not be as free. While German shorthaired pointers have, as advertised, very short hair, she said that she could feel the dirt the dog was carting in on his coat. And now she claimed to be allergic. In fact, Teddy said, she had definitely seemed more stuffed up. He had to give her that, he said.

I was livid. "Can't you see what she's *doing*?" I said. "Can't you see how she twists things to have you all to herself?"

"I don't want to get into that," said Teddy firmly. He was grim and clearly pained. "But I've got to do something." He looked at me hard and long. "Can *you* take him?"

"You want me to take *a dog*?" I practically yelped.

"I do," he said. The furrowed brow was back in spades. "George says that dogs that are returned to the shelter almost always are put down. People won't take a dog that's been returned."

You should put your damned mother in a shelter, Teddy, I thought, but it didn't leave my lips. Still, Teddy could see what I was thinking. "Your mother—" I began, but the look on Teddy's face stopped me.

"Joy, that's not helping things," he said through his teeth.

No, I knew it wasn't. I looked at Henry. His head was down and his ears were down, and he looked like a dog who might belong to Sylvia Plath.

"You can take him to work," Teddy said. "Josie will be okay with it. He's the easiest dog you could imagine. Just feed him and walk him and bring him home. He sleeps with me in my bed—but I have to tell you the truth, I do it because *I* like it. I like to hear him breathing. I don't think he cares whether he's with me or downstairs on his dog bed."

Teddy's eyes now filled with tears, and he tried to blink them away. "But I'm gonna *miss* him," he gulped, "like . . . you know . . . I miss *you*," which I thought he clearly added as an afterthought.

"That's very flattering, Teddy," I said sarcastically; and Teddy looked at me with a hurt and puzzled expression, as though he had no idea what I meant. But I looked at Henry again. He seemed so lost.

"There's nobody else you can think of who might take him?" I started to run down the list; the O'Sullivan girls or the Fortunata girls might love him. But, Teddy explained, that was part of the problem. Henry needed his space. He couldn't be hurried into relating. He was just going to need to come to trust and love slowly.

"You should understand that," he said.

And he brought in the blanket and the dog bed and the brown Rockingham bowls, and he cried openly when he kneeled and stroked Henry's glossy head and said good-bye. The dog and I both looked away.

I t's Thanksgiving. The trees are bare and it gets dark early, and my house is lit up like a jack-o'-lantern. There is a half-eaten turkey on the table; my first—but I followed Josie's instructions to the letter, from the butter-soaked cheesecloth to the stuffing, and it seems to have been a success.

Donna is walking with a cane but moving gracefully. She's brought a file of magazine clippings to share her ideas for dresses to be considered for her wedding to Allen Catsup on Valentine's Day. Her girls, Marta and Ava, seem so much taller, as though the events of caring for and about their mother have matured them physically, as well as mentally, beyond their years. They can't seem to keep their hands off Henry, who is lying on his back with his feet up, offering his pink human-skin belly for their strokes and patting. It's possible he's eaten far more than his share of turkey, as I think the girls see Thanksgiving as much a dog's feast of overindulgence as one for humans.

Adele Grant sits on the couch with a pretty woman named Martha, a therapist from New York, who is about Adele's age. They've just bought an apartment together in Brooklyn Heights around the corner from the house Adele shared with Laura. Martha and Adele drove up to Amherst this afternoon in Martha's Porsche convertible.

"We kept the top down and the heat cranked on high," laughed Adele, and she described the surprised expressions from the passengers of the cars they passed on their way. "First they expect a man to be driving. Then, when they see the scarves and sunglasses, they think they might be getting Scarlett Johansson and Natalie Portman—or some other *babes*. And when it turns out to be women old enough to be their mothers—"

"*Grand*mothers," Martha interjected, laughing and enjoying the moment.

"Well, no matter," answered Adele. "No one *ever* expects a woman of a certain age to be tooling around in a sports car." She ran a hand through her pixie haircut. "I think it's grand!" Clearly we agreed, and Adele continued, "Sets the world on its ear, don't you think? About time too!" She slapped her knee for emphasis. "Age is the *next* frontier we conquer!"

Martha and Adele had stashed their gear in one of the guest rooms I'd just finished, making sense, at last, of some of the references I'd pulled out of decorating books and magazines more than a year ago. They will spend the long weekend with me in Amherst.

I was getting used to having guests. My brunch recipe file was growing, and the design and layout of my house seemed to support friends who could look after themselves or share activities with equal grace. I found that I was especially valuing the exchange of ideas that only comes with intimacy and conversations allowed to drift over days, to be reconsidered over dinner, over tea, after the afternoon walk, settled only when a larger truth or greater insight might emerge. Nothing buys this luxury but time and proximity in an unhurried house on a quiet weekend. How lucky am I to have found it. Thanksgiving, indeed.

If my own Pilgrim journey had brought me to this point, I'd imported some New York Indians; Martha and Adele, of course, and Harry Fox, who had driven up to share the meal and finally see the house he's heard so much about. He's pursuing a program that might bring him to U Mass with some regularity, as a special adviser and lecturer to its journalism and media school, but his time away from Columbia has uncovered another love, and it's fiction, of all things. I sometimes send him iPhone pictures of rooms I've painted or furniture I'm considering, and he sends me drafts of chapters from a novel he's begun about boxing. Life, he announced on the phone the other day, is nothing less than a chance to "roll with the punches."

"Well, Harry," I answered, knowing he couldn't see me shaking my head at the receiver, "it seems to me, we need to do a bit more than roll. I think the trick is being open to change, while making the best of the chaos that change tracks into our lives—you know, like debris from a storm."

In a bit of good luck, Harry seems to be neither storm nor debris, but it's all a little too early in that game to judge. Never mind. As Bernadette reminds us each week, it's all lemonade from lemons, and probably no more profound than that. No less profound, either, I'm quick to add.

Catsup and Donna have taken to Harry already, and Marta, always drawn to the most attractive man, has tried to charm him with bowls of nuts and dishes of olives and the offerings of more to drink, calling him Harry-Fox this and Harry-Fox that. My speckled brown hound, however, has been eying him warily from across the room. This is not an indictment, I've explained. Henry takes his time. But he'll come around.

We miss Laura and Charlie. They'd been invited, of course, but they took the holiday break between classes to explore Lake Como. Charlie had, a few months before, moved into the house Adele and Laura shared for forty years, with Adele "selling" Laura her floor-through for a dollar. The professional Grant Girls continued to use the ground floor as their office and writing studio.

"Isn't it funny," Adele said to Catsup as they talked about weddings, "I never had the fantasy of settling down with someone romantically. I suppose sharing the house with Laura was family enough for me, and that whole Virginia Woolf idea of *a room of one's own,* you know. I could just go upstairs, close the door and be by myself. And then . . . I suppose the idea of a public statement . . ." She let the idea drift off.

Catsup seemed about to fill in the uncomfortable space, but Adele picked up steam. "I didn't know I was even open to the *possibility* of real romance until Laura married Charlie. There it was. A happy ending in front of my own eyes. Undeniable. It was as though I'd been released to . . . I don't know . . . *trust,* I guess . . . to go and find my own way." She looked bemused. "And I'm the happiest I've ever been. Imagine that. At *my* age."

Martha put her hand gently on Adele's arm as she read out an e-mail that Laura sent, wishing us all a good Thanksgiving, from a hotel in Varenna.

I still have my moments. It occurs to me, every now and then, that a life so comfortable and intent on balance and good cannot possibly be a fertile matrix for art or intellect. But there are too many truths, within touching distance, to contradict this; and, frankly, I know far too many contrarians who use this position to justify their own bad behavior. So all right, I may be one of those very contrarians, holding on to my own bits of dear and treasured bitterness. But when it threatens to ruin a perfectly good afternoon, Josie or Fran simply call me out. I can count on it.

People return to the table to help themselves to more food, patting their stomachs and saying that they've already had two helpings of the stuffing or three of the squash, onion and apple puree. Even covered with smears of cranberry sauce, mashed potatoes, green beans, bits of meat, stuffing, gravy and puree, my grandmother's china looks beautiful. It fills the room, as people have left their plates scattered about like leaves in autumn. The pale robin's-egg blue border on the tiny pleats of Wedgwood porcelain feel as though they've always lived in this house. My mother's Fostoria is on the mantel and the sideboard and the coffee table, filled with varying levels of white and red wine, ginger ale and water.

Earlier this year, while poking through the deep drawers of a chest in an antique shop here in town, I unearthed eighteen huge napkins of pale watery green damask, monogrammed, in handwork no one in this country has produced in the last fifty years, with a big swashy *JMH*. I laughed out loud. My husband's last name was Martin. So *what* if they were meant for me in another lifetime? I bought them anyway, and they look just wonderful in the room.

Yesterday morning, before she and the O'Sullivan brood took off for Palm Beach, Josie delivered a huge bouquet of autumn flowers, heavy with branches of bittersweet. I placed it on a low stack of leather-bound books in the middle of the sideboard, in front of a deeply carved, oak Jacobean mirror I'd found in Brimfield last July. If I stepped back and looked objectively, it was now all, finally, a scene of style and comfort any magazine might have been proud to print, illustrating, so clearly, the truth of the moment; a gracious Thanksgiving at home. At my home.

In what I'd come to recognize as a typical German shorthaired pointer gesture, Henry got up and stretched; his bottom high, cropped tail straight up, his elbows and nose low to the ground. He came over to me, laying his head and his silken ears on my knee. He looked up soulfully, and I knew exactly what he meant. Time to go out. He made what we called the "out-mouth," a kind of yawn with a little yowl and a considered look from the side of his eyes, as though checking to see I'd gotten the message.

"I got it. I *got* it, Henry," I said, and we headed to the door. He scampered down the steps and sniffed all the wintered plants, lifting his leg and marking the brown forsythia bush at the side of the house. I stood on the porch, gathering my thoughts in the soft blue shawl around my shoulders. Looking back into the warm light of the windows, I could see the family I'd chosen gathered and fed, laughing and safe. This was my home. My flag was planted here.

Explorers who'd set out to conquer new worlds on behalf of their kings had, at least, begun with a goal, a map, a plan. Okay, maybe they did think the world was flat. Maybe they did believe that China was roughly where Hoboken turned out to be. But at least they knew what they were looking for. I'd only known what I was not looking for. And that was more of the same. If I had known the territories would be so vast, if I'd understood they were so deep and internal as to be mythically subterranean, would I have made this journey?

This question, which suggests I had an element of will or control in the events, flatters me. As I see it, I didn't do much. Leaving a job one hates for what anyone would call a great new chance does not take an act of courage. Finding oneself swept along in love affairs with knaves and fools is hardly a reason for self-congratulations.

Long, long ago, when I was disappointed at some school friend's slight, my brother reminded me of an idea I've just remembered. "Don't you get it?" Timmy said. "No one is using the same yardstick. Their idea of a full measure is rarely yours—or anyone else's." My time with Will, and the massive, blind gratitude I now see as neurotic beyond the pale, was still a leap of faith, greater than any in *my* life to date. It was, at *that* moment, *my* full measure. And I'd allowed Teddy Hennessy, my pot-addled, darling, talented, emotional wreck of a momma's-boy-handyman, to teach me more about what it meant to be connected to my own life than any text of Henry James or Edith Wharton, whatever their intent or cultural status. That Teddy could not build his own home and his own life was a mark of *his* own yardstick at the moment. But life has a current, things change, I thought. Things are always changing. Look at me.

Other houses were lit and active, but there was little traffic on the street. I searched for the headlights of Howard and Edward's Lexus. They were due for dessert and running late. Henry bounded back up the steps as I saw a car turn onto our street and slow as it approached the house.

"Here comes your friend, Speedstick," I guessed, and said to Henry, who looked up into my face, dog brows raised and head cocked as though he wondered what Speedstick might be wearing this holiday; but the car didn't stop, and it didn't pull into the driveway. As I ruffled Henry's soft neck, I saw the winking, broken taillight at the back of the Subaru turn at the corner and head toward the center of town.

ACKNOWLEDGMENTS

Early readers are, essentially, a group assembled in a field to see if your kite will fly. You float this and that before them, and watch them react to the dips and sails. If you are very lucky, you have a group who respond with good humor, good sense and unlimited support. My group—John Colapinto, Donna Mehalko, Katherine Lanpher, the treasured Amys (Attas and Churgin), Ken Skalski and Jan Roberts—did just that. Hats off to each of them, acknowledging their kindness and their generosity (and the great good fortune of finding them in my green field).

My agent, Mitchell Waters, understood this book from the very first page and, even more important, knew who else might feel the same way. He directed it to my editor, Marjorie Braman. Teddy Hennessy and Joy showed up before she'd even unpacked her new office, but she managed to create a gracious and nurturing home for them at Holt. And I am delighted, filled with anticipation and full of appreciation for Mitchell and Marjorie.

And finally, the two godparents of this book: my friend Sara-Gwen Pritchard and my husband, Frank Delaney. With huge reservoirs of talent, skill and success to back them up, their concern for me was exceeded only by their insistence that I *could* do this. And I thank them more than words can say.

DIANE MEIER is the author of *The New American Wedding* and the president of Meier, a NYC-based marketing agency. She lives in north-western Connecticut with her husband, BBC broadcaster and writer Frank Delaney. This is her first novel.

To learn more, go to www.dianemeier.com.

THE SEASON OF SECOND CHANCES

by Diane Meier

About the Author

- A Conversation with Diane Meier

In Her Own Words

- "Why I Wrote *The Season of Second Chances*"
  An Original Essay by the Author

Keep on Reading

- Recommended Reading
- Reading Group Questions

For more reading group suggestions,
visit www.readinggroupgold.com.

 ST. MARTIN'S GRIFFIN

A Conversation with Diane Meier

Why did you choose to make your heroine, Joy Harkness, a university teacher?

I needed her to have authority and, just as important, to be seen as having authority. I didn't want her mixed into the commercial world, the world I know so well, because her lack of style and her discomfort with those choices wouldn't have allowed her to be successful.

She could get away with ignoring or rejecting the expression of personal style in her life on campus. The academic world, in fact, is one where style has been seen as suspect. And for feminists of Joy's age (forty-eight at the start of the book), style, and in general most things feminine (as opposed to female), have also been seen as less than worthy, as less than credible. I believe academics and many hard-line feminists have done a disservice to both women and men, in giving license, or worse, a more than subtle directive, to discourage issues of style as bourgeois, frivolous, and antifeminist. Nothing, in my opinion, could be further from the truth. And it certainly isn't a truth that would have been embraced by Yeats or Wilde, Byron or Keats, Chopin or Liszt, Rembrandt or Vermeer—and certainly not Joy's beloved Edith Wharton or Henry James.

And why the discipline of English literature?

It allowed me to show a character who related to the full nature of life, in all its passion and emotion—but only within the safety and distance of literature. So we could see that she had the depth, the intellect, and the instincts for a life of emotional connection, but not the courage to face it—in the flesh—so to speak.

What connection—if any—were you trying to forge between the restoration of a beautiful old house and the teaching of English?

Less, I think, between the restoration of a house and teaching—since we don't actually get to see Joy teach

(that's the next book—and another character!)—but more between the restoration of a house and the restoration of a civilized and emotionally integrated life.

How much were you launching a discussion of the way women make community among themselves?

Most women know very well how friends can form a kind of protective, emotional layer around the hard corners of life. But I do think that literature has given the fact of this kind of community very short shrift.

In our books, we get stories about men and women in passion and out, and tales of women and children from every possible angle—but the less obsessive and more socially integrated nature of friendship is rarely celebrated. I did, very consciously, want to show this part of life as valuable.

It was also important to me to develop that community as not exclusively female. Josie's husband, Dan, Dr. Catsup, and the two professors, Howard and Edward, all step up to meet a variety of challenges through the unfolding of this book.

Throughout the book, there's a delicate balance going on between Joy's physical surroundings—the renovation and opening of this falling-down house—and the restoration of her own emotional values. In other words, as the house recovers its old beauty, Joy emerges as a woman prepared to engage with friends. How consciously did you plot this or did it just unfold?

It was the inherent "business" of the book—so it didn't need much management. But I did, in the end, find that I had to go back and create a few moments where the reader was able to actually see Joy change in more discernable increments.

She has a very clear and distinctive voice. Some writers struggle for years to find such a bell ringing inside them. Did you?

Nope. I've always had the ability to write in voices. That's what copywriting is. If you're asking where this talent comes from, I don't have an answer, but I do have a story: Thirty years ago I created a series of little witty "playlets" that I dashed off on postcards in the clear voices of characters I might see on the street or imagine shopping in a particular kind of store. I loved the irony, sometimes pathetic, sometimes rather noble, that we could find in their circumstances, as we seemed to overhear bits of their lives.

Many of the pals to whom I sent these morsels of fluff continue to refer to their characters—three decades on. I suppose, in writing them, I was playing with a talent I didn't yet know how to harness.

The other main character in the book—the jobbing handyman/genius, Teddy Hennessy—becomes the project within the project. What is that relationship about?

Teddy is so very central that I wanted to call the book, *Teddy Hennessy*—and I still think that's the natural title of this story. He is, I believe, the truly original work in this piece. Teddy is an intelligent, thoughtful, and talented designer and craftsman, locked within an adolescent position of development, and held there by forces within and very much outside of himself. We're allowed to see this as both pathetic and funny—as so much of life—or at least as so much of what I enjoy in life so often is.

But I also like the joke that the reader is ahead of the narrator. All we are supposed to know of Joy's world comes from her to us, but rather early in the game the

"I wanted to show two characters who …integrate their passions with their lives, something I've found so rewarding in my own."

reader begins to sense that she's an unreliable witness.
Joy believes that this is a story about Teddy Hennessy
and *his* potential for growth, but we understand that
it is really a book about Joy. She's angry, negative,
sardonic, and alarmingly guarded; however, she's also
funny, smart, and so insightful that we recognize how
the conflict of that insight, when paired with her self-
protection, must be searingly painful. Teddy, in his
goofy T-shirts and pot-infused fog, is equally protected.
They are, a bit, like the blind leading the blind. And
certainly, they do not, in any way suggest a typical
literary love story.

**Marketing/advertising is a field concerned with the
making of style. What effect did your career in that field
have on this book?**

As a breed, successful marketers have infinite curiosity about the kinds of things that delight and motivate,
fulfill and define people; and we learn how to speak the
varied languages of subtle detail in words and visuals
that reflect and ignite the choices of their lives.

It's very difficult to know now whether my fascination with those issues of style and choice came from
my thirty years of working in this field—or whether I
became a marketer because I was so damned fascinated
with those delicate, ephemeral but discernable issues of
style and choice.

**After years of writing advertising copy, how different
was writing fiction?**

Not different at all. Dedicated copywriters hear the
voices of their target customers. We need to write compelling prose. We need to hear the music of language.

The strategic drafts I create for clients, which define a
position, a launch, or the turnaround of a brand, have

to be clear, clean, and convincing. They must be smart and solid. But they also have to be persuasive and seductive enough for a business executive and a team of disparate employees, each with their own agenda, to want to sign on to a course of action.

A novel is just a longer form of what I've done all my working life.

Joy Harkness is strong, clear, and, by the end of the book, directed forward into a new life. Will you write about her again?

I don't think so. She may show up as a tiny character in a book I'm working on now—but I think I've said everything I want to say about Joy. We've given her all the tools, now it's her job to get on with her life.

"I've been . . . sensitive to the . . . ways we cope with a world that feels too precarious."

An Original Essay by the Author

"Why I Wrote *The Season of Second Chances*"

Childhood traumas damage two families decades before we meet Joy Harkness and Teddy Hennessy, the off-center characters of *The Season of Second Chances*. While we can easily identify the ways in which their individual brands of self-protection have kept them insulated from the emotional tolls of real life, it is their talent, intelligence, humor, and heart that make us care about them. And it's those things that made these two characters so much fun to write about. Given my own childhood and family background, I've been, I suppose, especially sensitive to the inventive, self-protective, and sometimes funny ways we cope with a world that feels too precarious. And I look for the hints that might show us how to move beyond the comfort levels that baffle our own terrors and tears.

The family in which I grew up was pretty high WASP, in all the denial and quiet good behavior that cliché suggests. No one ever raised their voice. Scenes were avoided at (almost) all cost. But there was more than a small amount of tragedy in that house that carried into our daily lives. From a brother who was intermittently ill throughout my childhood to the ghost of my grandmother—dead at the age of thirty-three, daily remembered and mourned by my equally fragile and intermittently ill mother, my great-grandmother, and my grandfather. All lived (ghosts and otherwise) under our roof, and were my daily caretakers. And yet, in the face of their losses, there was the remarkable staff of strength, irony, and humor that extended grace and protection and made me feel well loved and safe despite their fears about what turn life might next take.

The insulating nature of humor—the good manners of the gentle joke in the face of terror or loss—might lighten the burden a bit, and remind us we are not the only person in the room (or on the planet). Or it might remind us that if there is a small thing to smile about today, perhaps there will be a larger thing to laugh about tomorrow. That's the atmosphere in which I grew up and that approach to life—both good and bad—is what I wanted to write about in my main character, Joy Harkness, an intelligent, successful college professor.

To the outside world, Joy's professional life seems an unmitigated success, yet she's taken very little pleasure in it, and has systematically learned to step away from people and emotional involvements. But a new job in a new town, and a new house that needs a lot of work, force Joy to face, if not embrace, change. The other character who figures quite large in the book is a very talented but emotionally stunted handyman/restoration artist, Teddy Hennessy. Teddy has limited his life to include little outside of his work and his mother, with whom he lives; but Joy and Teddy each allow larger joys of creativity in design and literature to enrich their days. As I wrote the book, I wanted to show two characters who, in spite of themselves, find a way to integrate their passions with their lives, something I've found so rewarding in my own life.

I believe that the celebration of an authentic personal style can enhance a person's life, both as an outward gesture of one's personality, and internally, for the comfort of personal recognition. Allowing Joy's house to come together as a home is a metaphor for that process. That it happens as she integrates her life into those around her feels emotionally accurate to me. From noting her "colors" to asking her to care for—and about—a critically ill acquaintance, Joy's world of intellect and cynicism are shaken hard until she finds a way to develop a real life that can stand up to the written lives she's treasured between the pages of her beloved books.

My career as a marketer has been about little *but* Style—with a capital S. From my earliest assignments, I have had to interpret cultural signs to set the look and strategy for brands and products that we've all known and used, from cosmetics and fashions to home furnishings and food. What we choose and the ways we choose to express ourselves, as individuals and as a culture, is a subject of endless fascination to me. I suspect the subject will surface in any story I might address. In life and in work, we can see the evidence of our lives as collages of choice, showing us, pretty clearly, how we communicate in signs, infinite and specific, which is another definition of style.

To separate these choices from those driven by status or commercial intent can only be done when we are allowed to find and express authentic ideas of delight and self-knowledge. Joy learns from Teddy, and from the rich community of friends and coworkers who fill her life, how to *express herself,* in the truest sense of that word.

In a culture as commercially driven as ours, this is a challenge many people find overwhelming. But if they demur, what joys they're missing! Our lives are our canvases. The only eye we need to delight is our own, reading the signs of our lives in our choices. My job has always been reading the signs. This time I got to write about them.

*In Her Own
Words*

Recommended Reading

I'm not sure there is enough paper in the world to hold this list—but I'll give it a try:

Literature

Everything O'Hara

Most of all, I love his short stories—but I have great affection for every novel and novella John O'Hara penned. Sanctioned for children or not, he was my childhood's Robert Louis Stevenson. And I've been hooked on his Gibbsville, PA, characters ever since. I return, year after year, to reread a novel or collection of stories, to touch base with the incipient idea of the adult I hoped to become, and to see again the vestiges of the once-familiar tribes and worlds I now suspect are gone forever.

Everything Wharton

Everything, except *The Decoration of Houses*—which you *must* have, of course. It changed everything; it was a landmark in the evolution of American design. So naturally, one has to respect it. After all, it threw out the idea of formal. It lightened things up. Heavy layers of velvets vanished from windows, fake copies of French furniture were tossed out, to be replaced with something simple—like wicker. It was groundbreaking. It should have felt like freedom. But good grief, it is written in a style so filled with contempt, so devoid of delight or release, that I wonder how anyone chose to follow what reads like just another set of rules. And yet in her glorious, compassionate, and deep body of fiction, everything is a reaction against rules. Go figure.

Reading Group Gold

Most of Henry James

At the risk of sounding like a cretin, let me just say: I like the early stuff. I like the stories in the later stuff; but, by this time, he's become so terribly self-conscious, so irrevocably hurt, so desperate for status and thrown off the track by the intellectual fringe, that his brilliant, moral core is nearly suffocated by his sentences. Inside all of that, though, is glorious, darling, compassionate, insightful, solid old Henry. No one better.

Biography

Amanda Vaill

Somewhere: The Life of Jerome Robbins

Everybody Was So Young: Gerald and Sara Murphy: A Lost Generation Love Story

James Kaplan

Frank: The Voice

It may be that the biographer's task is the most difficult of all writing. You can't make the facts up, and you have to find a way to hold readers by the lapels—when we all know that most of life is paying bills and waiting for the train to show up.

Still, when one has characters who made their marks upon the surface of the globe with as many sparks, style, courage—and sometimes, simply abrasion—as Sinatra, Robbins, and Gerald and Sara Murphy, the biographer owes his subjects a debt of nothing less than brilliance. Sadly, it rarely happens. Those of us who love biography, more often than not, live a life of dashed hopes.

Keep on Reading

Here are two wonderful exceptions:

Amanda Vaill and James Kaplan more than deliver on their promise to tender flesh and blood characters, full of issues and fears, subtext and contradictions. The folks they write about are as different as chalk and cheese—but they've wrapped them all up in books I could not put down. And I would go anywhere and read anything either of them writes, from now and forever. I advise you to do the same.

Memoir

Alan Bennett

Untold Stories

I couldn't have liked it more. It's a lot of things—funny and touching and serious—and very moving. It's intimate in a way that I find personally resonant: the small ironic detail that keeps the terror at bay, a bit of business to mitigate the sadness or make you smile in spite, *in spite,* of very real loss. Somehow, that *spite* in the face of loss is a kind of pluck I recognize in myself and admire in Bennett. What better skill to have as a writer of one's life than the wit to find irony in both the tragedy and success of one's life.

Katherine Lanpher

Leap Days

Another book of wit and loss and courage. A wonderful set of pieces about her move to New York from the Midwest when she was forty and newly single (talk about second chances!).

Quirky Choices

Two of my favorite books are more than a little quirky,
I suppose. But then, I'm more than a little quirky.

Craig Seligman

Sontag and Kael: Opposites Attract Me

Allen Shawn

Wish I Could Be There: Notes from a Phobic Life

What holds these two wonderful books together is a
deeply personal and almost obsessive degree of attention to a very narrow subject. As I happen to feel
strongly (and positively) about both Sontag and Kael,
my interest in the Seligman book was piqued from the
get-go. But I fell in love with Seligman's writing (and
his values) in the process. The book felt like one of
those great long conversations that one returns to over
a weekend in the country, when you're lucky enough to
bring along a good friend—and a very thoughtful, very
witty, very brilliant friend, indeed.

I'm not sure how I stumbled across Shawn's book, but
it's become a favorite. He's produced an unwavering
report of clear-eyed honesty within a subject that wants
nothing more than to hide. A brave and captivating
book. And, selfishly, a great lesson for a novelist who
writes in the first person.

Reference

I have a thing for reference books. I'd almost rather
retire with a guidebook or a book on paint formulas
and techniques than any fantasy you could dream up.

Roget's Thesaurus (1964)

My affection for my 1964 *Roget's Thesaurus* was so specific, so nontransferable—that when the poor book, rubbed nearly to death like *The Velveteen Rabbit,* was about to bite the dust, I sent it off to a great book-binder to be dressed up in new clothes. It returned in brilliant red linen, struck with gold letters that say: "Diane Meier's Beloved Thesaurus." I know, I know: There are a lot of NEW words since 1964. But this is the book I like. Sometimes, when I don't know what to write or how to write it, I just open it up and look at words. Words. What they look like. What they mean. What other words you might want to use. What they make you think of . . . and, lo and behold, I'm all fired up again.

Jenifer Lang (Editor)

Larousse Gastronomique (1988)

Same deal as my thesaurus. You may find another copy but you WANT the 1988 version. Hardcover. Jenifer Lang edited.

In this book you will find all the wonders of the food world (at least the French food world) made completely understandable. Hard to believe? Listen to this: Gratin? Look it up under G. There it is—the explanation, the history, a recipe. Magic! Béchamel? Under B, of course. It will not only give you a recipe, but tell you about the aristocrat for which it was named. You may never get around to cooking.

Isabel O'Neil

The Art of the Painted Finish

How many books did your mother work on? Well, mine worked on this. And helped to teach some of the most skilled decorative and restorative painters in this country during her more than forty-year career. I use some of the techniques—at least the inspiration, if

Reading Group Gold

not the skills—throughout our homes and offices. But I could sit and just read it for hours. It's everything I love. Recipes. Ideas. Color. And it just inspires all kinds of good things.

Stephen Sondheim

Finishing the Hat: Collected Lyrics (1954–1981)

Are books of lyrics reference books? I think so. And I have 'em all. Rogers and Hart. Rogers and Hammerstein, Ira Gershwin, Cole Porter, Noël Coward—you name it, we could prop it up on the piano and have a go. This Sondheim hybrid is something else: Part memoir, part gossip, all lyrics. If you are a Sondheim fan, that "something else" is simply heaven. If not, well, it won't mean much to you. Go sing your own song.

Diane Meier

The New American Wedding

Are we allowed to put our own work in these lists? Why not. I love this book. A fresh way to approach a ritual whose time has come to change. When the rite was cast in stone (only about a hundred years ago), brides were seventeen, grooms were eighteen, and parents were launching them out into the wide world in a shower of hope and support. Now, with first-time brides and grooms marrying at an age close to thirty, it's a whole new ball game.

Here at MEIER, we interviewed about a thousand people, visited a hundred, and brought their experiences of New Ritual to the forefront. We clarified the differences and shared example after example of new thinking, fresh starts, and completely authentic ideas of personal style in fashion, entertaining, ceremony, and celebration. It's a beauty of a book and we're very proud of it.

Keep on Reading

Plays

Theater is my secret passion. Well maybe not such a secret. But did you know about it? And I love reading plays.

Right now I'm reading Philip Barry. Working through everything he wrote. I pretty well hated a *Hotel Universe,* but I couldn't like *Holiday* or *The Philadelphia Story* more. That's generally the way the critics treated Barry in the 1930s and '40s, not unlike Woody Allen (we really like your funny stuff better). But maybe sometimes, and only sometimes, the critics are right.

Eugene O'Neill is devastatingly good in print. Try *A Moon for the Misbegotten* first. It's tenderness and brutality in equal parts and you can see every move you'd make on stage.

Tom Stoppard. Well, I'm not very original in my tastes, I know, but you've asked for the favorites. I've read just about all of Stoppard. Love them. I'd vote for *The Real Thing* and *Rock 'n' Roll.* But it depends on the week. I might change my mind by Tuesday and have a new favorite. Check in with me often.

You have to read Oscar Wilde's plays. For some odd reason, they're better than seeing them performed. *The Importance of Being Earnest,* for instance, reads like a goofy, sliding, delightful satire by a good friend. A send-up of a bunch of stiffs. All of a sudden you know what they mean by "romp." And inside of it all is a kind of respect for the authentic that I only saw in print.

Contemporary Fiction

John Colapinto

About the Author

An original voice in a book about plagiarism. Funny. Great ear. Great energy. It came out the week of 9/11 and consequently, no one ever heard about it. But now you have. You'll love it.

Sara Pritchard

Crackpots

The kind of talent you didn't think they'd discover anymore, a completely unique point of view. Sort of flea-market magic realism, if you can imagine that. Sublime passages will make you think of a paint-by-number versions of Chagall's floating ladies, offering jars of Cheese Wiz, Marshmallow Fluff, and Play-Doh to the wacky but seriously wonderful crowds below.

Frank Delaney

Ireland, Tipperary, Shannon, Venetia Kelly's Traveling Show, The Matchmaker of Kenmare

When people ask me whose work, besides your husband's, do you like, I want to reply, "What's this *besides*?" I do love Frank's work. They're fabulous reads. Moving, big, sprawling novels. Like they used to write. With characters you'll never forget. And if you don't see yourself toting these big books around, try the audio books and let Frank read them to you. I promise you'll be hooked. They're heart-stopping.

Reading Group Questions

1. Do you find Joy to be a reliable narrator? Is she capable of providing insights about her own life? Does this change from the beginning to the end of the novel?

2. How did your opinion of Joy change throughout the novel? Did you find her endearing at first? In a way, do you think your perception of the narrator over the course of the novel mimics Joy's own coming to terms with herself?

3. Joy heads off to Amherst thinking that it will be a fresh change from what she perceives as the politics and bureaucracy at Columbia. Is Amherst truly different from Columbia? Did Adele Grant's wedding change your opinion of the life Joy left behind?

4. At first, Joy finds Fran and Josie's attempts at friendship intrusive. What is it that finally gets her to accept them as her friends? Why do you think it takes Joy so long to open up to them?

5. When Teddy first starts working on Joy's house, he takes her completely by surprise when he recites Yeats to her. What do you make of this incident? How does it foreshadow the events still to come?

6. Joy's sharp wit pervades the novel. Do you think that in some ways she uses her wit to distract herself from the reality at hand? Is it a kind of guard for her?

7. Consider the effect that Joe's death had on Teddy, and the effects of Tim's death on Joy. Were their reactions to losing an older brother at all similar? How did Joy and Teddy each respond to this loss? Joy mentions that once she moved to New York, she no longer felt that Timmy was with her. Why do you think this changes when she arrives in Amherst?

8. At one point in the novel, Joy goes to Will's apartment, where she is met by a half-naked Will, and, moments later, a neighbor knocking at the door in a negligee who claims to have stopped by because she thought she smelled gas. What do you make of this incident? How is it that Will manages to make her try to talk herself out of what she's seen? Is she willing to be manipulated? Why?

9. In what ways is the night Joy leaves Will a major turning point for her? Is there anything different about her afterward?

10. How does Joy deal with the attack on Donna? Does she surprise herself in some ways? Did she surprise you?

11. What does this novel have to say about feminism?
Consider Bernadette Lowell's opinions about
women taking care of each other, and also what
Theo (the hairdresser) has to say about looking
good to get ahead. What is Joy's definition of feminism? Does it change over the course of the novel?

12. Joy, Josie, and Dan all want to get Teddy to go
back to school, but he doesn't seem particularly
interested. Why do you think that is? What are
Joy's reasons for wanting Teddy to go back to
school? Do her actions in this arena demonstrate
a deeper understanding of Teddy or not? Do you
think, at times, academic learning can be overly
important to her?

13. Parts of the novel's plot turn on Teddy's relationship with his mother, Maureen. Why do you think
she treats him the way that she does? Why does he
submit to it? Do you think that Teddy is genuinely
his own person? Do you think he can be his own
person while he's still under his mother's wing?